WOODSTOCK™
MASTER OF DISGUISE

A **PEANUTS**™ Collection

CHARLES M. SCHULZ

Andrews McMeel
Publishing®

Kansas City • Sydney • London

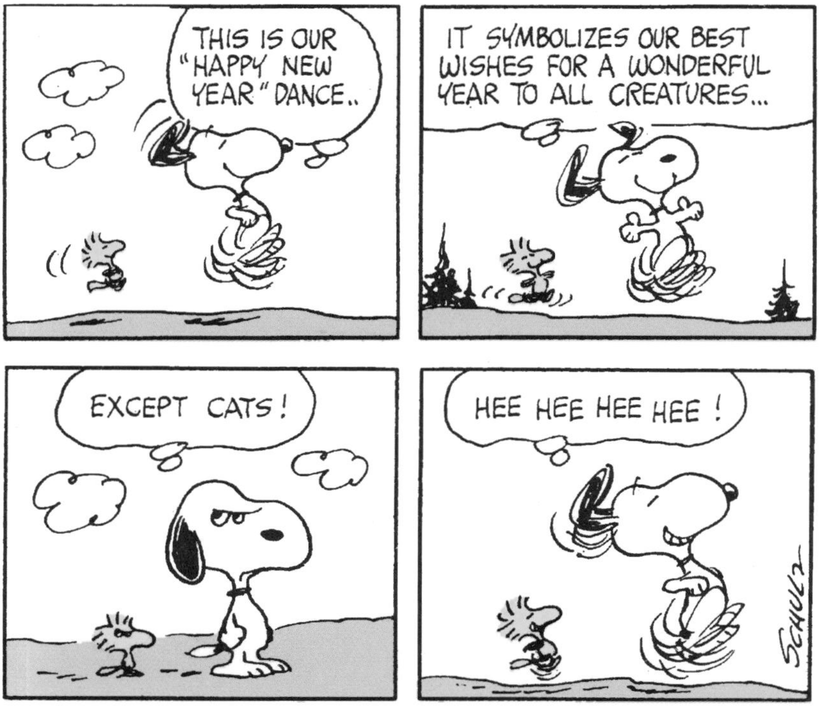
THIS IS OUR "HAPPY NEW YEAR" DANCE..
IT SYMBOLIZES OUR BEST WISHES FOR A WONDERFUL YEAR TO ALL CREATURES...
EXCEPT CATS!
HEE HEE HEE HEE!

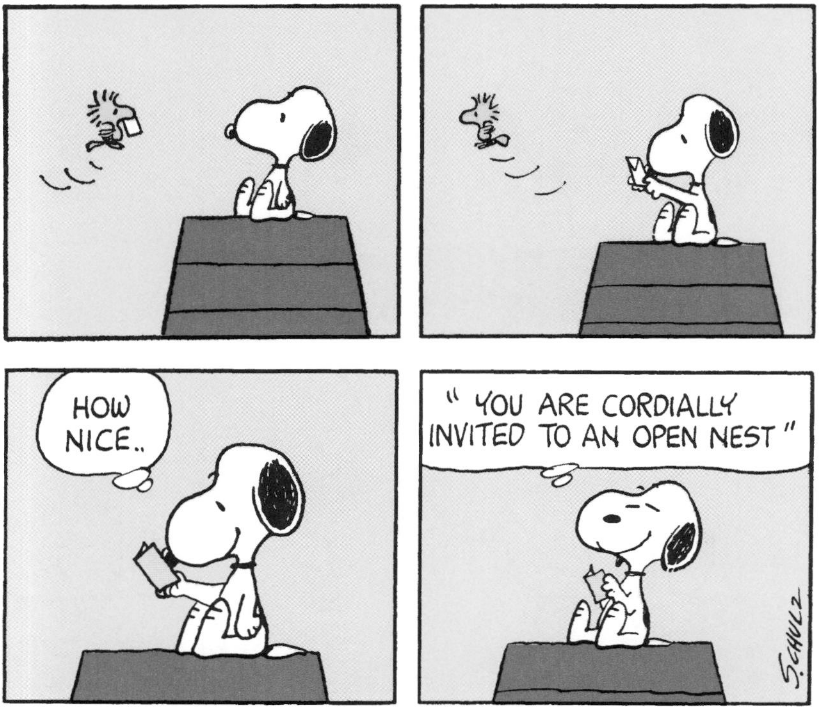
HOW NICE..
" YOU ARE CORDIALLY INVITED TO AN OPEN NEST "

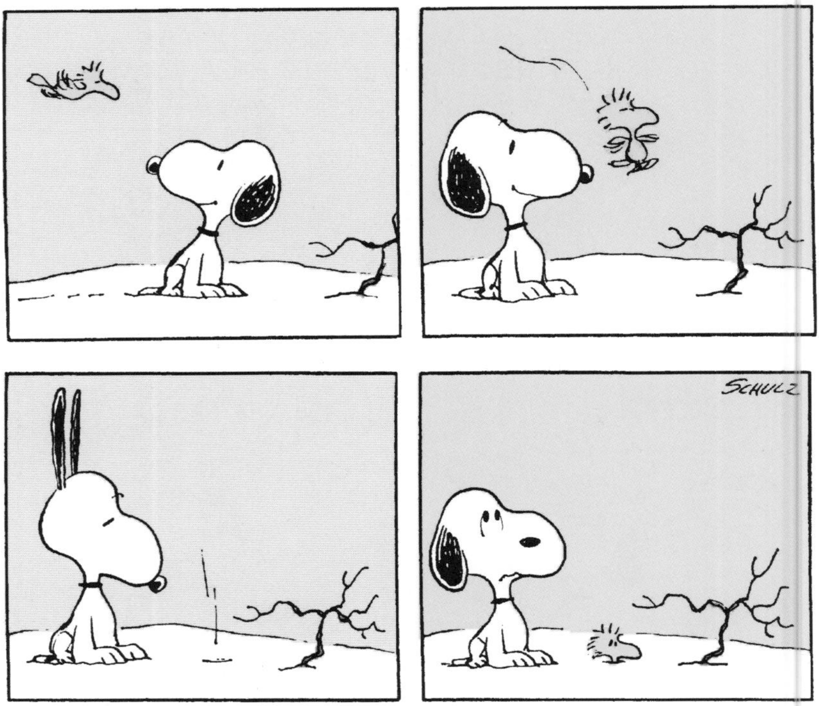
SCHULZ

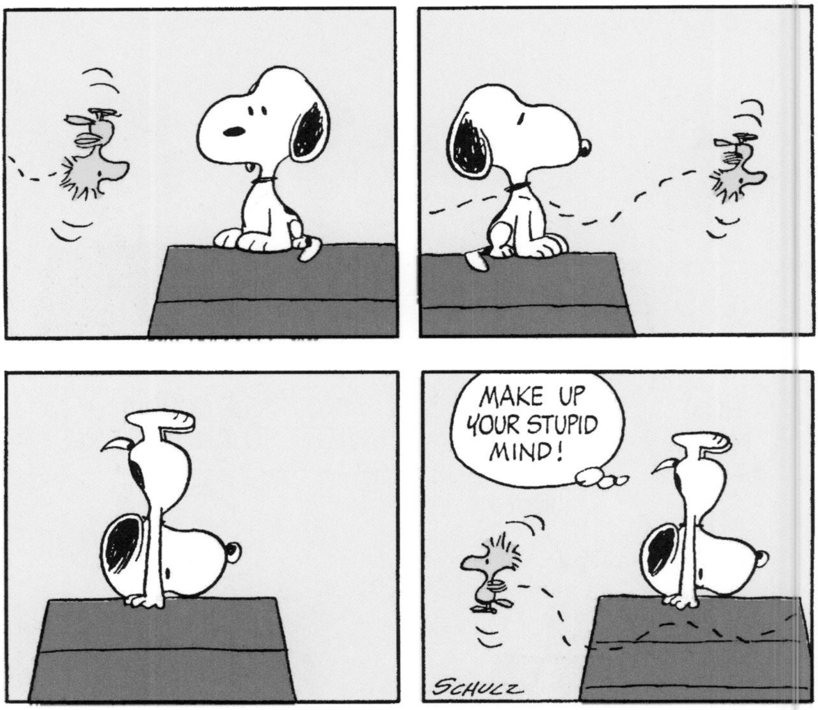
MAKE UP YOUR STUPID MIND!
SCHULZ

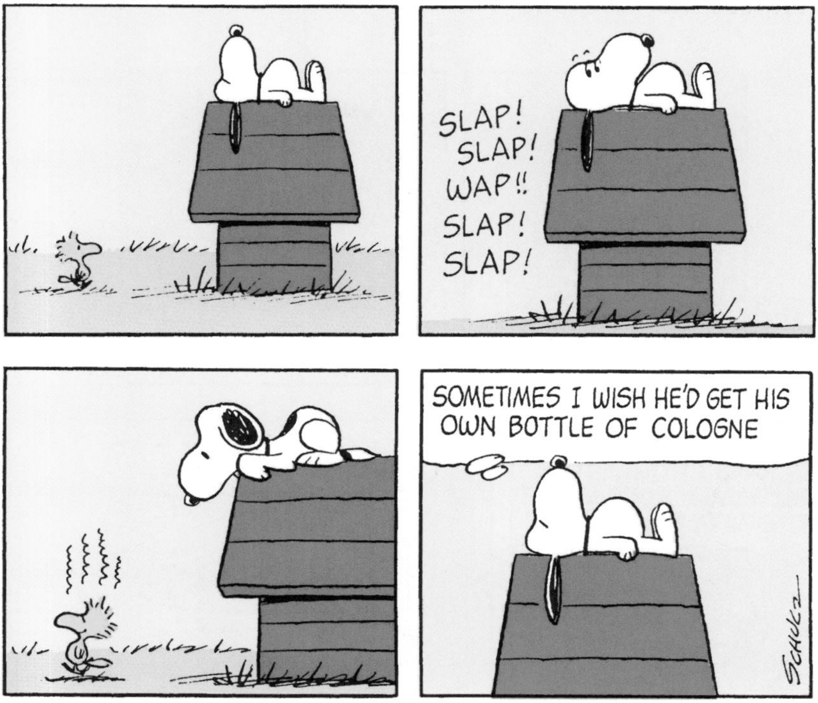
SLAP!
SLAP!
WAP!!
SLAP!
SLAP!
SOMETIMES I WISH HE'D GET HIS OWN BOTTLE OF COLOGNE
SCHULZ

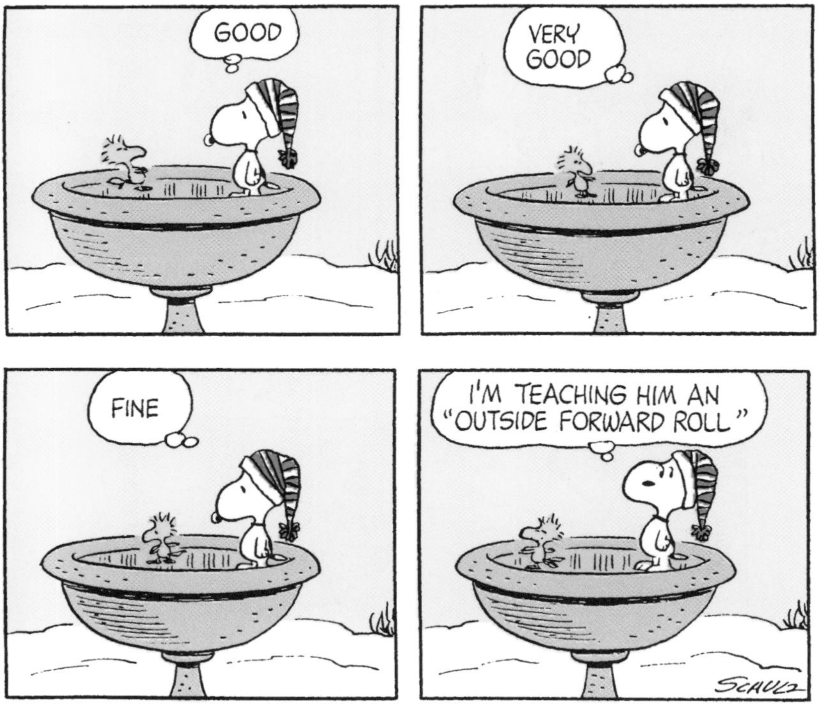
GOOD
VERY GOOD
FINE
I'M TEACHING HIM AN "OUTSIDE FORWARD ROLL"
SCHULZ

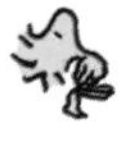

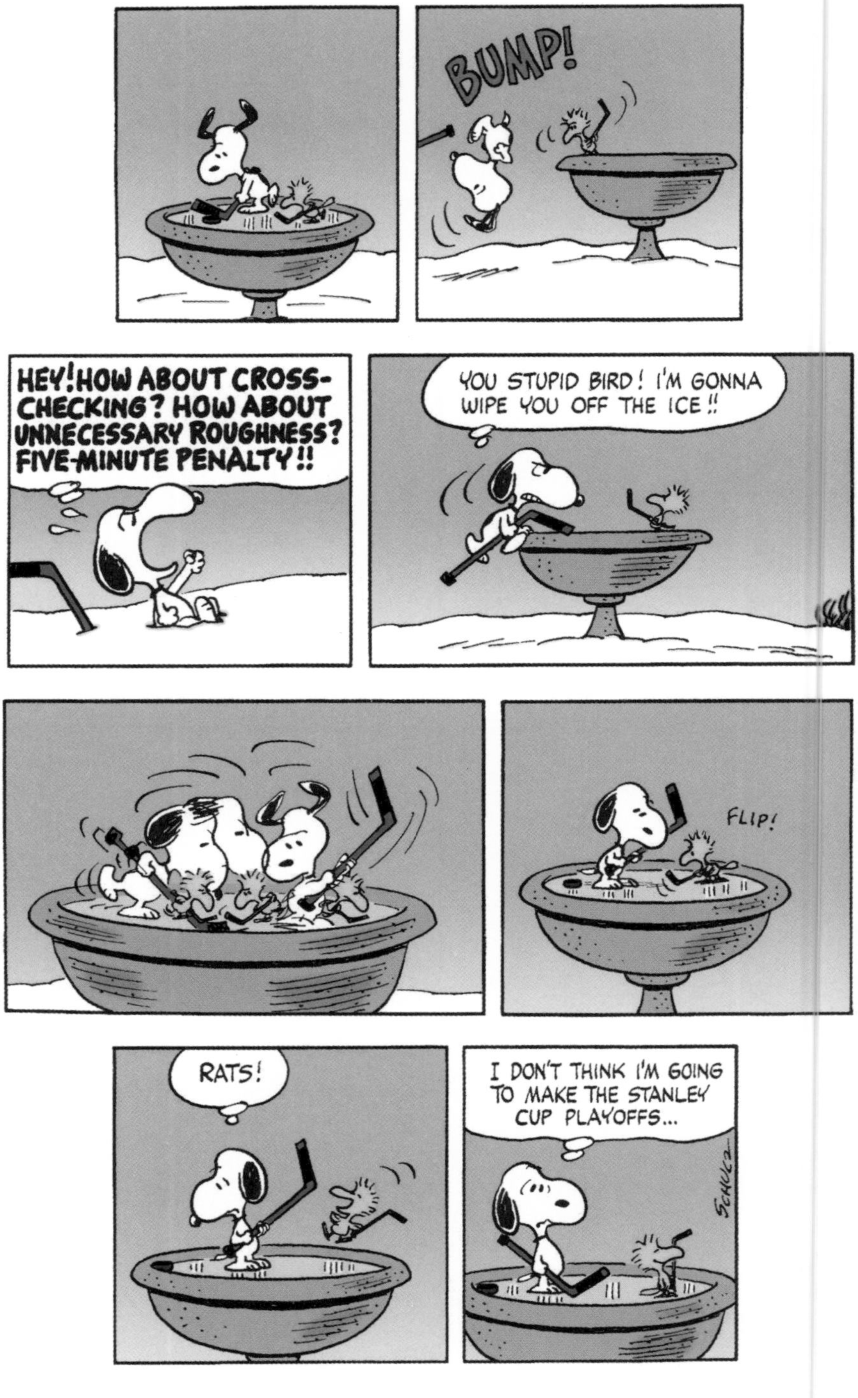
BUMP!
HEY! HOW ABOUT CROSS-CHECKING? HOW ABOUT UNNECESSARY ROUGHNESS? FIVE-MINUTE PENALTY!!
YOU STUPID BIRD! I'M GONNA WIPE YOU OFF THE ICE!!
FLIP!
RATS!
I DON'T THINK I'M GOING TO MAKE THE STANLEY CUP PLAYOFFS...
SCHULZ

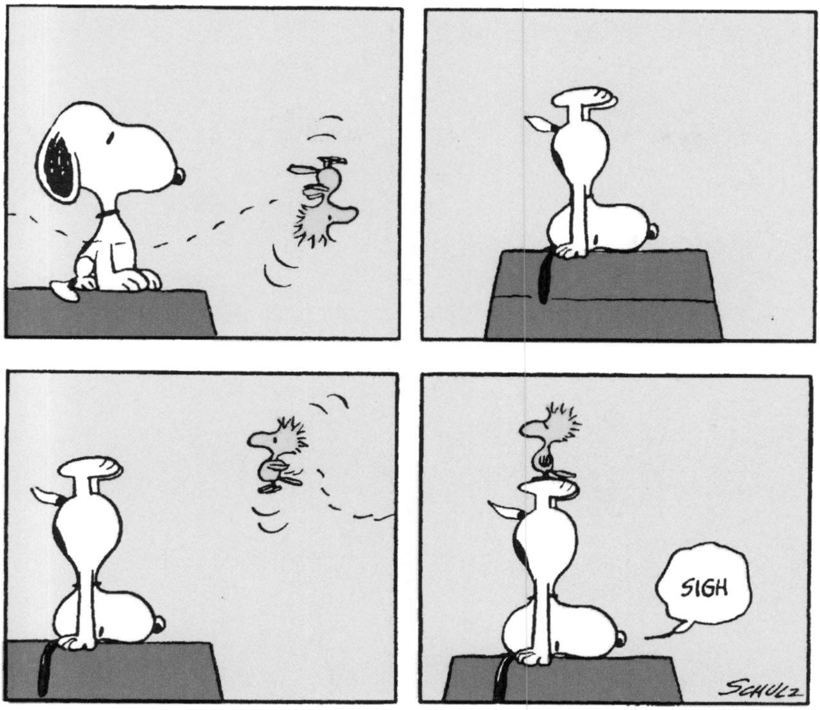
SIGH
SCHULZ

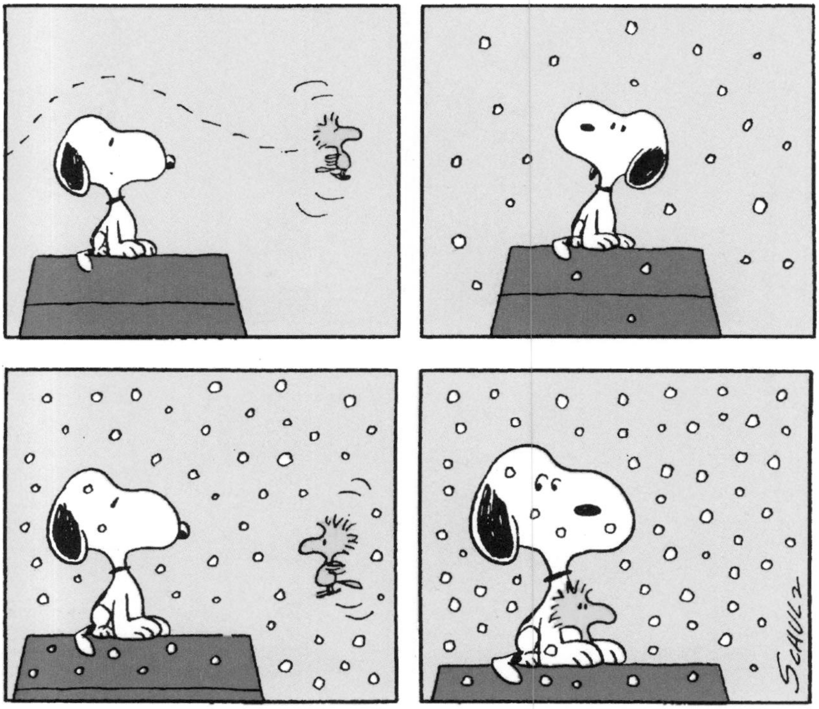
SCHULZ

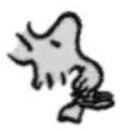

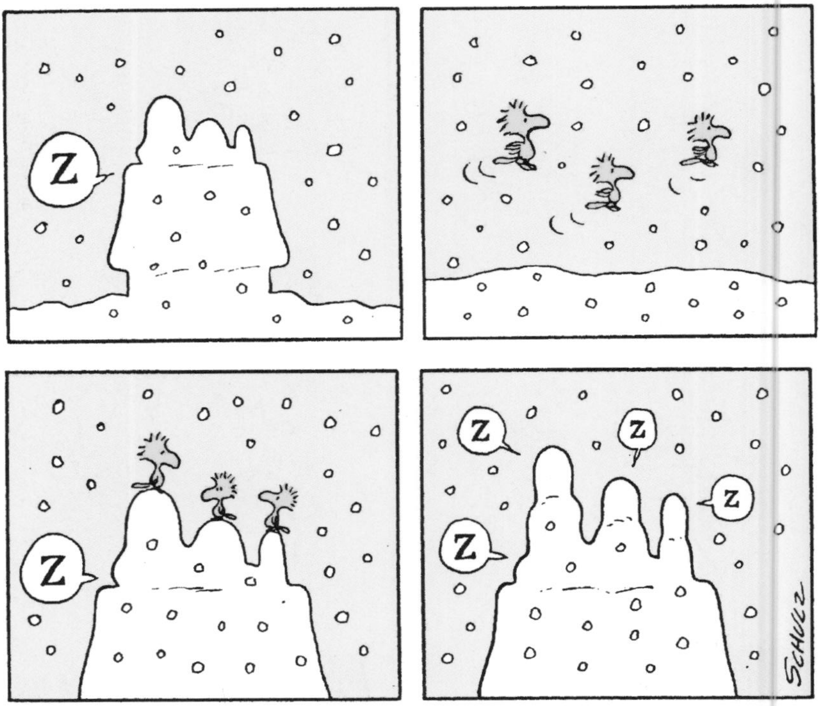
Z
Z
Z
Z
Z
Z
SCHULZ

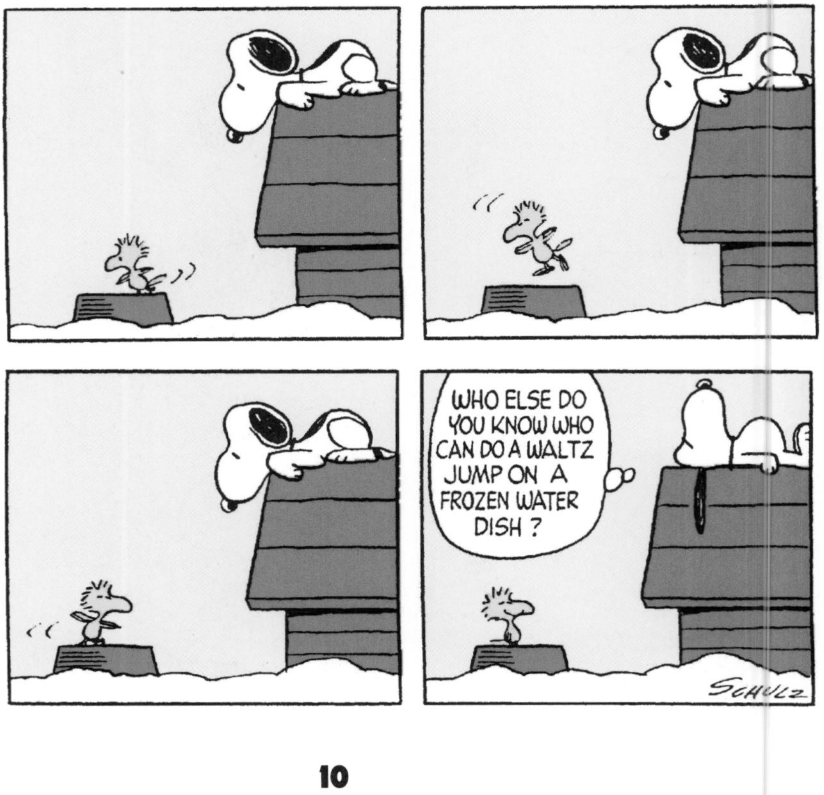
WHO ELSE DO YOU KNOW WHO CAN DO A WALTZ JUMP ON A FROZEN WATER DISH ?
SCHULZ

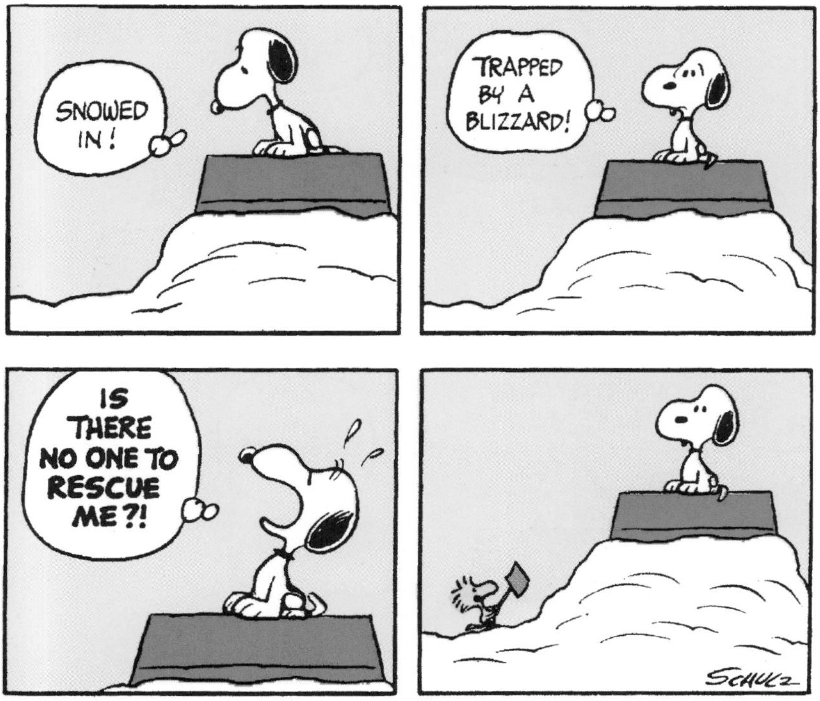
SNOWED IN!
TRAPPED BY A BLIZZARD!
IS THERE NO ONE TO RESCUE ME?!
SCHULZ

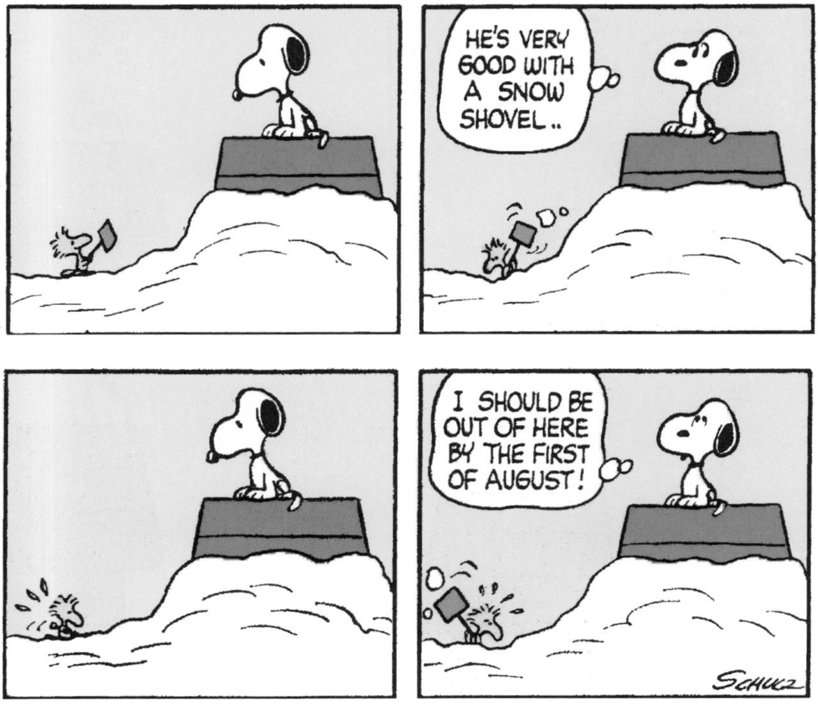
HE'S VERY GOOD WITH A SNOW SHOVEL..
I SHOULD BE OUT OF HERE BY THE FIRST OF AUGUST!
SCHULZ

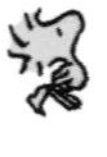

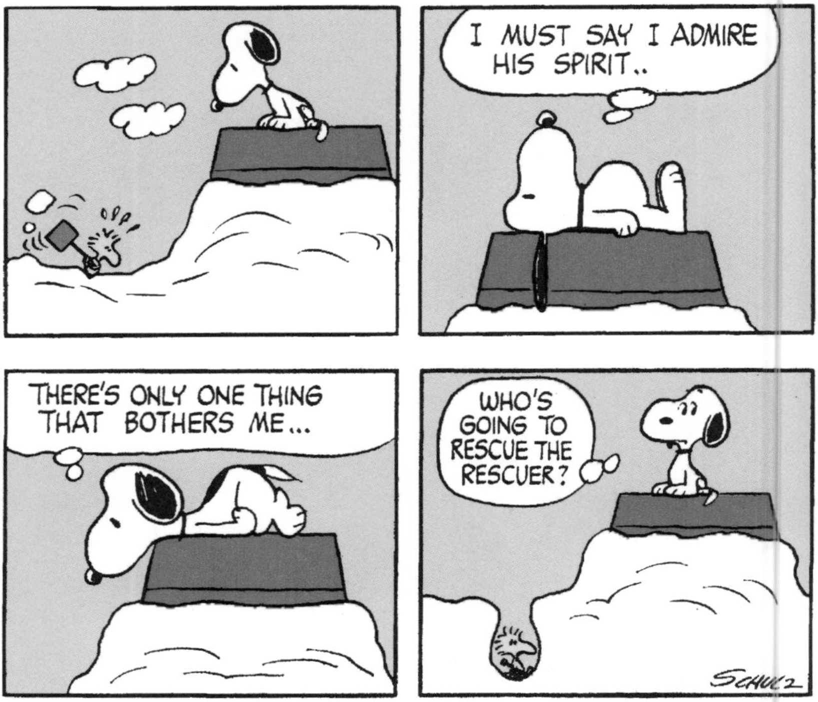
I MUST SAY I ADMIRE HIS SPIRIT..
THERE'S ONLY ONE THING THAT BOTHERS ME...
WHO'S GOING TO RESCUE THE RESCUER?
SCHULZ

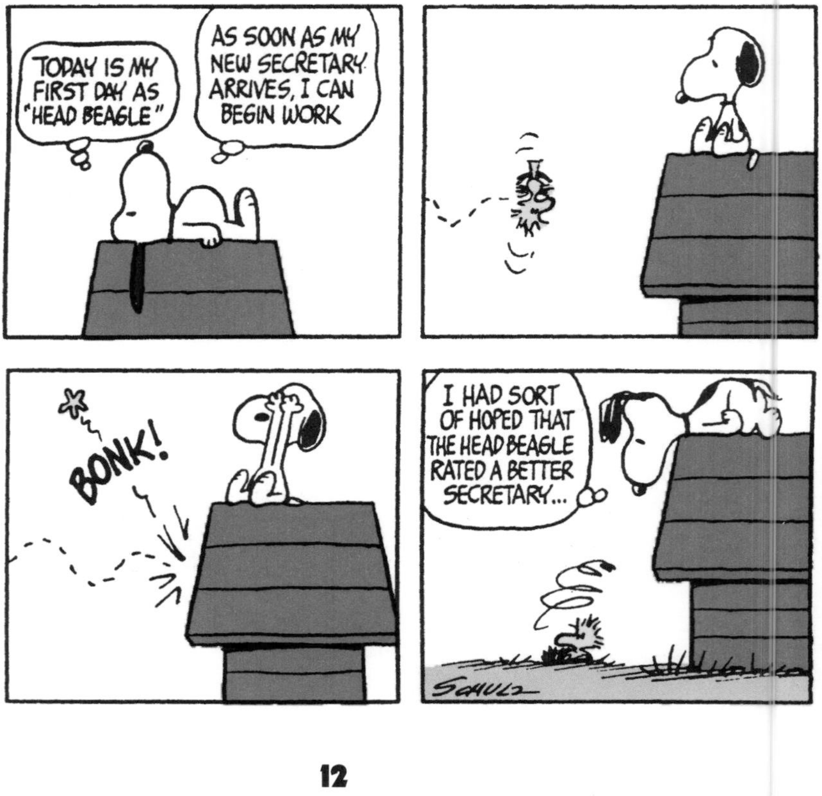
TODAY IS MY FIRST DAY AS "HEAD BEAGLE"
AS SOON AS MY NEW SECRETARY ARRIVES, I CAN BEGIN WORK
BONK!
I HAD SORT OF HOPED THAT THE HEAD BEAGLE RATED A BETTER SECRETARY...
SCHULZ

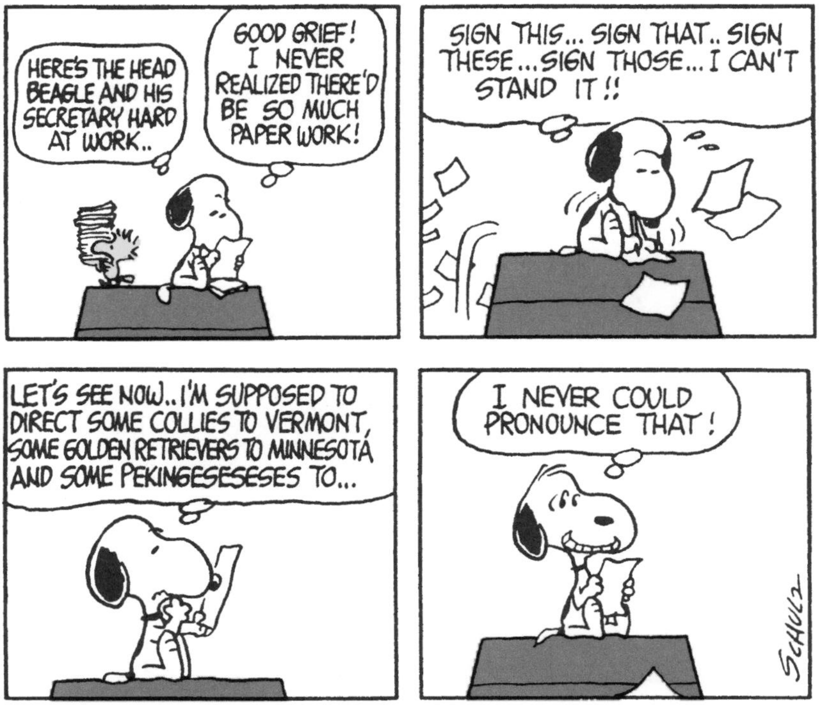
HERE'S THE HEAD BEAGLE AND HIS SECRETARY HARD AT WORK..
GOOD GRIEF! I NEVER REALIZED THERE'D BE SO MUCH PAPER WORK!
SIGN THIS... SIGN THAT.. SIGN THESE...SIGN THOSE...I CAN'T STAND IT!!
LET'S SEE NOW..I'M SUPPOSED TO DIRECT SOME COLLIES TO VERMONT, SOME GOLDEN RETRIEVERS TO MINNESOTA AND SOME PEKINGESESESES TO...
I NEVER COULD PRONOUNCE THAT!
SCHULZ

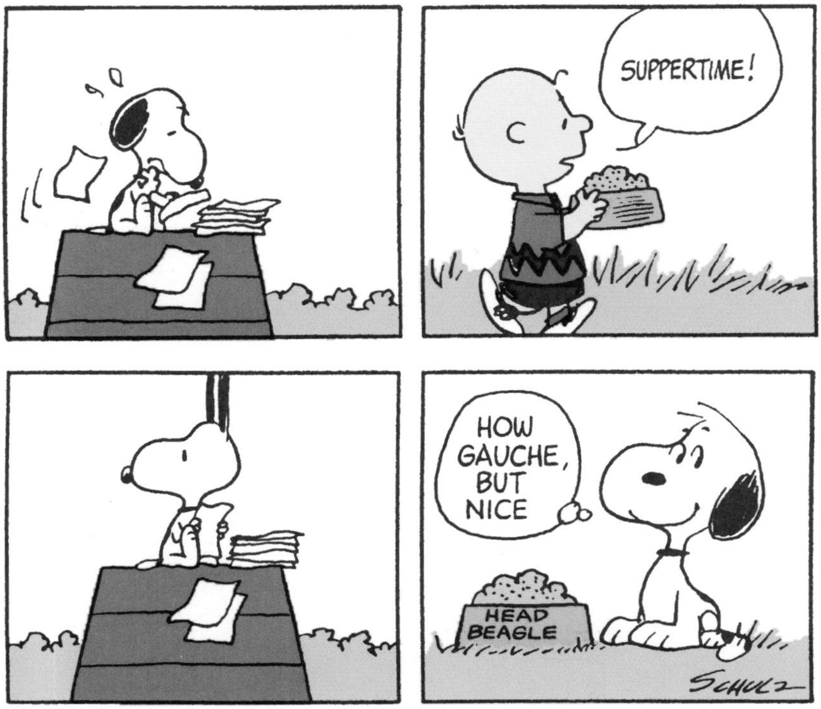
SUPPERTIME!
HOW GAUCHE, BUT NICE
HEAD BEAGLE
SCHULZ

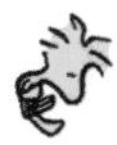

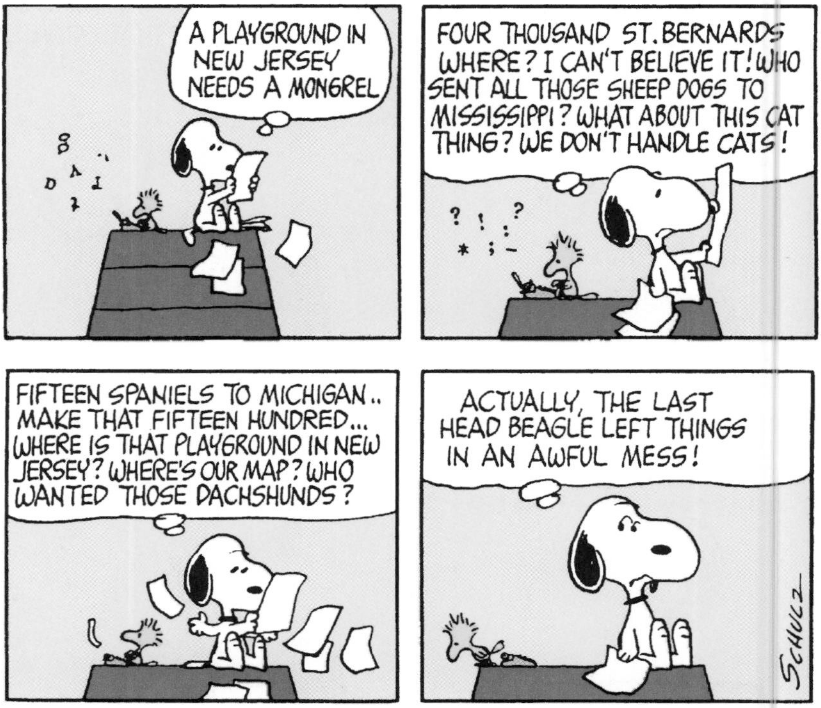
A PLAYGROUND IN NEW JERSEY NEEDS A MONGREL
FOUR THOUSAND ST. BERNARDS WHERE? I CAN'T BELIEVE IT! WHO SENT ALL THOSE SHEEP DOGS TO MISSISSIPPI? WHAT ABOUT THIS CAT THING? WE DON'T HANDLE CATS!
FIFTEEN SPANIELS TO MICHIGAN.. MAKE THAT FIFTEEN HUNDRED... WHERE IS THAT PLAYGROUND IN NEW JERSEY? WHERE'S OUR MAP? WHO WANTED THOSE DACHSHUNDS?
ACTUALLY, THE LAST HEAD BEAGLE LEFT THINGS IN AN AWFUL MESS!
SCHULZ

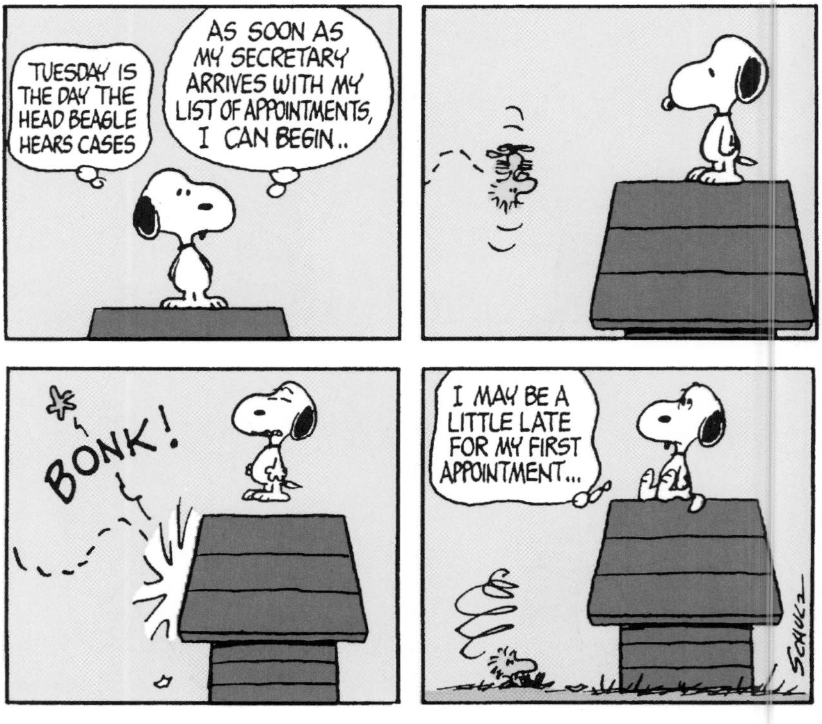
TUESDAY IS THE DAY THE HEAD BEAGLE HEARS CASES
AS SOON AS MY SECRETARY ARRIVES WITH MY LIST OF APPOINTMENTS, I CAN BEGIN..
BONK!
I MAY BE A LITTLE LATE FOR MY FIRST APPOINTMENT...
SCHULZ

Dear Sir,
THAT'S VERY NICE
PAT PAT
ALL SECRETARIES NEED A LITTLE COMPLIMENT NOW AND THEN..
Plx?g
SCHULZ

NOW, THIS NEXT LIST WILL HAVE THE NAMES OF TEN MILLION DOGS..
I NEED A DETAILED REPORT ON EACH DOG'S ACTIVITIES TYPED UP IN TRIPLICATE
KLUNK!
I HATE IT WHEN MY SECRETARY FAINTS!
SCHULZ

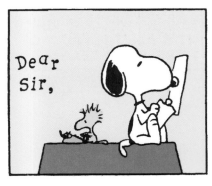

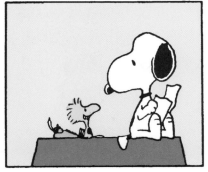

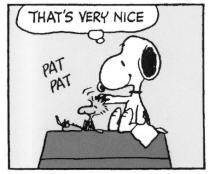

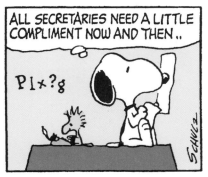

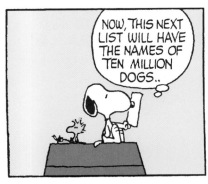

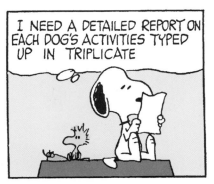

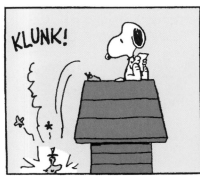

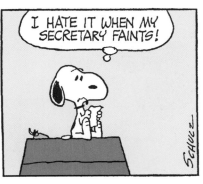

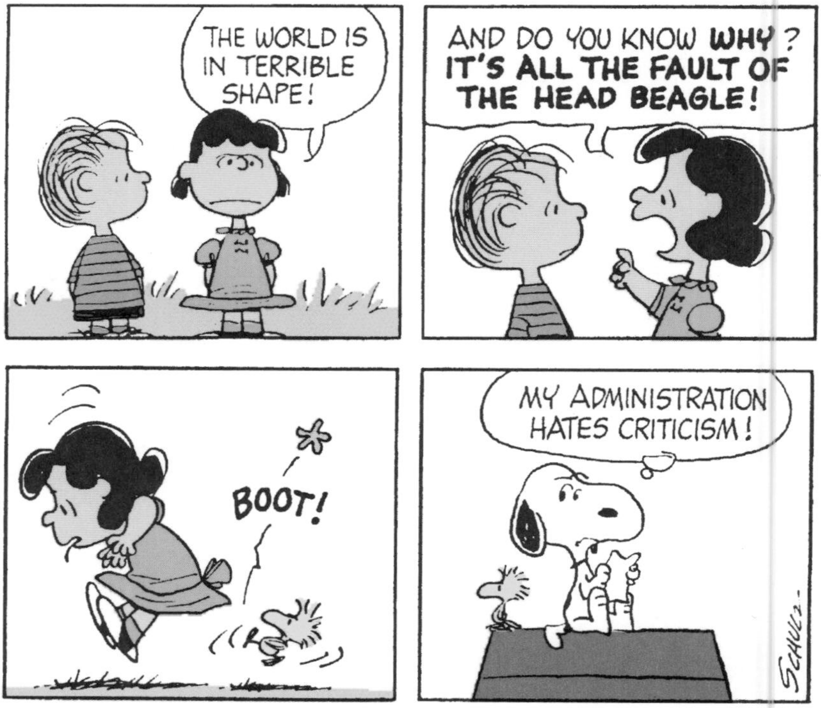
THE WORLD IS IN TERRIBLE SHAPE!
AND DO YOU KNOW **WHY**? **IT'S ALL THE FAULT OF THE HEAD BEAGLE!**
BOOT!
MY ADMINISTRATION HATES CRITICISM!
SCHULZ

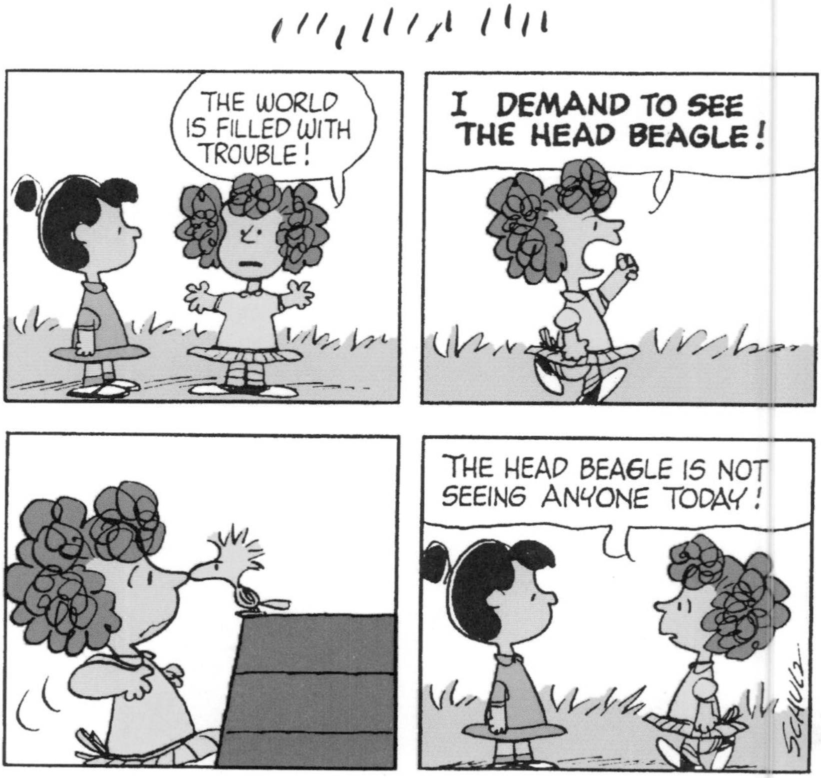
THE WORLD IS FILLED WITH TROUBLE!
I DEMAND TO SEE THE HEAD BEAGLE!
THE HEAD BEAGLE IS NOT SEEING ANYONE TODAY!
SCHULZ

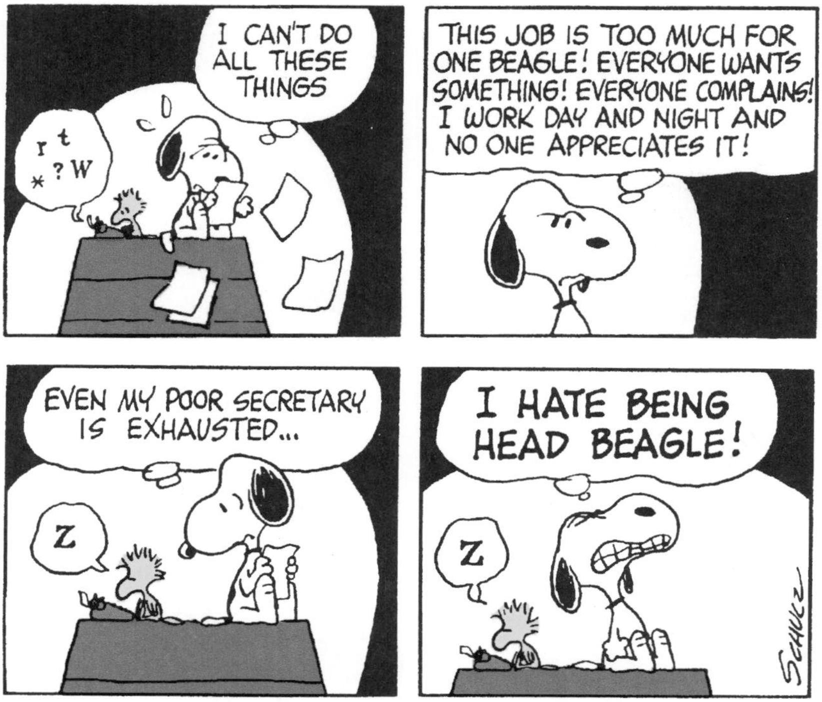
I CAN'T DO ALL THESE THINGS
r t * ? W
THIS JOB IS TOO MUCH FOR ONE BEAGLE! EVERYONE WANTS SOMETHING! EVERYONE COMPLAINS! I WORK DAY AND NIGHT AND NO ONE APPRECIATES IT!
EVEN MY POOR SECRETARY IS EXHAUSTED...
Z
I HATE BEING HEAD BEAGLE!
Z
SCHULZ

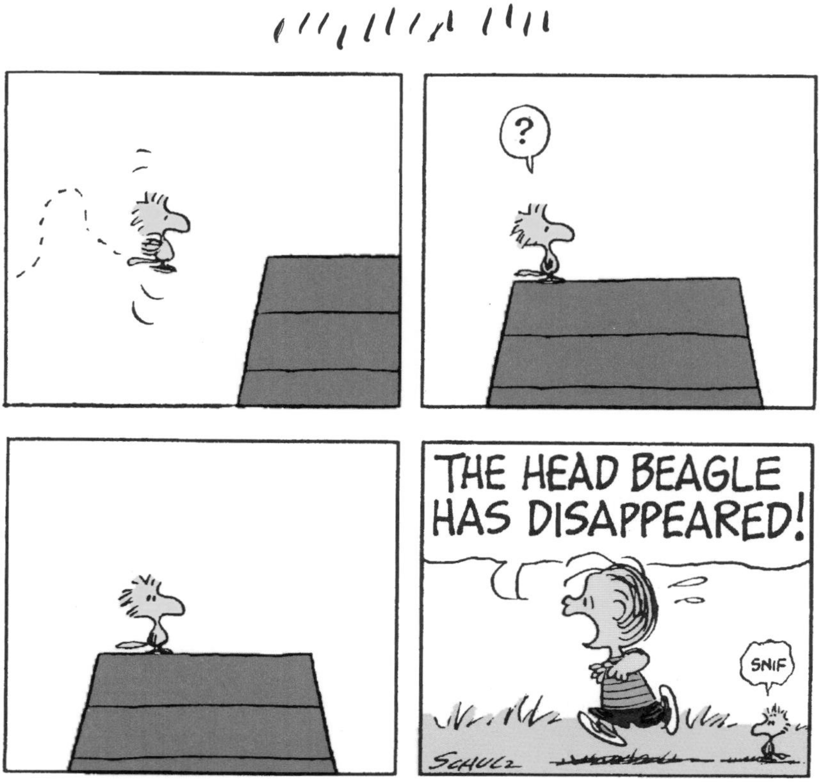
?
THE HEAD BEAGLE HAS DISAPPEARED!
SNIF
SCHULZ

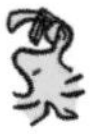

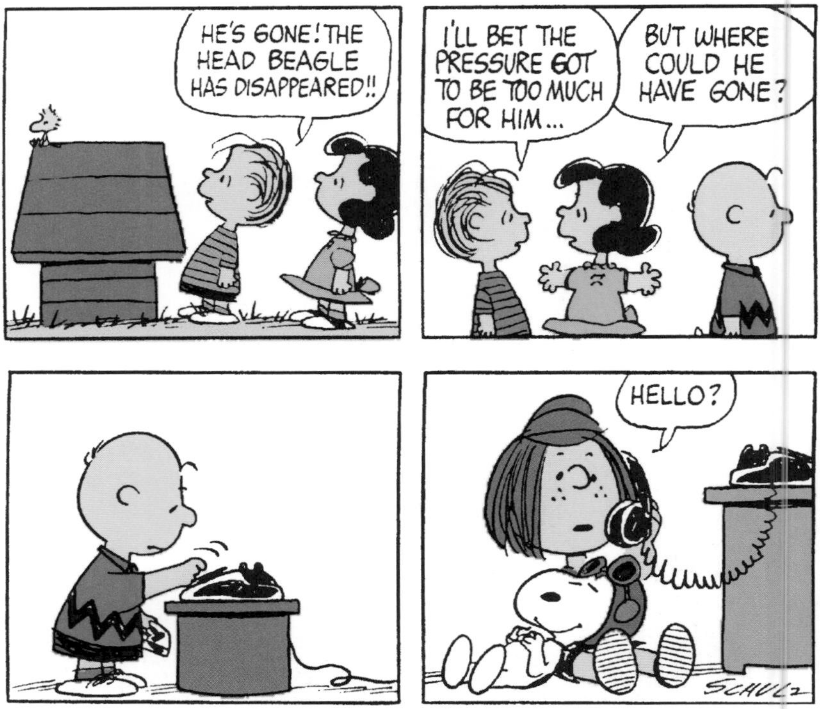
HE'S GONE! THE HEAD BEAGLE HAS DISAPPEARED!!
I'LL BET THE PRESSURE GOT TO BE TOO MUCH FOR HIM...
BUT WHERE COULD HE HAVE GONE?
HELLO?
SCHULZ

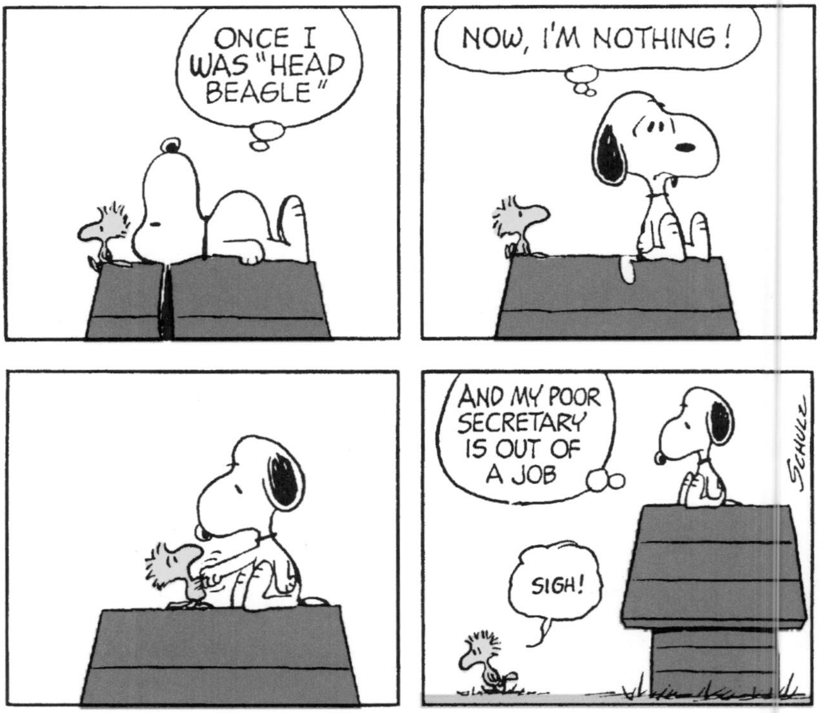
ONCE I WAS "HEAD BEAGLE"
NOW, I'M NOTHING!
AND MY POOR SECRETARY IS OUT OF A JOB
SIGH!
SCHULZ

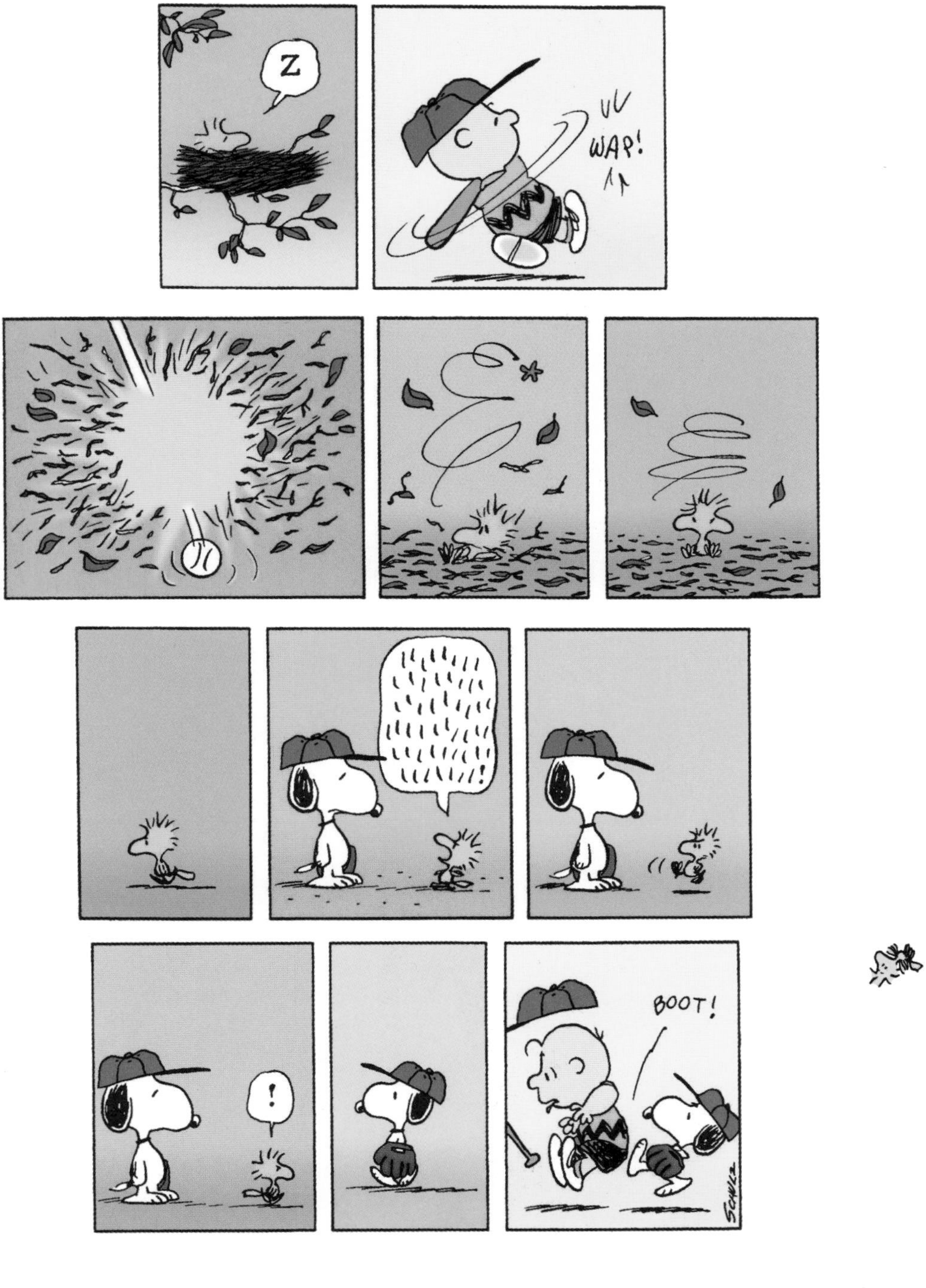
Z
WAP!
BOOT!

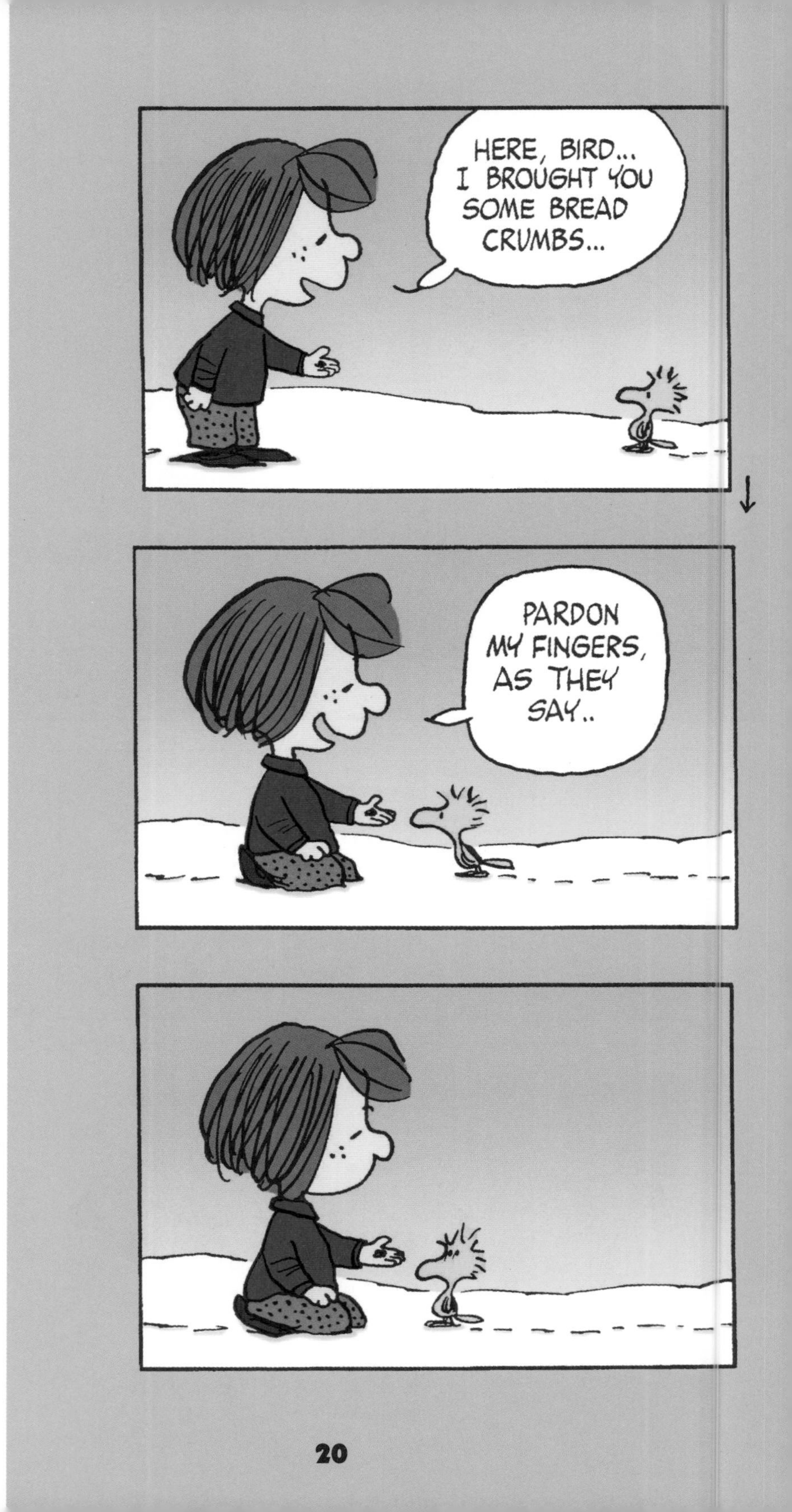
HERE, BIRD... I BROUGHT YOU SOME BREAD CRUMBS...
PARDON MY FINGERS, AS THEY SAY..

BLEAH!
MY HANDS ARE CLEAN, YOU STUPID BIRD!
SCHULZ

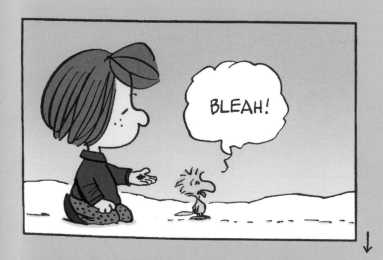

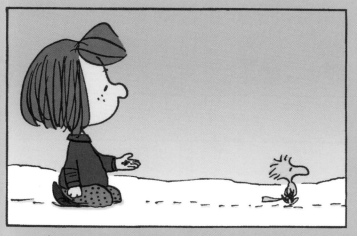

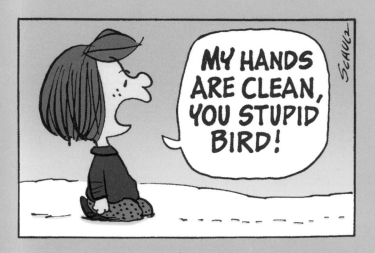

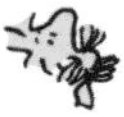

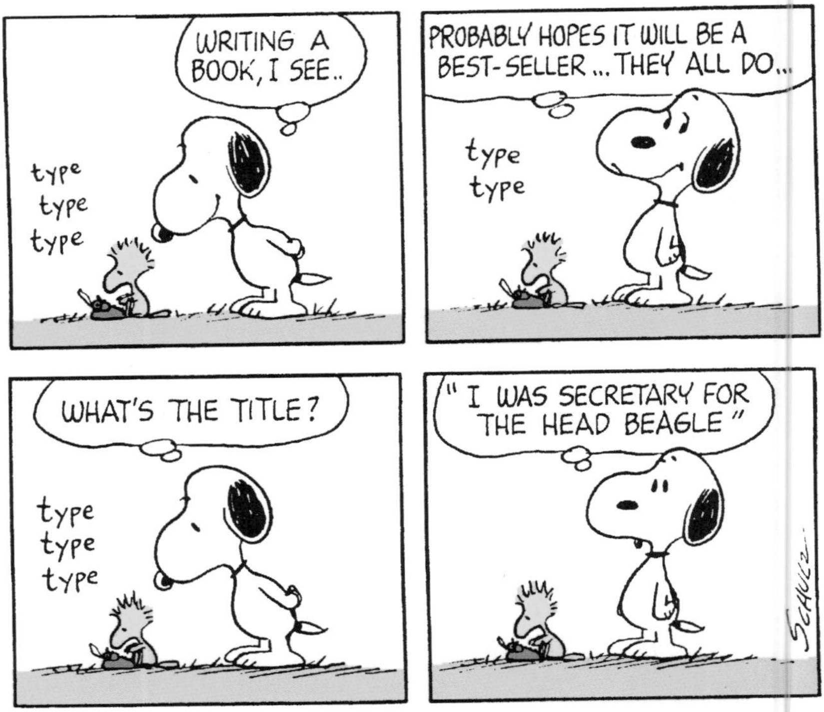
WRITING A BOOK, I SEE..
type
type
type
PROBABLY HOPES IT WILL BE A BEST-SELLER ... THEY ALL DO...
type
type
WHAT'S THE TITLE?
type
type
type
" I WAS SECRETARY FOR THE HEAD BEAGLE "

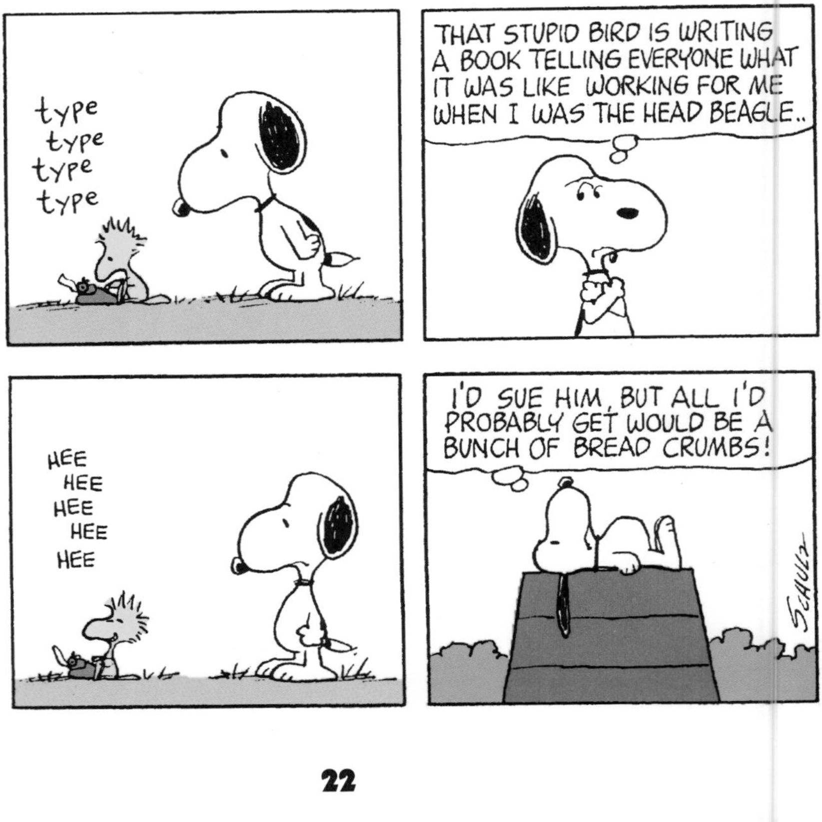
type
type
type
type
THAT STUPID BIRD IS WRITING A BOOK TELLING EVERYONE WHAT IT WAS LIKE WORKING FOR ME WHEN I WAS THE HEAD BEAGLE..
HEE
HEE
HEE
HEE
HEE
I'D SUE HIM, BUT ALL I'D PROBABLY GET WOULD BE A BUNCH OF BREAD CRUMBS!

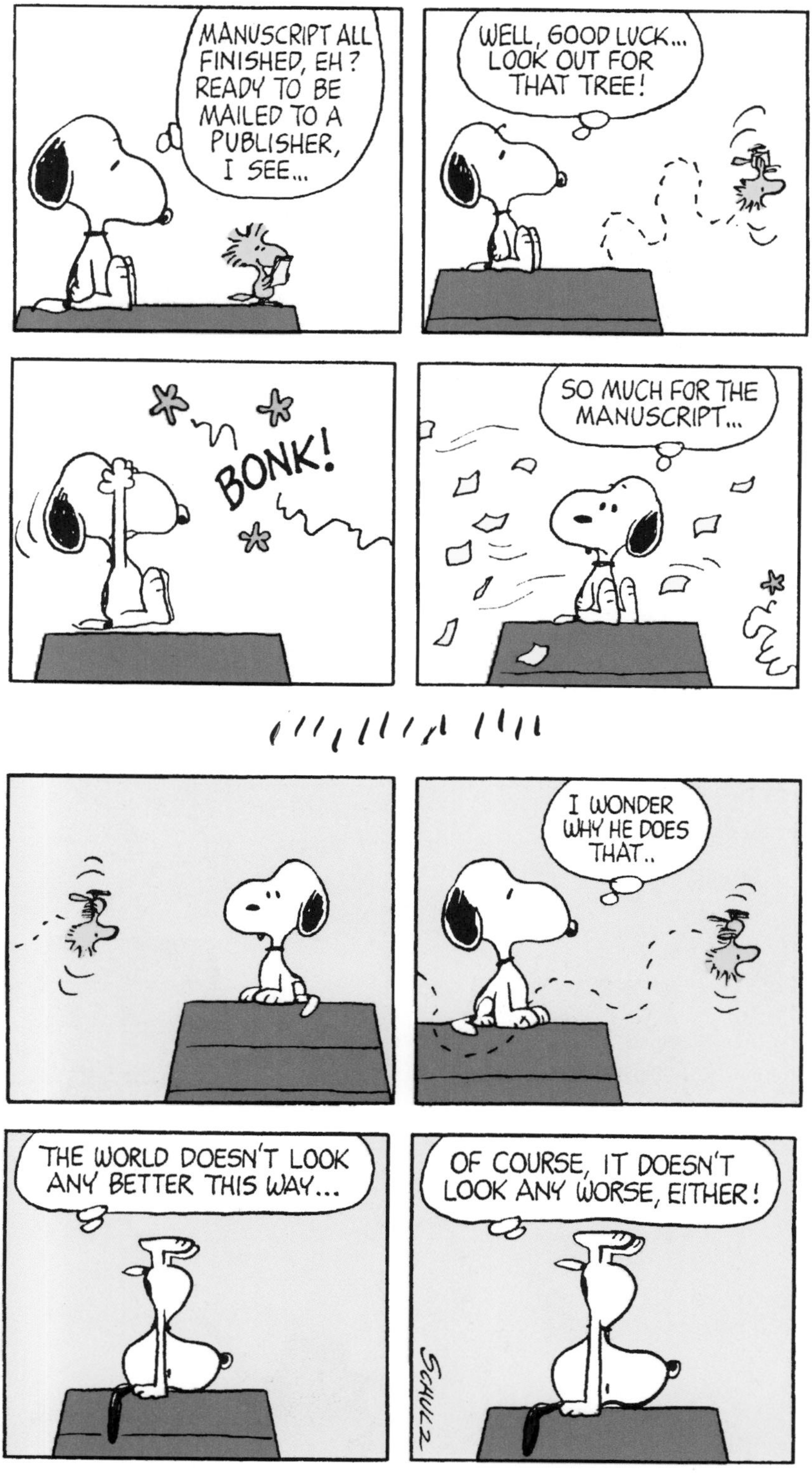
MANUSCRIPT ALL FINISHED, EH? READY TO BE MAILED TO A PUBLISHER, I SEE...
WELL, GOOD LUCK... LOOK OUT FOR THAT TREE!
BONK!
SO MUCH FOR THE MANUSCRIPT...
I WONDER WHY HE DOES THAT..
THE WORLD DOESN'T LOOK ANY BETTER THIS WAY...
OF COURSE, IT DOESN'T LOOK ANY WORSE, EITHER!
SCHULZ

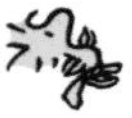

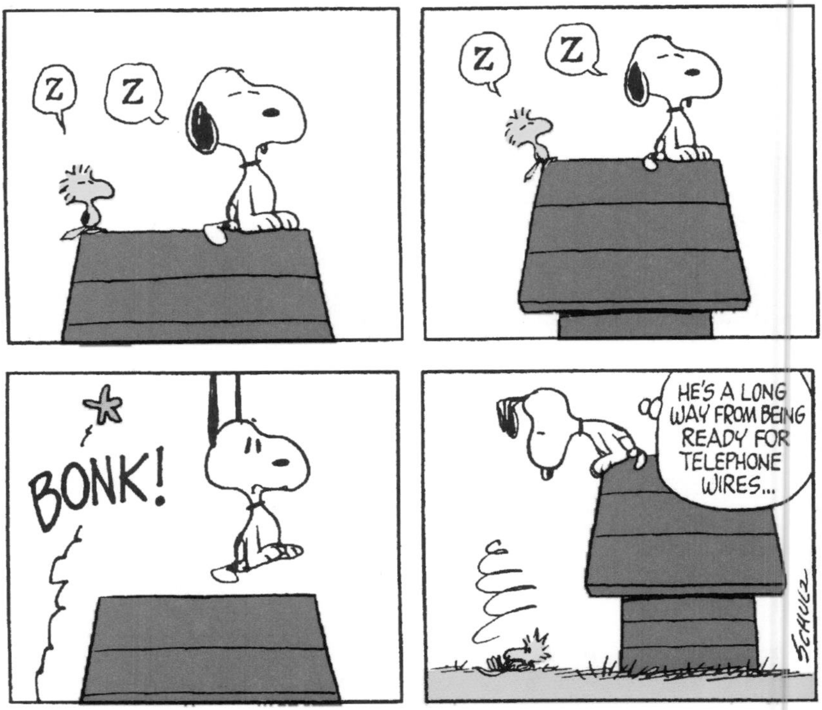
Z
Z
Z
Z
BONK!
HE'S A LONG WAY FROM BEING READY FOR TELEPHONE WIRES...

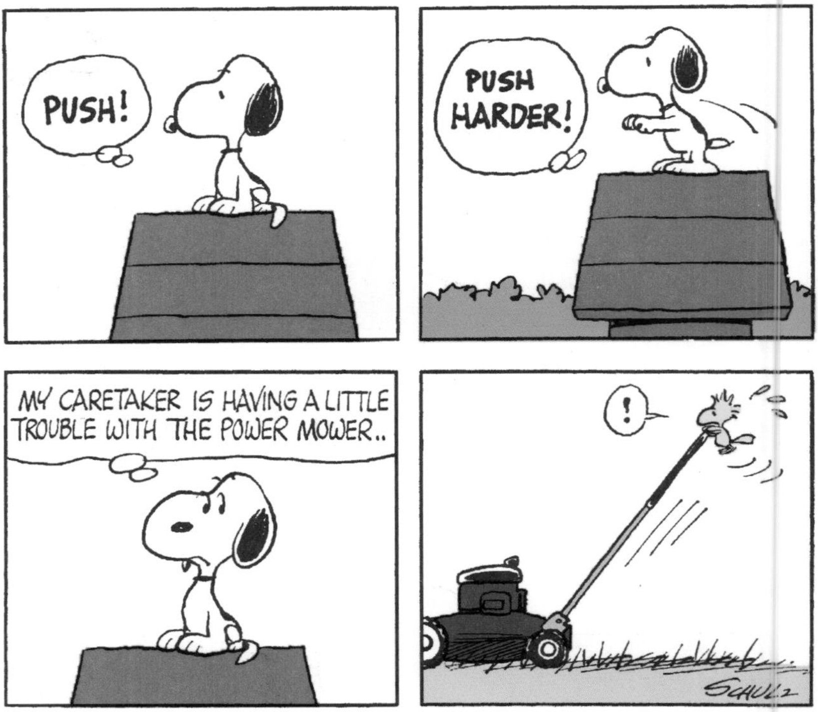
PUSH!
PUSH HARDER!
MY CARETAKER IS HAVING A LITTLE TROUBLE WITH THE POWER MOWER..
!

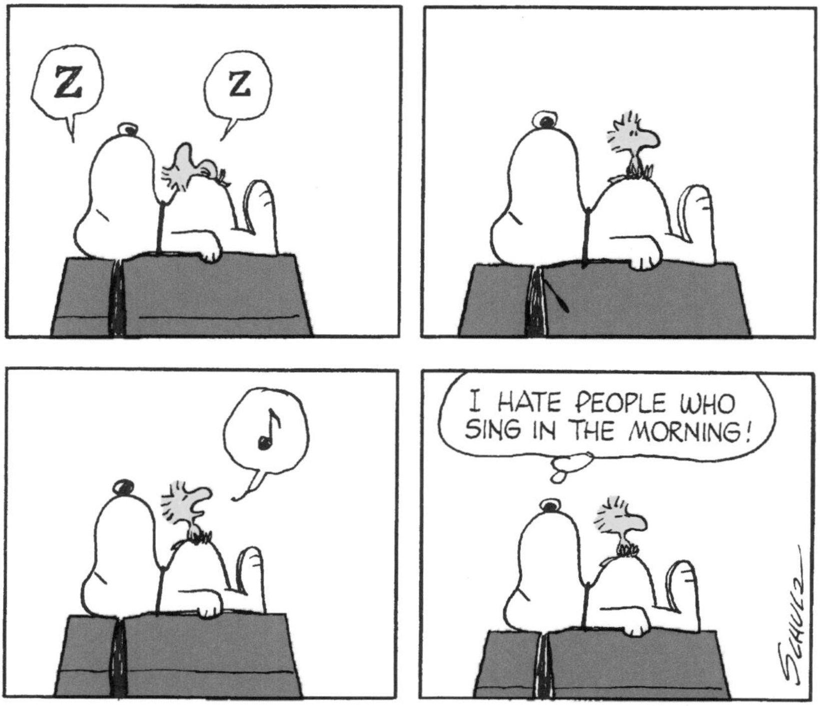
Z
Z
♪
I HATE PEOPLE WHO SING IN THE MORNING!
SCHULZ

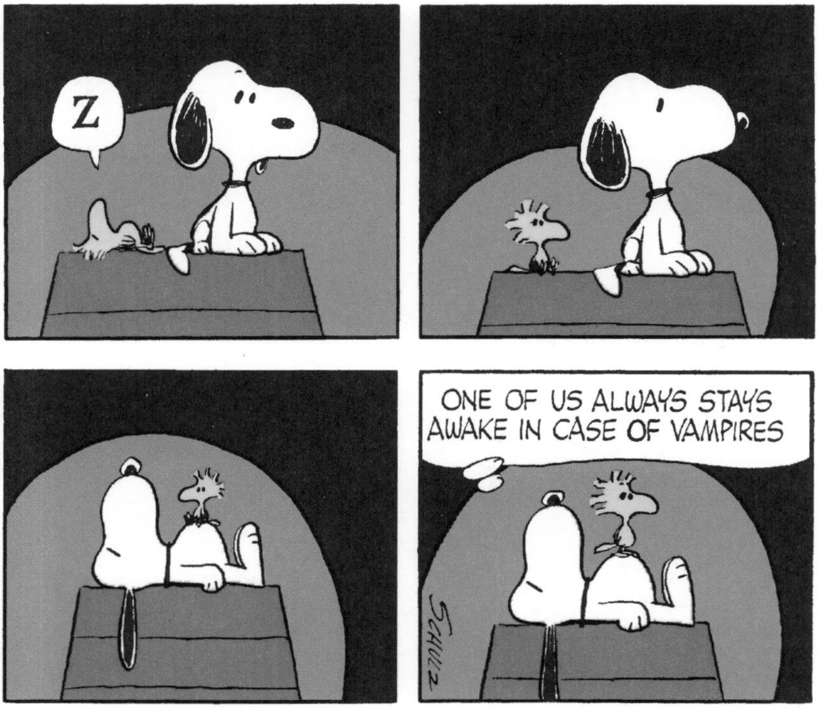
Z
ONE OF US ALWAYS STAYS AWAKE IN CASE OF VAMPIRES
SCHULZ

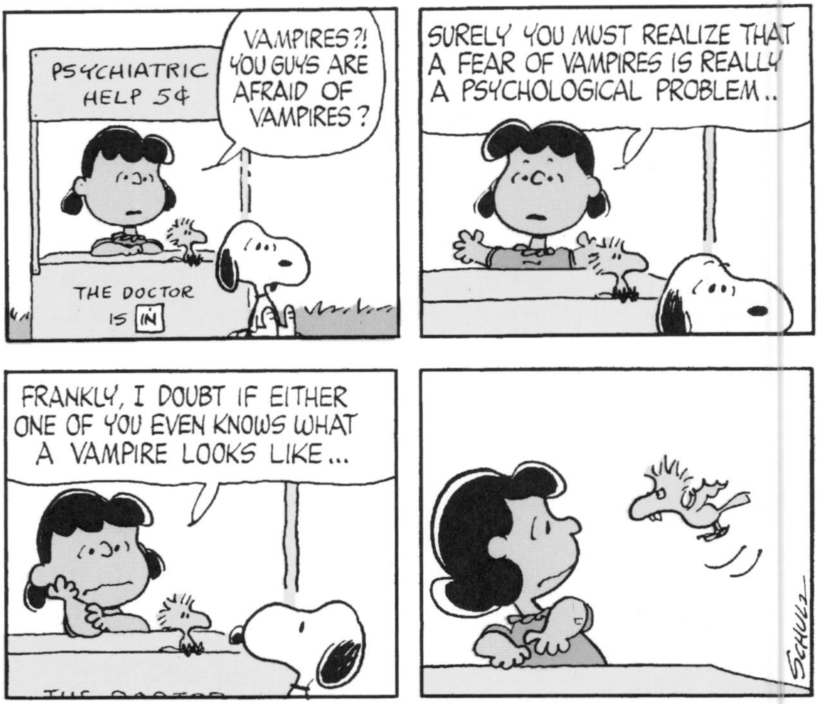
PSYCHIATRIC HELP 5¢
THE DOCTOR IS IN
VAMPIRES?! YOU GUYS ARE AFRAID OF VAMPIRES?
SURELY YOU MUST REALIZE THAT A FEAR OF VAMPIRES IS REALLY A PSYCHOLOGICAL PROBLEM..
FRANKLY, I DOUBT IF EITHER ONE OF YOU EVEN KNOWS WHAT A VAMPIRE LOOKS LIKE...
SCHULZ

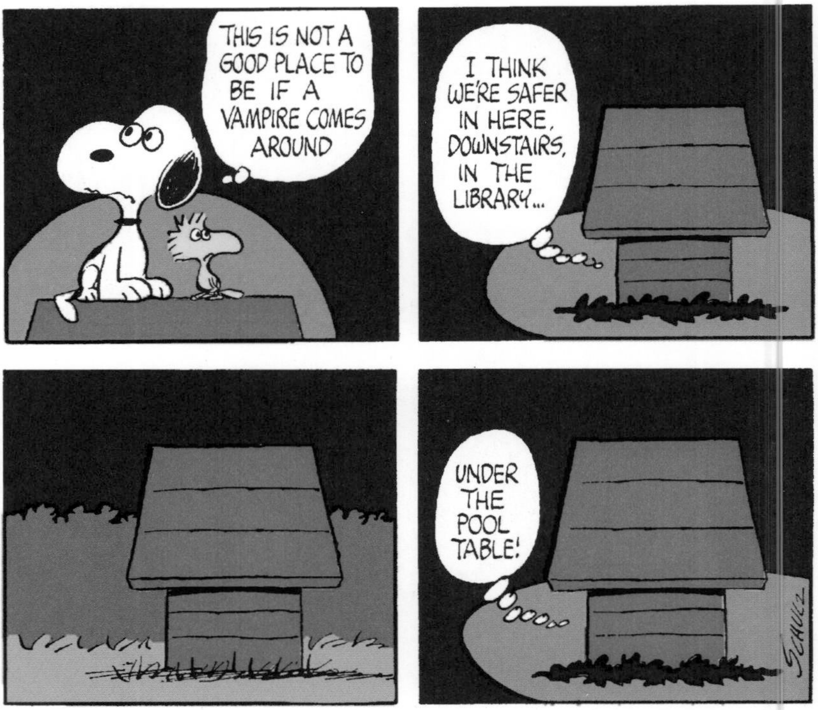
THIS IS NOT A GOOD PLACE TO BE IF A VAMPIRE COMES AROUND
I THINK WE'RE SAFER IN HERE, DOWNSTAIRS, IN THE LIBRARY...
UNDER THE POOL TABLE!
SCHULZ

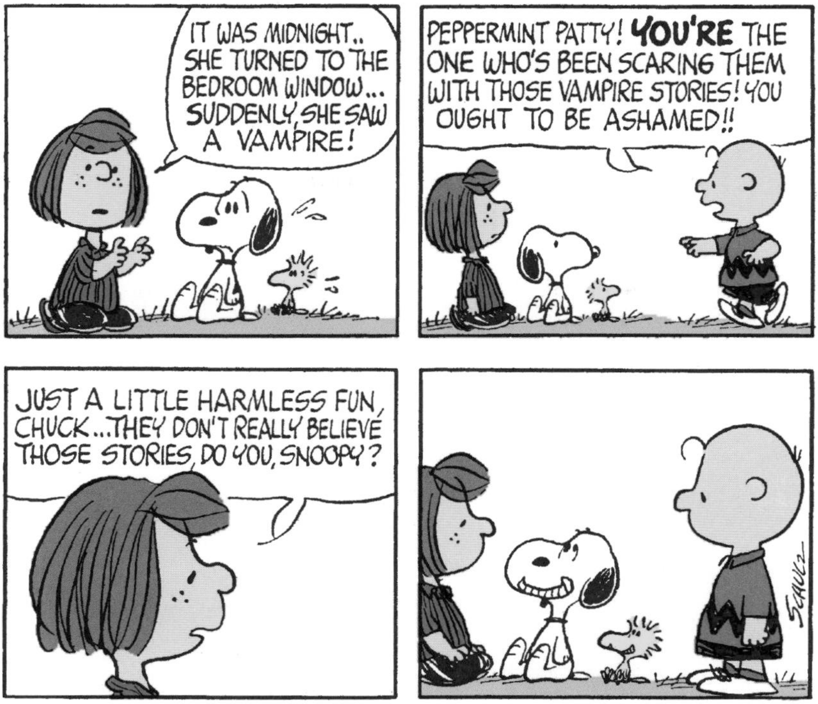
IT WAS MIDNIGHT.. SHE TURNED TO THE BEDROOM WINDOW... SUDDENLY, SHE SAW A VAMPIRE!
PEPPERMINT PATTY! **YOU'RE** THE ONE WHO'S BEEN SCARING THEM WITH THOSE VAMPIRE STORIES! YOU OUGHT TO BE ASHAMED!!
JUST A LITTLE HARMLESS FUN, CHUCK...THEY DON'T REALLY BELIEVE THOSE STORIES, DO YOU, SNOOPY?
SCHULZ

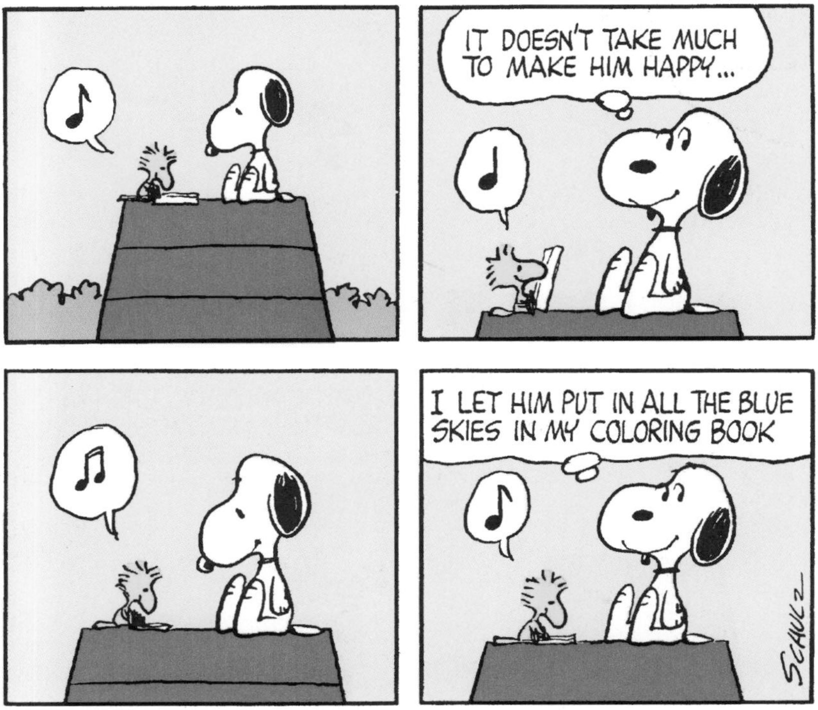
IT DOESN'T TAKE MUCH TO MAKE HIM HAPPY...
I LET HIM PUT IN ALL THE BLUE SKIES IN MY COLORING BOOK
SCHULZ

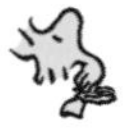

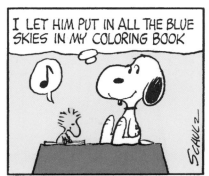

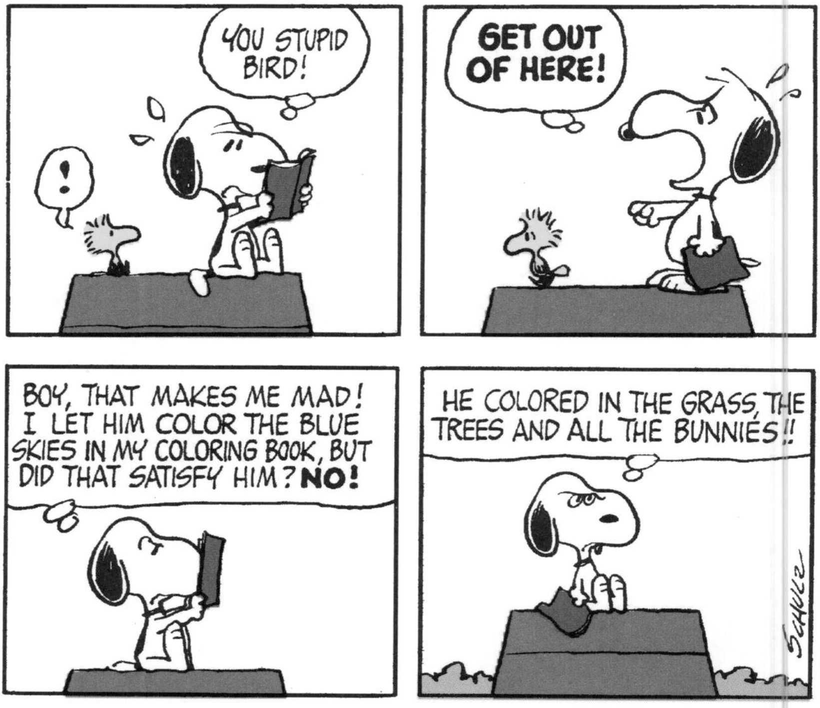
YOU STUPID BIRD!
!
GET OUT OF HERE!
BOY, THAT MAKES ME MAD! I LET HIM COLOR THE BLUE SKIES IN MY COLORING BOOK, BUT DID THAT SATISFY HIM? NO!
HE COLORED IN THE GRASS, THE TREES AND ALL THE BUNNIES!!

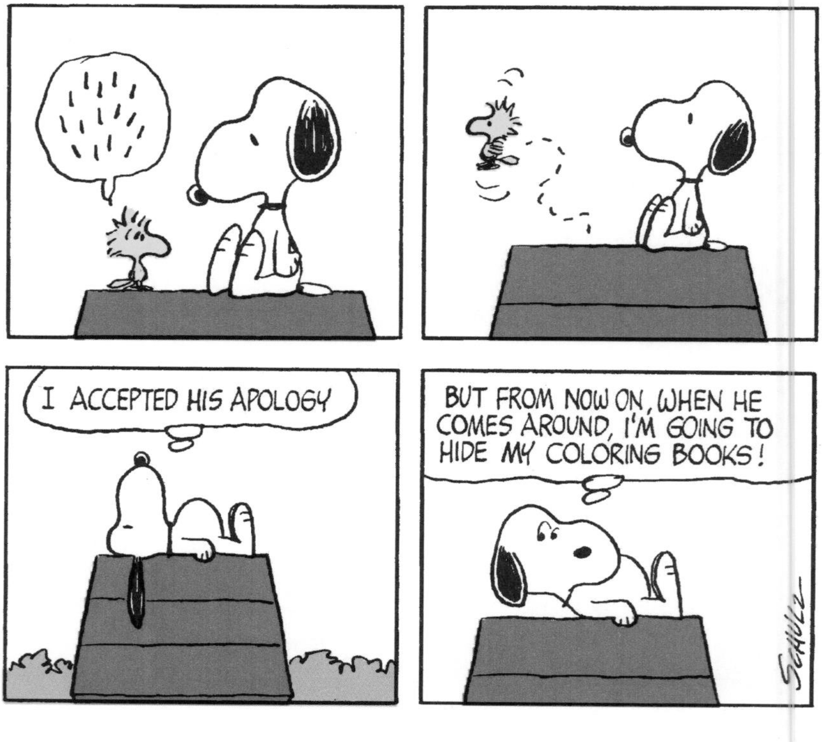
I ACCEPTED HIS APOLOGY
BUT FROM NOW ON, WHEN HE COMES AROUND, I'M GOING TO HIDE MY COLORING BOOKS!

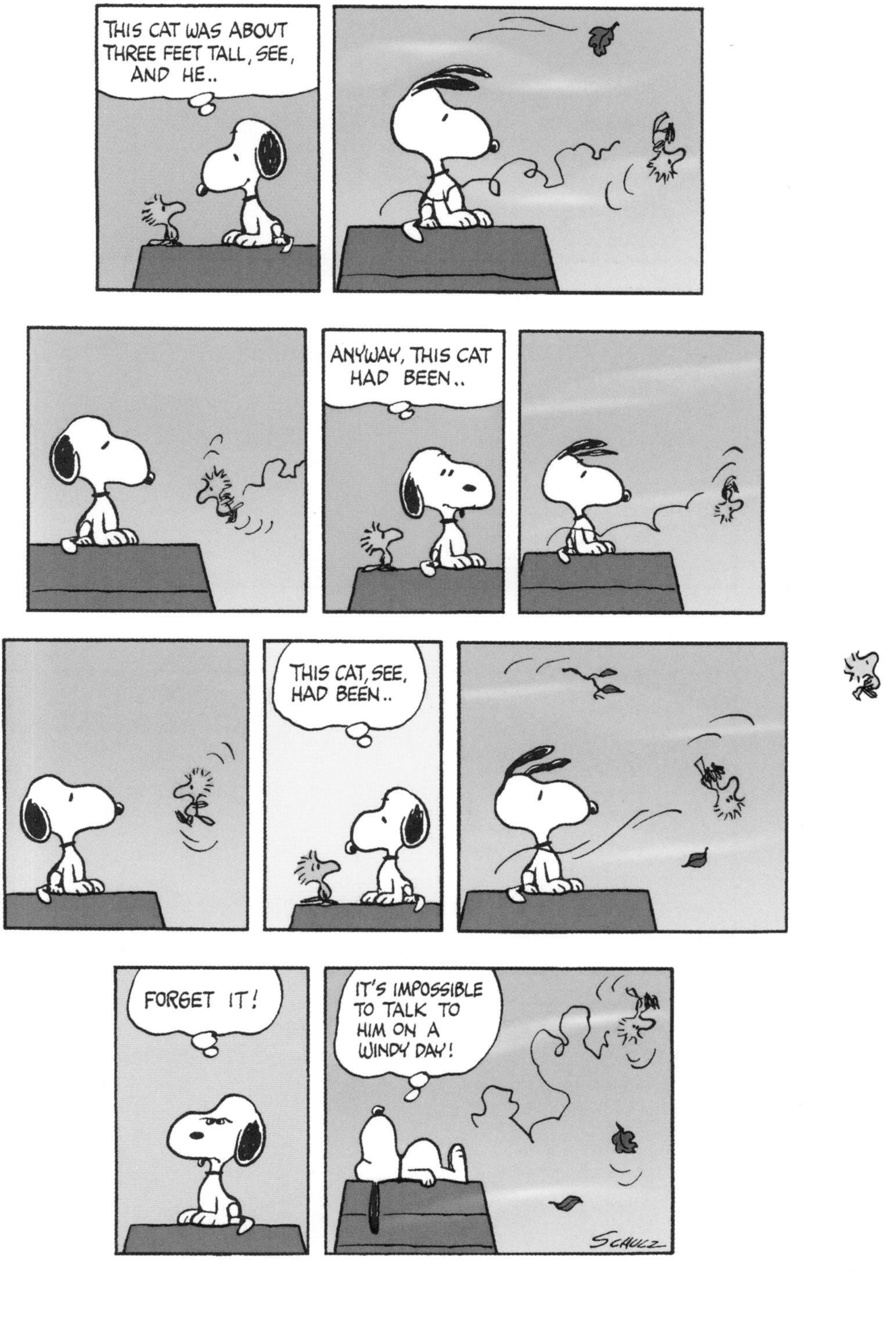
THIS CAT WAS ABOUT THREE FEET TALL, SEE, AND HE..
ANYWAY, THIS CAT HAD BEEN..
THIS CAT, SEE, HAD BEEN..
FORGET IT!
IT'S IMPOSSIBLE TO TALK TO HIM ON A WINDY DAY!
SCHULZ

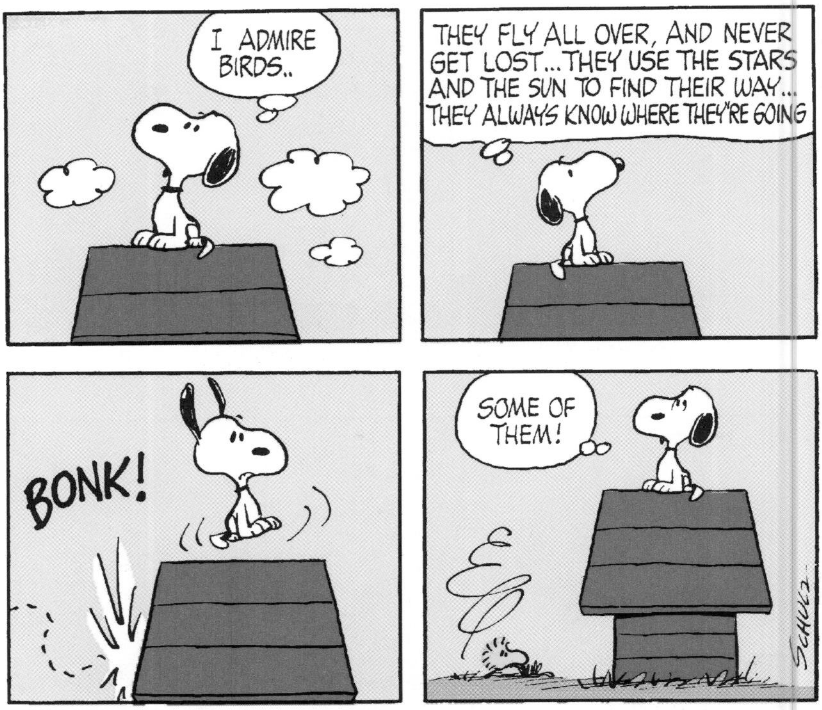
I ADMIRE BIRDS..
THEY FLY ALL OVER, AND NEVER GET LOST...THEY USE THE STARS AND THE SUN TO FIND THEIR WAY... THEY ALWAYS KNOW WHERE THEY'RE GOING
BONK!
SOME OF THEM!
SCHULZ

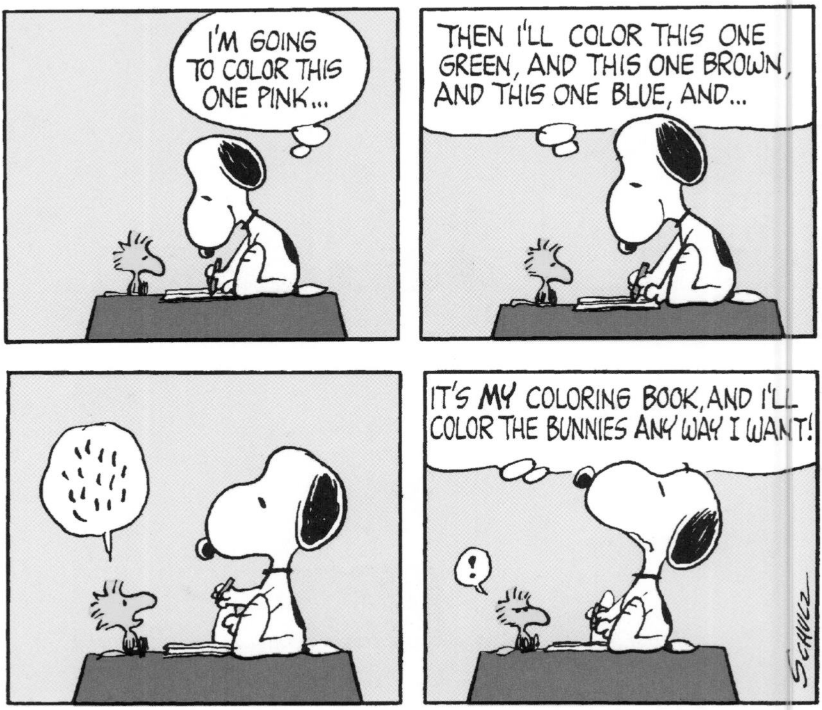
I'M GOING TO COLOR THIS ONE PINK...
THEN I'LL COLOR THIS ONE GREEN, AND THIS ONE BROWN, AND THIS ONE BLUE, AND...
IT'S **MY** COLORING BOOK, AND I'LL COLOR THE BUNNIES ANY WAY I WANT!
!
SCHULZ

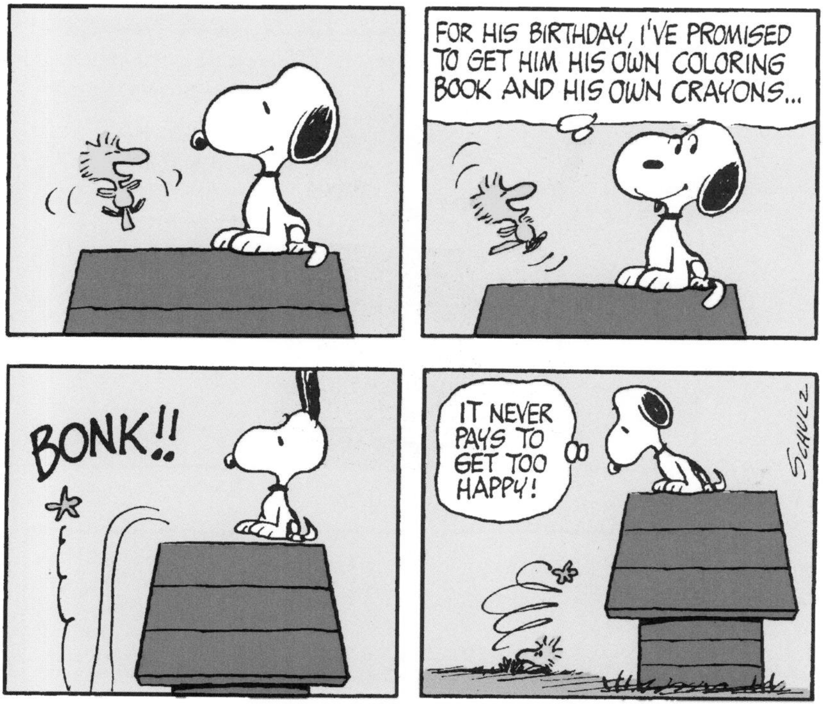
FOR HIS BIRTHDAY, I'VE PROMISED TO GET HIM HIS OWN COLORING BOOK AND HIS OWN CRAYONS...
BONK!!
IT NEVER PAYS TO GET TOO HAPPY!
SCHULZ

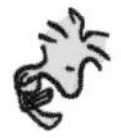

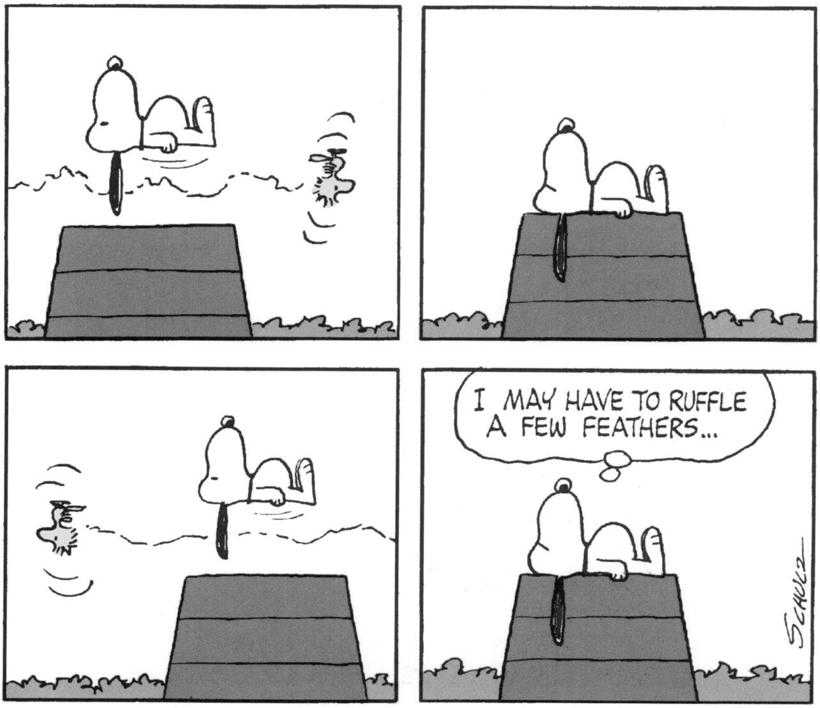
I MAY HAVE TO RUFFLE A FEW FEATHERS...
SCHULZ

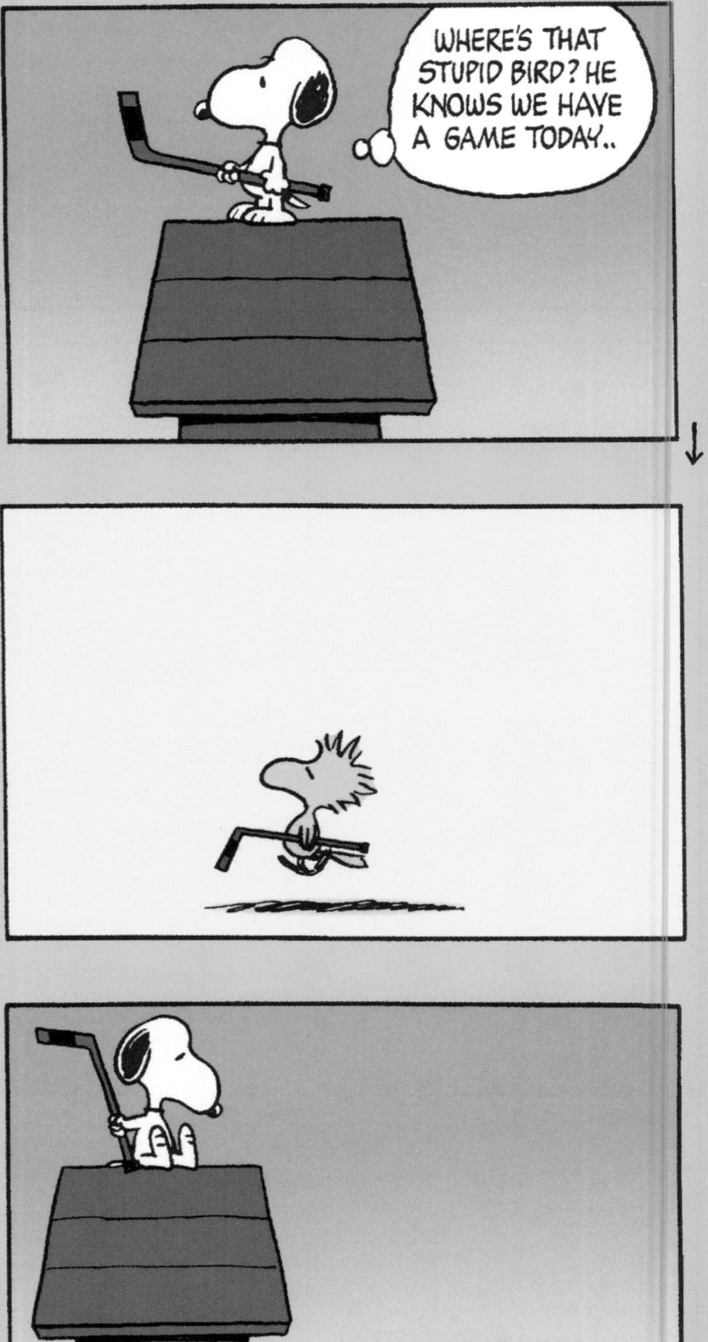
WHERE'S THAT STUPID BIRD? HE KNOWS WE HAVE A GAME TODAY..

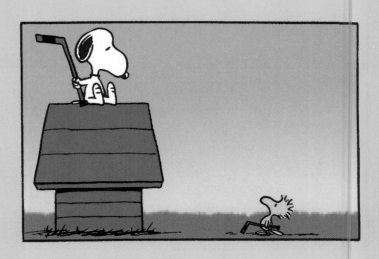

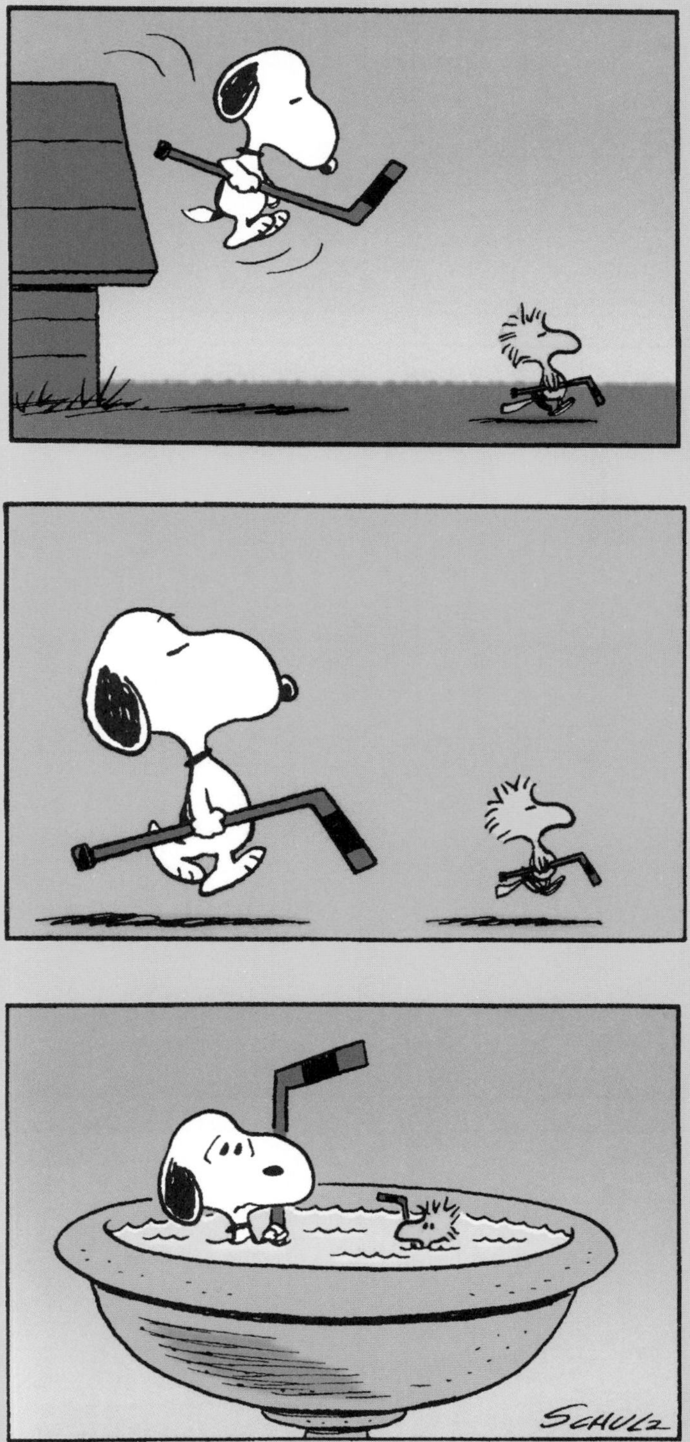
SCHULZ

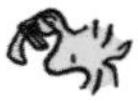

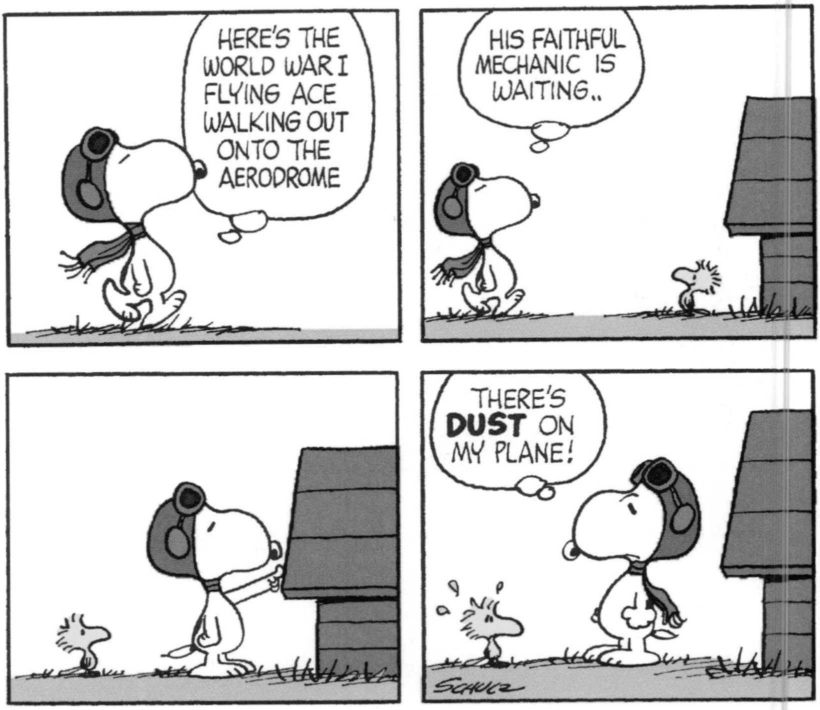
HERE'S THE WORLD WAR I FLYING ACE WALKING OUT ONTO THE AERODROME
HIS FAITHFUL MECHANIC IS WAITING..
THERE'S **DUST** ON MY PLANE!
SCHULZ

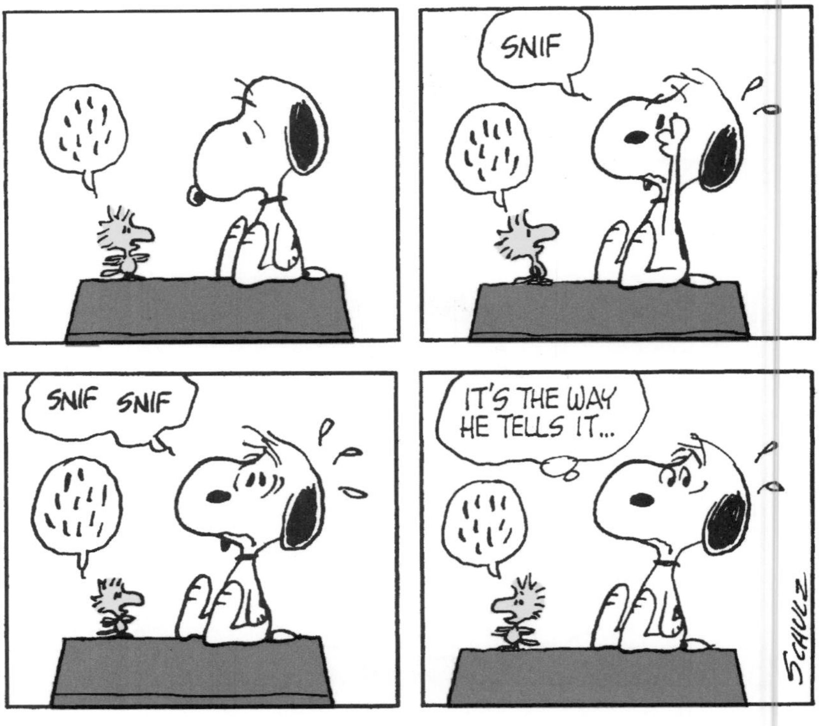
SNIF
SNIF SNIF
IT'S THE WAY HE TELLS IT...
SCHULZ

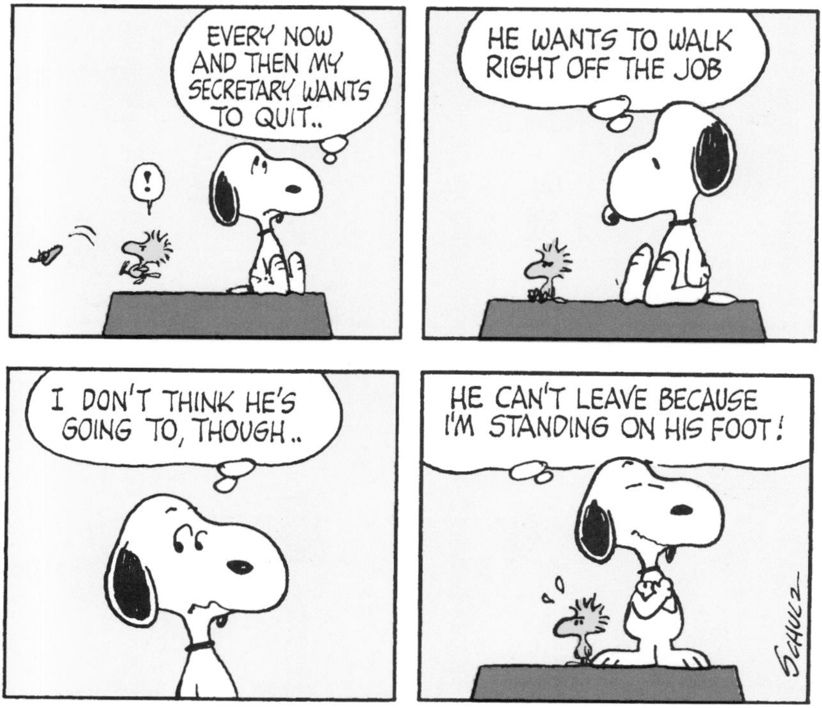
EVERY NOW AND THEN MY SECRETARY WANTS TO QUIT..
HE WANTS TO WALK RIGHT OFF THE JOB
I DON'T THINK HE'S GOING TO, THOUGH..
HE CAN'T LEAVE BECAUSE I'M STANDING ON HIS FOOT!
SCHULZ

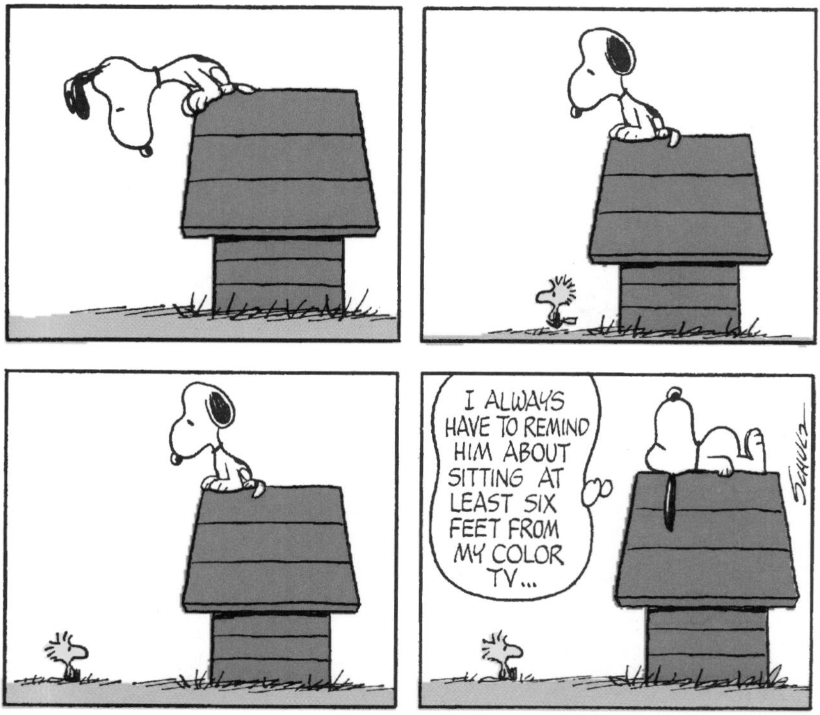
I ALWAYS HAVE TO REMIND HIM ABOUT SITTING AT LEAST SIX FEET FROM MY COLOR TV...
SCHULZ

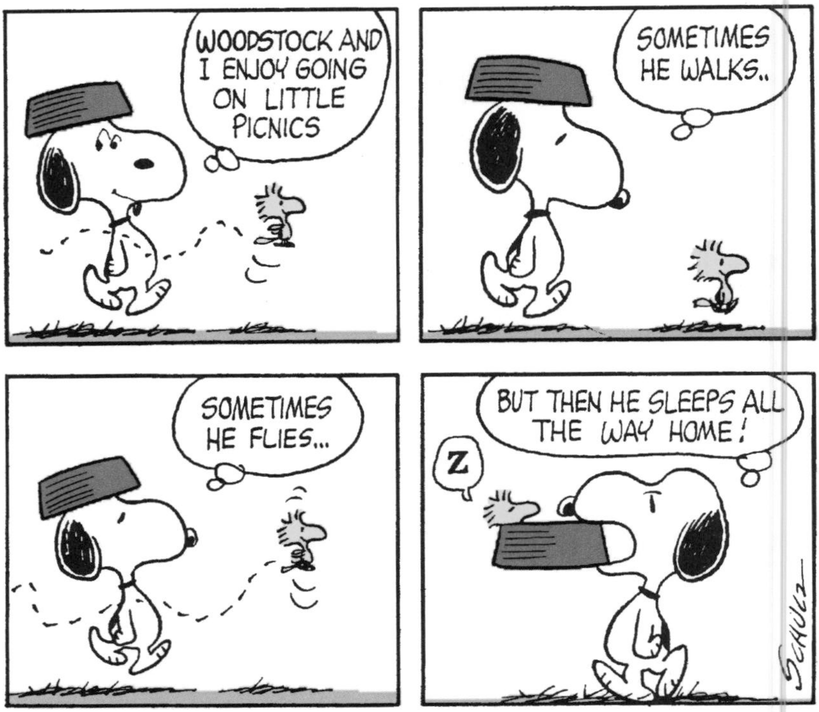
WOODSTOCK AND I ENJOY GOING ON LITTLE PICNICS
SOMETIMES HE WALKS..
SOMETIMES HE FLIES...
BUT THEN HE SLEEPS ALL THE WAY HOME!
Z
SCHULZ

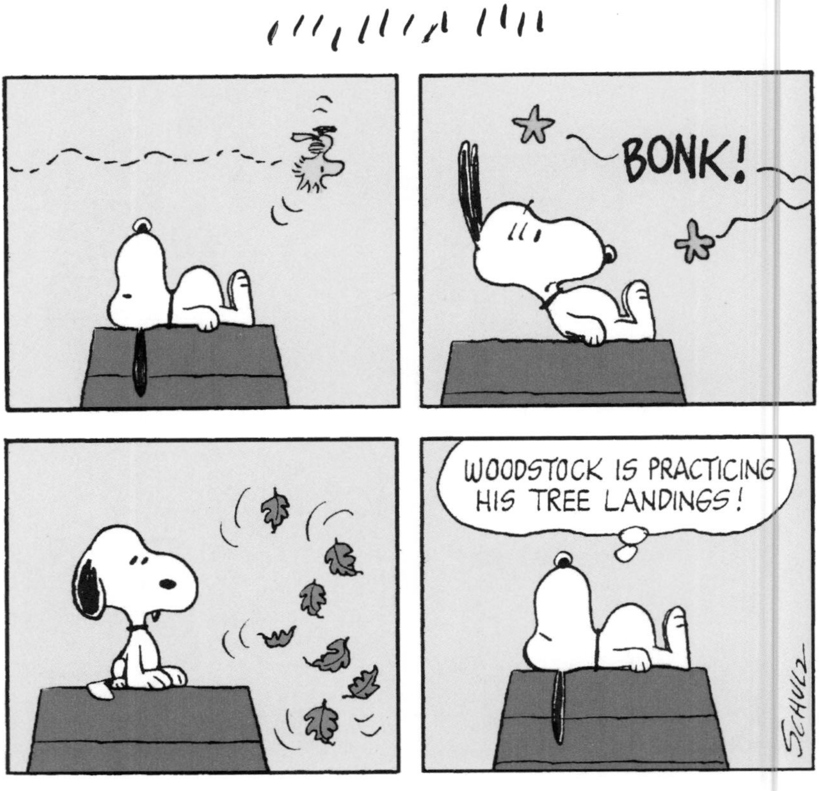
BONK!
WOODSTOCK IS PRACTICING HIS TREE LANDINGS!
SCHULZ

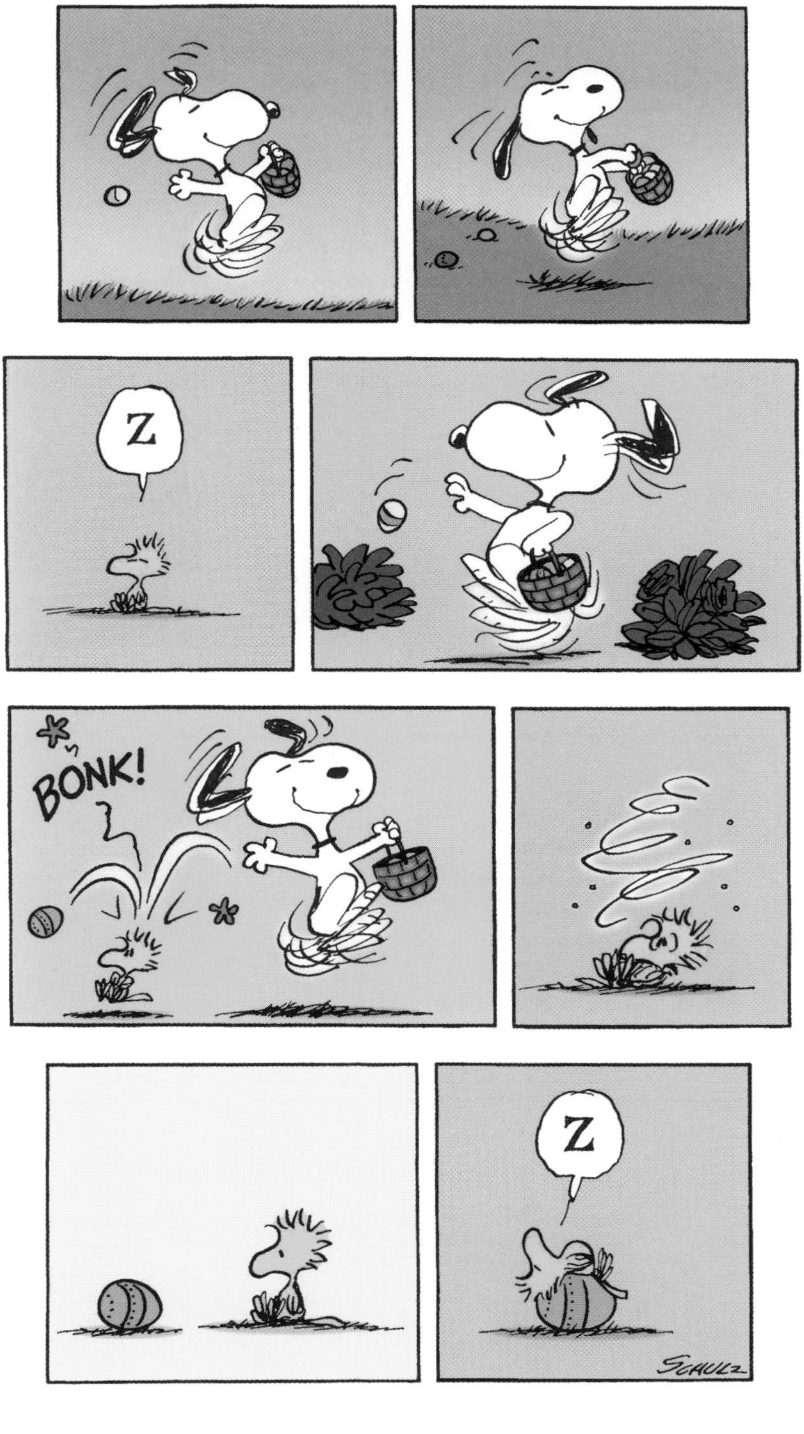
Z
BONK!
Z
SCHULZ

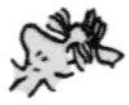

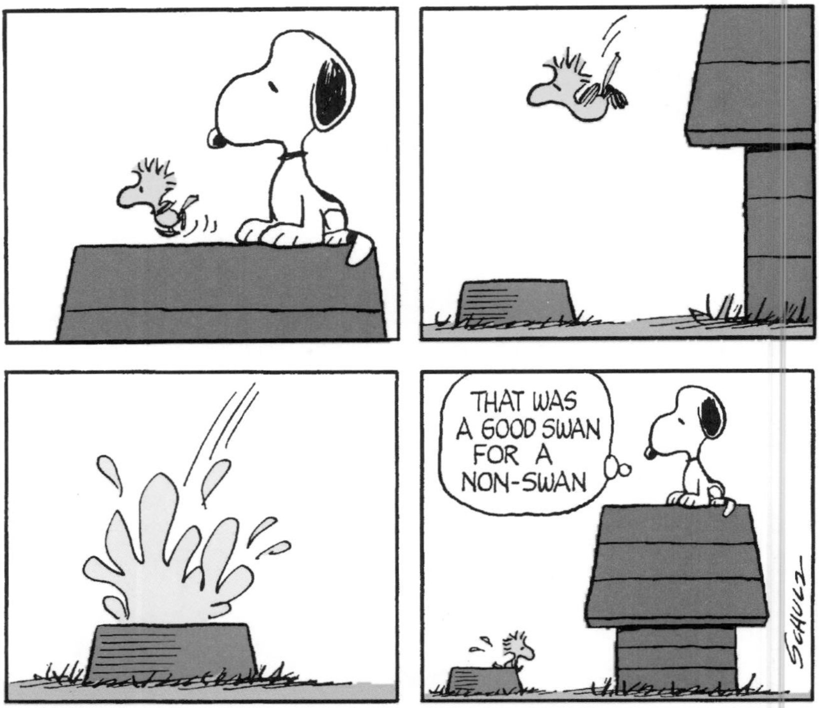
THAT WAS A GOOD SWAN FOR A NON-SWAN
SCHULZ

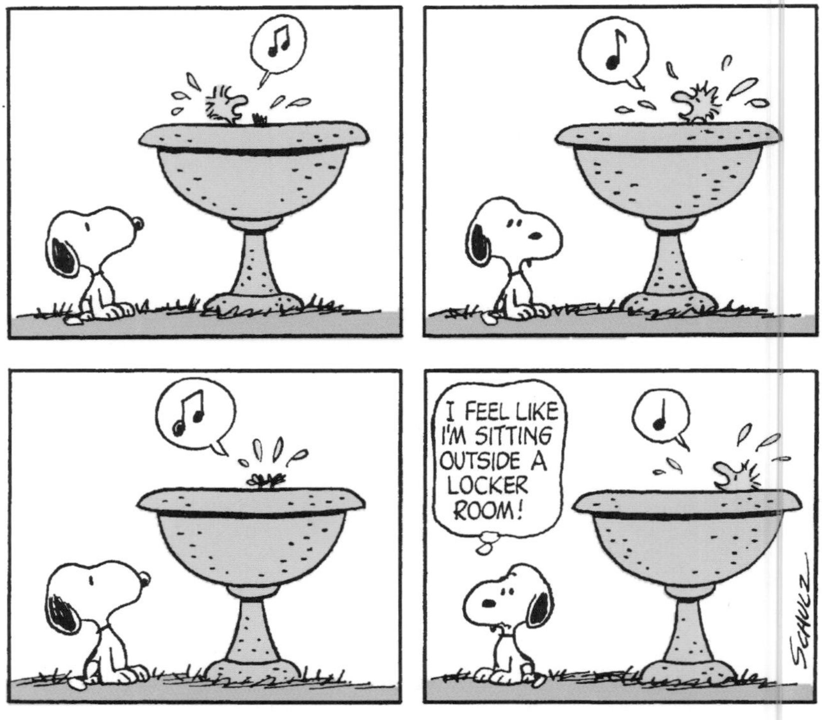
I FEEL LIKE I'M SITTING OUTSIDE A LOCKER ROOM!
SCHULZ

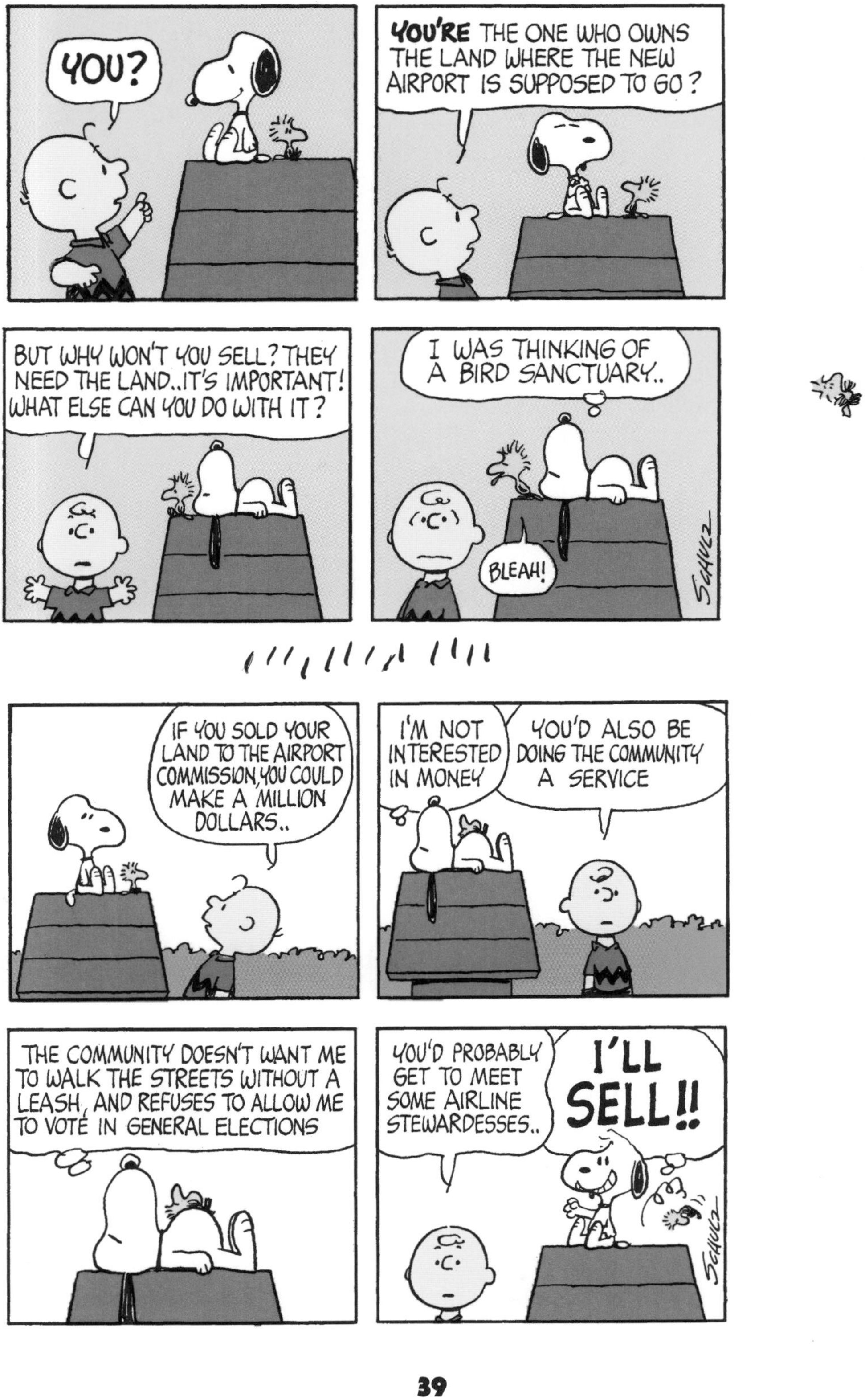
YOU?
YOU'RE THE ONE WHO OWNS THE LAND WHERE THE NEW AIRPORT IS SUPPOSED TO GO?
BUT WHY WON'T YOU SELL? THEY NEED THE LAND..IT'S IMPORTANT! WHAT ELSE CAN YOU DO WITH IT?
I WAS THINKING OF A BIRD SANCTUARY..
BLEAH!
SCHULZ
IF YOU SOLD YOUR LAND TO THE AIRPORT COMMISSION, YOU COULD MAKE A MILLION DOLLARS..
I'M NOT INTERESTED IN MONEY
YOU'D ALSO BE DOING THE COMMUNITY A SERVICE
THE COMMUNITY DOESN'T WANT ME TO WALK THE STREETS WITHOUT A LEASH, AND REFUSES TO ALLOW ME TO VOTE IN GENERAL ELECTIONS
YOU'D PROBABLY GET TO MEET SOME AIRLINE STEWARDESSES..
I'LL SELL!!
SCHULZ

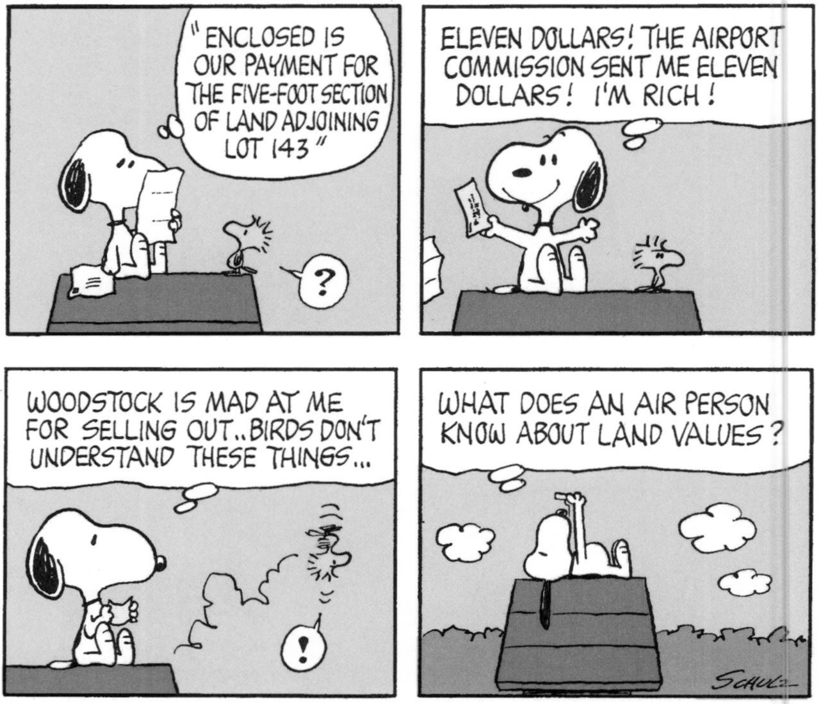
"ENCLOSED IS OUR PAYMENT FOR THE FIVE-FOOT SECTION OF LAND ADJOINING LOT 143"
?
ELEVEN DOLLARS! THE AIRPORT COMMISSION SENT ME ELEVEN DOLLARS! I'M RICH!
WOODSTOCK IS MAD AT ME FOR SELLING OUT..BIRDS DON'T UNDERSTAND THESE THINGS...
!
WHAT DOES AN AIR PERSON KNOW ABOUT LAND VALUES?

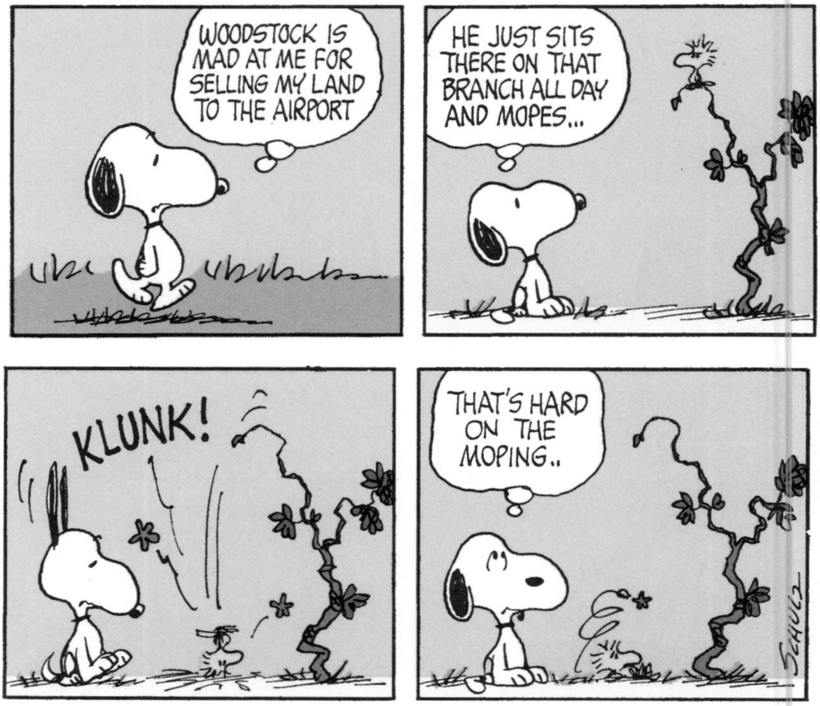
WOODSTOCK IS MAD AT ME FOR SELLING MY LAND TO THE AIRPORT
HE JUST SITS THERE ON THAT BRANCH ALL DAY AND MOPES...
KLUNK!
THAT'S HARD ON THE MOPING..

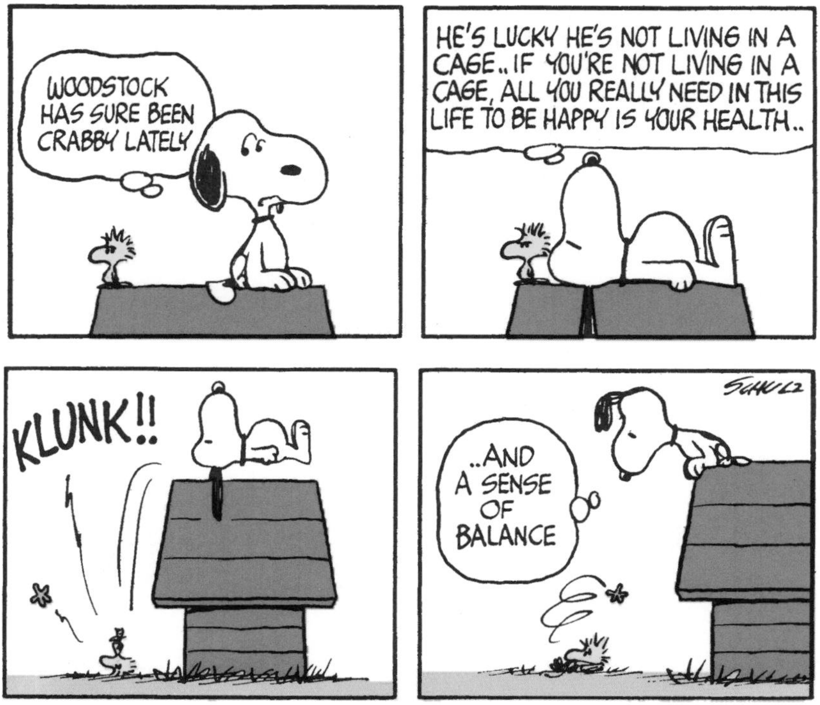
WOODSTOCK HAS SURE BEEN CRABBY LATELY
HE'S LUCKY HE'S NOT LIVING IN A CAGE.. IF YOU'RE NOT LIVING IN A CAGE, ALL YOU REALLY NEED IN THIS LIFE TO BE HAPPY IS YOUR HEALTH..
KLUNK!!
..AND A SENSE OF BALANCE

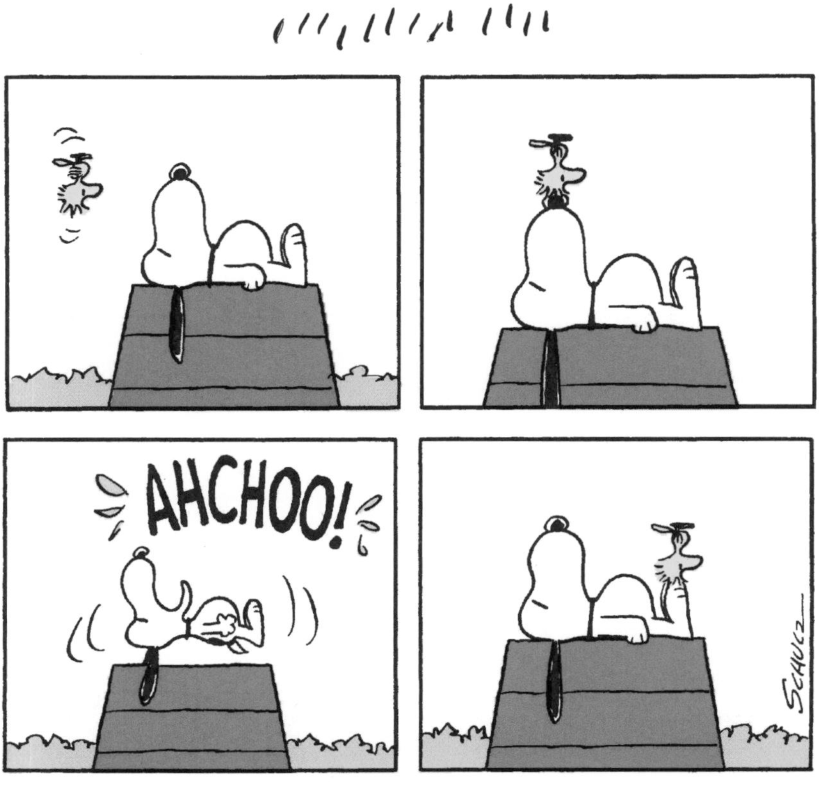
AHCHOO!

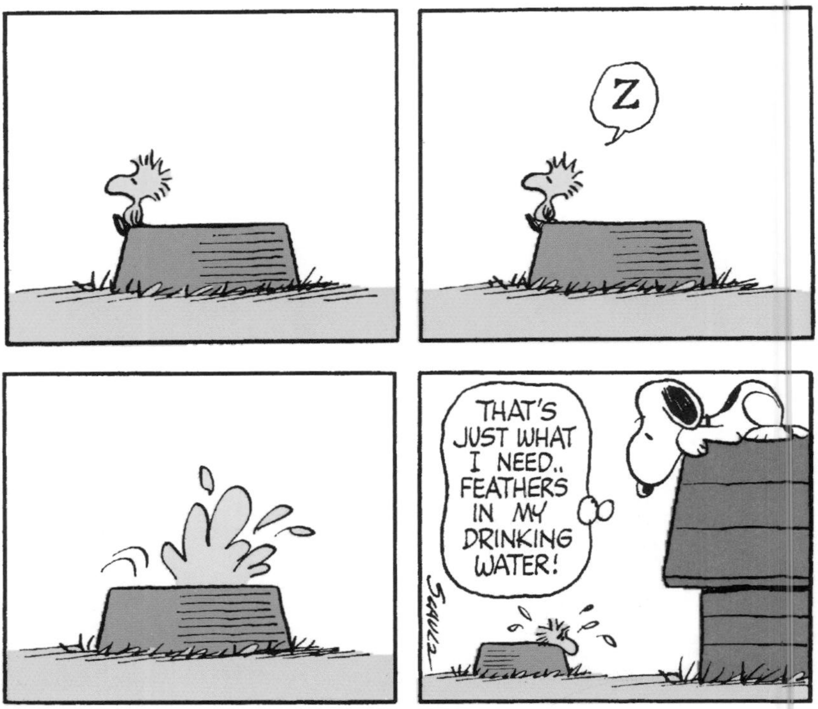
Z
THAT'S JUST WHAT I NEED.. FEATHERS IN MY DRINKING WATER!
SCHULZ

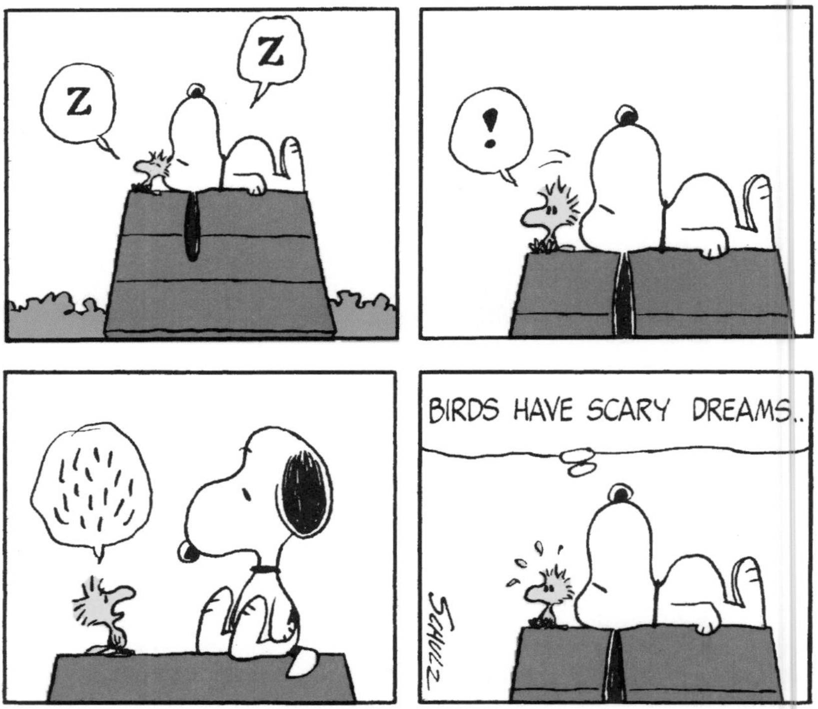
Z
Z
!
BIRDS HAVE SCARY DREAMS..
SCHULZ

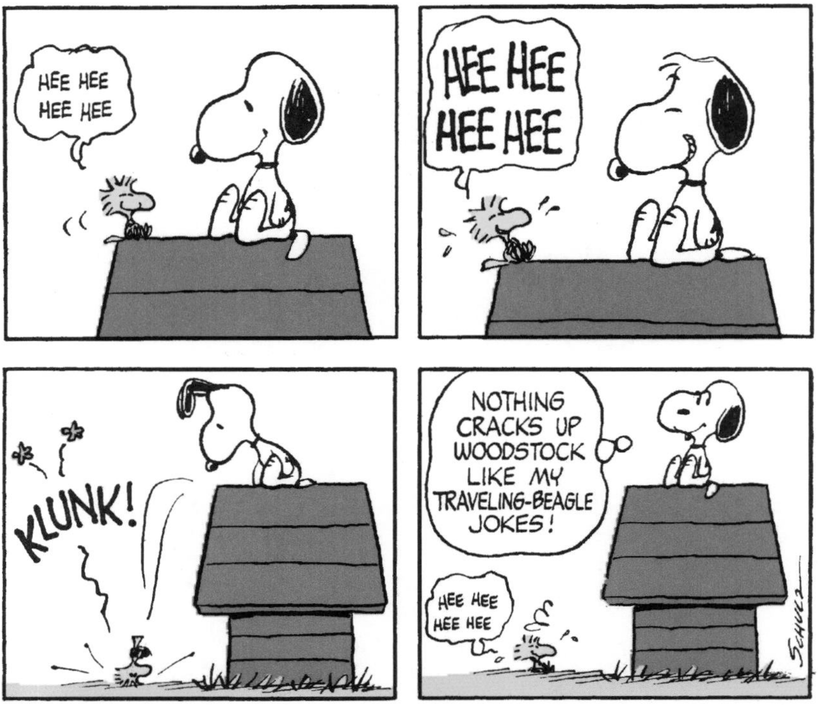
HEE HEE
HEE HEE
HEE HEE
HEE HEE
KLUNK!
NOTHING CRACKS UP WOODSTOCK LIKE MY TRAVELING-BEAGLE JOKES!
HEE HEE
HEE HEE
SCHULZ

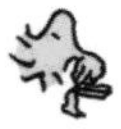

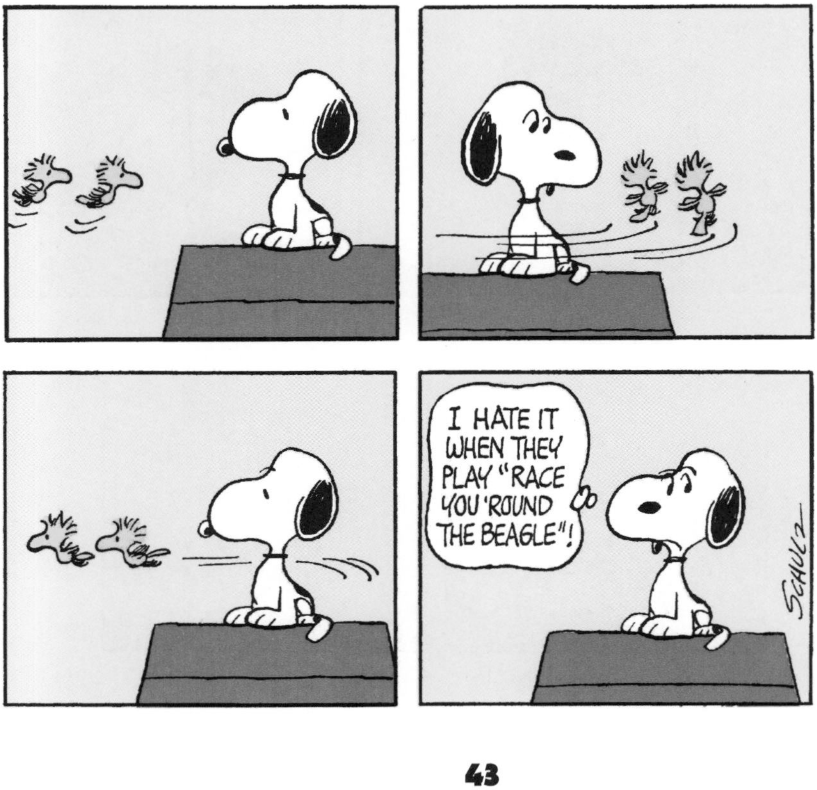
I HATE IT WHEN THEY PLAY "RACE YOU 'ROUND THE BEAGLE"!
SCHULZ

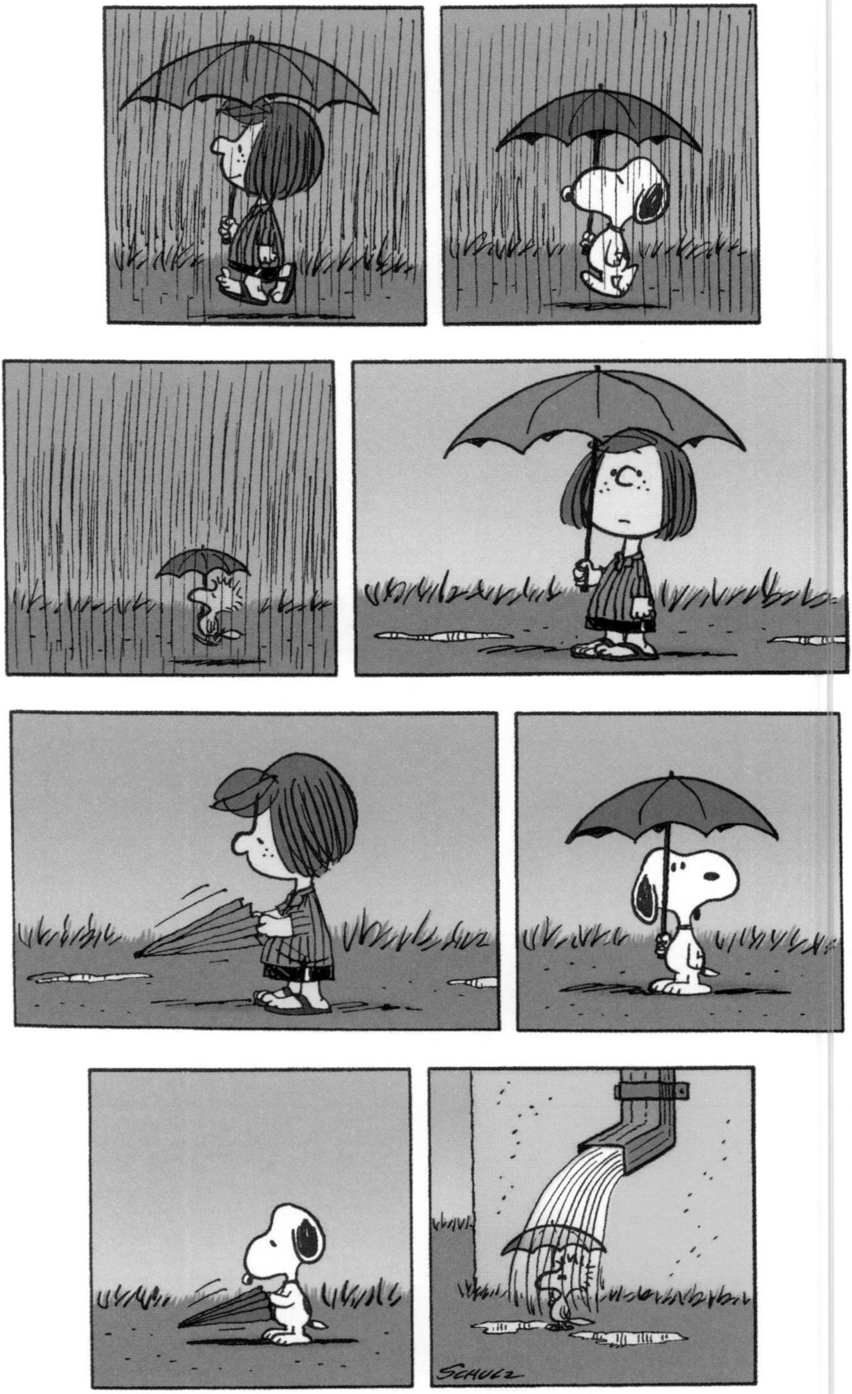
SCHULZ

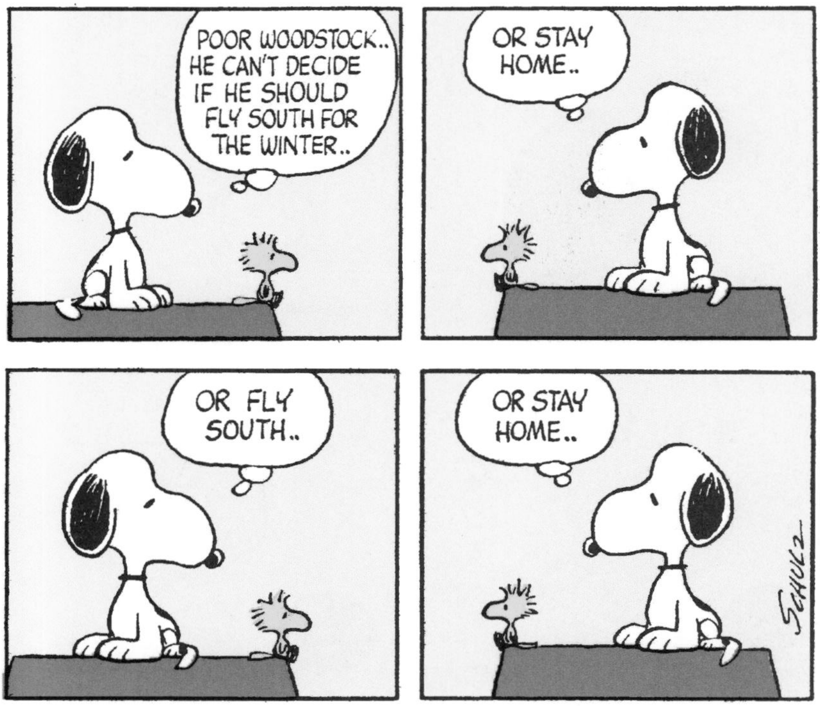
POOR WOODSTOCK.. HE CAN'T DECIDE IF HE SHOULD FLY SOUTH FOR THE WINTER..
OR STAY HOME..
OR FLY SOUTH..
OR STAY HOME..
SCHULZ

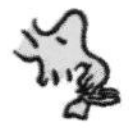

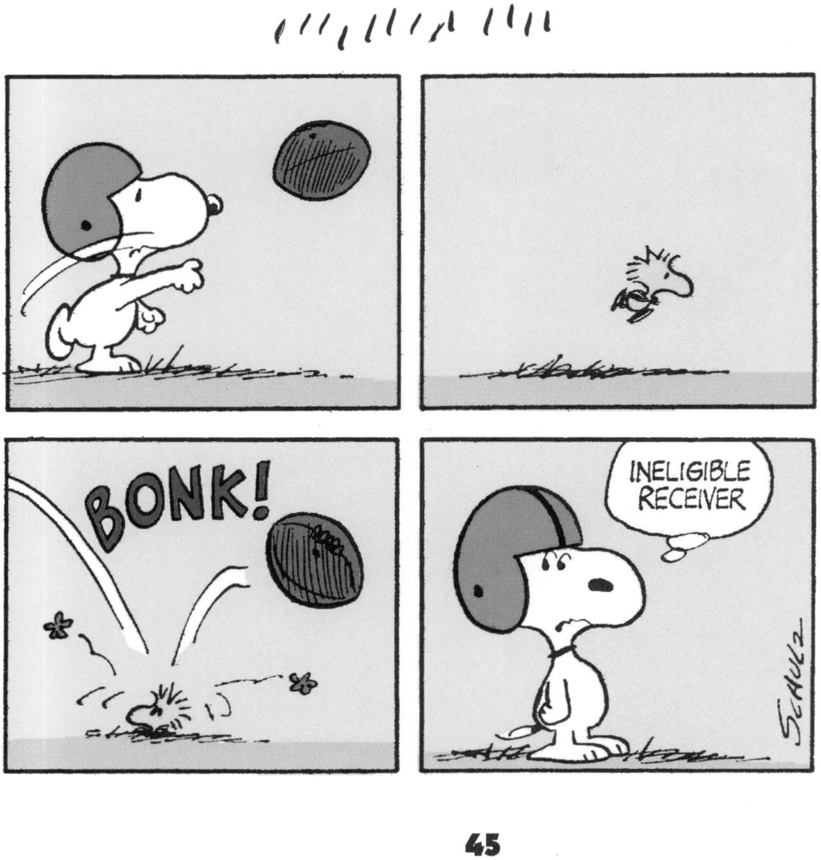
BONK!
INELIGIBLE RECEIVER
SCHULZ

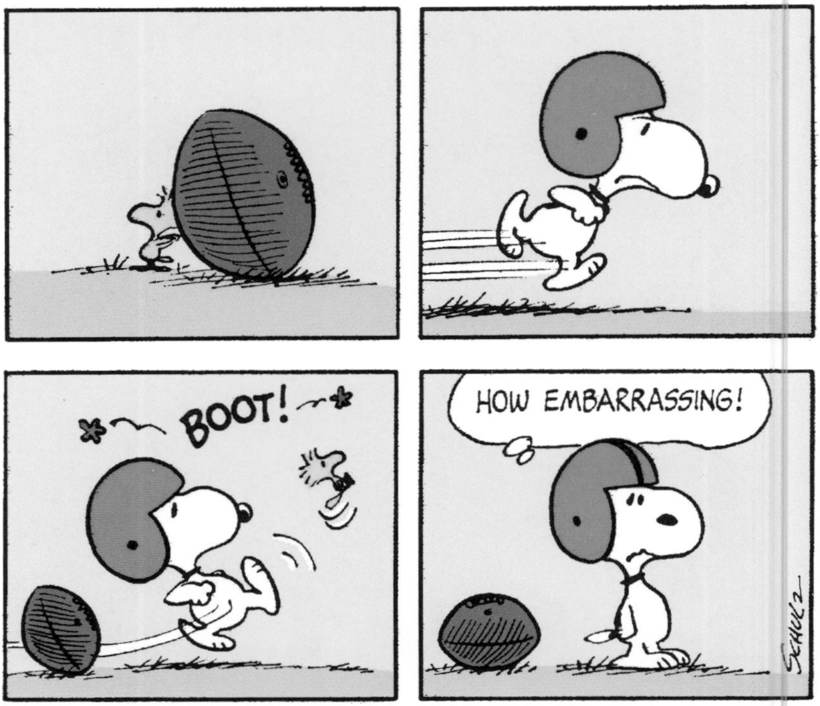
BOOT!
HOW EMBARRASSING!
SCHULZ

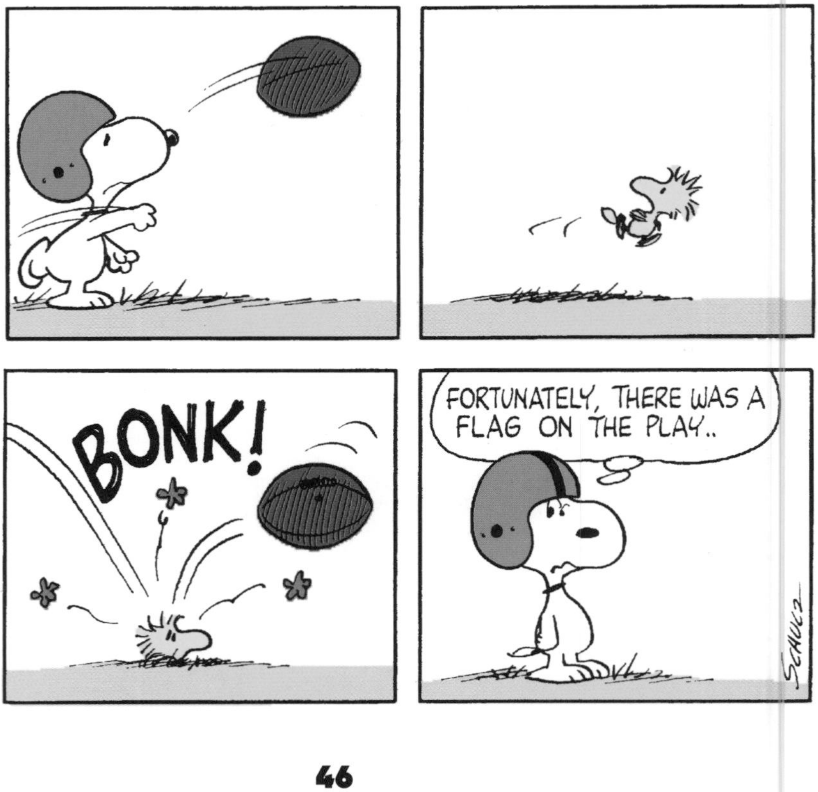
BONK!
FORTUNATELY, THERE WAS A FLAG ON THE PLAY..
SCHULZ

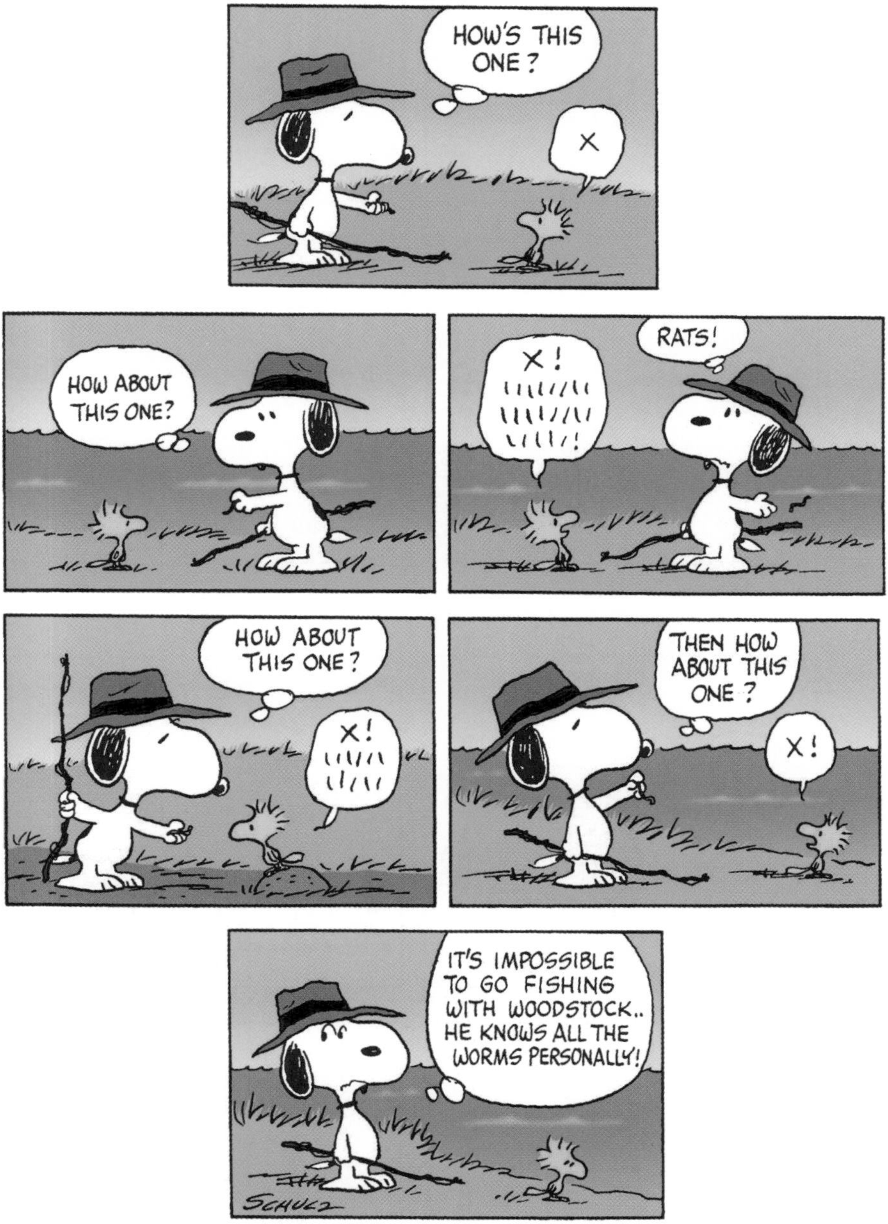
HOW'S THIS ONE?
X
HOW ABOUT THIS ONE?
X!
RATS!
HOW ABOUT THIS ONE?
X!
THEN HOW ABOUT THIS ONE?
X!
IT'S IMPOSSIBLE TO GO FISHING WITH WOODSTOCK.. HE KNOWS ALL THE WORMS PERSONALLY!
SCHULZ

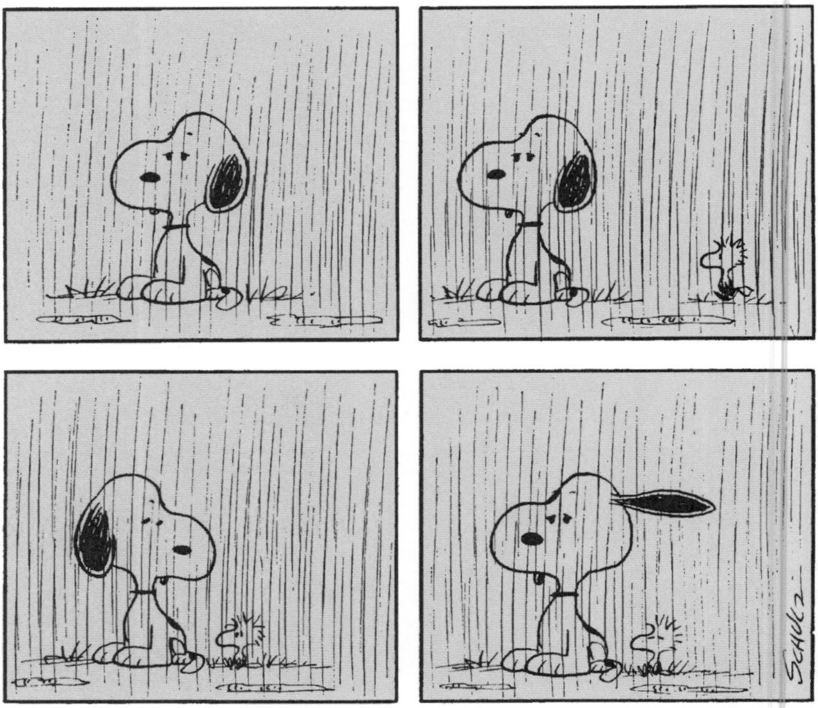

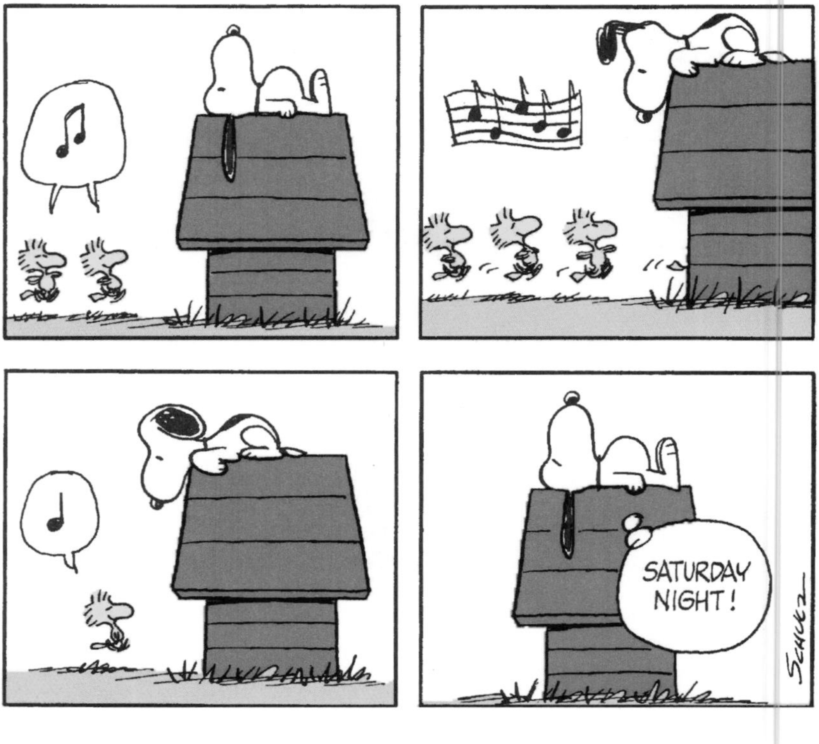
SATURDAY NIGHT!

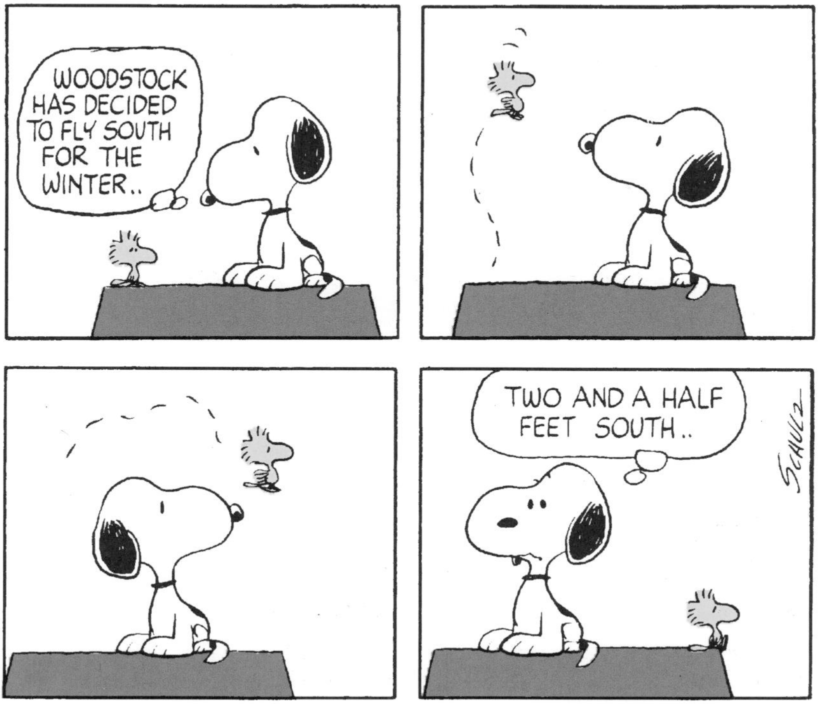
WOODSTOCK HAS DECIDED TO FLY SOUTH FOR THE WINTER..
TWO AND A HALF FEET SOUTH..

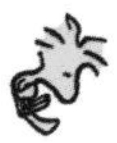

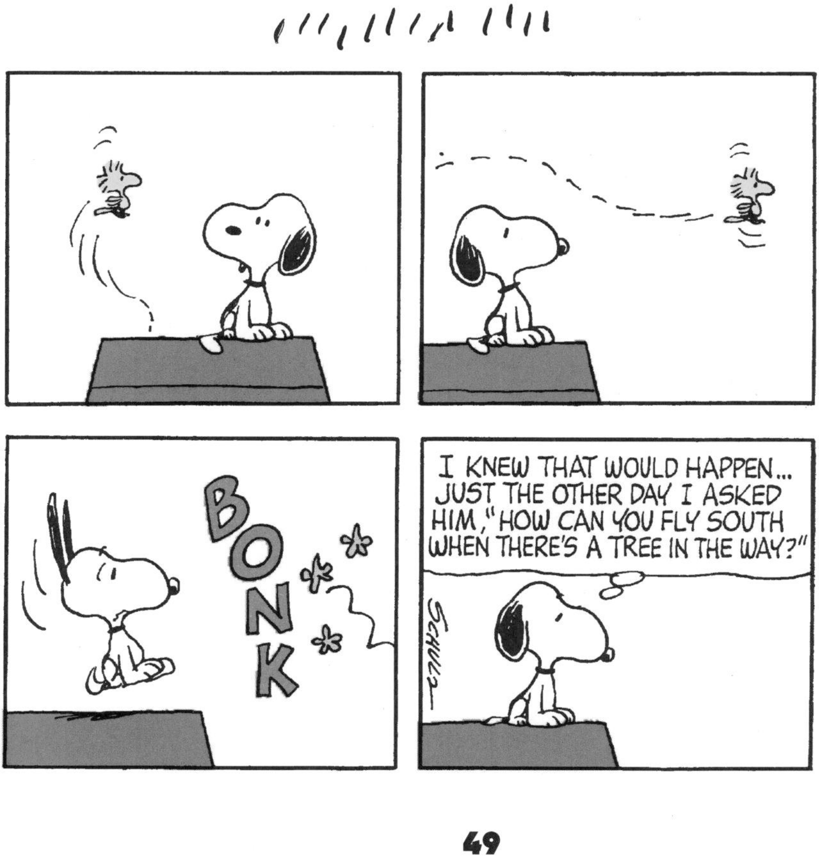
BONK
I KNEW THAT WOULD HAPPEN... JUST THE OTHER DAY I ASKED HIM, "HOW CAN YOU FLY SOUTH WHEN THERE'S A TREE IN THE WAY?"

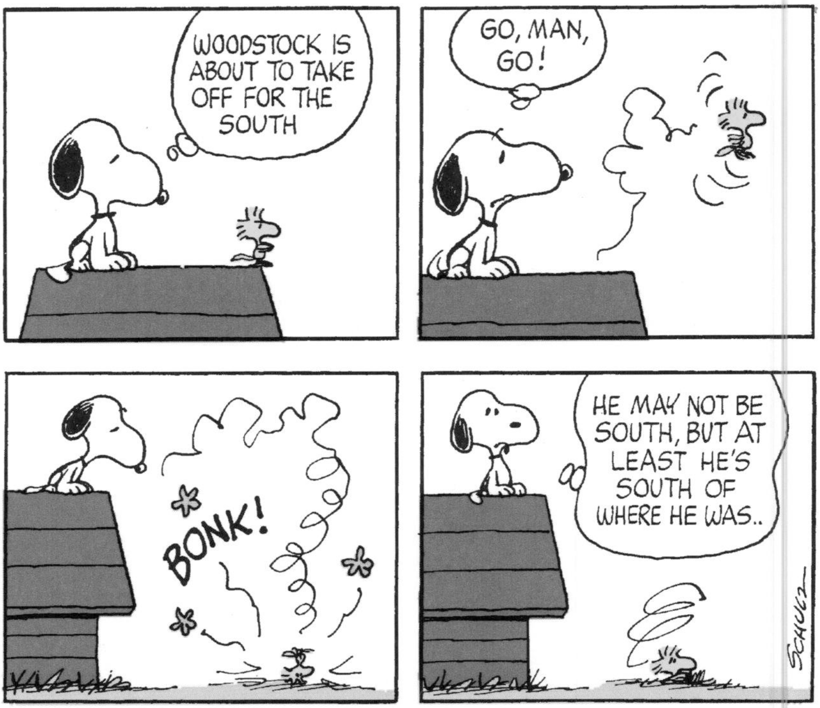
WOODSTOCK IS ABOUT TO TAKE OFF FOR THE SOUTH
GO, MAN, GO!
BONK!
HE MAY NOT BE SOUTH, BUT AT LEAST HE'S SOUTH OF WHERE HE WAS..
SCHULZ

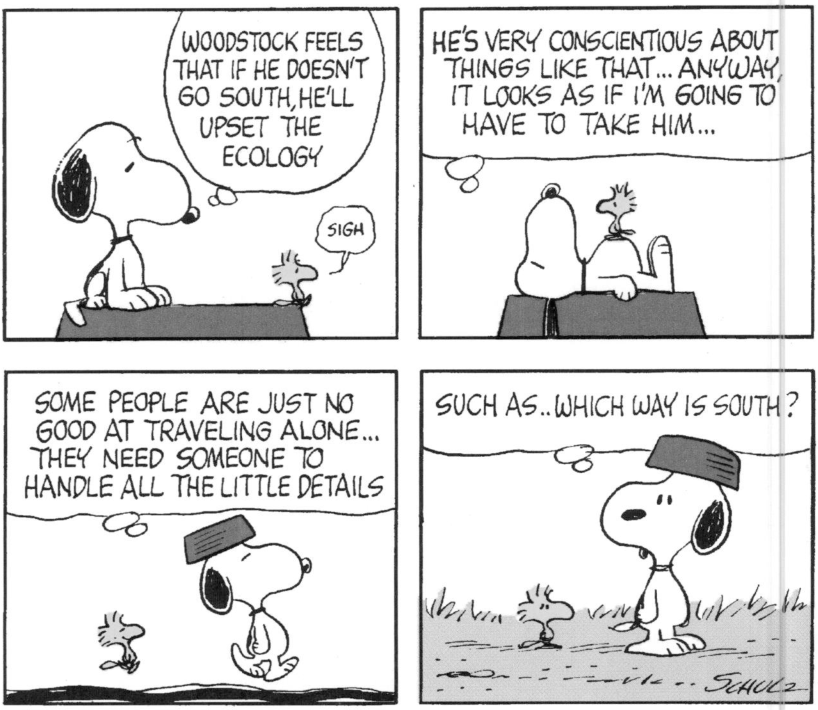
WOODSTOCK FEELS THAT IF HE DOESN'T GO SOUTH, HE'LL UPSET THE ECOLOGY
SIGH
HE'S VERY CONSCIENTIOUS ABOUT THINGS LIKE THAT... ANYWAY, IT LOOKS AS IF I'M GOING TO HAVE TO TAKE HIM...
SOME PEOPLE ARE JUST NO GOOD AT TRAVELING ALONE... THEY NEED SOMEONE TO HANDLE ALL THE LITTLE DETAILS
SUCH AS.. WHICH WAY IS SOUTH?
SCHULZ

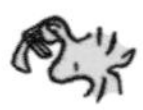

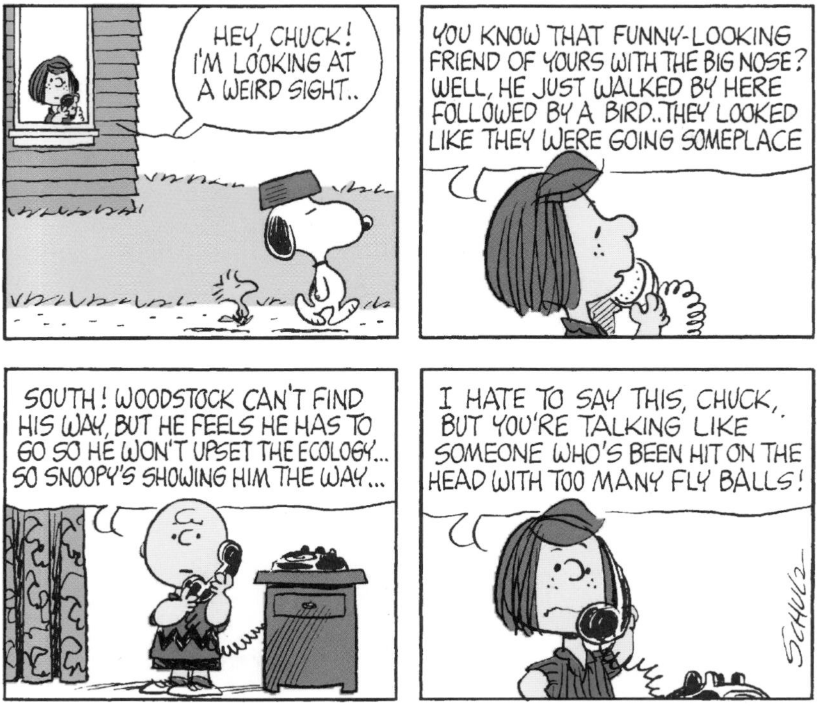
HEY, CHUCK! I'M LOOKING AT A WEIRD SIGHT..
YOU KNOW THAT FUNNY-LOOKING FRIEND OF YOURS WITH THE BIG NOSE? WELL, HE JUST WALKED BY HERE FOLLOWED BY A BIRD..THEY LOOKED LIKE THEY WERE GOING SOMEPLACE
SOUTH! WOODSTOCK CAN'T FIND HIS WAY, BUT HE FEELS HE HAS TO GO SO HE WON'T UPSET THE ECOLOGY... SO SNOOPY'S SHOWING HIM THE WAY...
I HATE TO SAY THIS, CHUCK, BUT YOU'RE TALKING LIKE SOMEONE WHO'S BEEN HIT ON THE HEAD WITH TOO MANY FLY BALLS!
SCHULZ

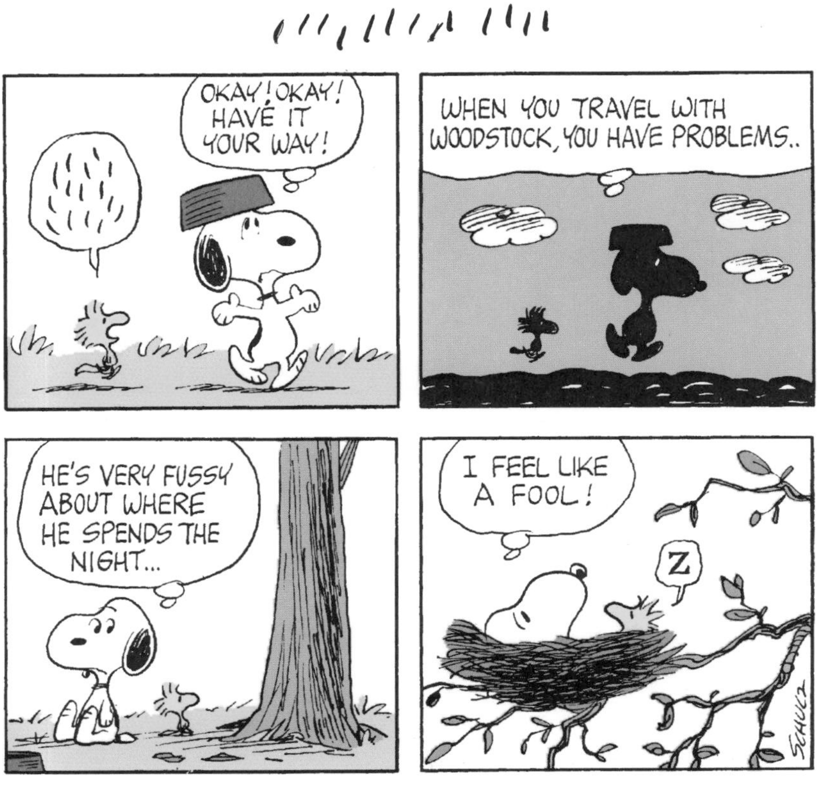
OKAY! OKAY! HAVE IT YOUR WAY!
WHEN YOU TRAVEL WITH WOODSTOCK, YOU HAVE PROBLEMS..
HE'S VERY FUSSY ABOUT WHERE HE SPENDS THE NIGHT...
I FEEL LIKE A FOOL!
Z
SCHULZ

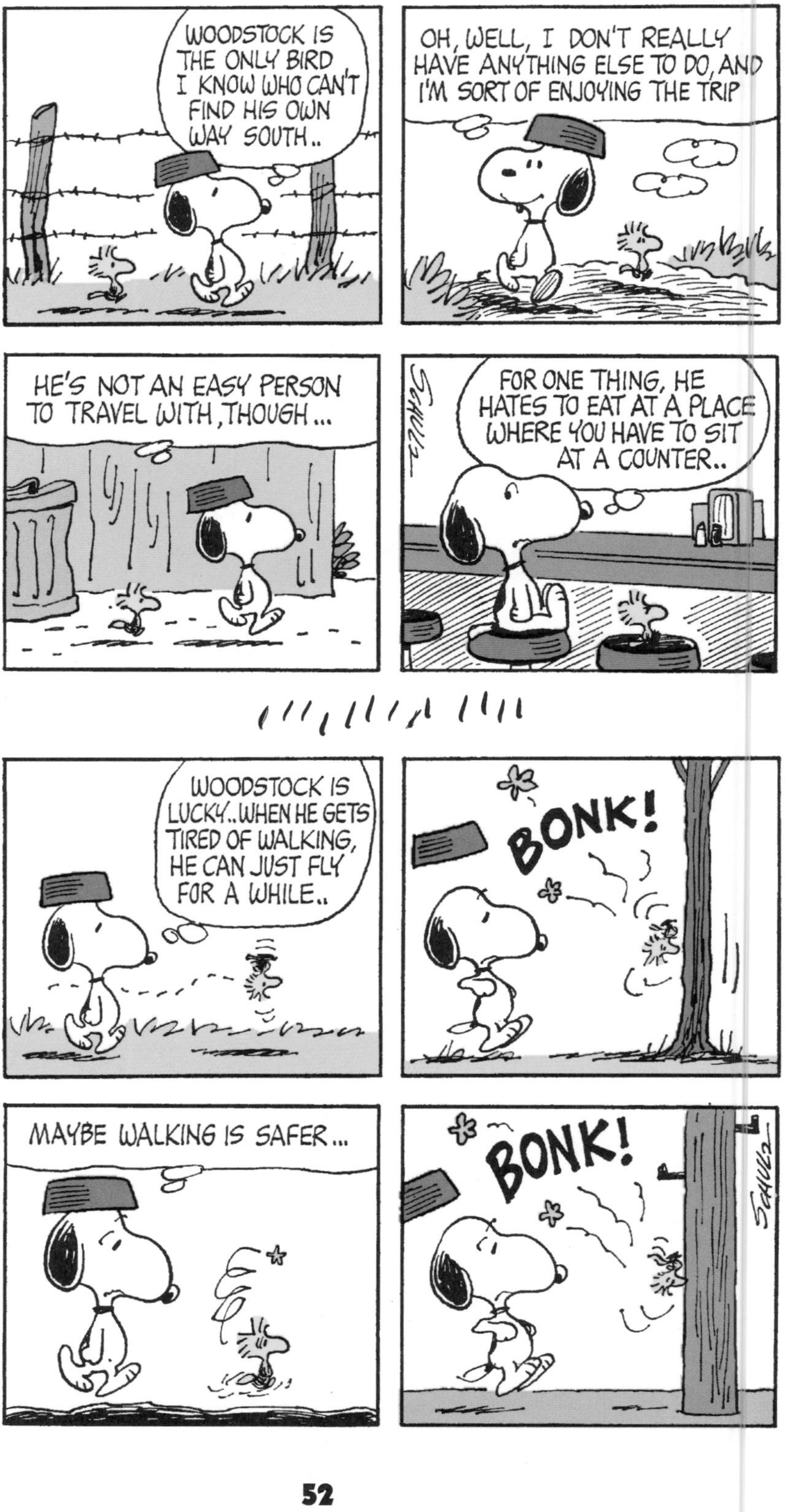
WOODSTOCK IS THE ONLY BIRD I KNOW WHO CAN'T FIND HIS OWN WAY SOUTH..
OH, WELL, I DON'T REALLY HAVE ANYTHING ELSE TO DO, AND I'M SORT OF ENJOYING THE TRIP
HE'S NOT AN EASY PERSON TO TRAVEL WITH, THOUGH...
SCHULZ
FOR ONE THING, HE HATES TO EAT AT A PLACE WHERE YOU HAVE TO SIT AT A COUNTER..
WOODSTOCK IS LUCKY..WHEN HE GETS TIRED OF WALKING, HE CAN JUST FLY FOR A WHILE..
BONK!
MAYBE WALKING IS SAFER...
BONK!
SCHULZ

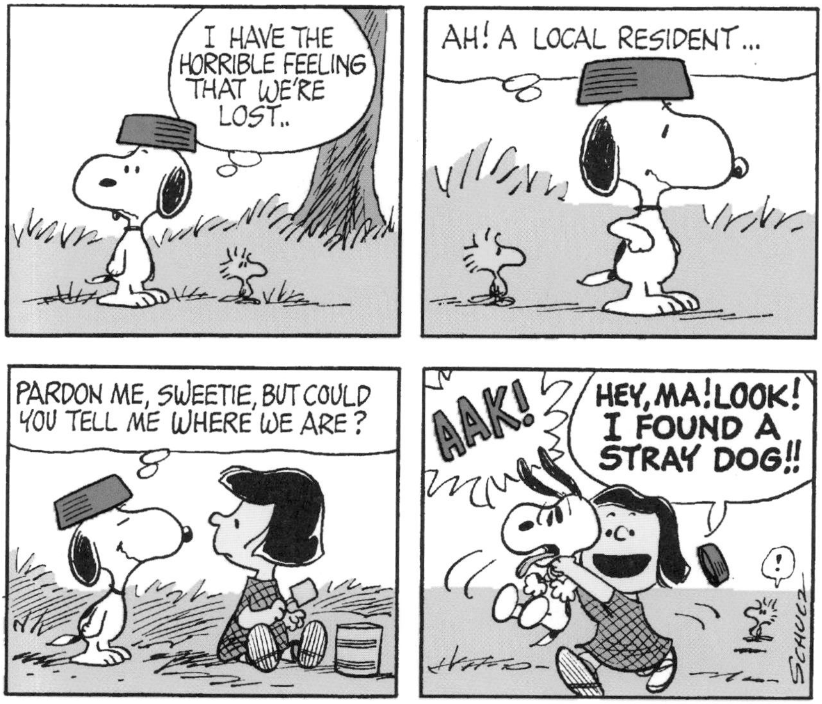
I HAVE THE HORRIBLE FEELING THAT WE'RE LOST..
AH! A LOCAL RESIDENT...
PARDON ME, SWEETIE, BUT COULD YOU TELL ME WHERE WE ARE?
AAK!
HEY, MA! LOOK! I FOUND A STRAY DOG!!
!
SCHULZ

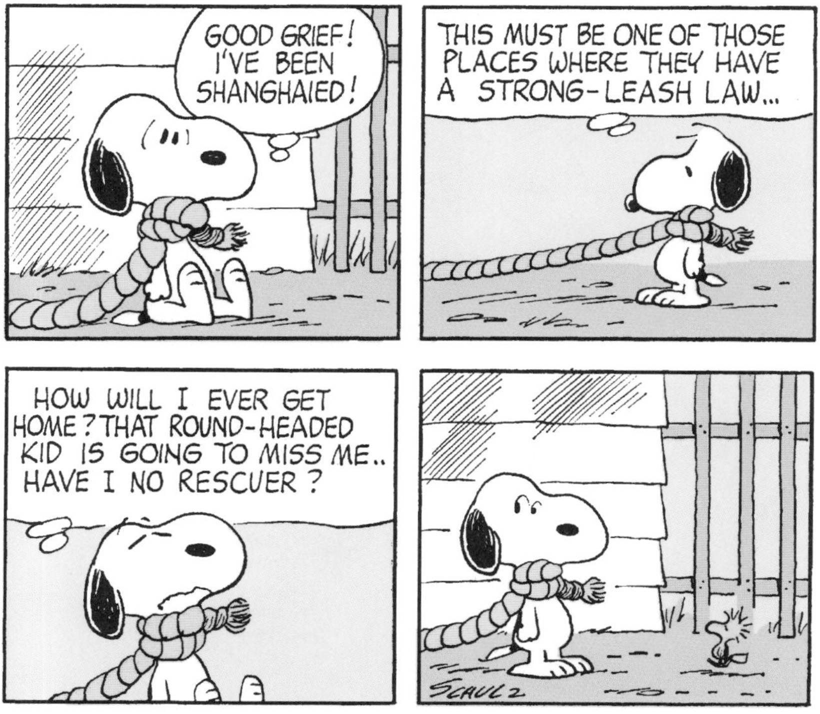
GOOD GRIEF! I'VE BEEN SHANGHAIED!
THIS MUST BE ONE OF THOSE PLACES WHERE THEY HAVE A STRONG-LEASH LAW...
HOW WILL I EVER GET HOME? THAT ROUND-HEADED KID IS GOING TO MISS ME.. HAVE I NO RESCUER?
SCHULZ

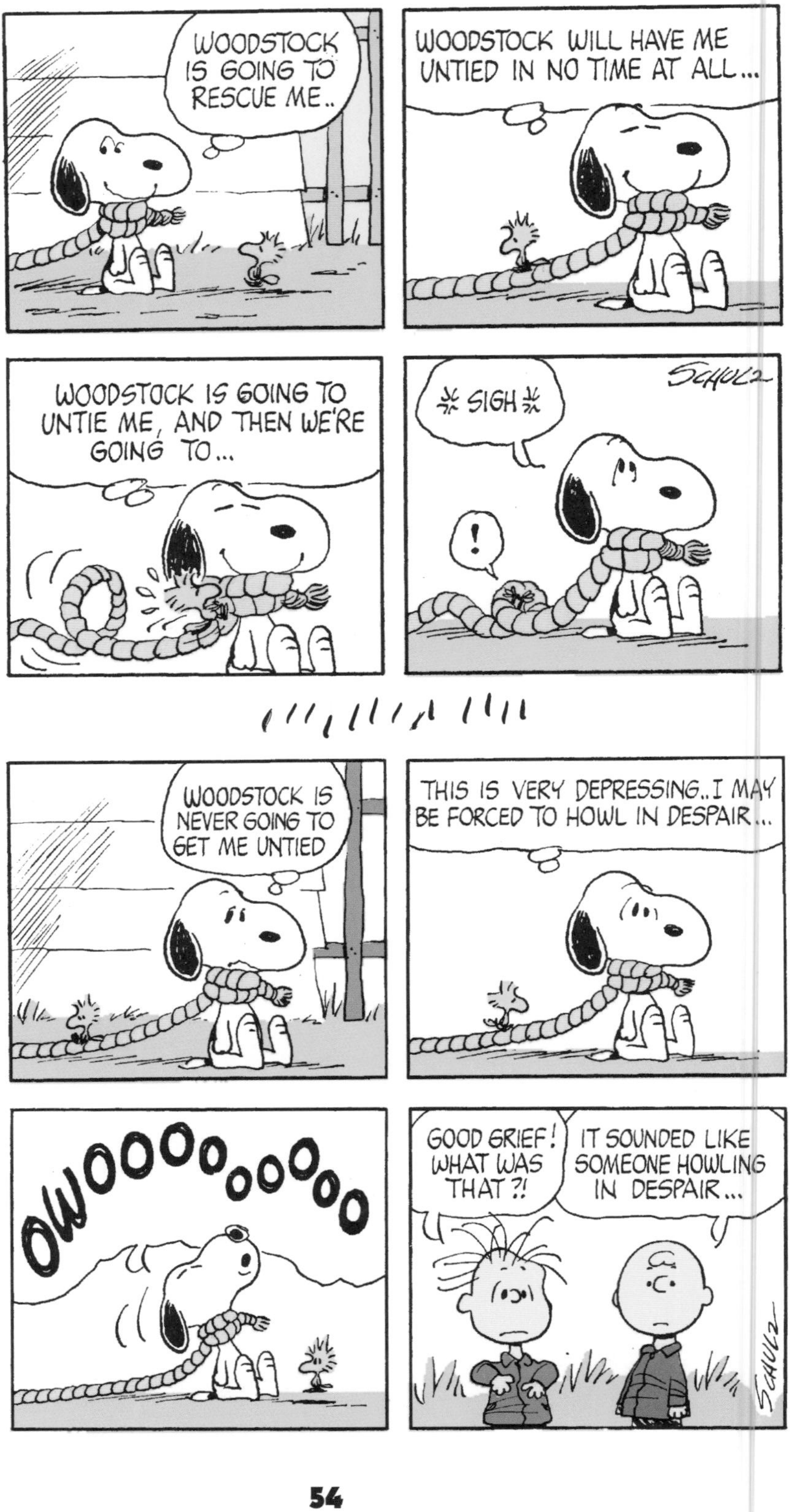
WOODSTOCK IS GOING TO RESCUE ME..
WOODSTOCK WILL HAVE ME UNTIED IN NO TIME AT ALL...
WOODSTOCK IS GOING TO UNTIE ME, AND THEN WE'RE GOING TO...
SCHULZ
☆ SIGH ☆
!
WOODSTOCK IS NEVER GOING TO GET ME UNTIED
THIS IS VERY DEPRESSING..I MAY BE FORCED TO HOWL IN DESPAIR...
OWOOOOOOOOOO
GOOD GRIEF! WHAT WAS THAT?!
IT SOUNDED LIKE SOMEONE HOWLING IN DESPAIR...
SCHULZ

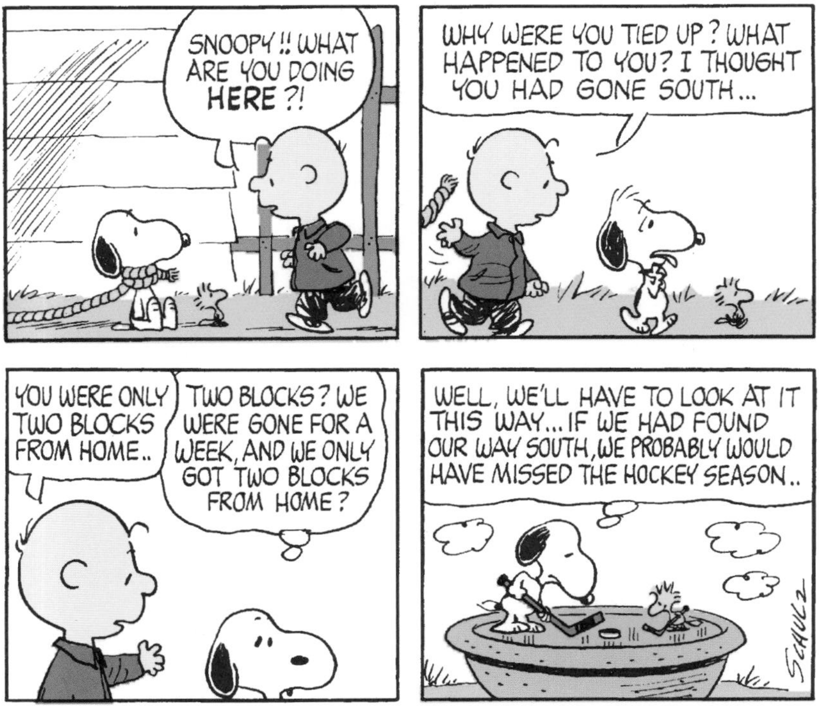
SNOOPY!! WHAT ARE YOU DOING HERE?!
WHY WERE YOU TIED UP? WHAT HAPPENED TO YOU? I THOUGHT YOU HAD GONE SOUTH...
YOU WERE ONLY TWO BLOCKS FROM HOME..
TWO BLOCKS? WE WERE GONE FOR A WEEK, AND WE ONLY GOT TWO BLOCKS FROM HOME?
WELL, WE'LL HAVE TO LOOK AT IT THIS WAY... IF WE HAD FOUND OUR WAY SOUTH, WE PROBABLY WOULD HAVE MISSED THE HOCKEY SEASON..
SCHULZ

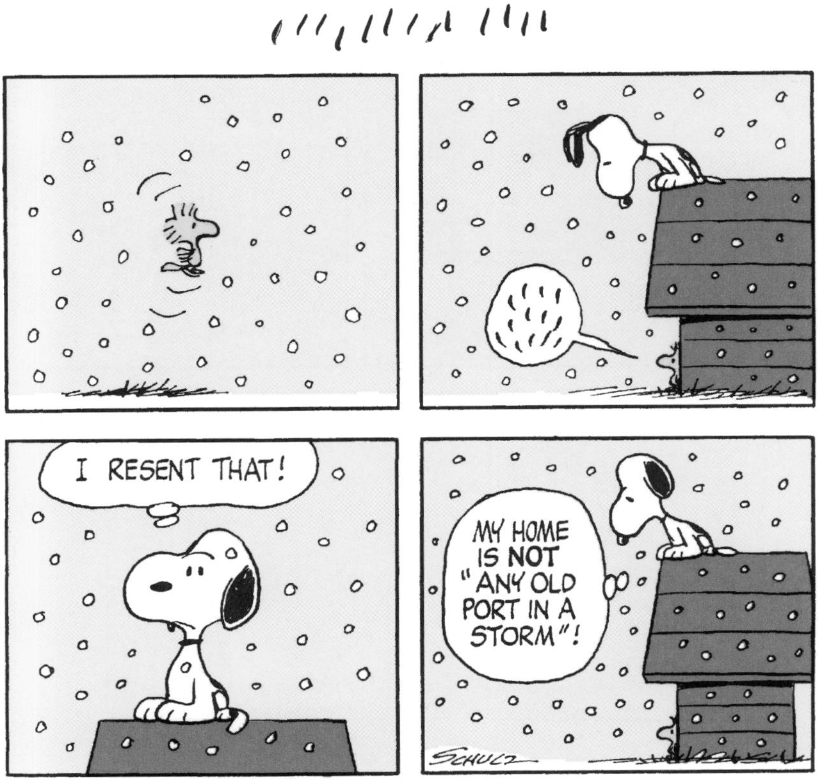
I RESENT THAT!
MY HOME IS NOT "ANY OLD PORT IN A STORM"!
SCHULZ

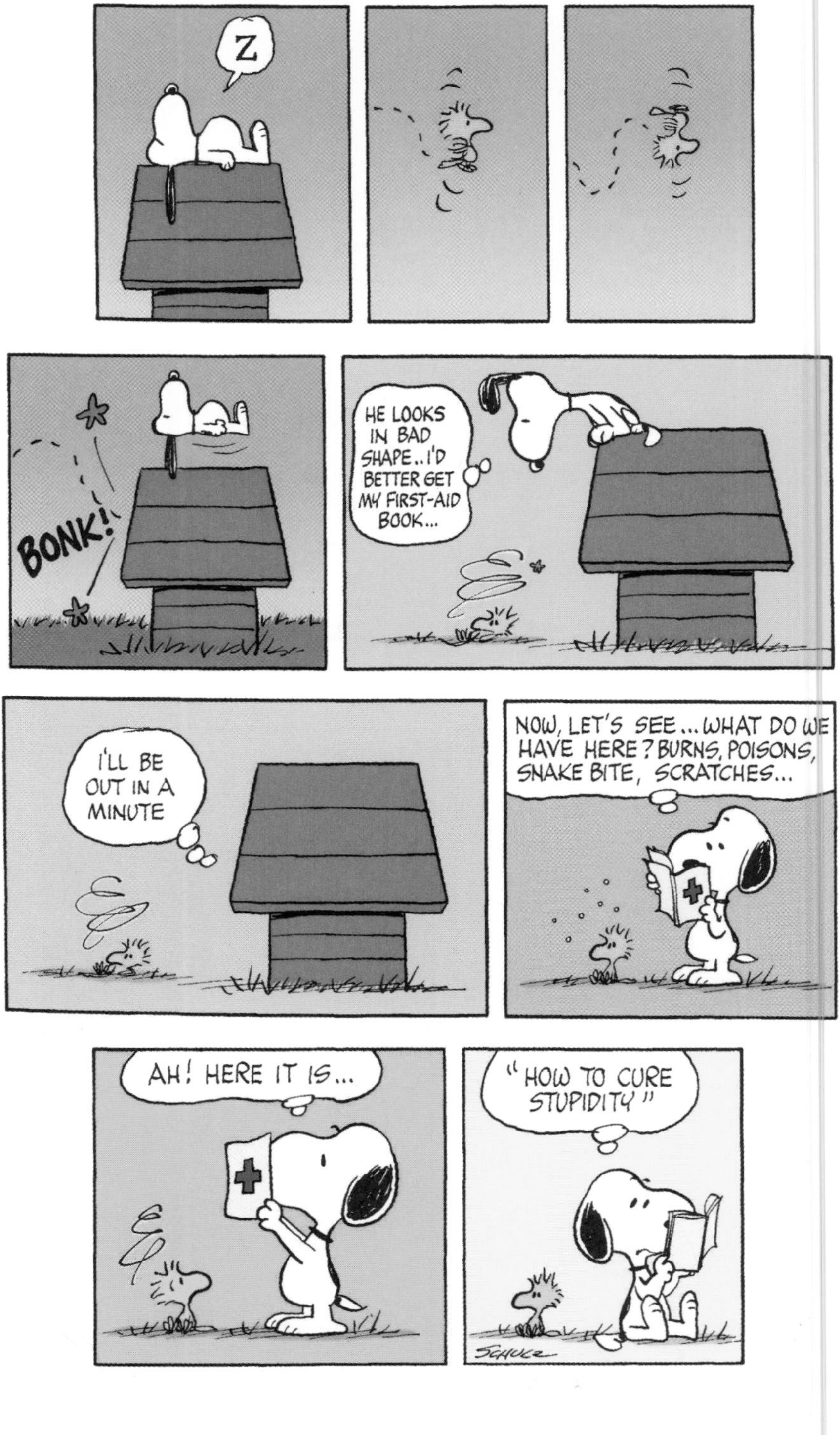
Z
BONK!
HE LOOKS IN BAD SHAPE..I'D BETTER GET MY FIRST-AID BOOK...
I'LL BE OUT IN A MINUTE
NOW, LET'S SEE...WHAT DO WE HAVE HERE? BURNS, POISONS, SNAKE BITE, SCRATCHES...
AH! HERE IT IS...
"HOW TO CURE STUPIDITY"
SCHULZ

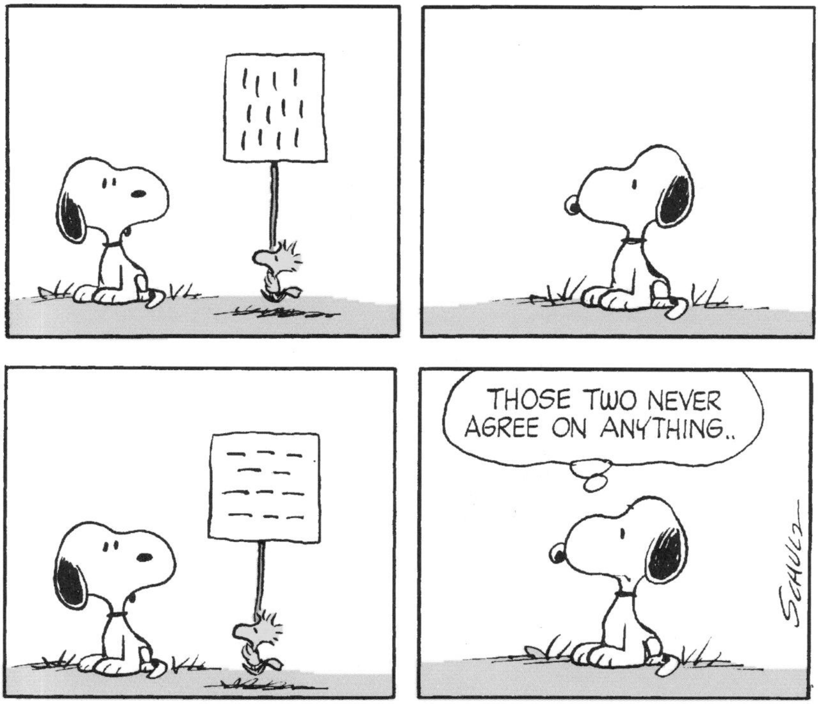
THOSE TWO NEVER AGREE ON ANYTHING..
SCHULZ

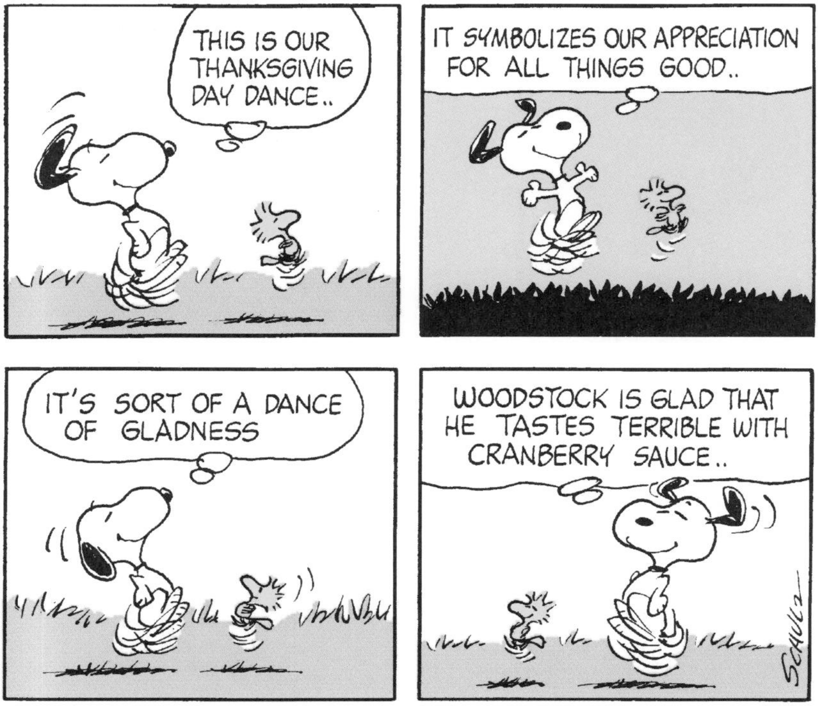
THIS IS OUR THANKSGIVING DAY DANCE..
IT SYMBOLIZES OUR APPRECIATION FOR ALL THINGS GOOD..
IT'S SORT OF A DANCE OF GLADNESS
WOODSTOCK IS GLAD THAT HE TASTES TERRIBLE WITH CRANBERRY SAUCE..
SCHULZ

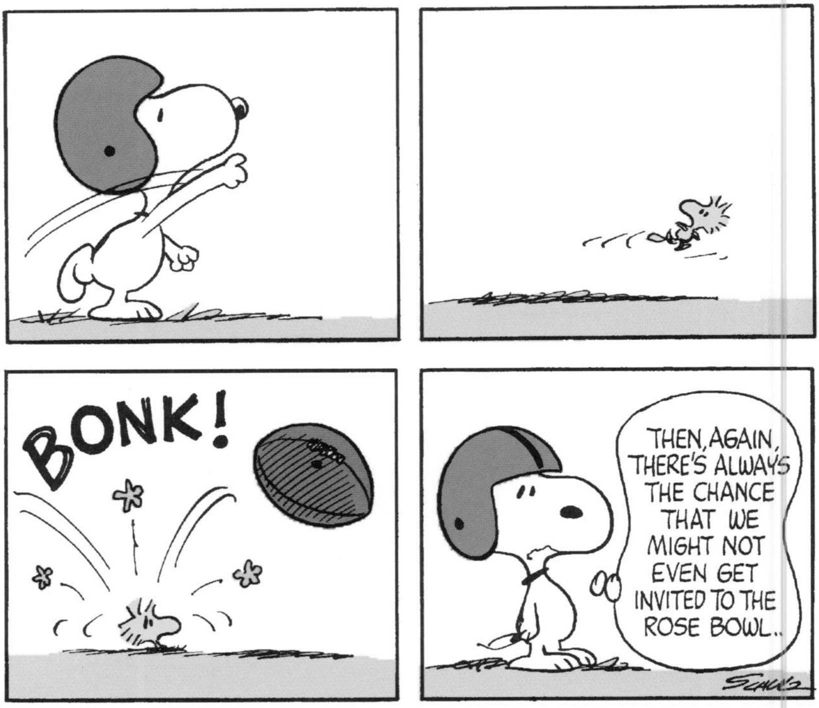
BONK!
THEN, AGAIN, THERE'S ALWAYS THE CHANCE THAT WE MIGHT NOT EVEN GET INVITED TO THE ROSE BOWL..

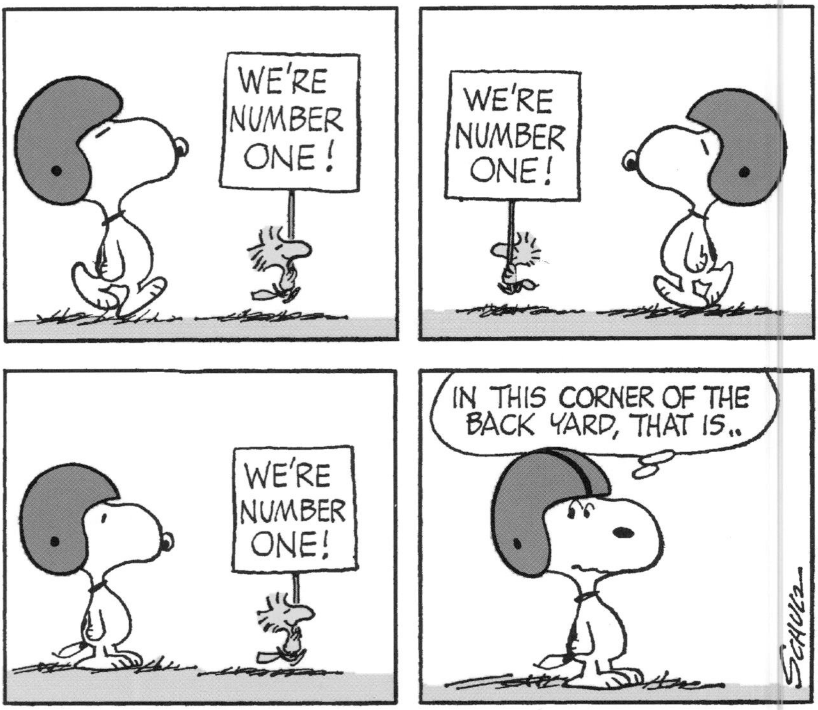
WE'RE NUMBER ONE!
WE'RE NUMBER ONE!
WE'RE NUMBER ONE!
IN THIS CORNER OF THE BACK YARD, THAT IS..

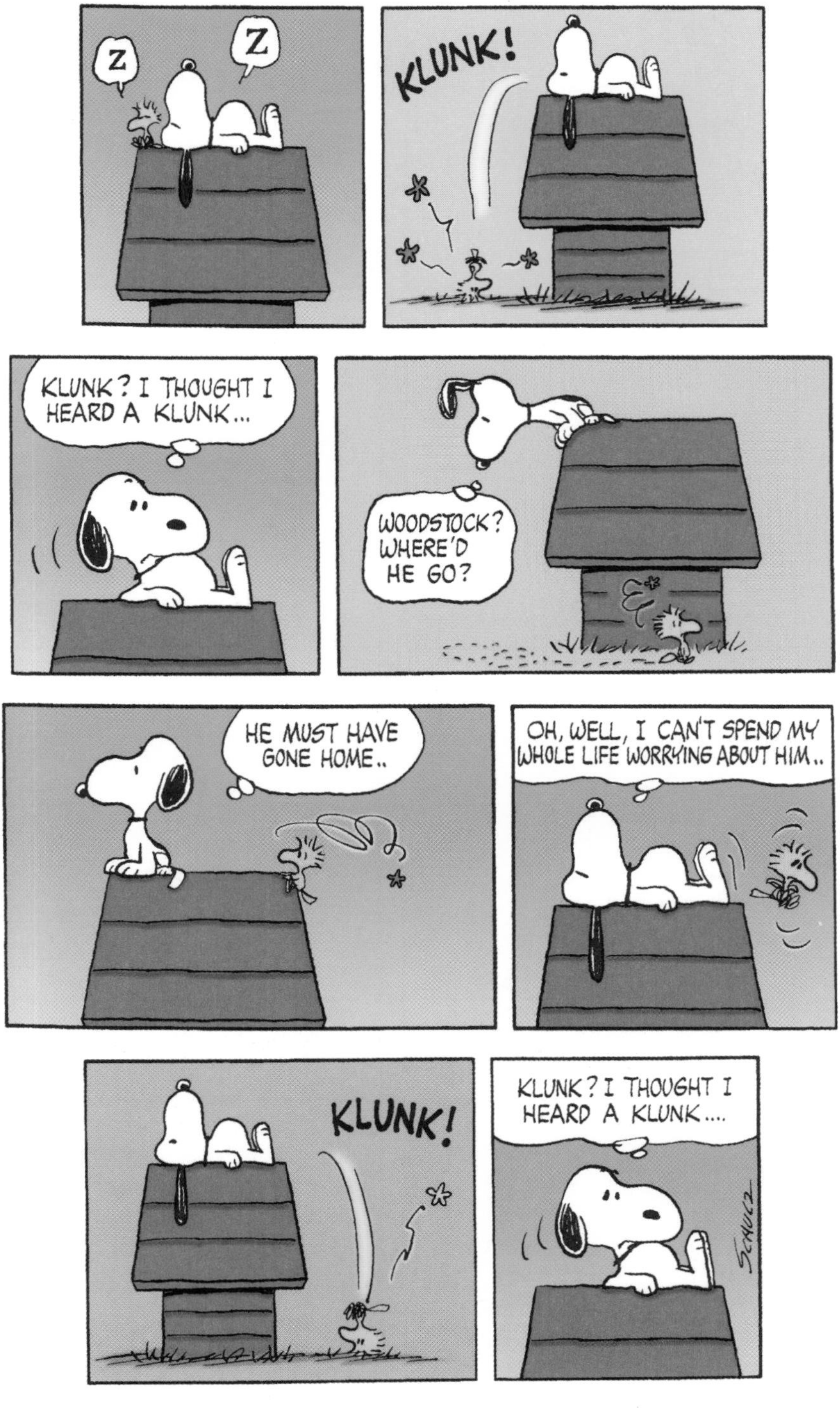
Z
Z
KLUNK!
KLUNK? I THOUGHT I HEARD A KLUNK...
WOODSTOCK? WHERE'D HE GO?
HE MUST HAVE GONE HOME..
OH, WELL, I CAN'T SPEND MY WHOLE LIFE WORRYING ABOUT HIM..
KLUNK!
KLUNK? I THOUGHT I HEARD A KLUNK....
SCHULZ

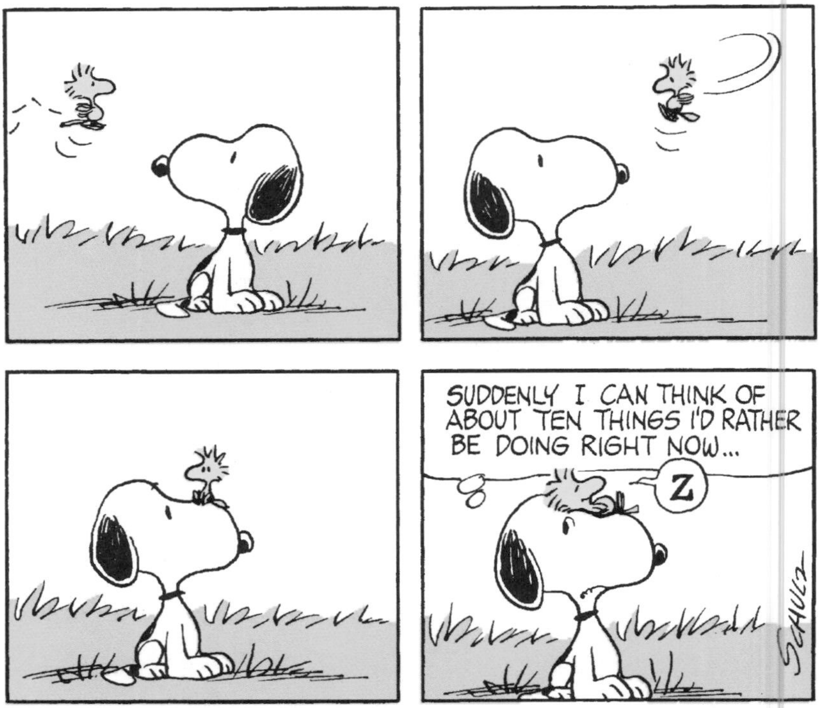
SUDDENLY I CAN THINK OF ABOUT TEN THINGS I'D RATHER BE DOING RIGHT NOW...
Z
SCHULZ

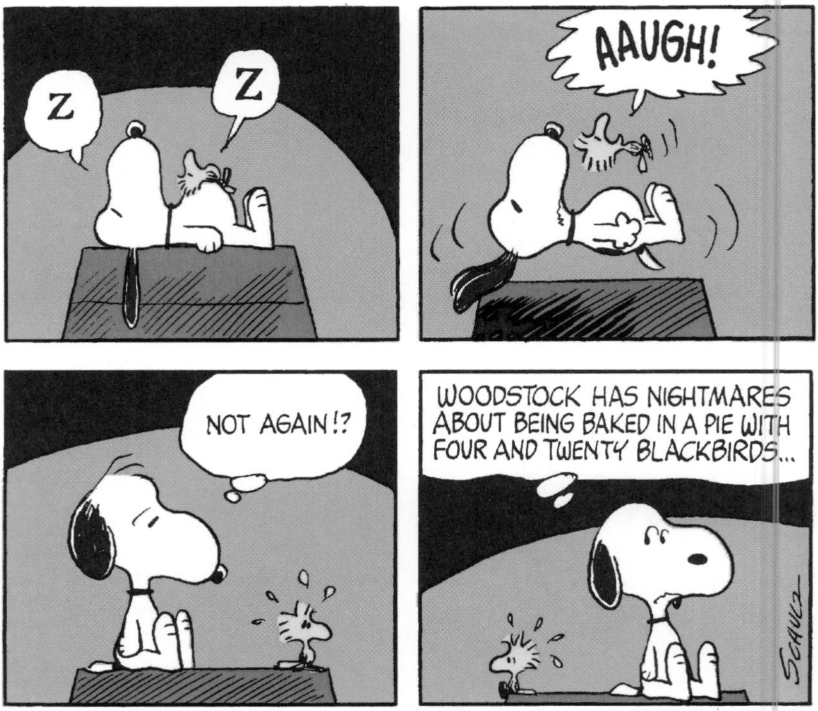
Z
Z
AAUGH!
NOT AGAIN!?
WOODSTOCK HAS NIGHTMARES ABOUT BEING BAKED IN A PIE WITH FOUR AND TWENTY BLACKBIRDS...
SCHULZ

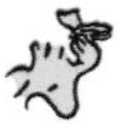

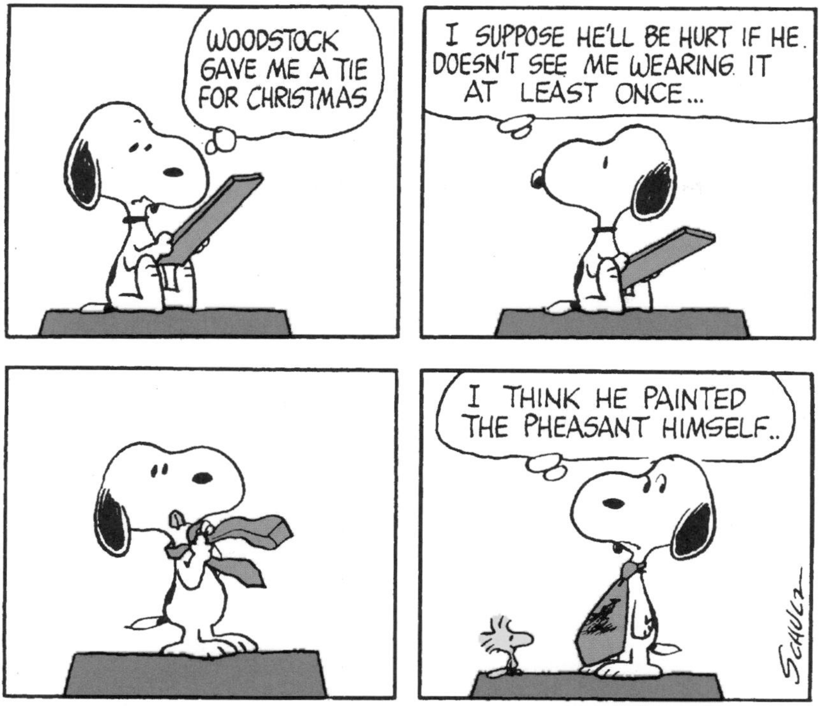
WOODSTOCK GAVE ME A TIE FOR CHRISTMAS
I SUPPOSE HE'LL BE HURT IF HE DOESN'T SEE ME WEARING IT AT LEAST ONCE...
I THINK HE PAINTED THE PHEASANT HIMSELF..
SCHULZ

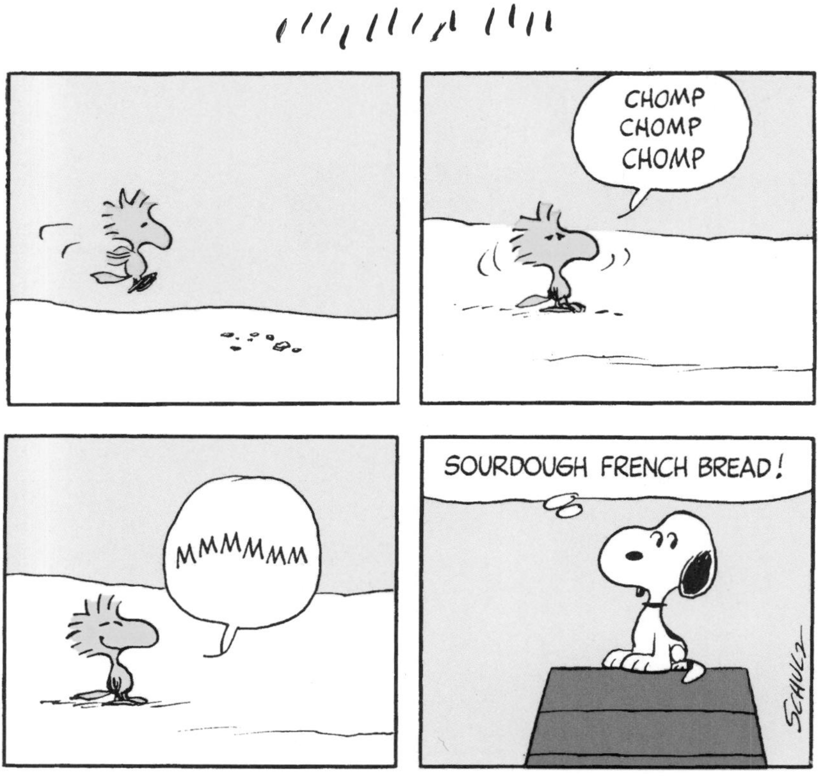
CHOMP CHOMP CHOMP
MMMMMMM
SOURDOUGH FRENCH BREAD!
SCHULZ

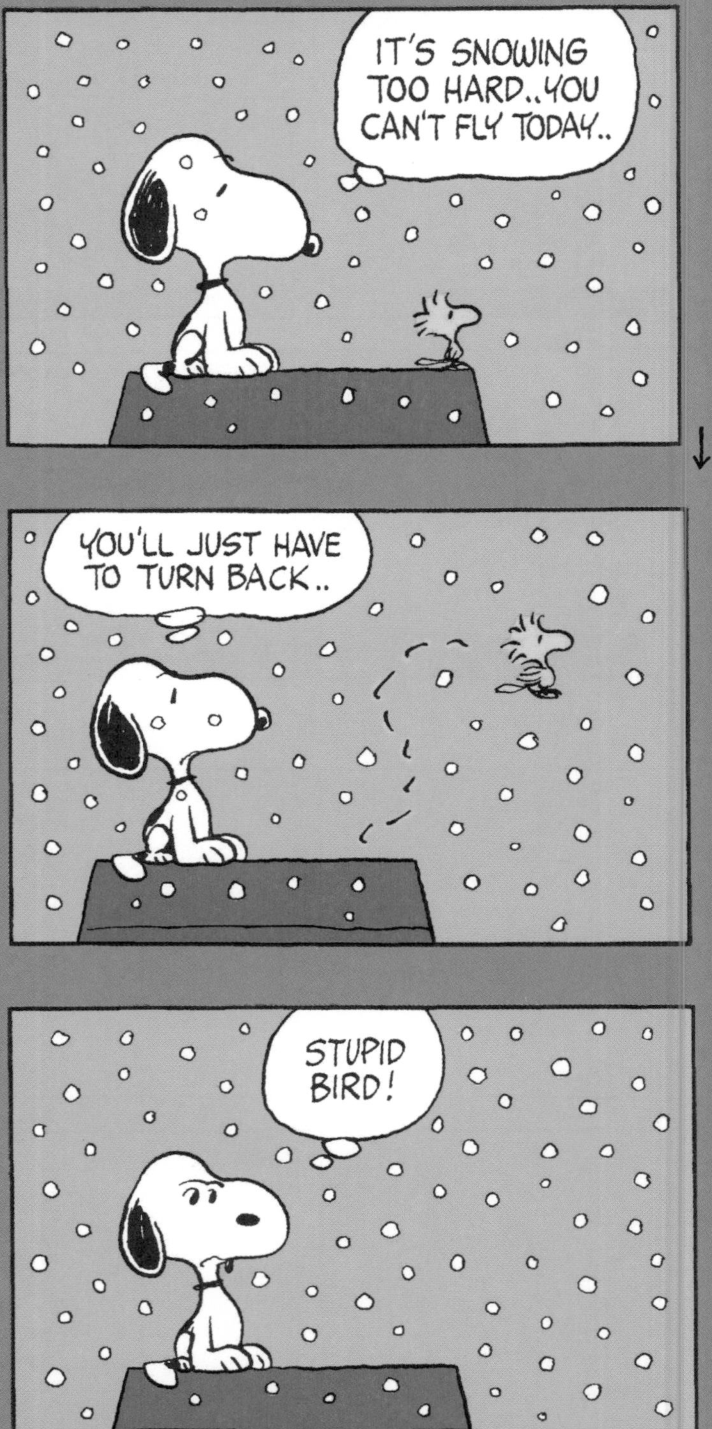
IT'S SNOWING TOO HARD..YOU CAN'T FLY TODAY..
YOU'LL JUST HAVE TO TURN BACK..
STUPID BIRD!

HA! I KNEW IT!
ALWAYS LISTEN TO THE CONTROL TOWER!
SIGH
SCHULZ

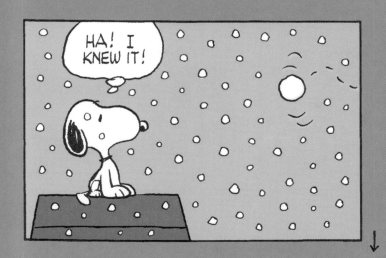

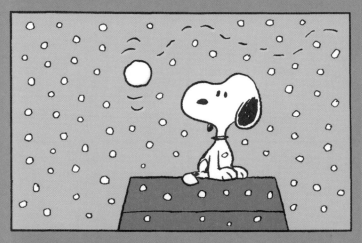

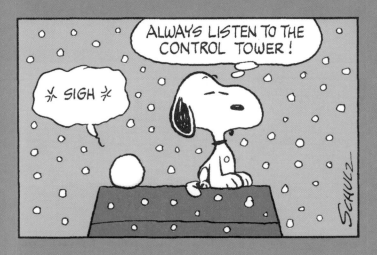

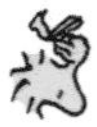

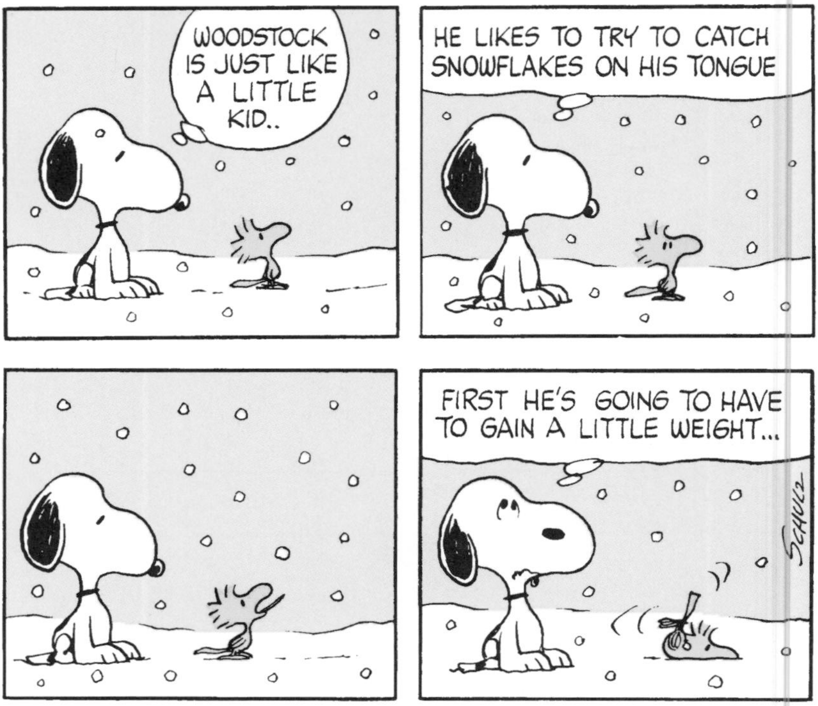
WOODSTOCK IS JUST LIKE A LITTLE KID..
HE LIKES TO TRY TO CATCH SNOWFLAKES ON HIS TONGUE
FIRST HE'S GOING TO HAVE TO GAIN A LITTLE WEIGHT...
SCHULZ

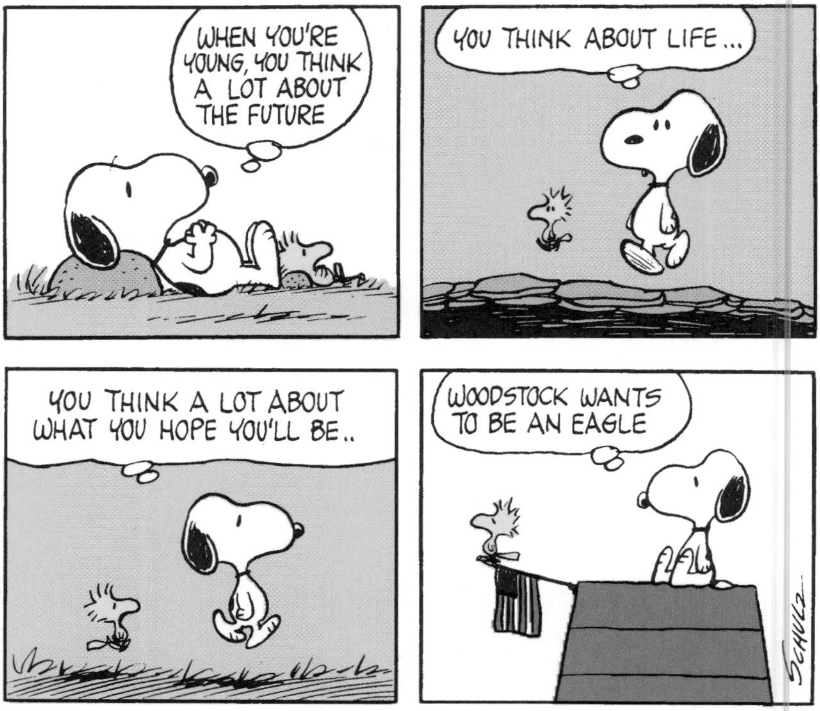
WHEN YOU'RE YOUNG, YOU THINK A LOT ABOUT THE FUTURE
YOU THINK ABOUT LIFE...
YOU THINK A LOT ABOUT WHAT YOU HOPE YOU'LL BE..
WOODSTOCK WANTS TO BE AN EAGLE
SCHULZ

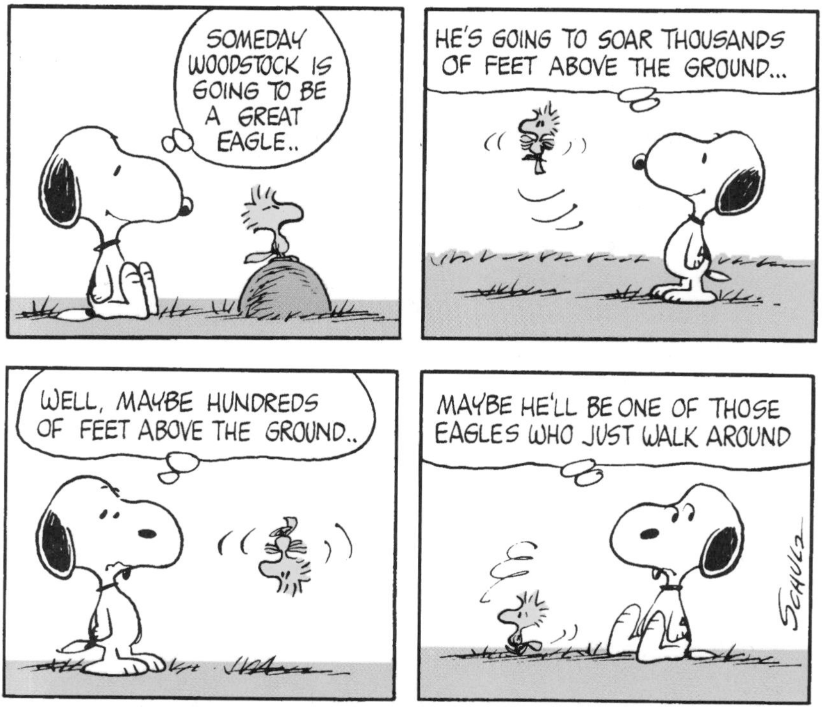
SOMEDAY WOODSTOCK IS GOING TO BE A GREAT EAGLE..
HE'S GOING TO SOAR THOUSANDS OF FEET ABOVE THE GROUND...
WELL, MAYBE HUNDREDS OF FEET ABOVE THE GROUND..
MAYBE HE'LL BE ONE OF THOSE EAGLES WHO JUST WALK AROUND
SCHULZ

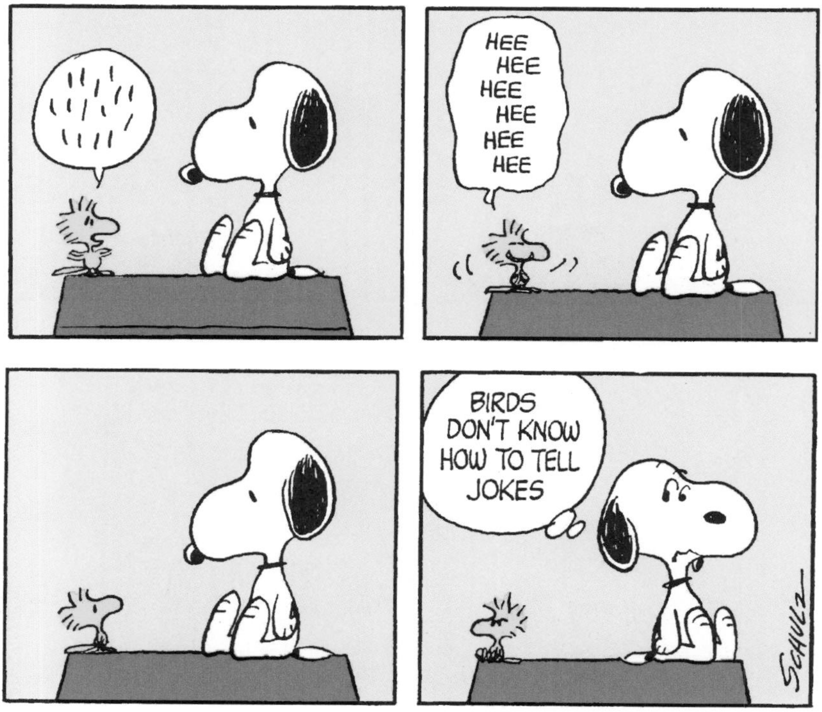
HEE HEE HEE HEE HEE HEE
BIRDS DON'T KNOW HOW TO TELL JOKES
SCHULZ

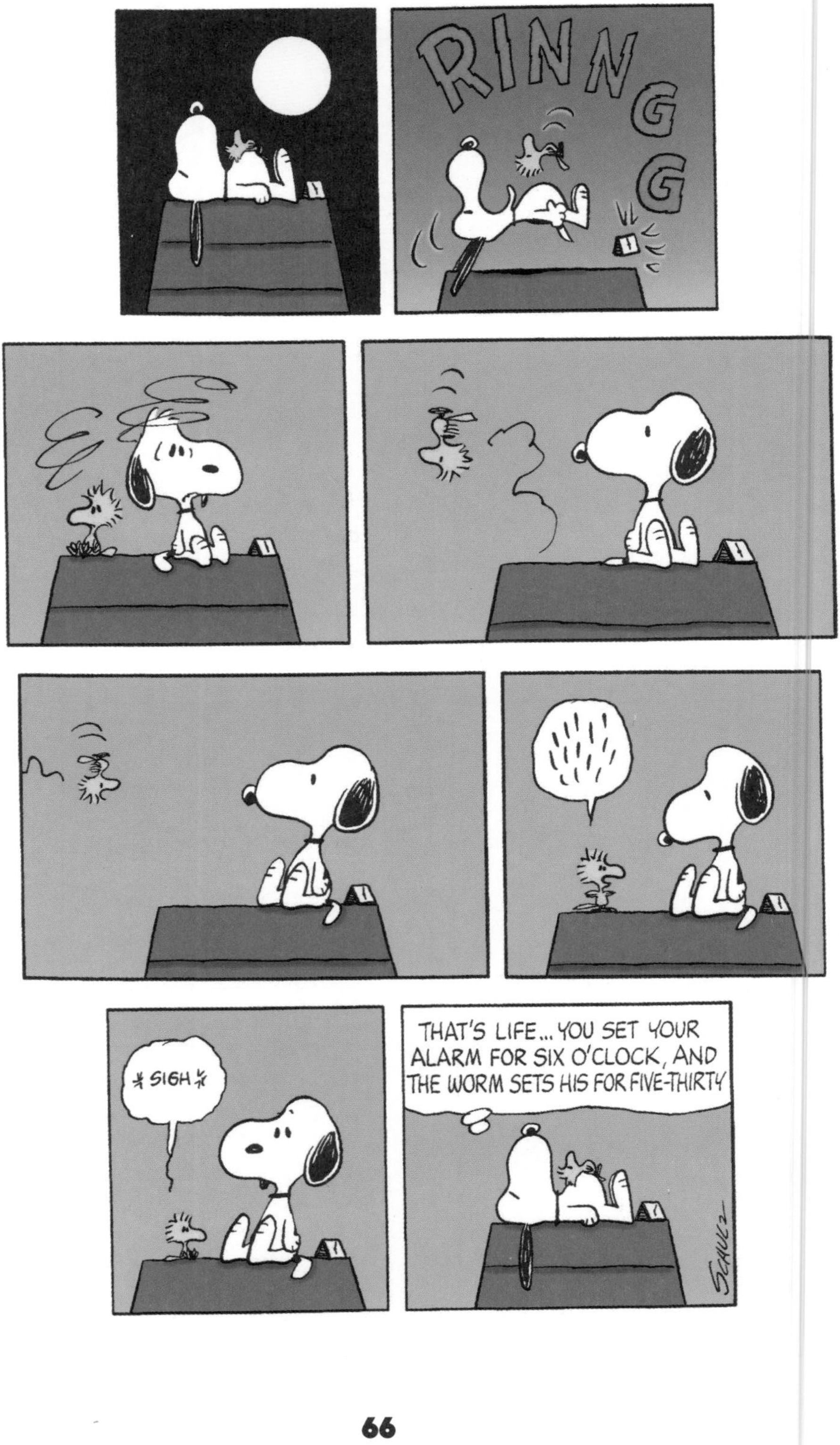
RINNG G
* SIGH *
THAT'S LIFE... YOU SET YOUR ALARM FOR SIX O'CLOCK, AND THE WORM SETS HIS FOR FIVE-THIRTY
SCHULZ

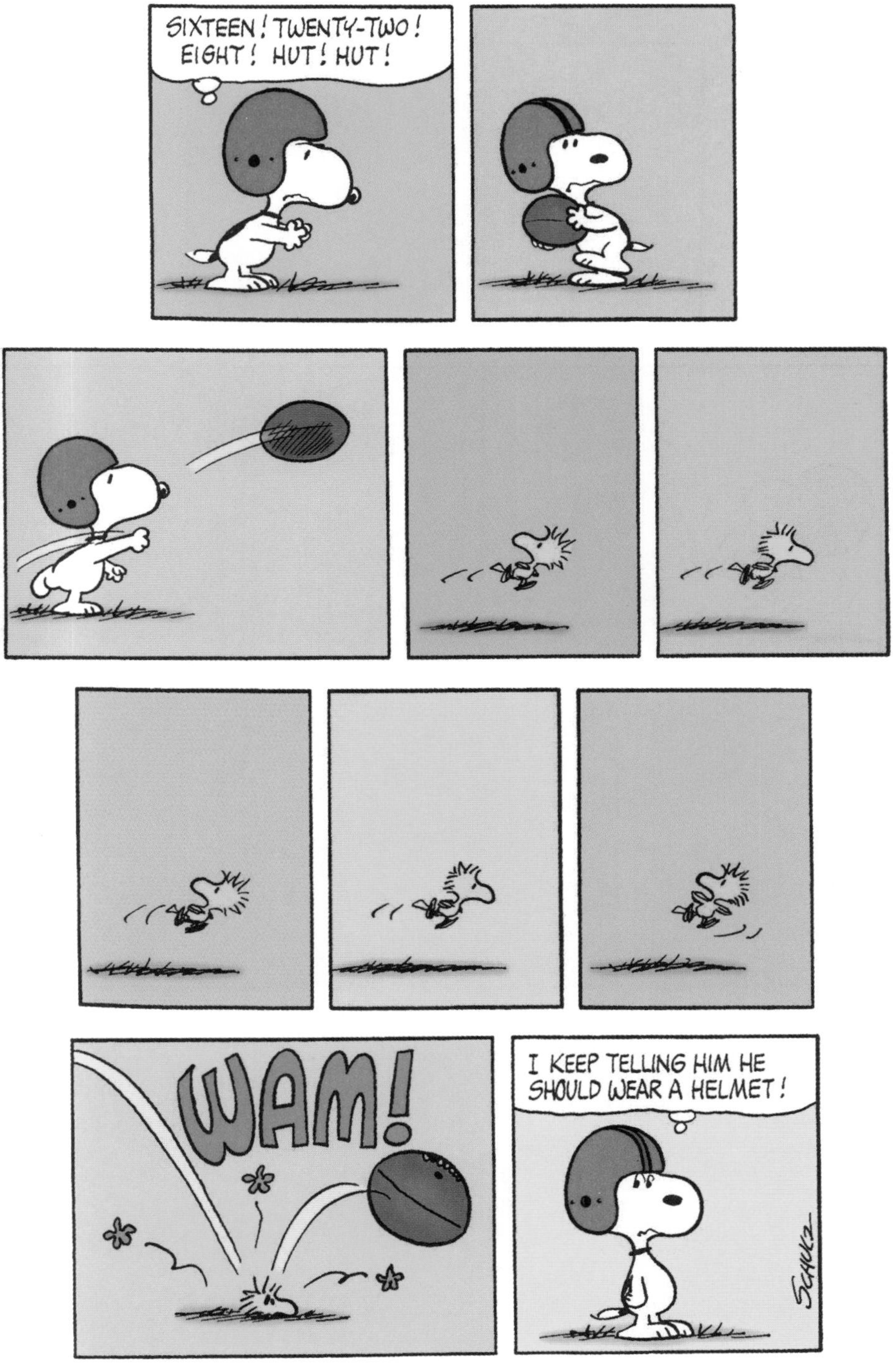
SIXTEEN! TWENTY-TWO! EIGHT! HUT! HUT!
WAM!
I KEEP TELLING HIM HE SHOULD WEAR A HELMET!
SCHULZ

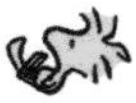

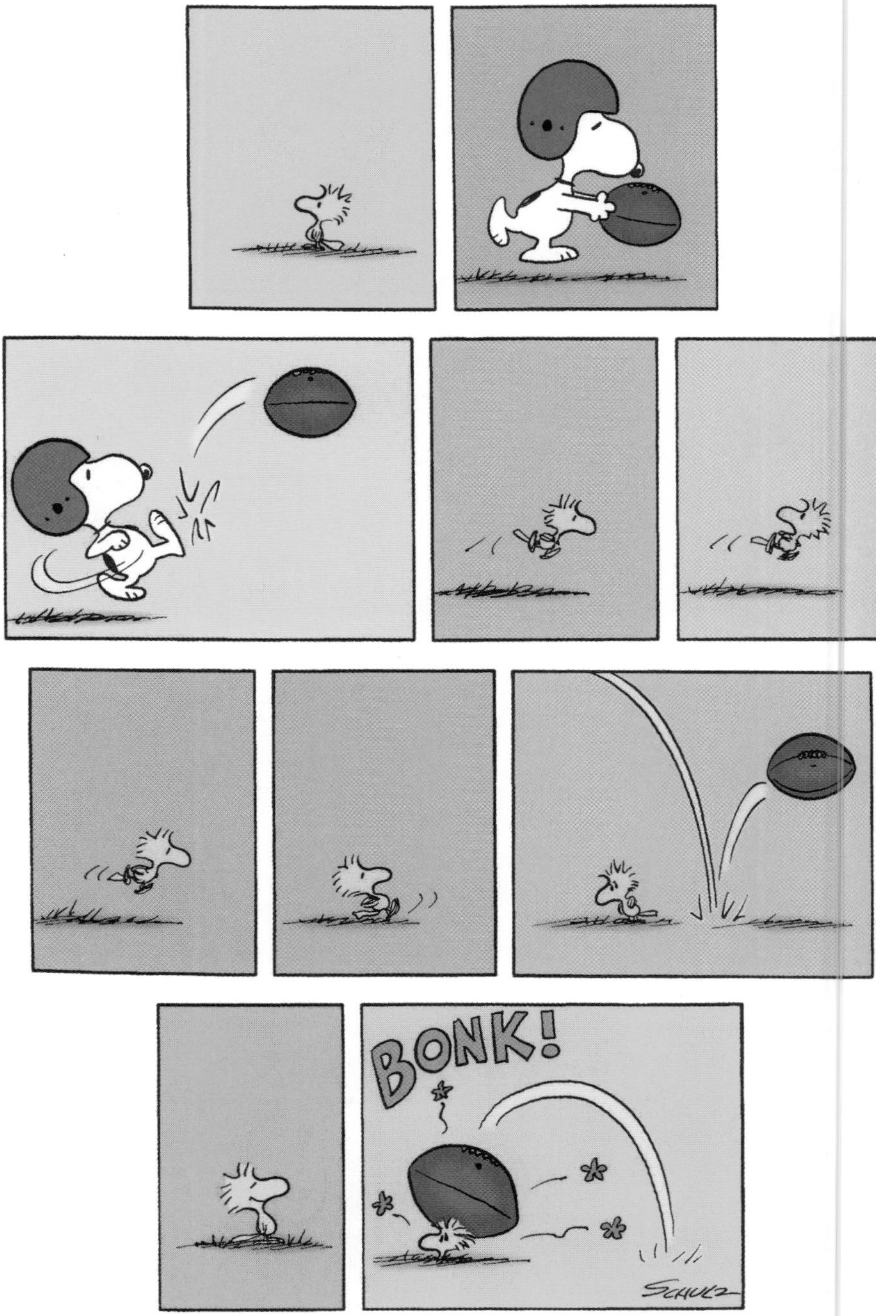
BONK!
SCHULZ

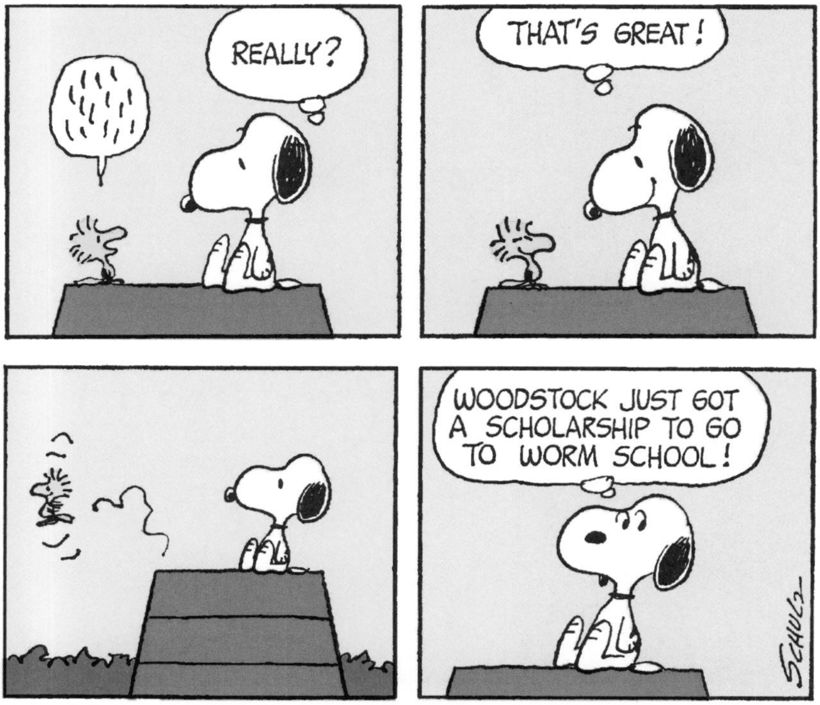
REALLY?
THAT'S GREAT!
WOODSTOCK JUST GOT A SCHOLARSHIP TO GO TO WORM SCHOOL!

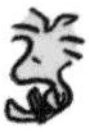

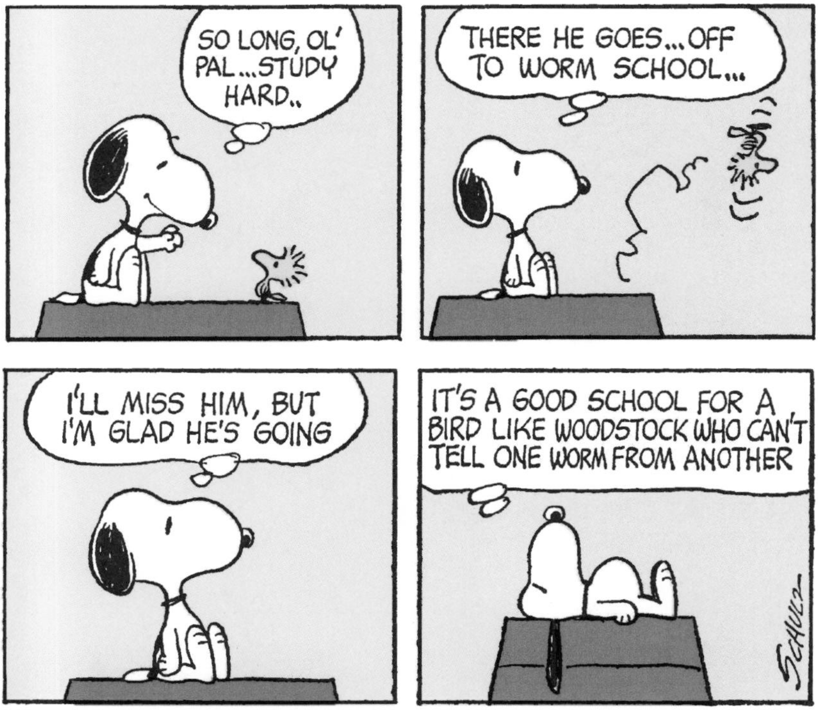
SO LONG, OL' PAL...STUDY HARD..
THERE HE GOES...OFF TO WORM SCHOOL...
I'LL MISS HIM, BUT I'M GLAD HE'S GOING
IT'S A GOOD SCHOOL FOR A BIRD LIKE WOODSTOCK WHO CAN'T TELL ONE WORM FROM ANOTHER

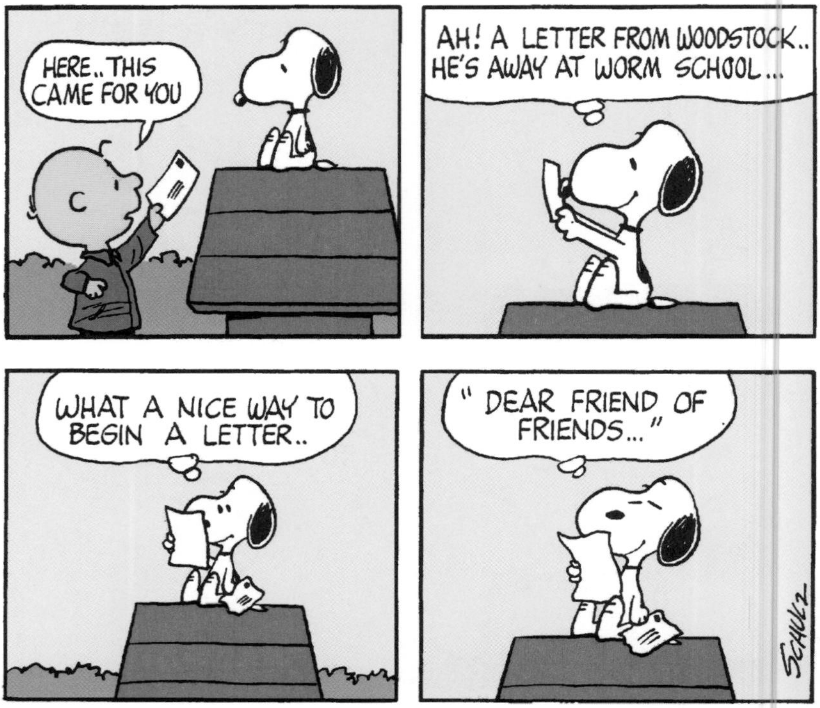
HERE.. THIS CAME FOR YOU
AH! A LETTER FROM WOODSTOCK.. HE'S AWAY AT WORM SCHOOL...
WHAT A NICE WAY TO BEGIN A LETTER..
" DEAR FRIEND OF FRIENDS..."
SCHULZ

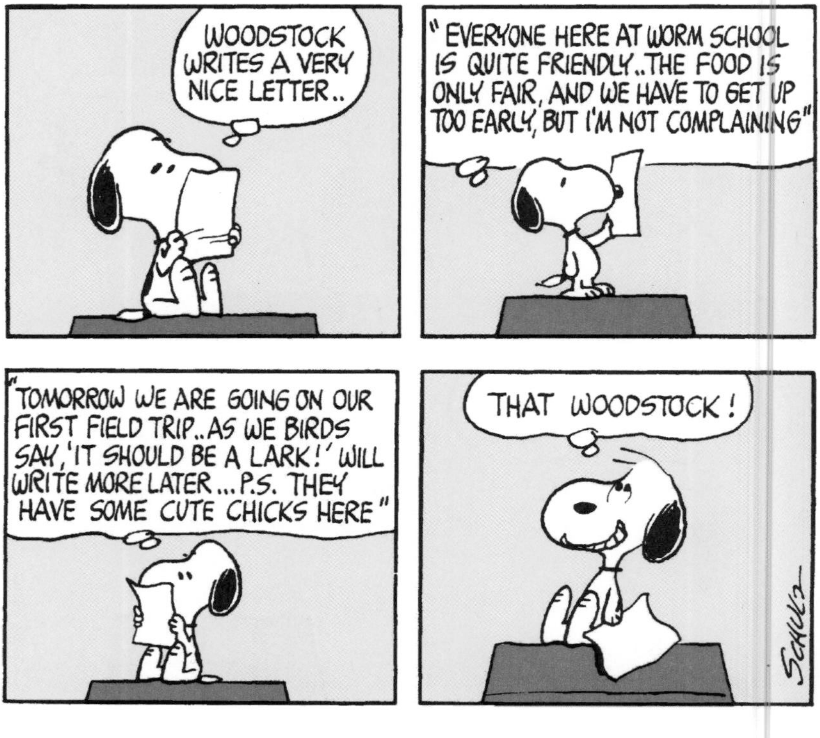
WOODSTOCK WRITES A VERY NICE LETTER..
" EVERYONE HERE AT WORM SCHOOL IS QUITE FRIENDLY..THE FOOD IS ONLY FAIR, AND WE HAVE TO GET UP TOO EARLY, BUT I'M NOT COMPLAINING"
"TOMORROW WE ARE GOING ON OUR FIRST FIELD TRIP..AS WE BIRDS SAY, 'IT SHOULD BE A LARK!' WILL WRITE MORE LATER ... P.S. THEY HAVE SOME CUTE CHICKS HERE"
THAT WOODSTOCK!
SCHULZ

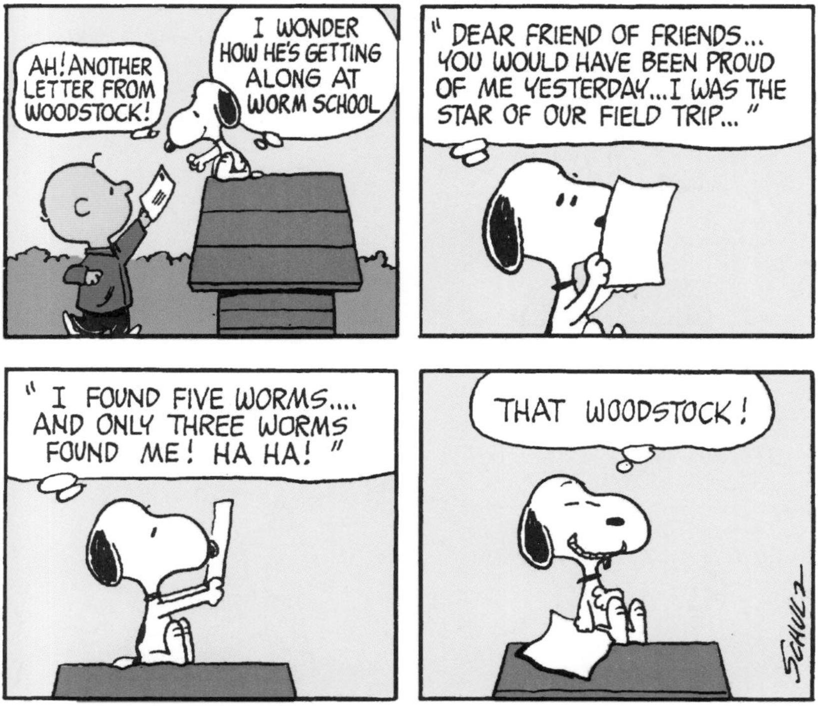
AH! ANOTHER LETTER FROM WOODSTOCK!
I WONDER HOW HE'S GETTING ALONG AT WORM SCHOOL
" DEAR FRIEND OF FRIENDS... YOU WOULD HAVE BEEN PROUD OF ME YESTERDAY...I WAS THE STAR OF OUR FIELD TRIP... "
" I FOUND FIVE WORMS.... AND ONLY THREE WORMS FOUND ME! HA HA! "
THAT WOODSTOCK!
SCHULZ

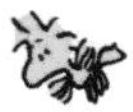

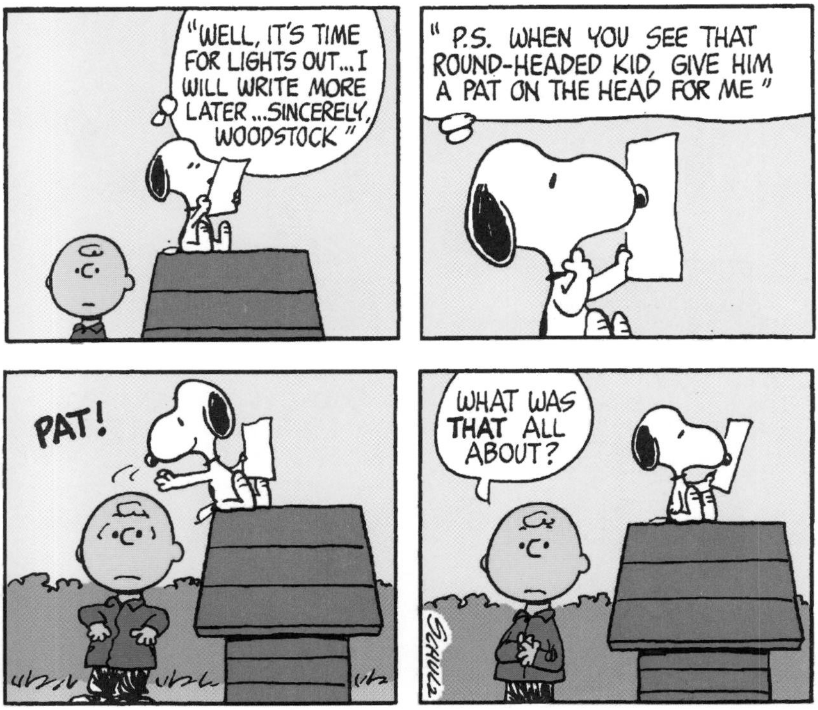
"WELL, IT'S TIME FOR LIGHTS OUT...I WILL WRITE MORE LATER...SINCERELY, WOODSTOCK "
" P.S. WHEN YOU SEE THAT ROUND-HEADED KID, GIVE HIM A PAT ON THE HEAD FOR ME "
PAT!
WHAT WAS THAT ALL ABOUT?
SCHULZ

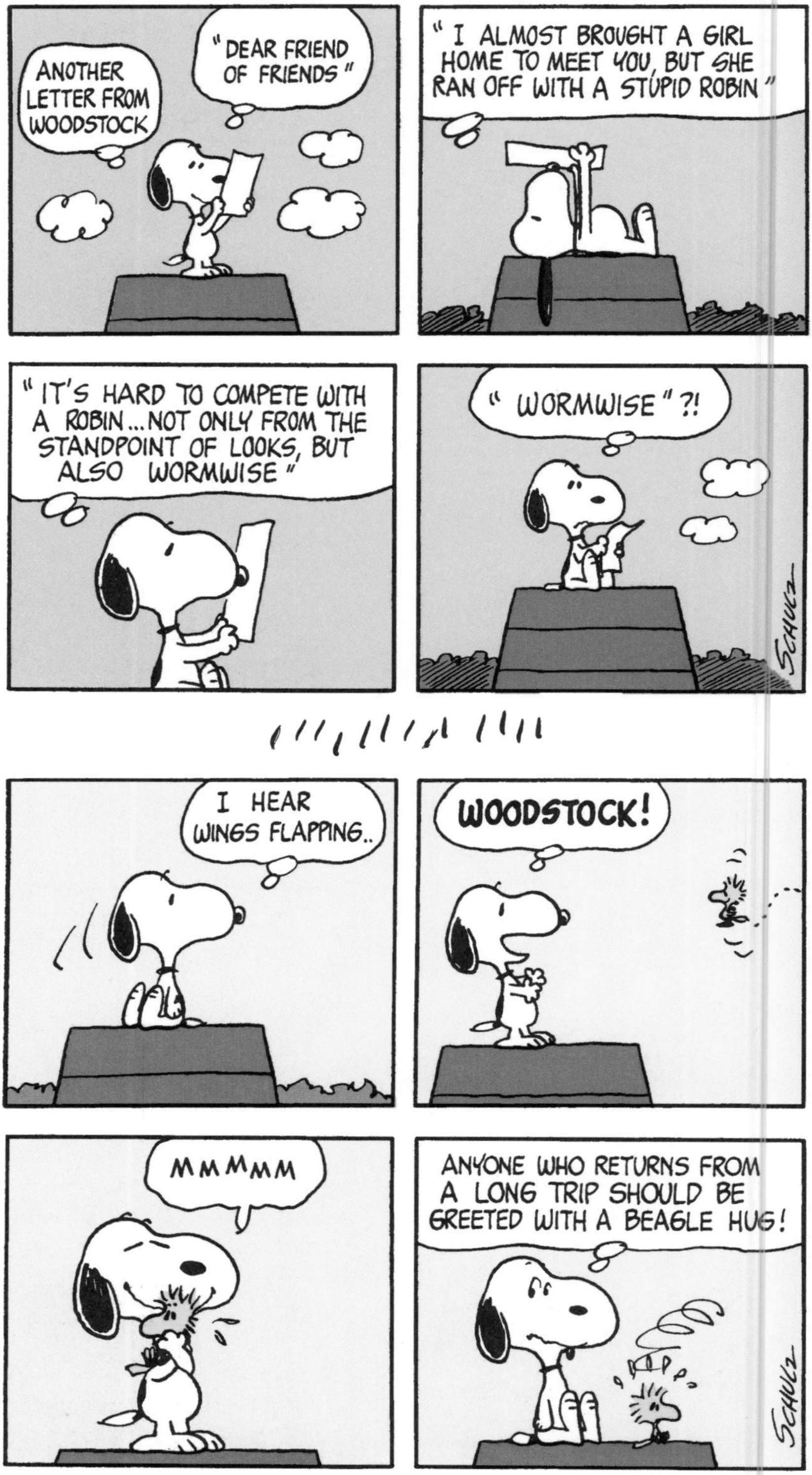
ANOTHER LETTER FROM WOODSTOCK
"DEAR FRIEND OF FRIENDS"
"I ALMOST BROUGHT A GIRL HOME TO MEET YOU, BUT SHE RAN OFF WITH A STUPID ROBIN"
"IT'S HARD TO COMPETE WITH A ROBIN...NOT ONLY FROM THE STANDPOINT OF LOOKS, BUT ALSO WORMWISE"
"WORMWISE"?!
SCHULZ
I HEAR WINGS FLAPPING..
WOODSTOCK!
MMMMM
ANYONE WHO RETURNS FROM A LONG TRIP SHOULD BE GREETED WITH A BEAGLE HUG!
SCHULZ

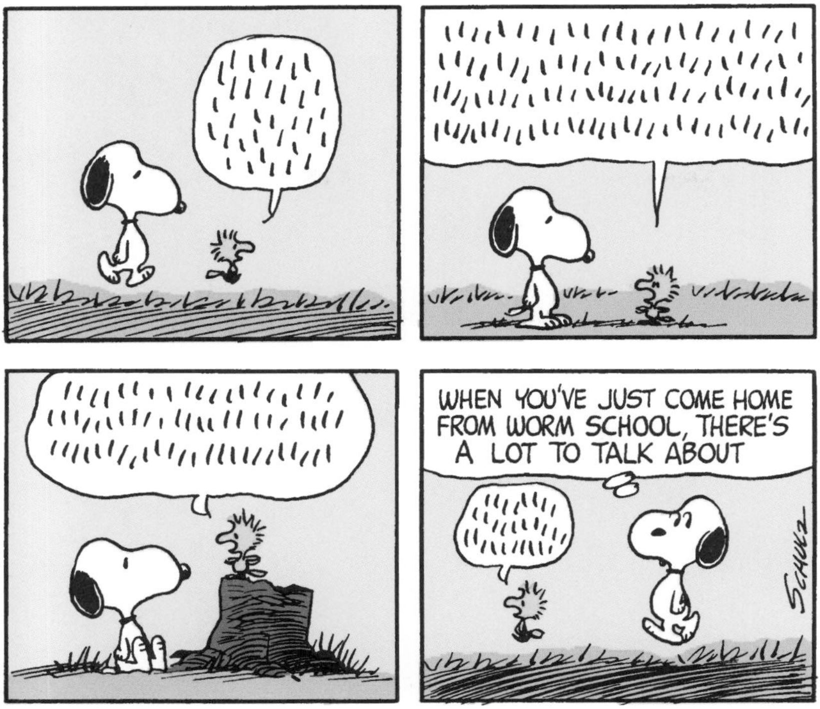
WHEN YOU'VE JUST COME HOME FROM WORM SCHOOL, THERE'S A LOT TO TALK ABOUT
SCHULZ

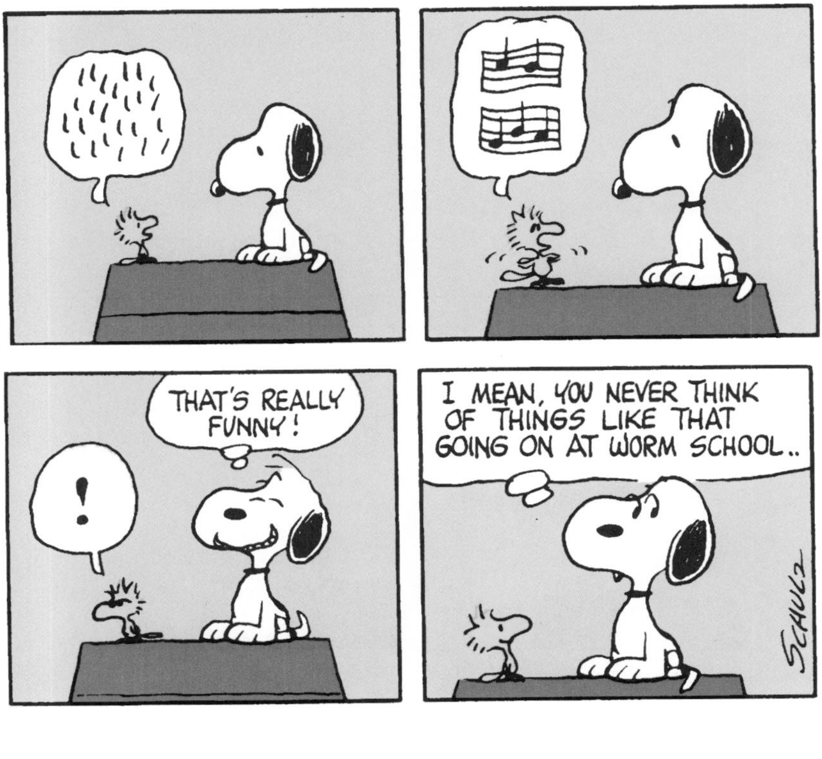
THAT'S REALLY FUNNY!
!
I MEAN, YOU NEVER THINK OF THINGS LIKE THAT GOING ON AT WORM SCHOOL..
SCHULZ

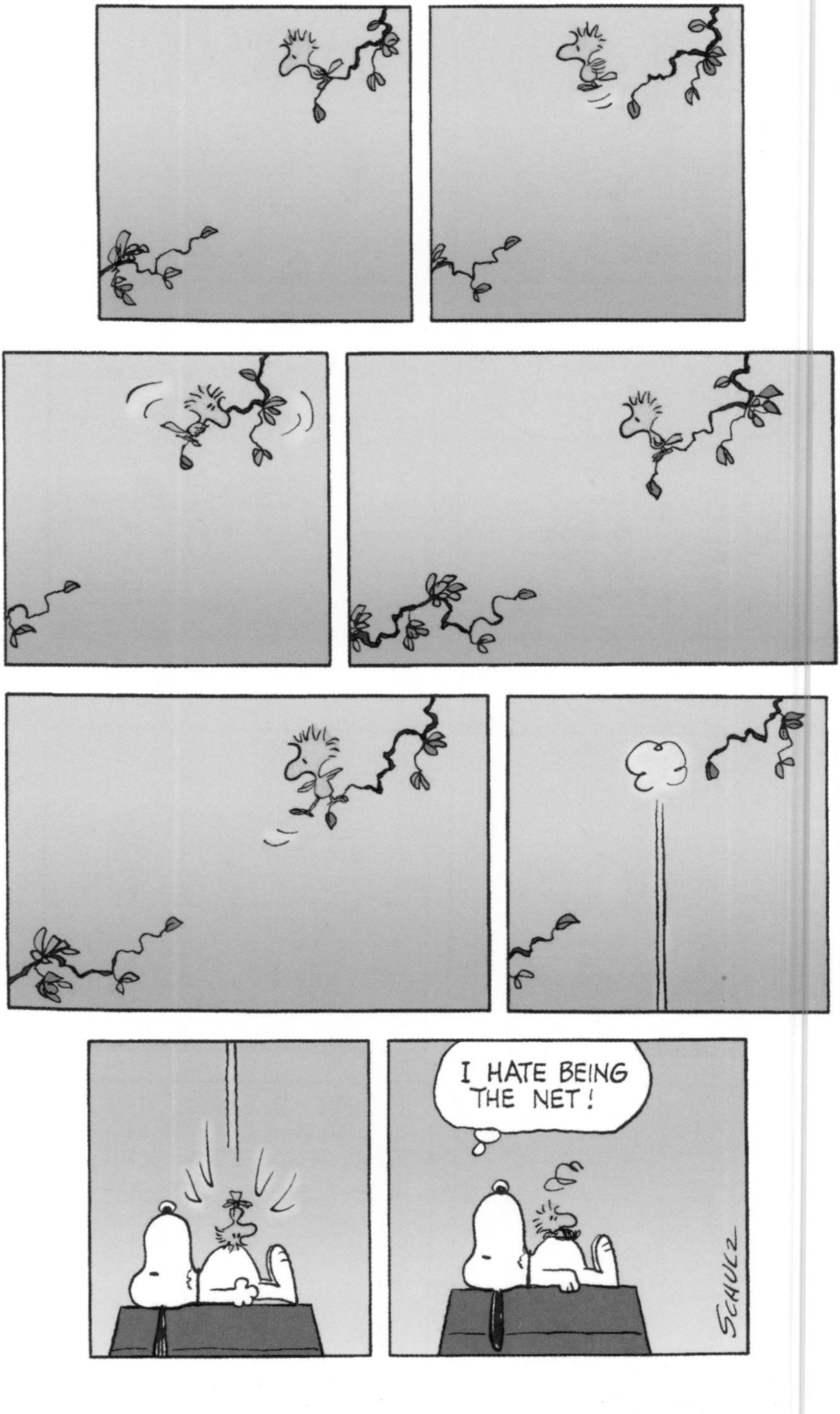
I HATE BEING THE NET!
SCHULZ

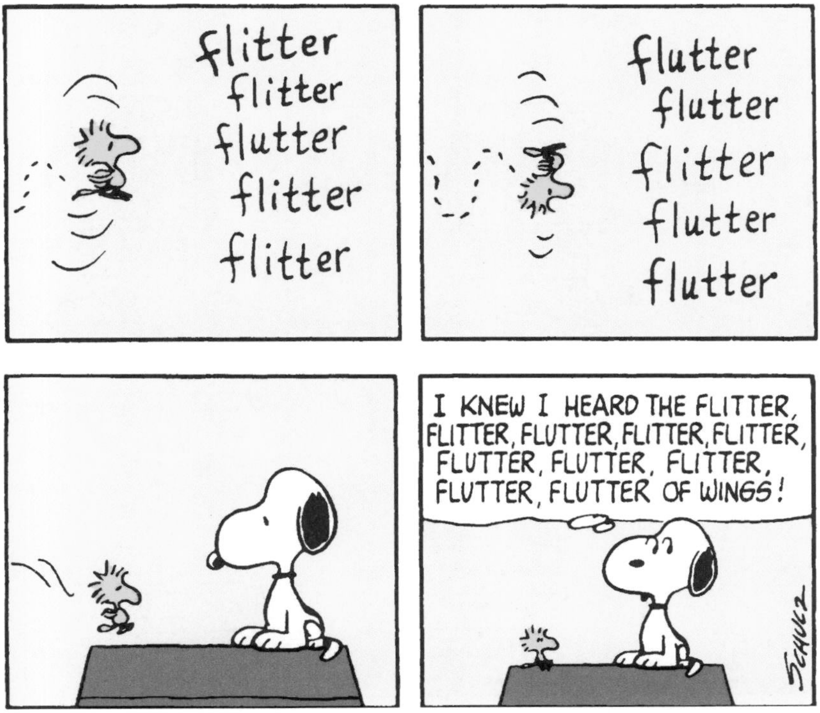
flitter
flitter
flutter
flitter
flitter
flutter
flutter
flitter
flutter
flutter
I KNEW I HEARD THE FLITTER, FLITTER, FLUTTER, FLITTER, FLITTER, FLUTTER, FLUTTER, FLITTER, FLUTTER, FLUTTER OF WINGS!
SCHULZ

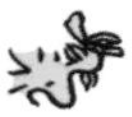

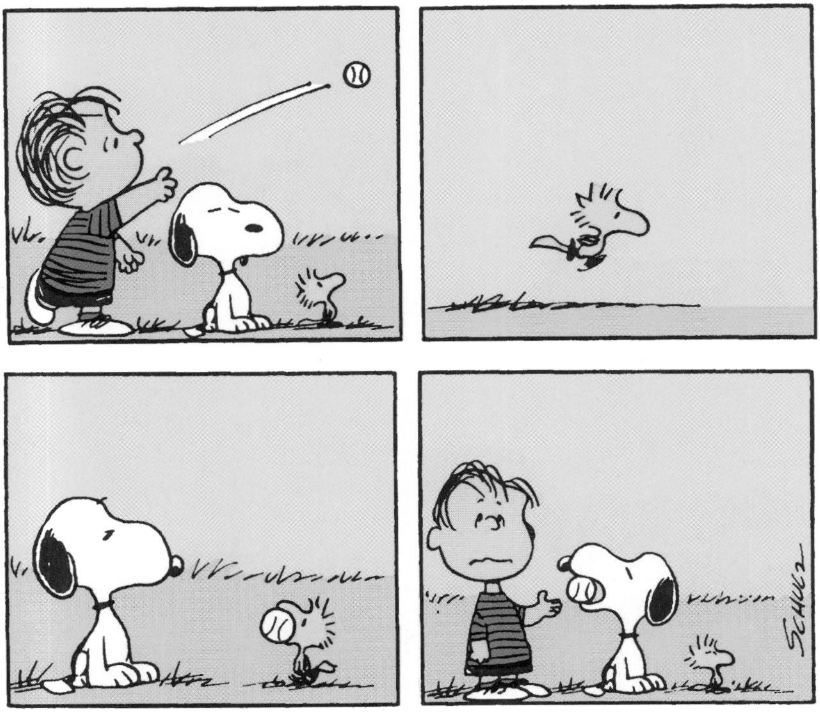
SCHULZ

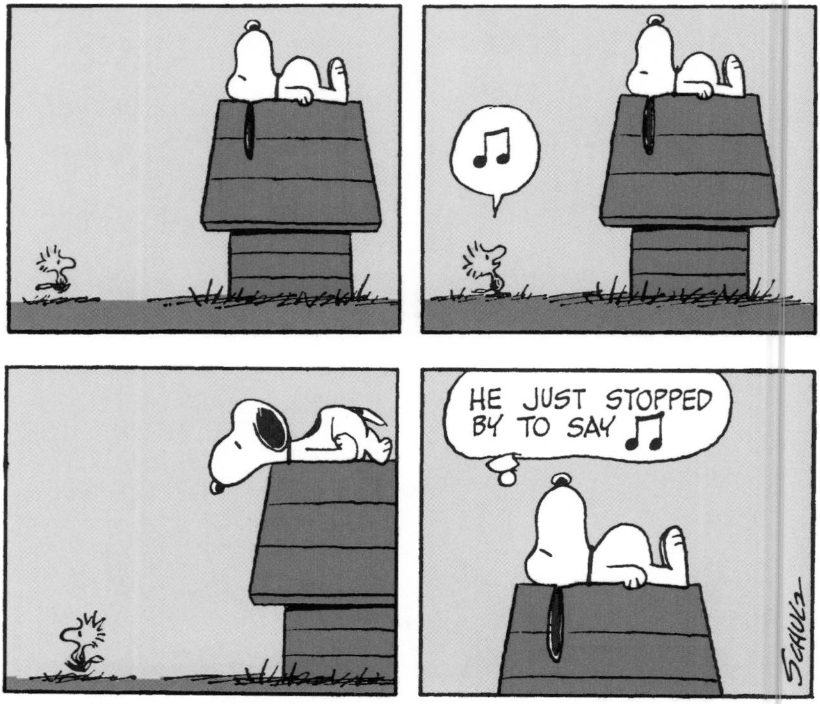
HE JUST STOPPED BY TO SAY
SCHULZ

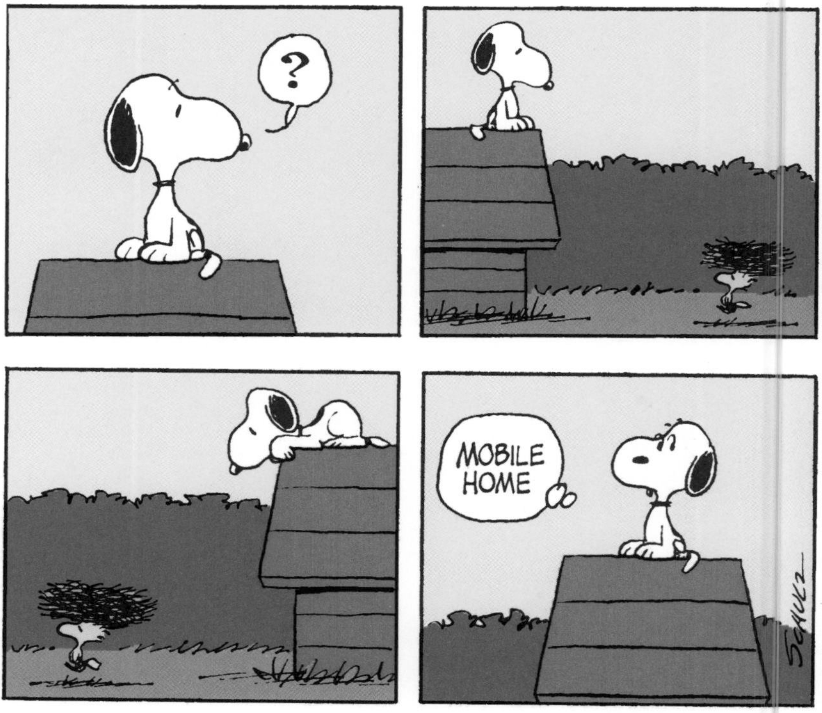
?
MOBILE HOME
SCHULZ

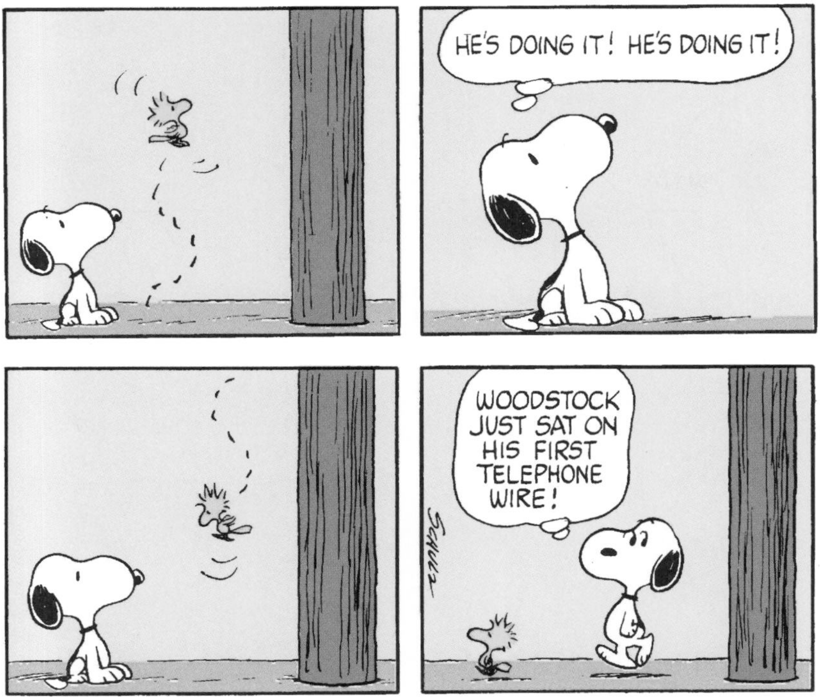

HE'S DOING IT! HE'S DOING IT!
WOODSTOCK JUST SAT ON HIS FIRST TELEPHONE WIRE!
SCHULZ

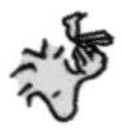

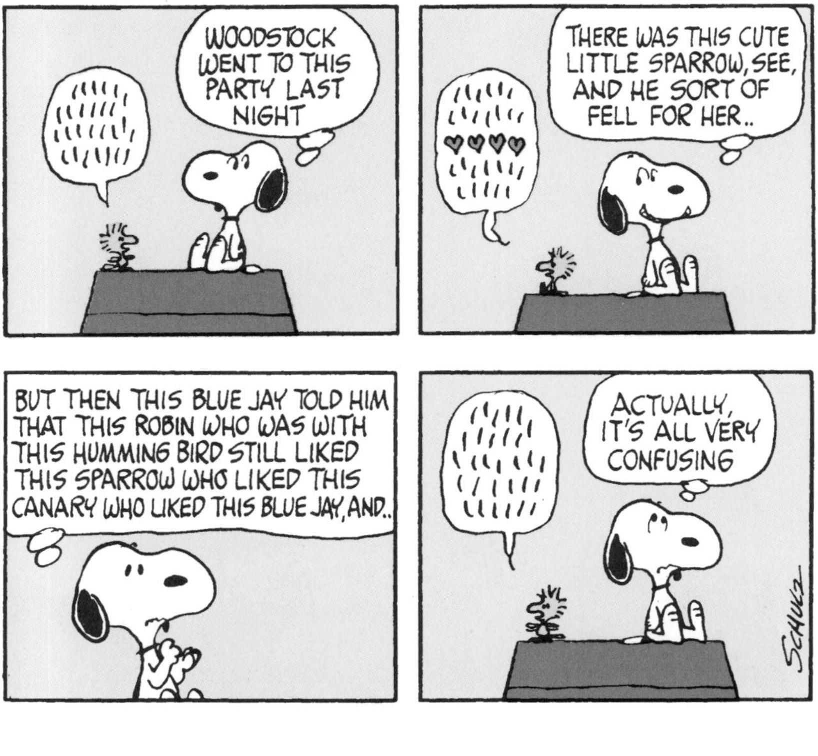

WOODSTOCK WENT TO THIS PARTY LAST NIGHT
THERE WAS THIS CUTE LITTLE SPARROW, SEE, AND HE SORT OF FELL FOR HER..
BUT THEN THIS BLUE JAY TOLD HIM THAT THIS ROBIN WHO WAS WITH THIS HUMMING BIRD STILL LIKED THIS SPARROW WHO LIKED THIS CANARY WHO LIKED THIS BLUE JAY, AND..
ACTUALLY, IT'S ALL VERY CONFUSING
SCHULZ

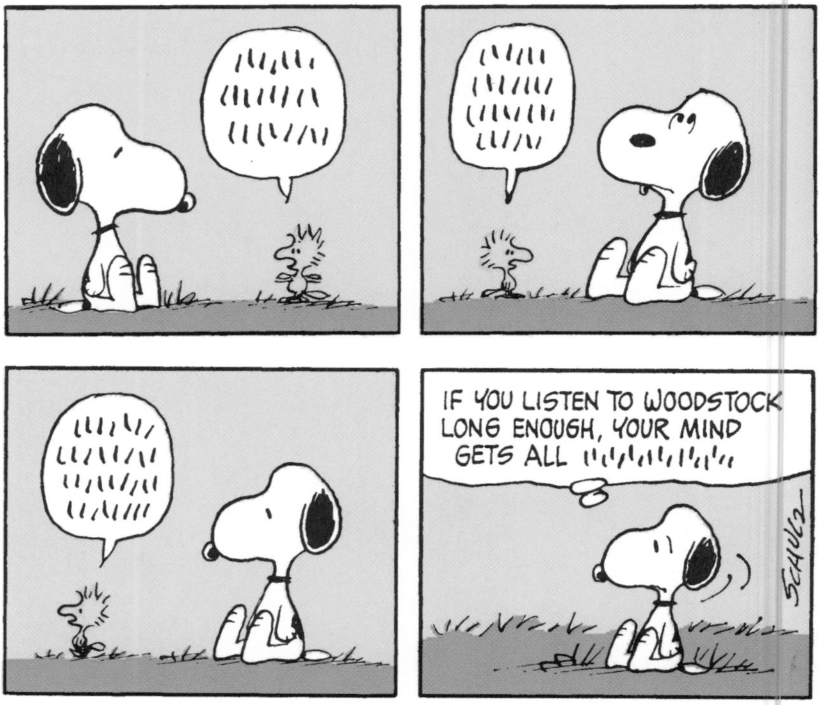
IF YOU LISTEN TO WOODSTOCK LONG ENOUGH, YOUR MIND GETS ALL
SCHULZ

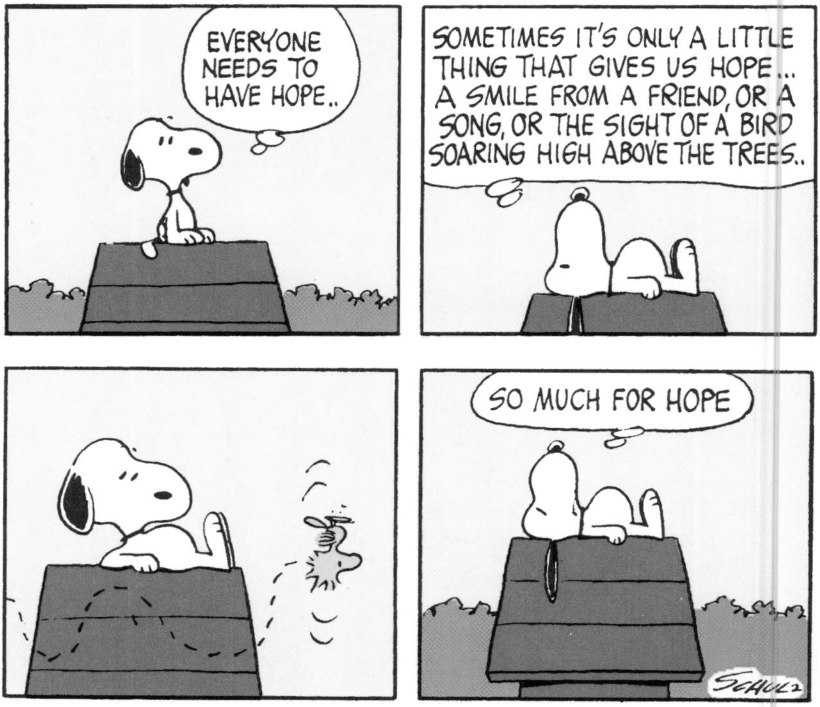
EVERYONE NEEDS TO HAVE HOPE..
SOMETIMES IT'S ONLY A LITTLE THING THAT GIVES US HOPE... A SMILE FROM A FRIEND, OR A SONG, OR THE SIGHT OF A BIRD SOARING HIGH ABOVE THE TREES..
SO MUCH FOR HOPE
SCHULZ

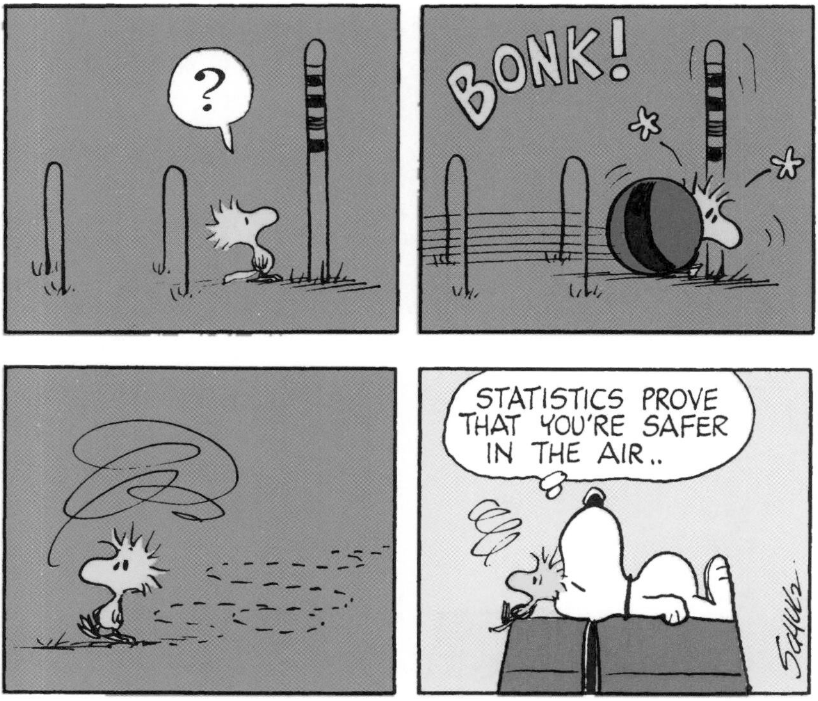
?
BONK!
STATISTICS PROVE THAT YOU'RE SAFER IN THE AIR..
SCHULZ

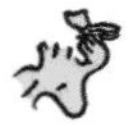

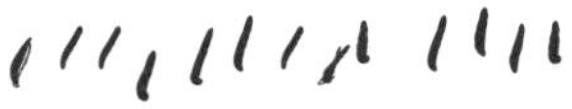

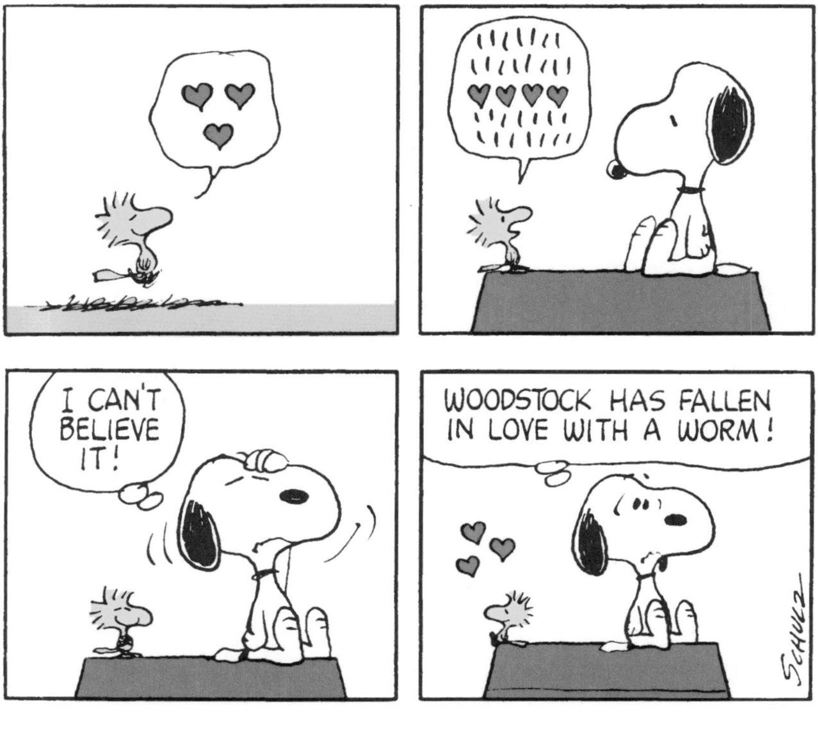
I CAN'T BELIEVE IT!
WOODSTOCK HAS FALLEN IN LOVE WITH A WORM!
SCHULZ

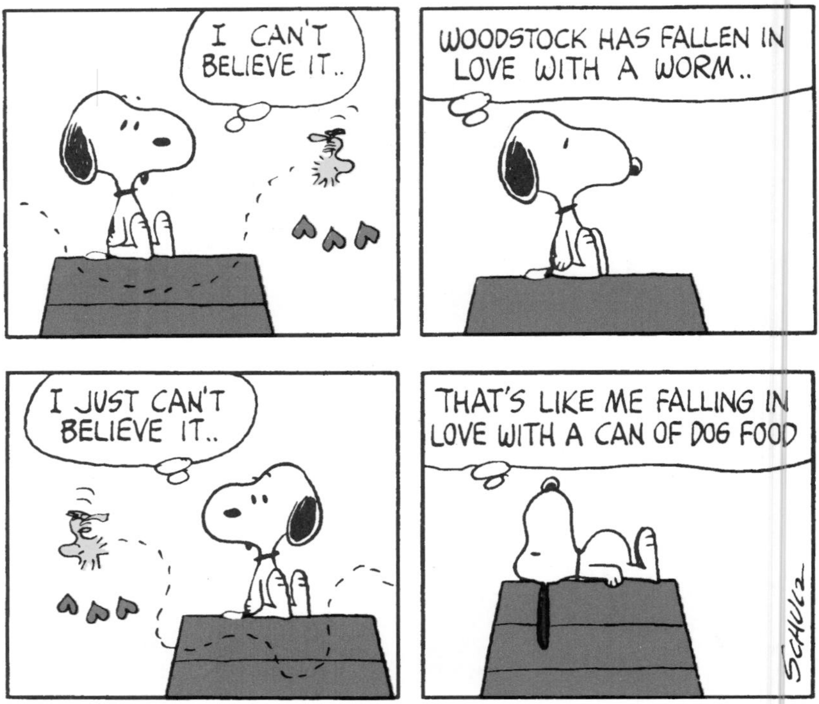
I CAN'T BELIEVE IT..
WOODSTOCK HAS FALLEN IN LOVE WITH A WORM..
I JUST CAN'T BELIEVE IT..
THAT'S LIKE ME FALLING IN LOVE WITH A CAN OF DOG FOOD
SCHULZ

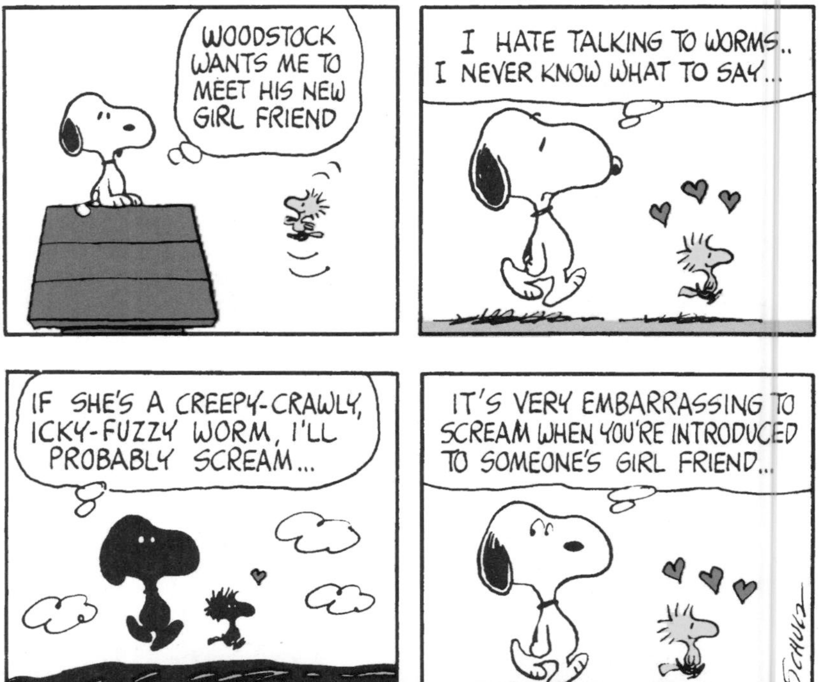
WOODSTOCK WANTS ME TO MEET HIS NEW GIRL FRIEND
I HATE TALKING TO WORMS.. I NEVER KNOW WHAT TO SAY...
IF SHE'S A CREEPY-CRAWLY, ICKY-FUZZY WORM, I'LL PROBABLY SCREAM...
IT'S VERY EMBARRASSING TO SCREAM WHEN YOU'RE INTRODUCED TO SOMEONE'S GIRL FRIEND...
SCHULZ

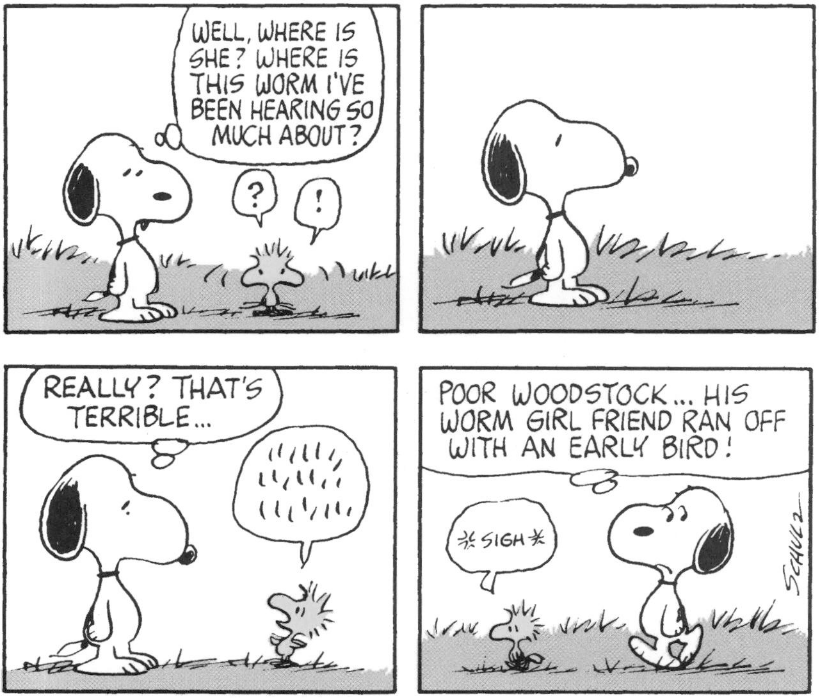
WELL, WHERE IS SHE? WHERE IS THIS WORM I'VE BEEN HEARING SO MUCH ABOUT?
?
!
REALLY? THAT'S TERRIBLE...
POOR WOODSTOCK... HIS WORM GIRL FRIEND RAN OFF WITH AN EARLY BIRD!
SIGH
SCHULZ

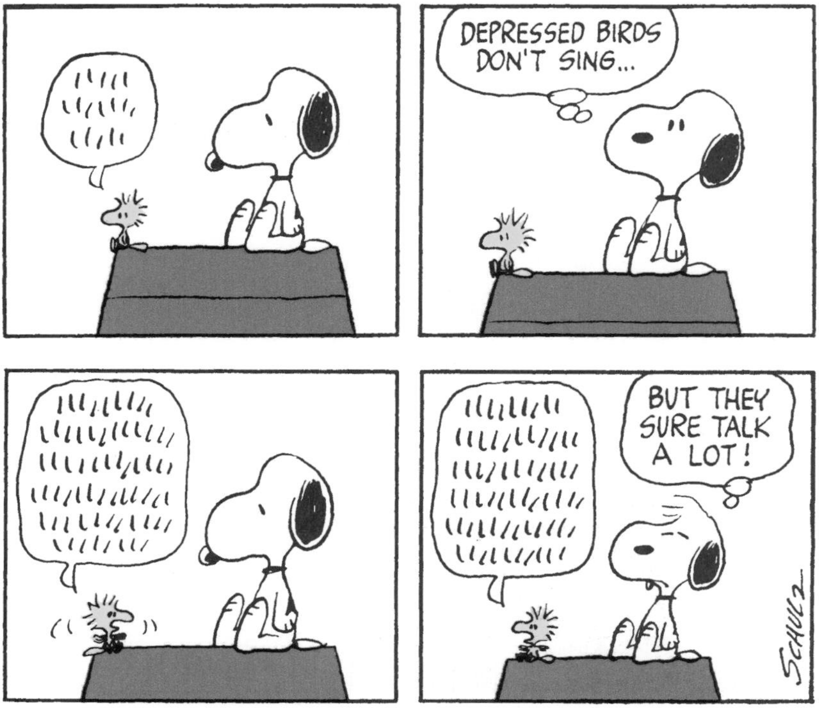
DEPRESSED BIRDS DON'T SING...
BUT THEY SURE TALK A LOT!
SCHULZ

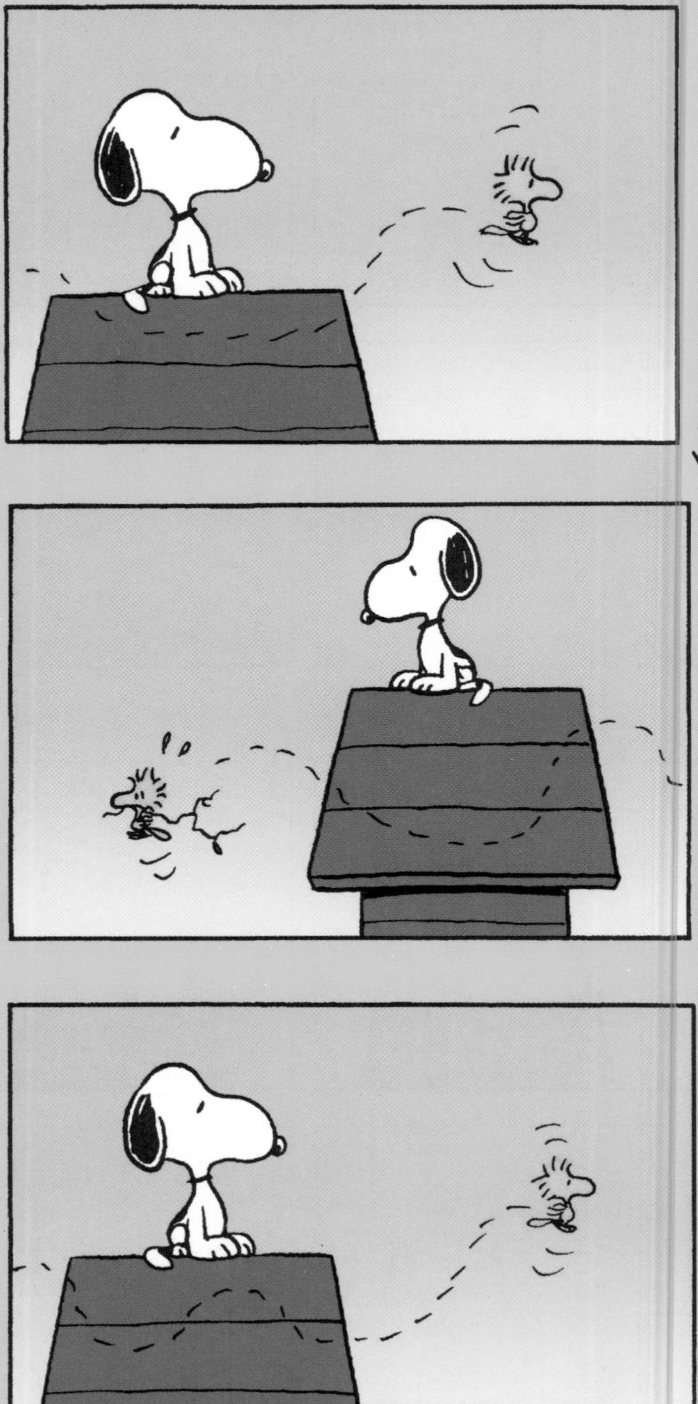

* SIGH *
I GUESS THERE'S NO WAY I CAN GET OUT OF IT..
I HATE HELPING WOODSTOCK BUILD NESTS!
SCHULZ

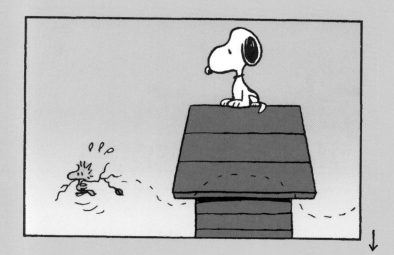

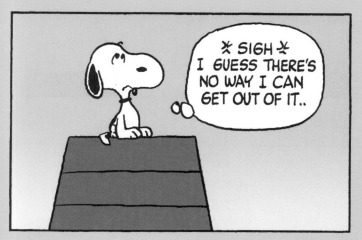

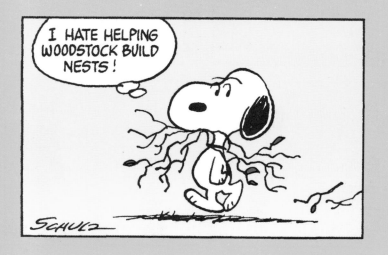

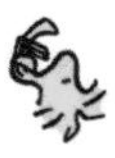

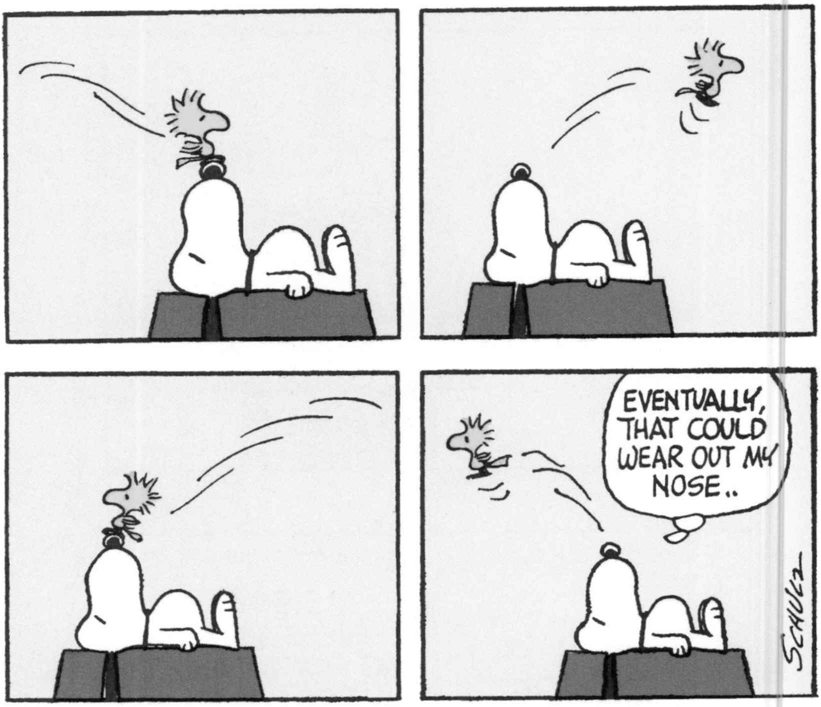
EVENTUALLY, THAT COULD WEAR OUT MY NOSE..
SCHULZ

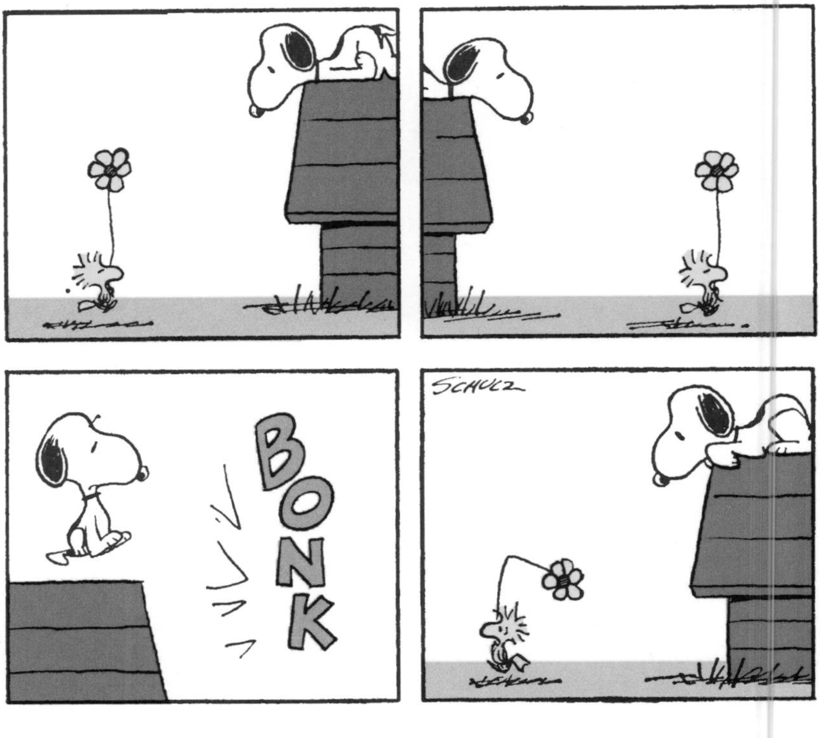
BONK
SCHULZ

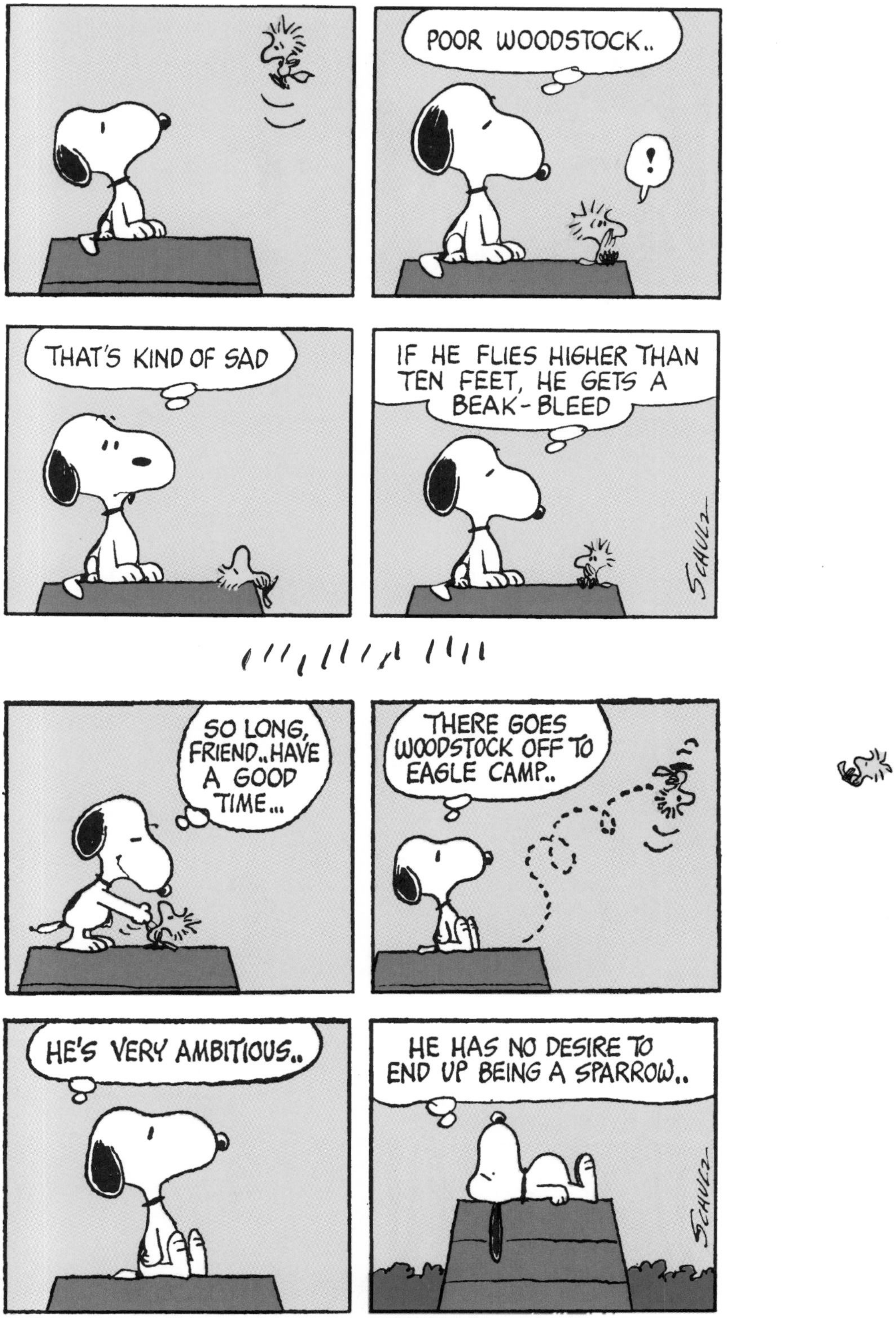
POOR WOODSTOCK..
!
THAT'S KIND OF SAD
IF HE FLIES HIGHER THAN TEN FEET, HE GETS A BEAK-BLEED
SCHULZ
SO LONG, FRIEND..HAVE A GOOD TIME...
THERE GOES WOODSTOCK OFF TO EAGLE CAMP..
HE'S VERY AMBITIOUS..
HE HAS NO DESIRE TO END UP BEING A SPARROW..
SCHULZ

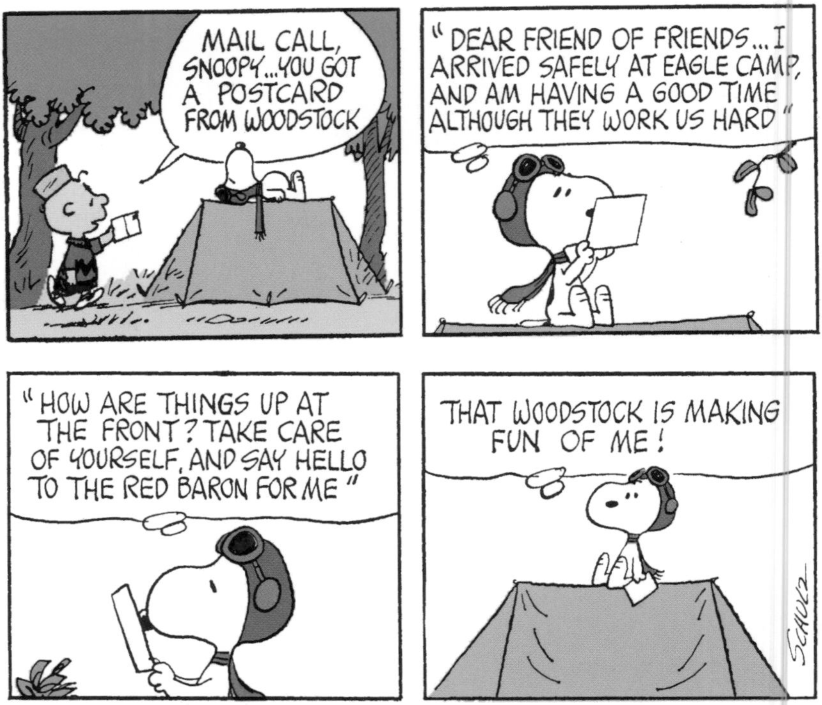
MAIL CALL, SNOOPY...YOU GOT A POSTCARD FROM WOODSTOCK
" DEAR FRIEND OF FRIENDS...I ARRIVED SAFELY AT EAGLE CAMP, AND AM HAVING A GOOD TIME ALTHOUGH THEY WORK US HARD "
" HOW ARE THINGS UP AT THE FRONT? TAKE CARE OF YOURSELF, AND SAY HELLO TO THE RED BARON FOR ME "
THAT WOODSTOCK IS MAKING FUN OF ME!
SCHULZ

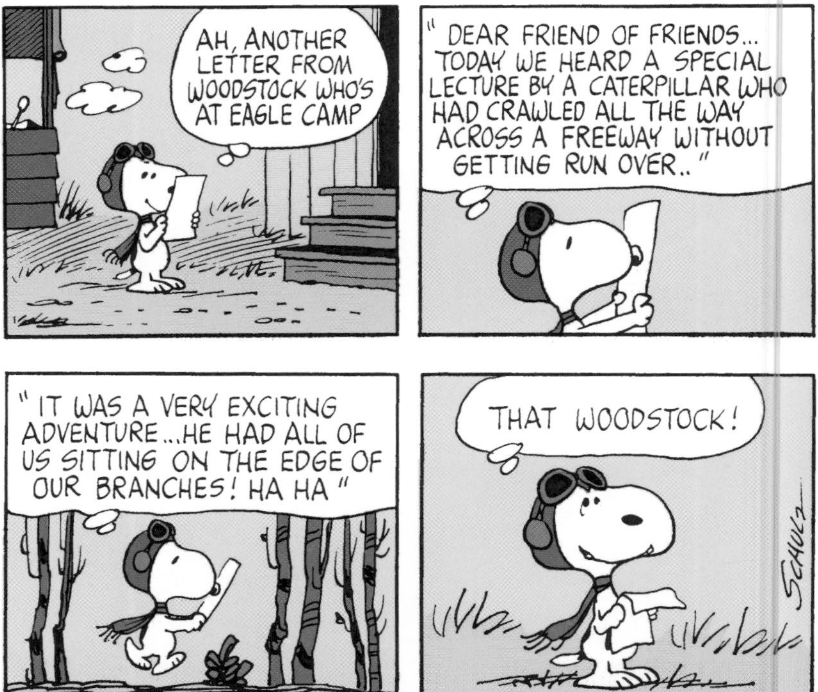
AH, ANOTHER LETTER FROM WOODSTOCK WHO'S AT EAGLE CAMP
" DEAR FRIEND OF FRIENDS... TODAY WE HEARD A SPECIAL LECTURE BY A CATERPILLAR WHO HAD CRAWLED ALL THE WAY ACROSS A FREEWAY WITHOUT GETTING RUN OVER.. "
" IT WAS A VERY EXCITING ADVENTURE...HE HAD ALL OF US SITTING ON THE EDGE OF OUR BRANCHES! HA HA "
THAT WOODSTOCK!
SCHULZ

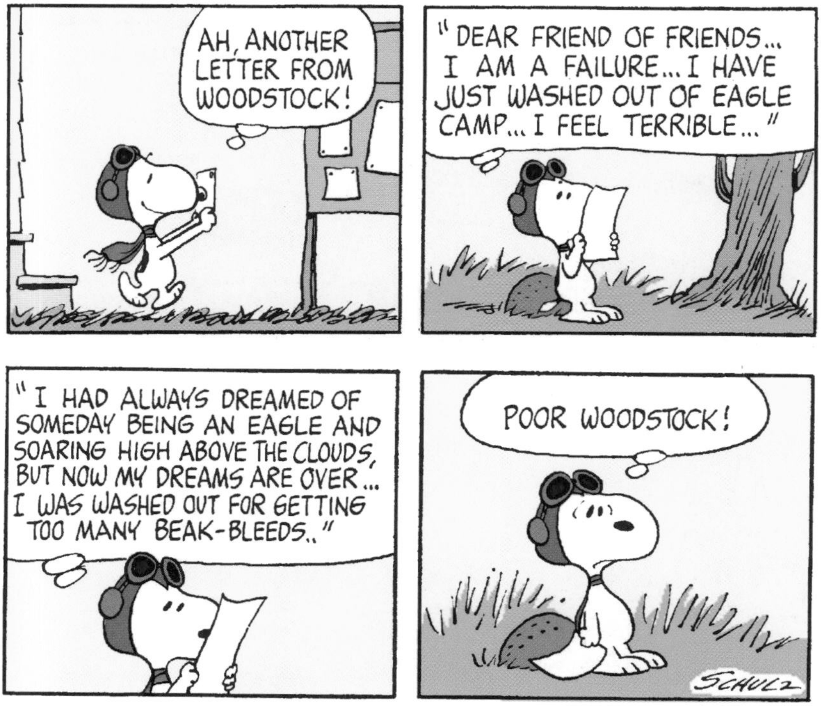
AH, ANOTHER LETTER FROM WOODSTOCK!
"DEAR FRIEND OF FRIENDS... I AM A FAILURE... I HAVE JUST WASHED OUT OF EAGLE CAMP... I FEEL TERRIBLE..."
"I HAD ALWAYS DREAMED OF SOMEDAY BEING AN EAGLE AND SOARING HIGH ABOVE THE CLOUDS, BUT NOW MY DREAMS ARE OVER... I WAS WASHED OUT FOR GETTING TOO MANY BEAK-BLEEDS.."
POOR WOODSTOCK!
SCHULZ

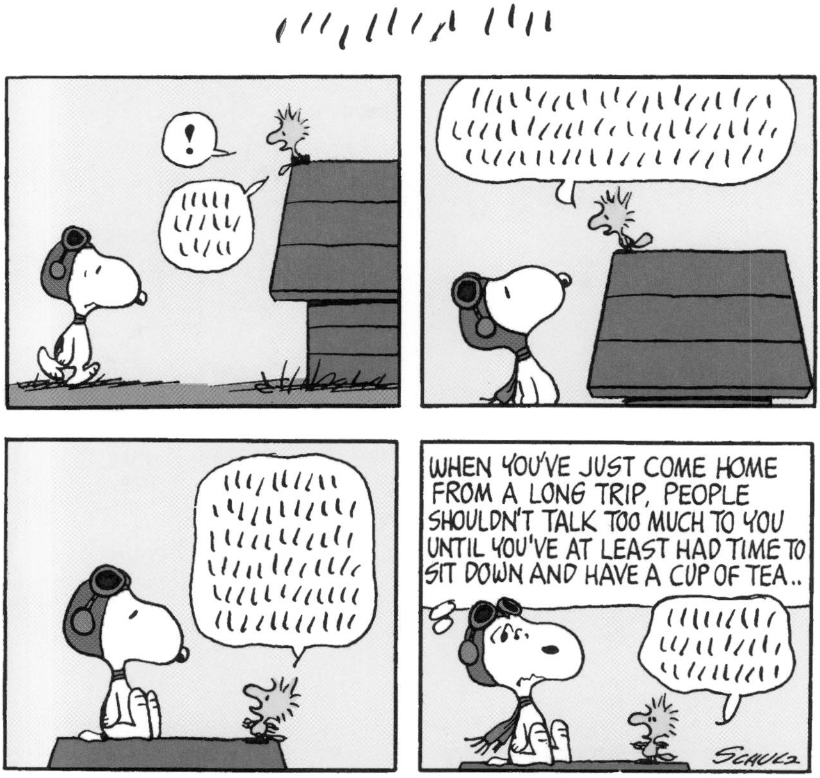
!
WHEN YOU'VE JUST COME HOME FROM A LONG TRIP, PEOPLE SHOULDN'T TALK TOO MUCH TO YOU UNTIL YOU'VE AT LEAST HAD TIME TO SIT DOWN AND HAVE A CUP OF TEA..
SCHULZ

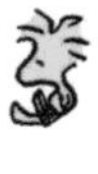

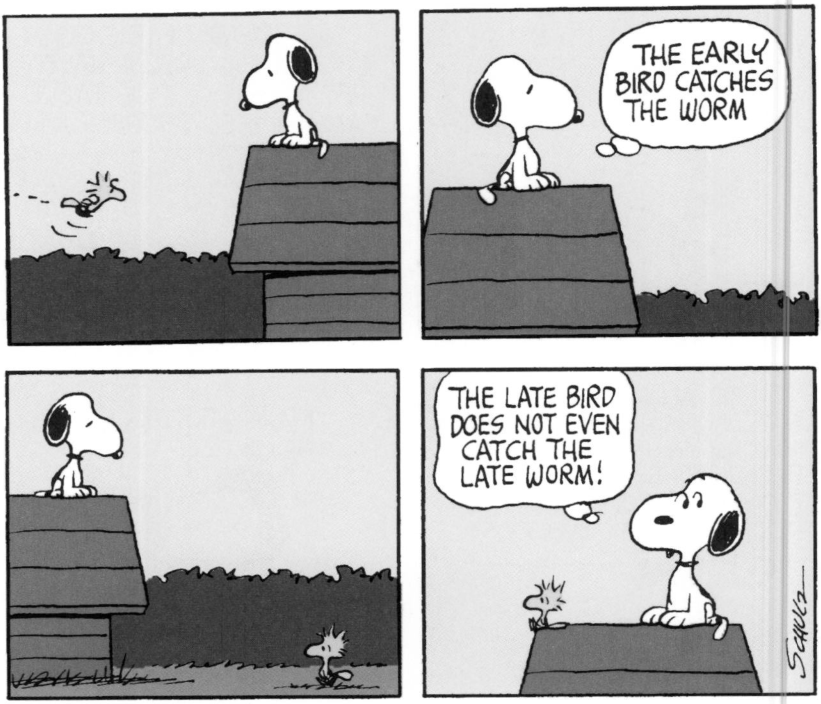
THE EARLY BIRD CATCHES THE WORM
THE LATE BIRD DOES NOT EVEN CATCH THE LATE WORM!
SCHULZ

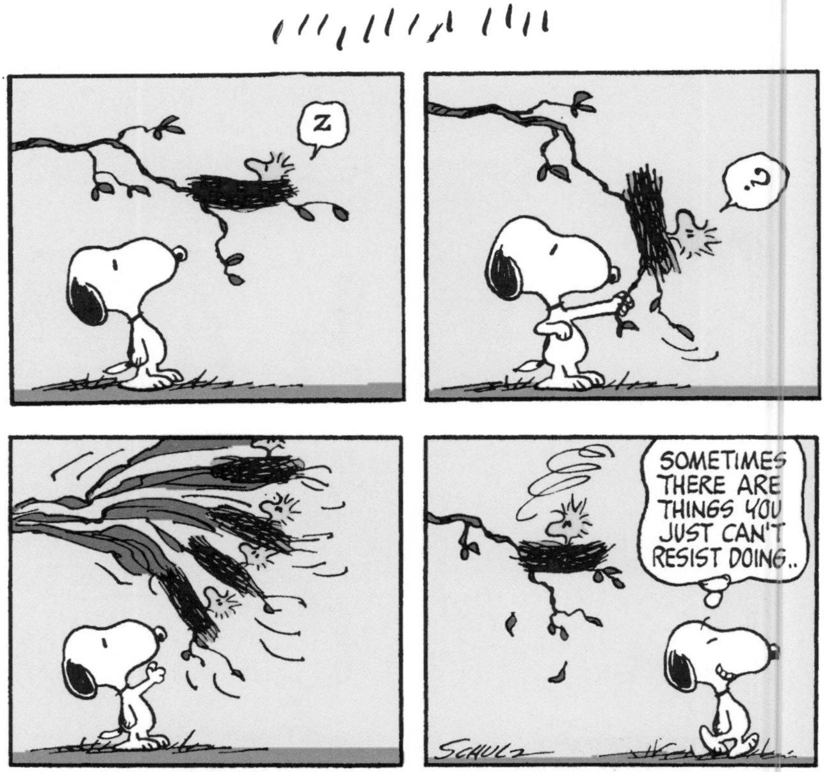
Z
?
SOMETIMES THERE ARE THINGS YOU JUST CAN'T RESIST DOING..
SCHULZ

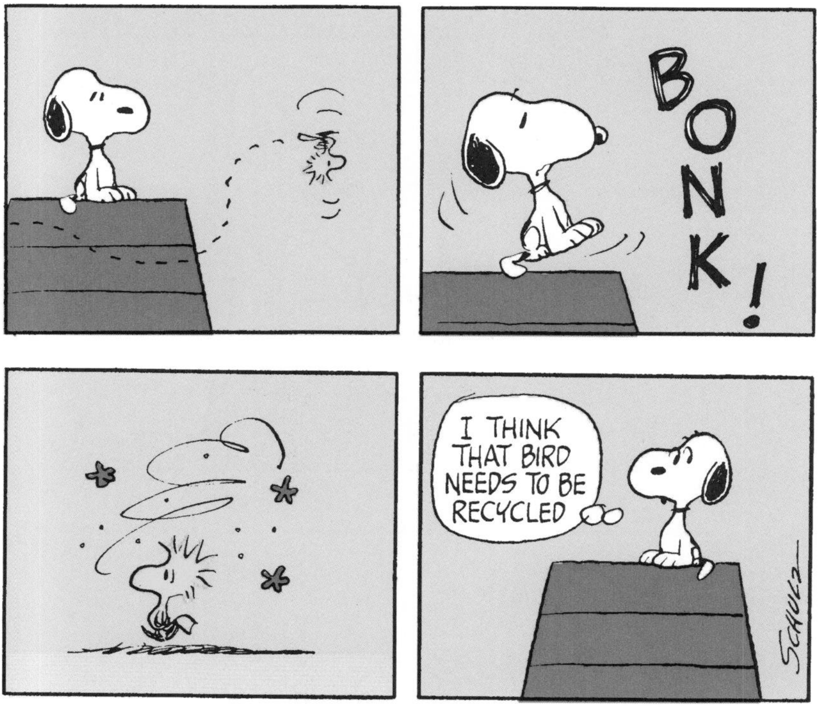
BONK!
I THINK THAT BIRD NEEDS TO BE RECYCLED
SCHULZ

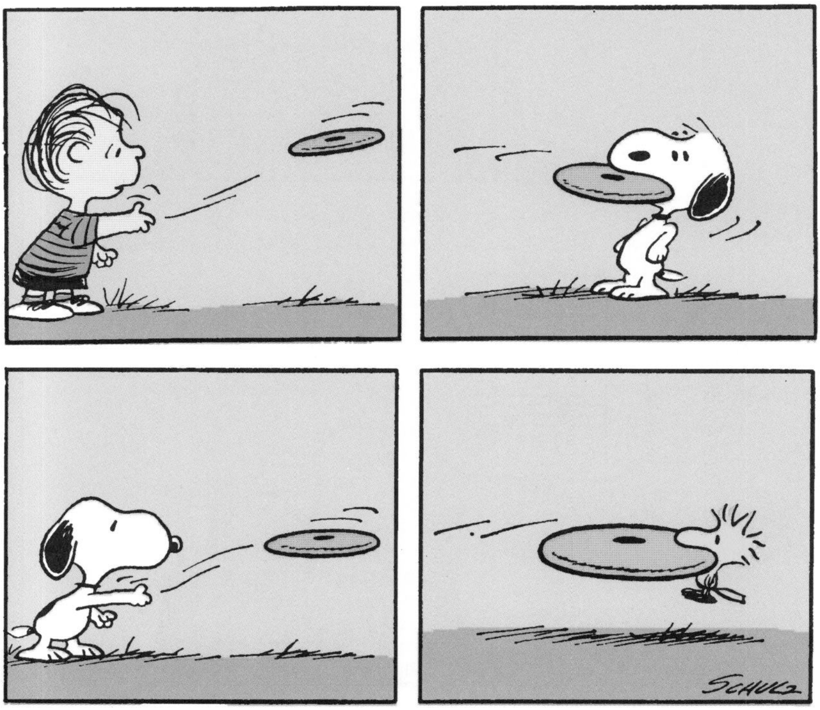
SCHULZ

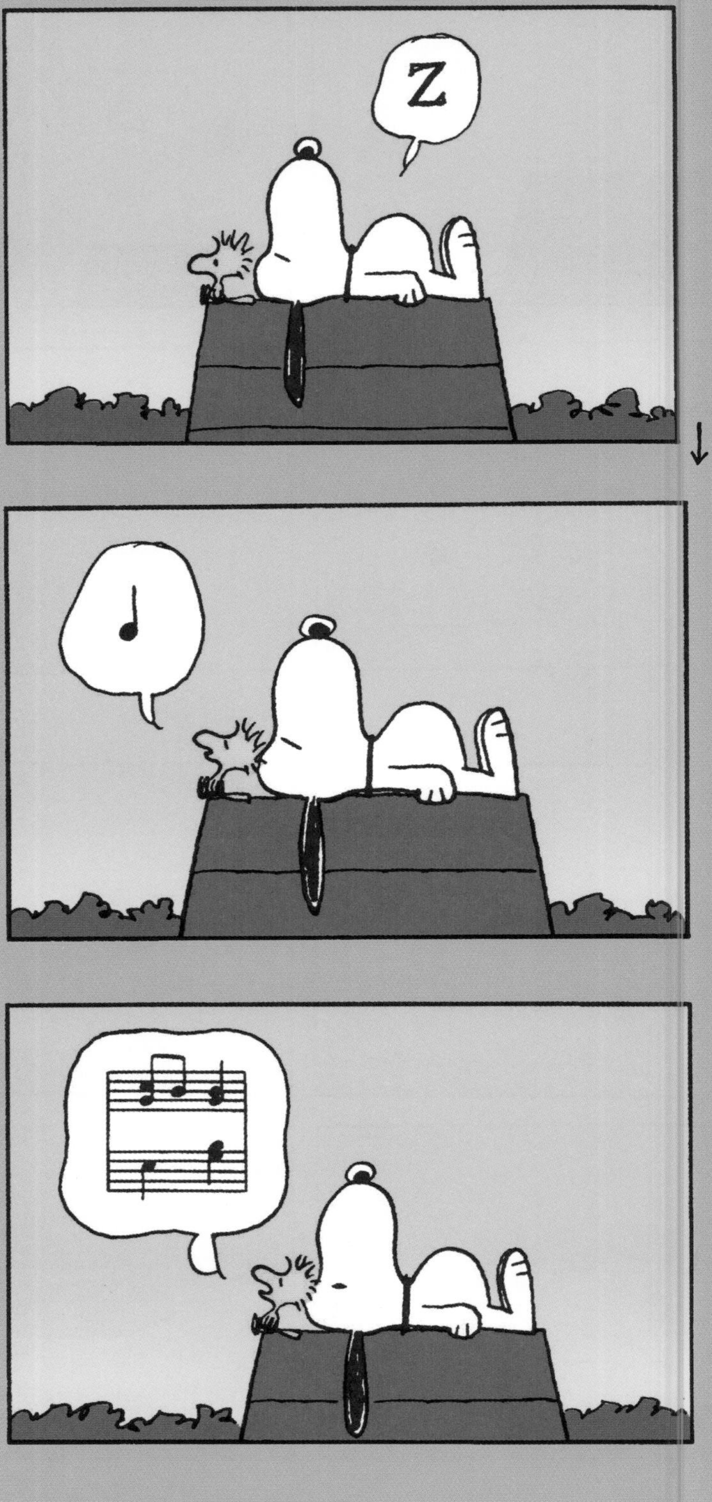
Z

!
Z
SCHULZ

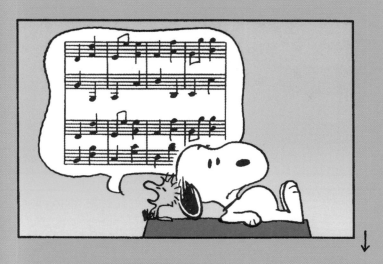

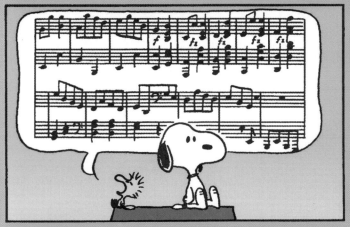

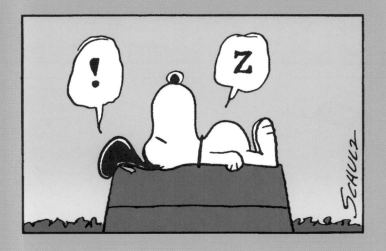

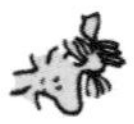

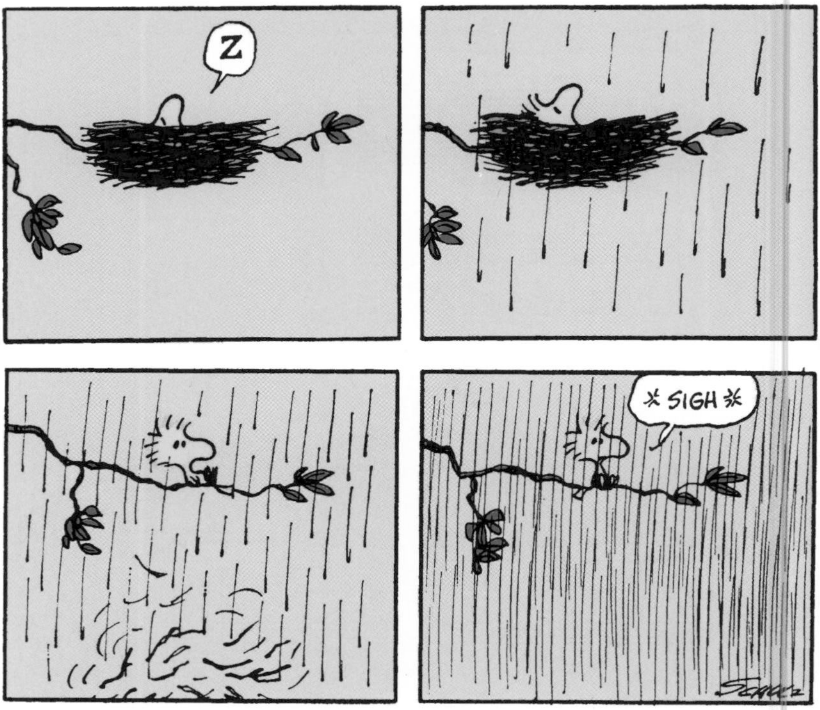
Z
* SIGH *

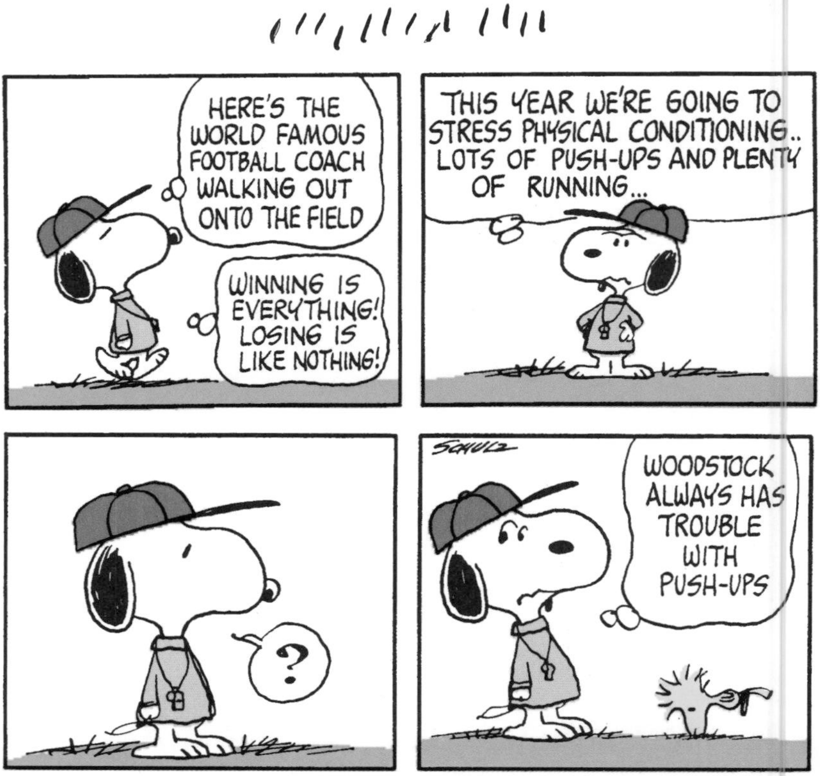
HERE'S THE WORLD FAMOUS FOOTBALL COACH WALKING OUT ONTO THE FIELD
WINNING IS EVERYTHING! LOSING IS LIKE NOTHING!
THIS YEAR WE'RE GOING TO STRESS PHYSICAL CONDITIONING.. LOTS OF PUSH-UPS AND PLENTY OF RUNNING...
?
WOODSTOCK ALWAYS HAS TROUBLE WITH PUSH-UPS

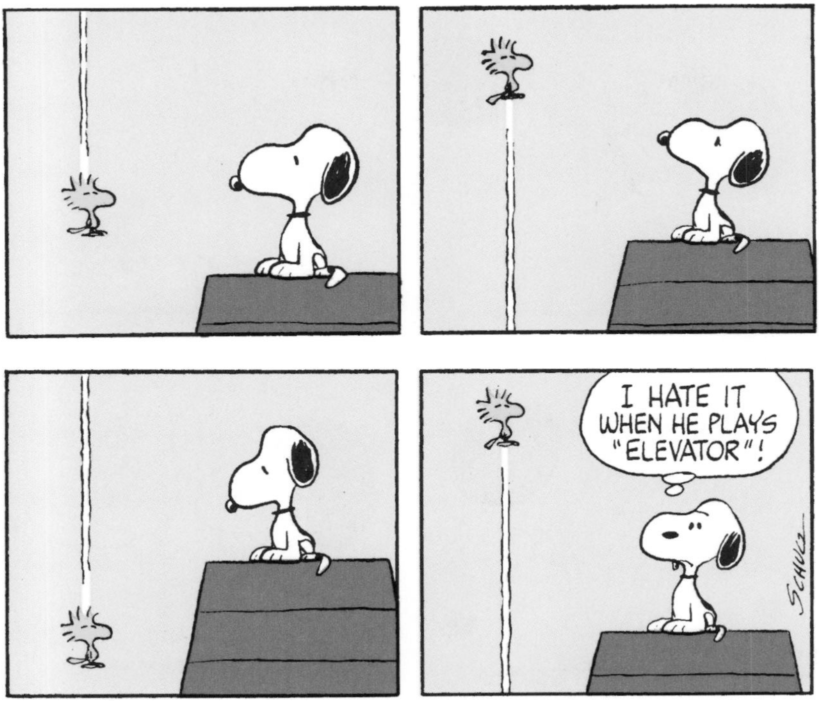
I HATE IT WHEN HE PLAYS "ELEVATOR"!

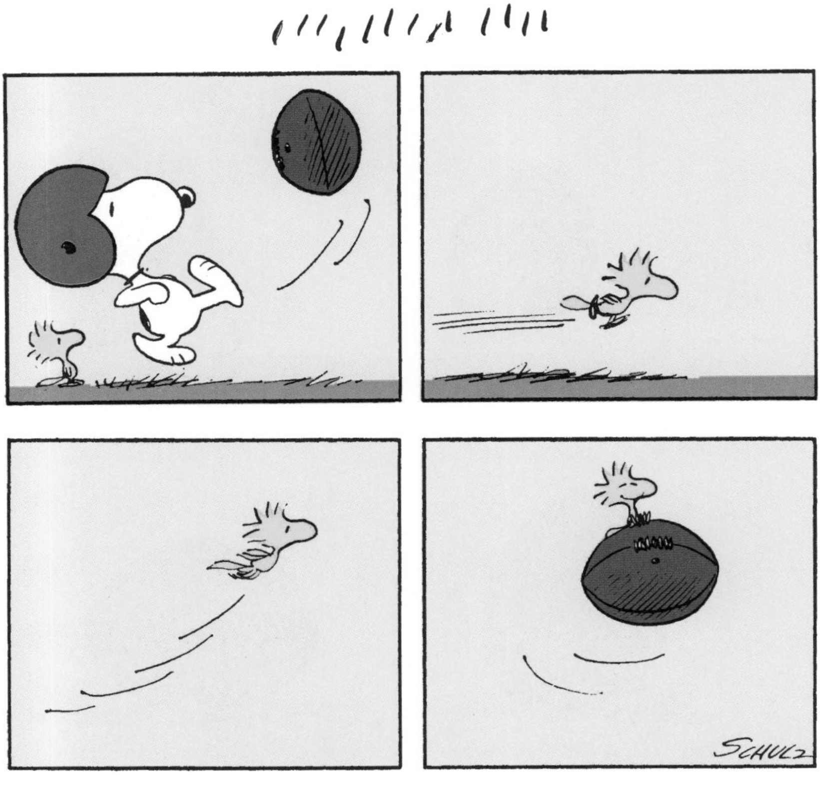

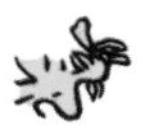

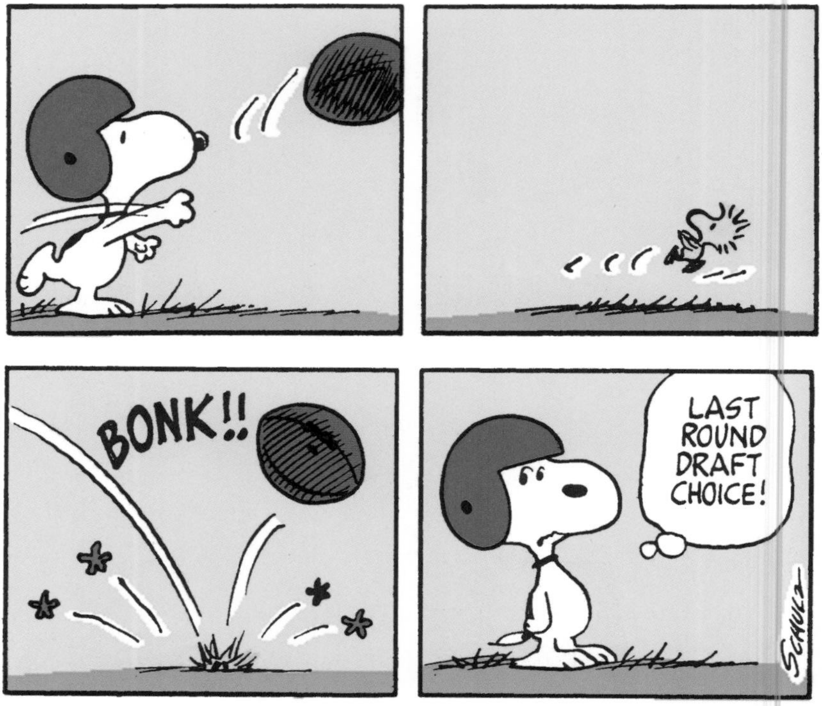
BONK!!
LAST ROUND DRAFT CHOICE!
SCHULZ

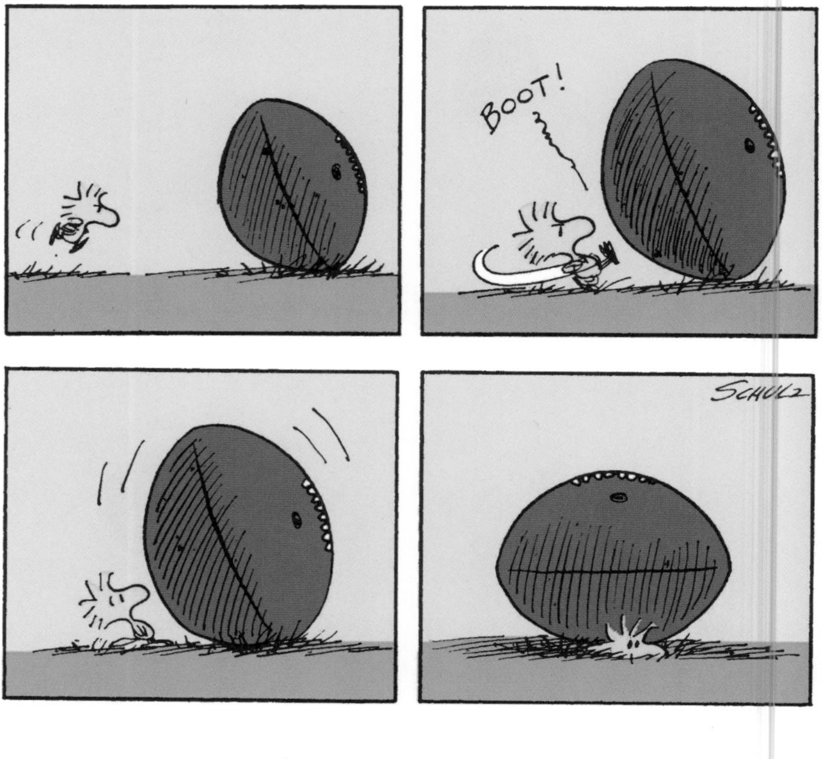
BOOT!
SCHULZ

BOOT!
OOF!
SCHULZ

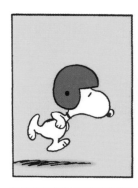

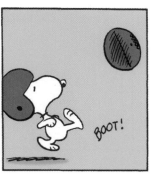

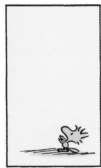

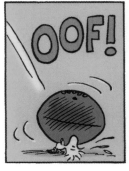

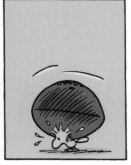

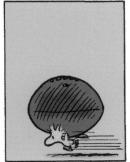

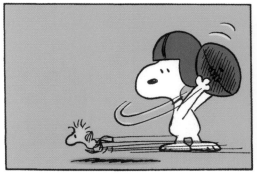

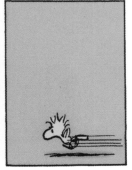

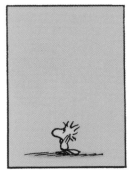

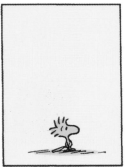

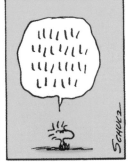

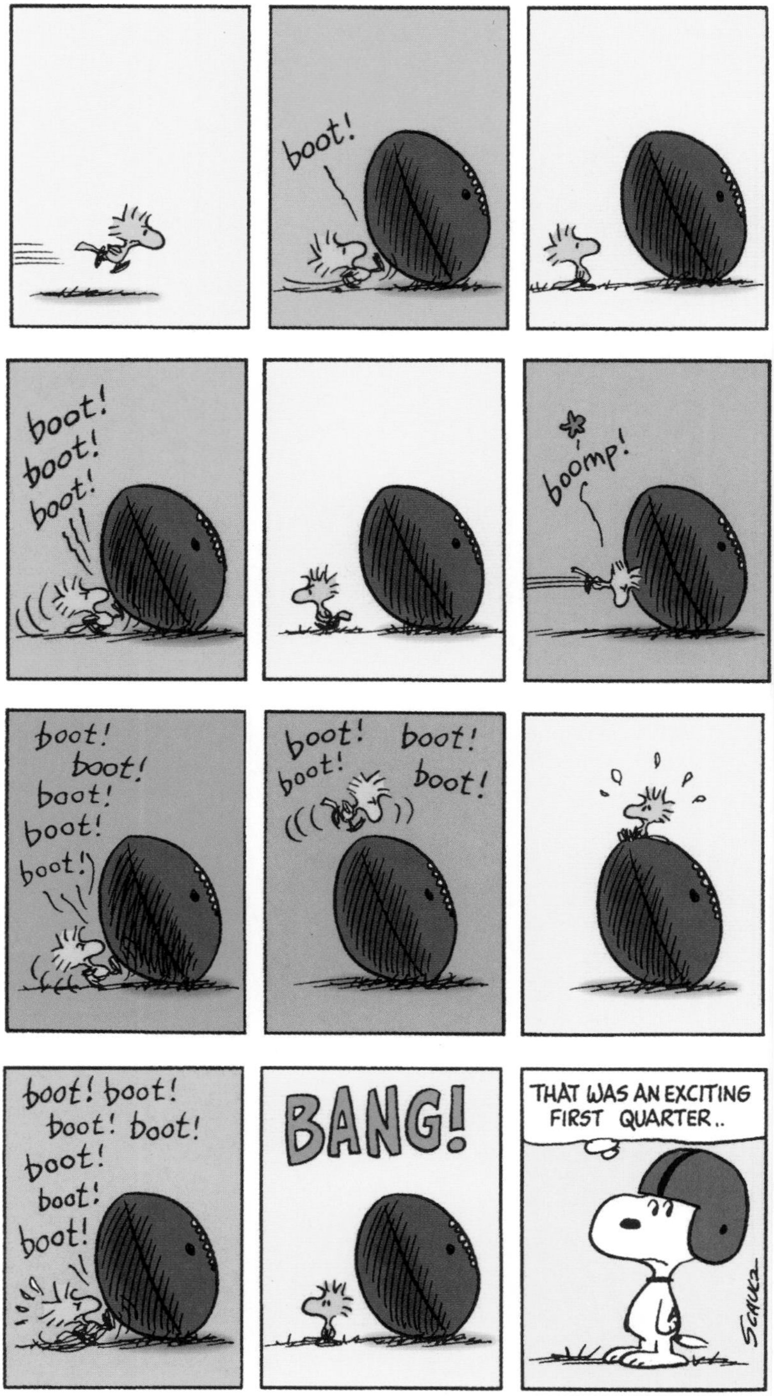

boot!
boot!
boot!
boot!
boomp!
boot!
boot!
boot!
boot!
boot!
boot!
boot!
boot!
boot!
boot! boot!
boot! boot!
boot!
boot!
boot!
BANG!
THAT WAS AN EXCITING FIRST QUARTER..
SCHULZ

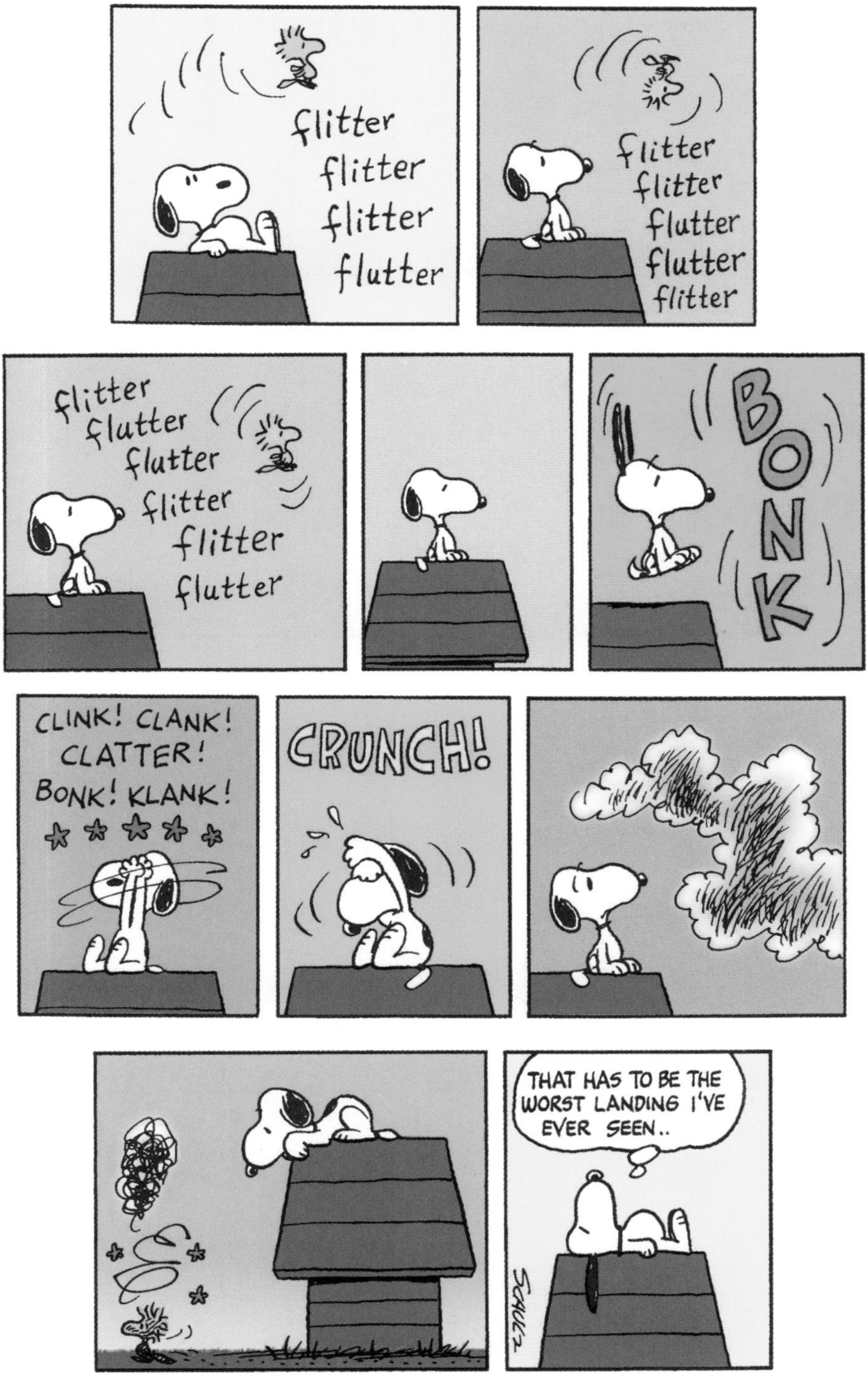
flitter
flitter
flitter
flutter
flitter
flitter
flutter
flutter
flitter
flitter
flutter
flutter
flitter
flitter
flutter
BONK
CLINK! CLANK! CLATTER! BONK! KLANK!
CRUNCH!
THAT HAS TO BE THE WORST LANDING I'VE EVER SEEN..
SCHULZ

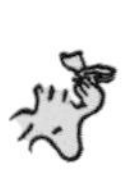

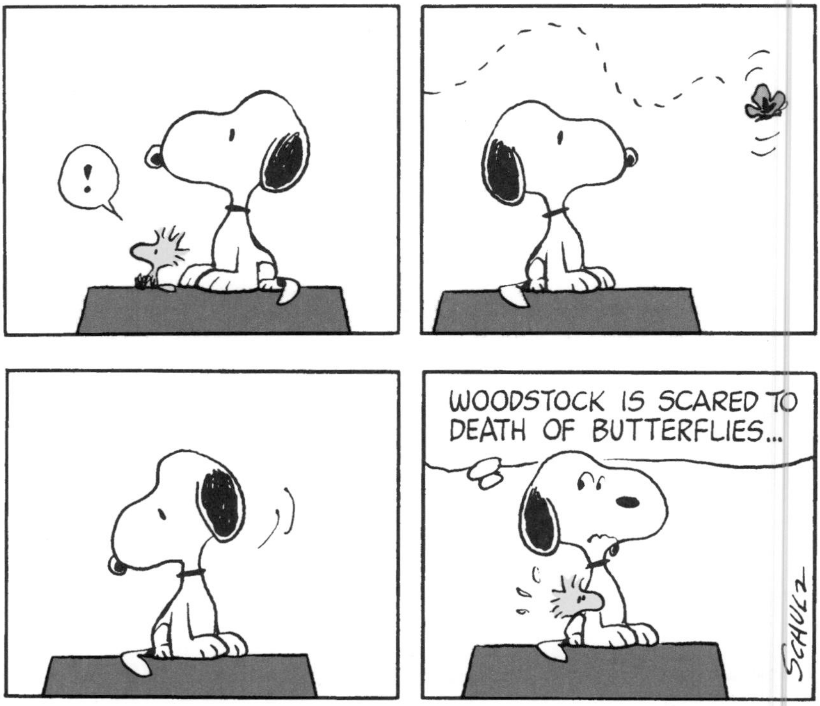
!
WOODSTOCK IS SCARED TO DEATH OF BUTTERFLIES...
SCHULZ

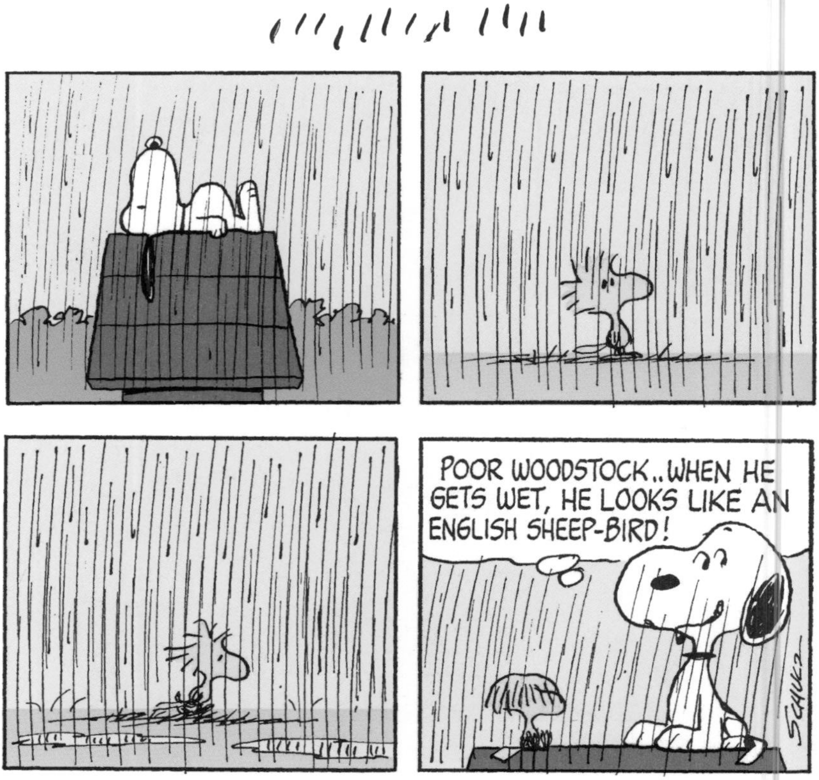
POOR WOODSTOCK..WHEN HE GETS WET, HE LOOKS LIKE AN ENGLISH SHEEP-BIRD!
SCHULZ

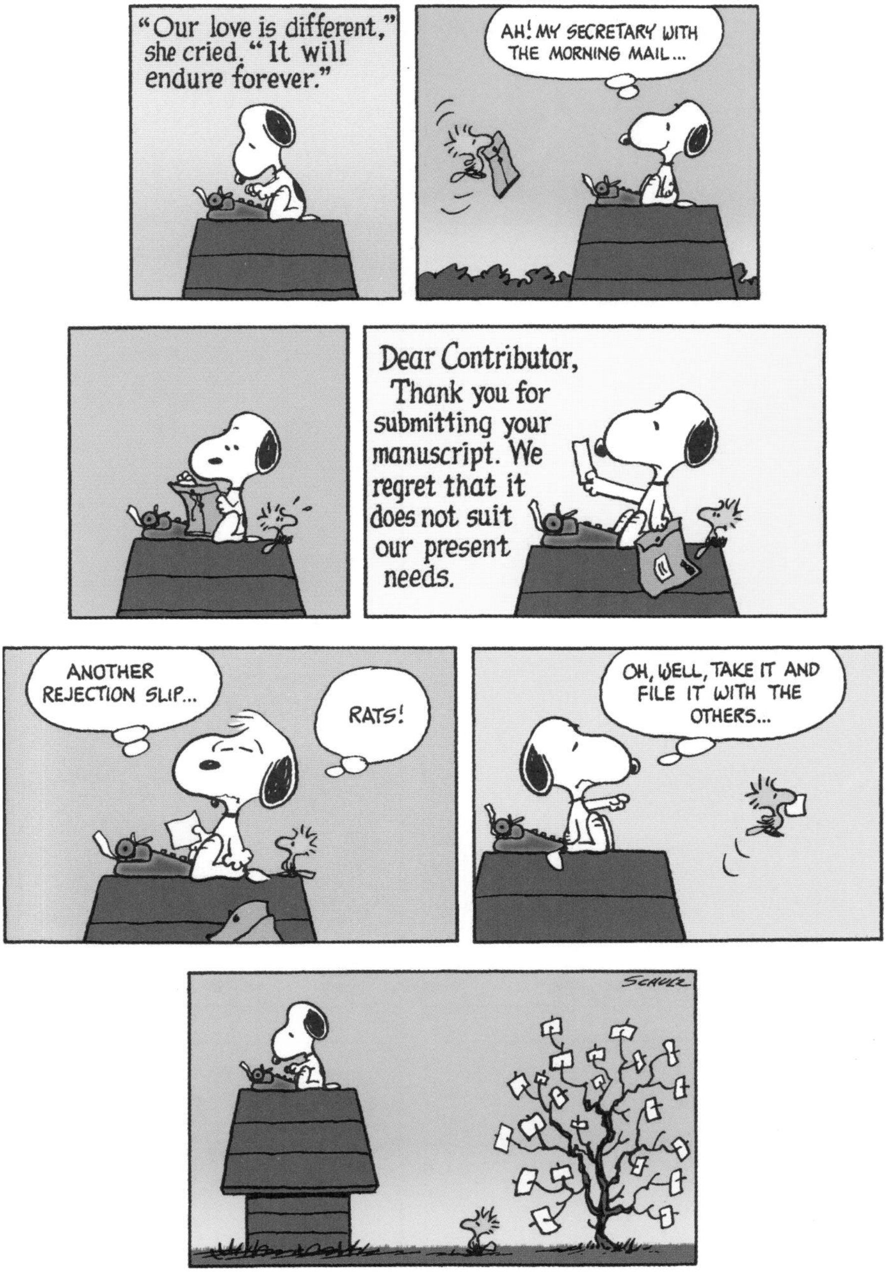
"Our love is different," she cried. "It will endure forever."
AH! MY SECRETARY WITH THE MORNING MAIL...
Dear Contributor, Thank you for submitting your manuscript. We regret that it does not suit our present needs.
ANOTHER REJECTION SLIP...
RATS!
OH, WELL, TAKE IT AND FILE IT WITH THE OTHERS...

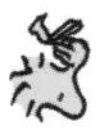

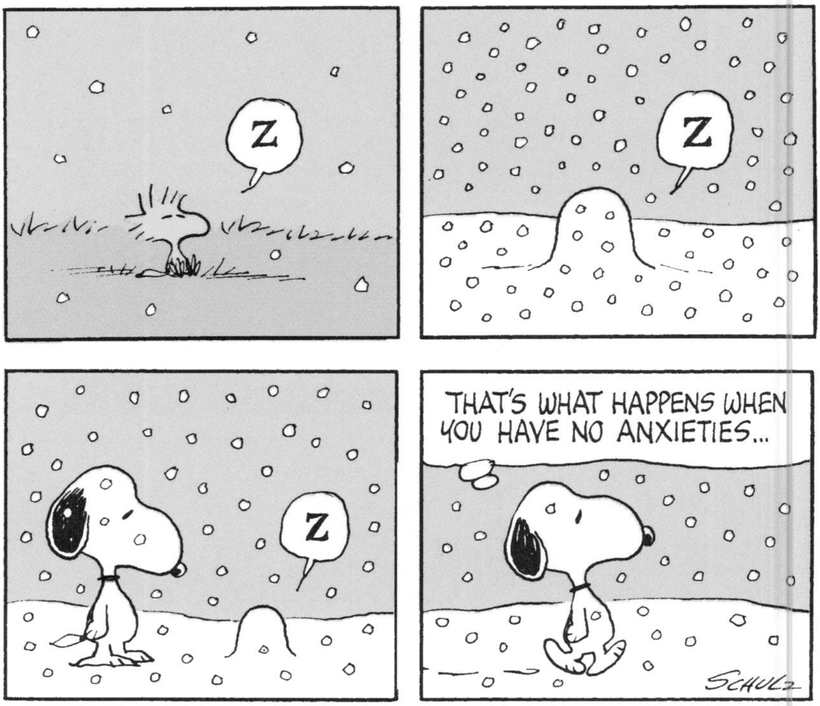
Z
Z
Z
THAT'S WHAT HAPPENS WHEN YOU HAVE NO ANXIETIES...
SCHULZ

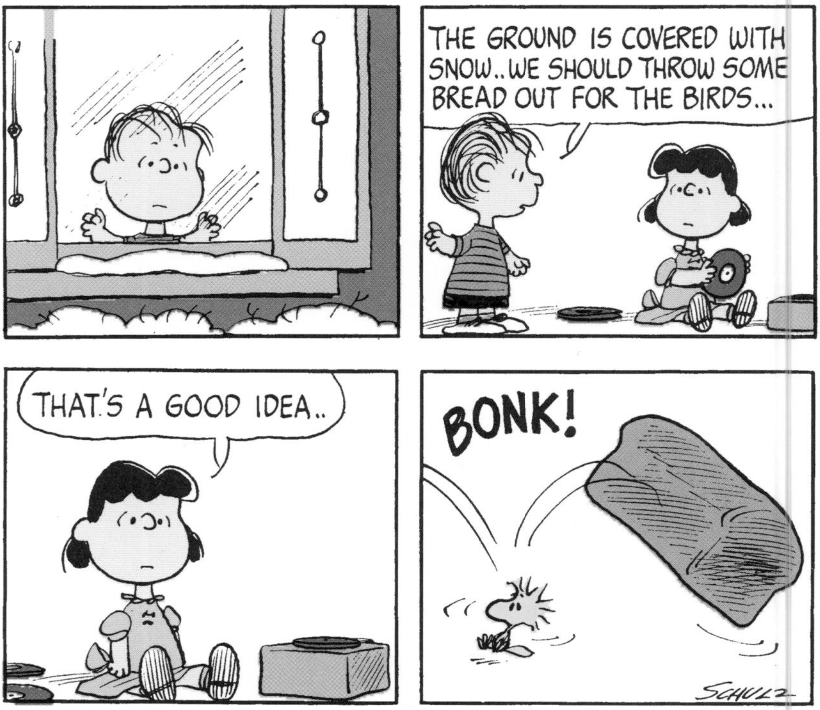
THE GROUND IS COVERED WITH SNOW..WE SHOULD THROW SOME BREAD OUT FOR THE BIRDS...
THAT'S A GOOD IDEA..
BONK!
SCHULZ

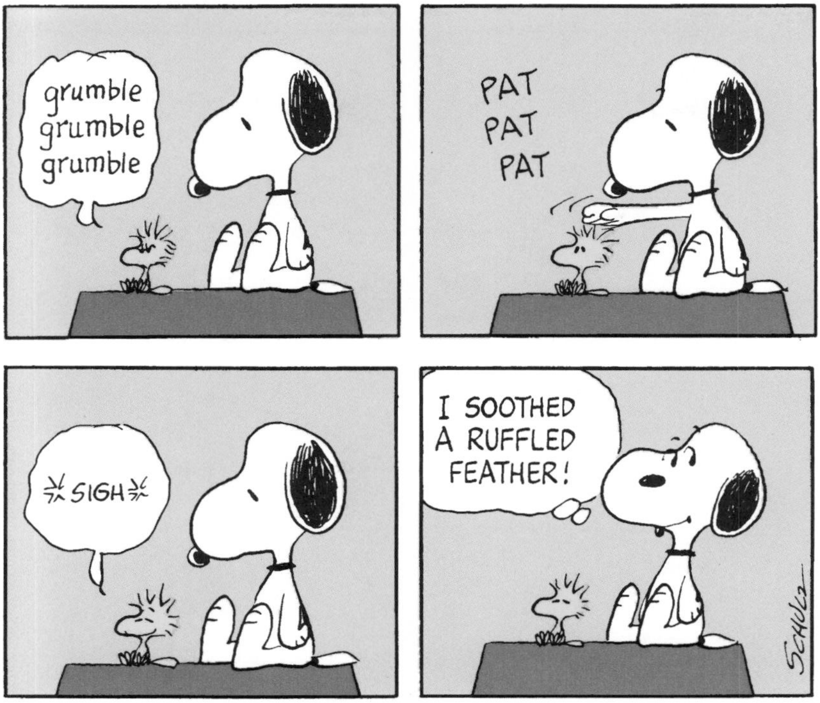
grumble grumble grumble
PAT PAT PAT
SIGH
I SOOTHED A RUFFLED FEATHER!
SCHULZ

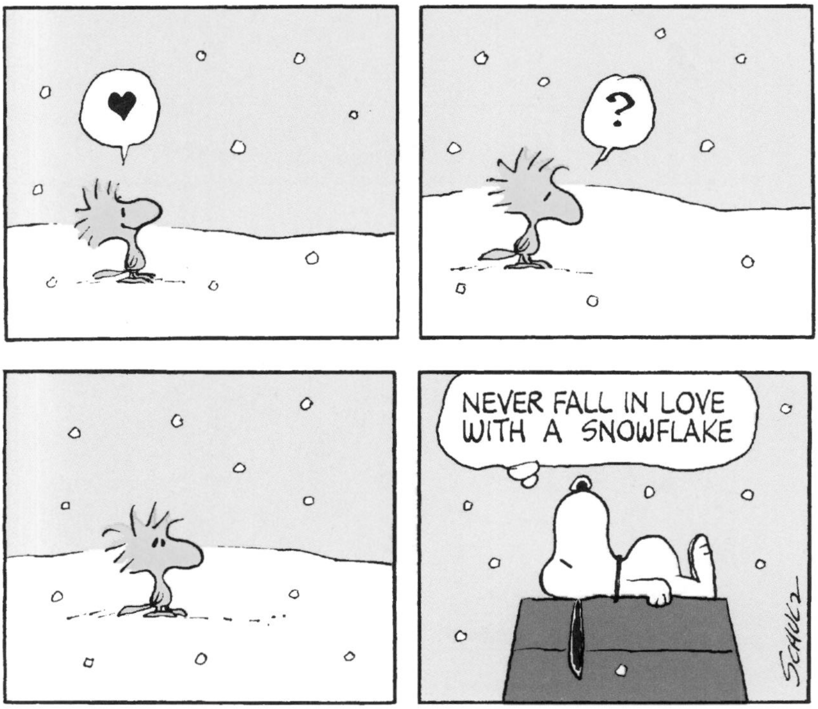
?
NEVER FALL IN LOVE WITH A SNOWFLAKE
SCHULZ

HERE'S THE FACE-OFF FOR THE START OF THE BIG HOCKEY GAME..
OW! HE HIT ME ON THE SHIN!
OW! OOOOO!! OW!

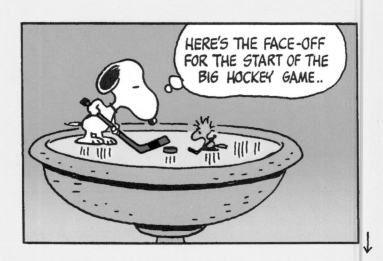

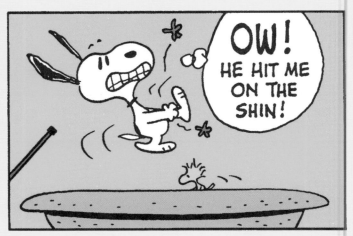

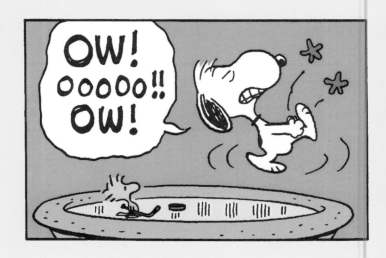

YOU STUPID BIRD! YOU KNEW I DIDN'T HAVE ANY SHIN PADS ON!
OW! OOOO! OW!! OW!! OOOOO!
NOW I HAVE TO SPEND THE NEXT HOUR SITTING IN MY WHIRLPOOL BATH...
SCHULZ

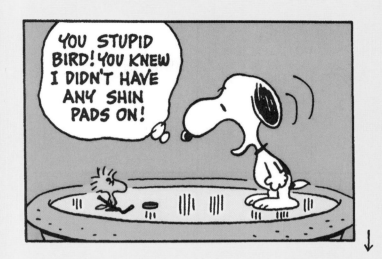

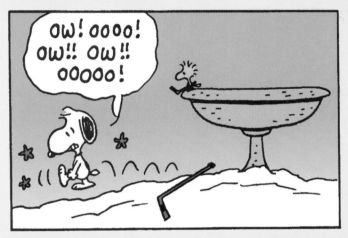

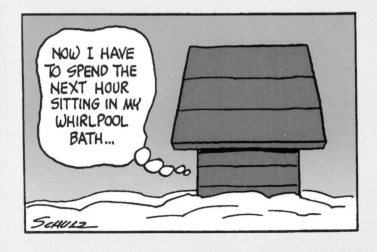

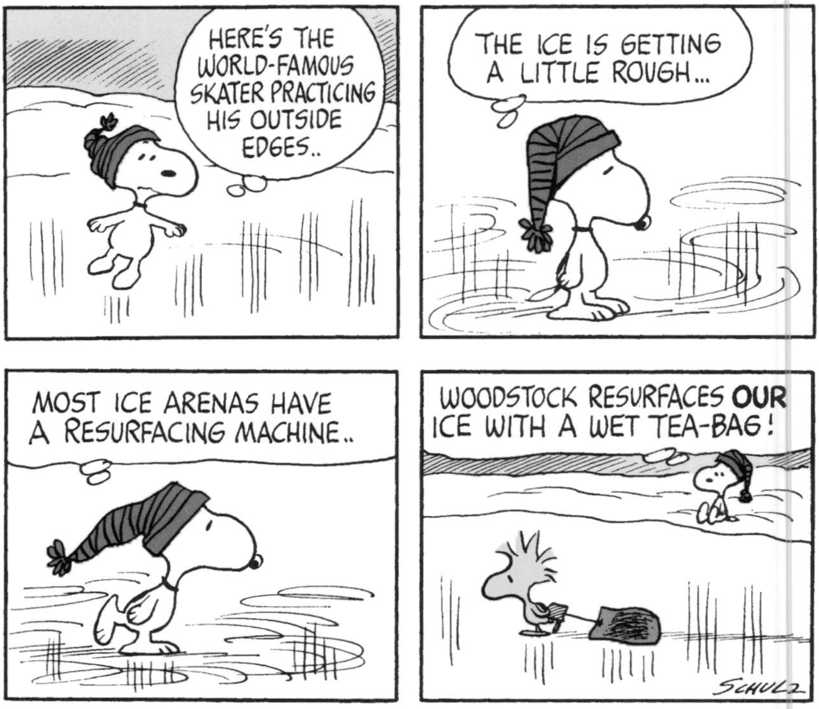
HERE'S THE WORLD-FAMOUS SKATER PRACTICING HIS OUTSIDE EDGES..
THE ICE IS GETTING A LITTLE ROUGH...
MOST ICE ARENAS HAVE A RESURFACING MACHINE..
WOODSTOCK RESURFACES **OUR** ICE WITH A WET TEA-BAG!
SCHULZ

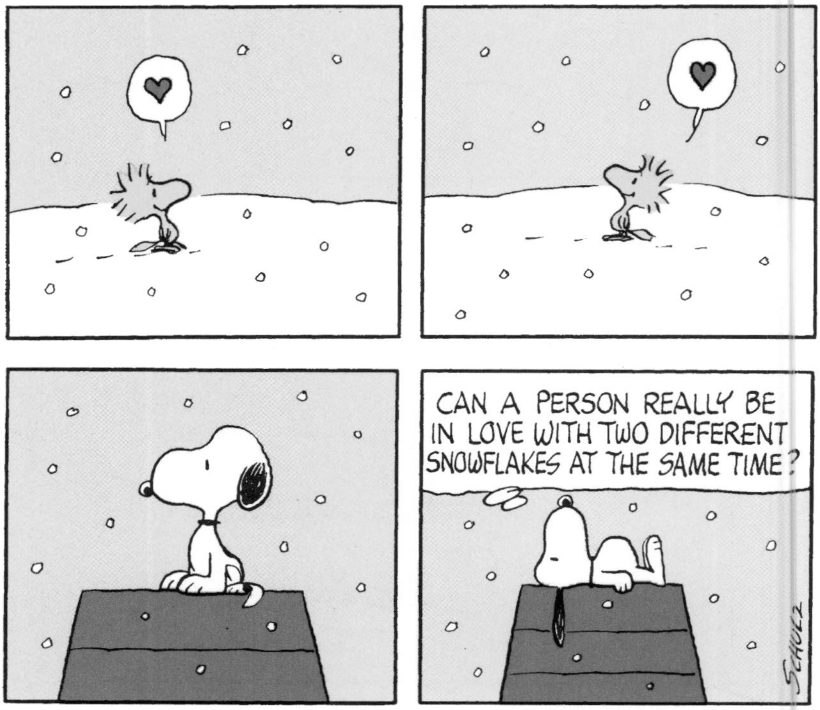
CAN A PERSON REALLY BE IN LOVE WITH TWO DIFFERENT SNOWFLAKES AT THE SAME TIME?
SCHULZ

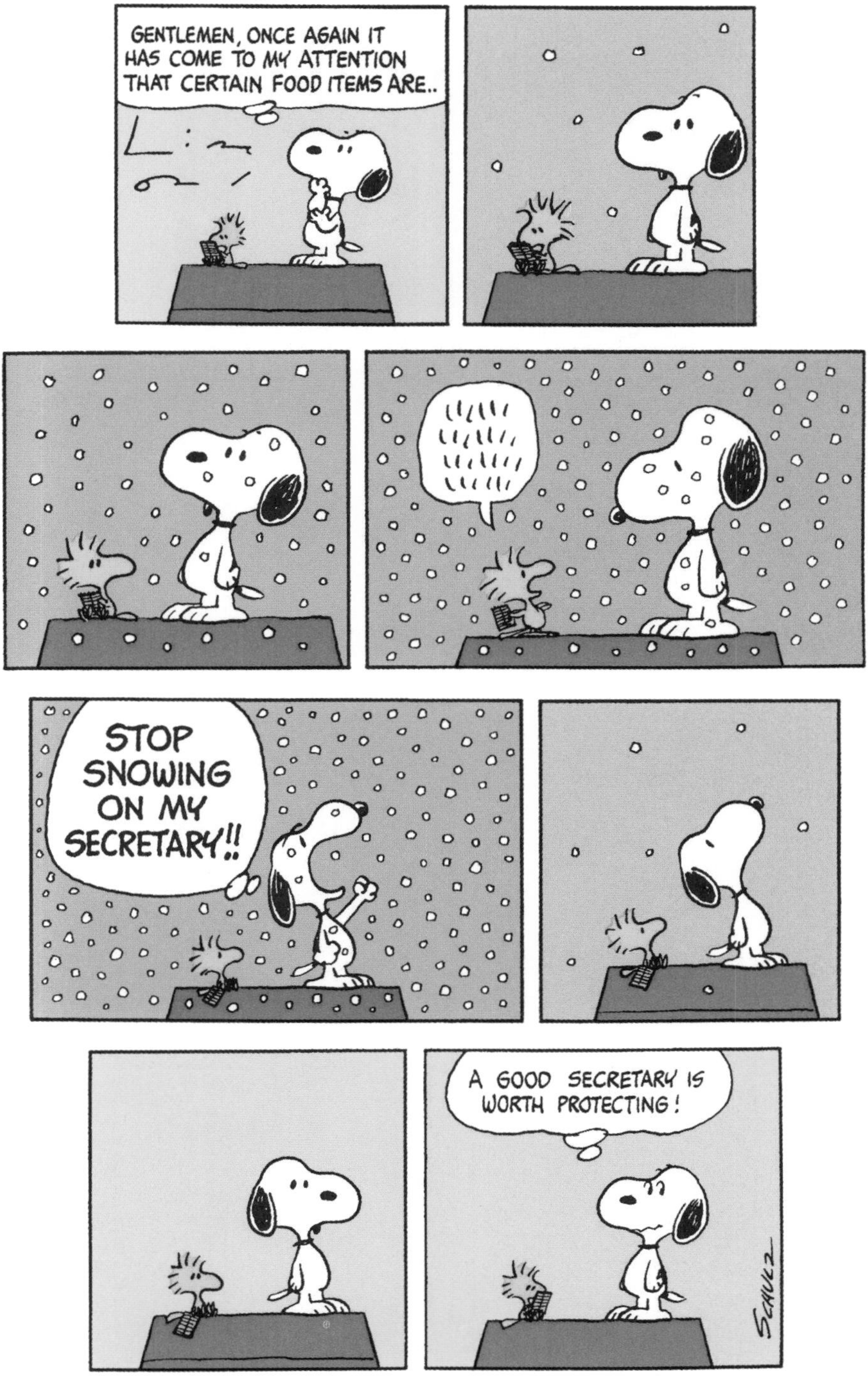
GENTLEMEN, ONCE AGAIN IT HAS COME TO MY ATTENTION THAT CERTAIN FOOD ITEMS ARE..
STOP SNOWING ON MY SECRETARY!!
A GOOD SECRETARY IS WORTH PROTECTING!
SCHULZ

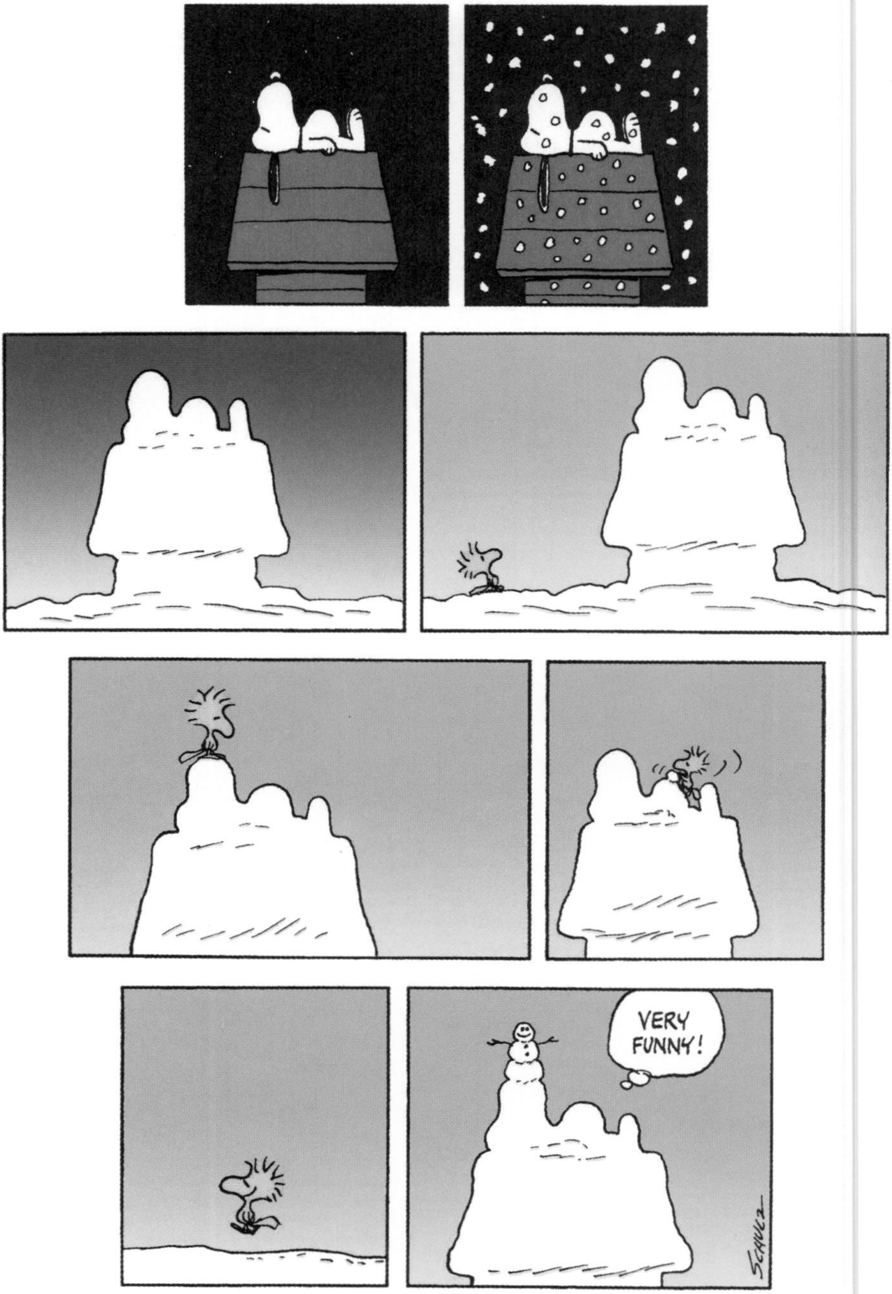
VERY FUNNY!
SCHULZ

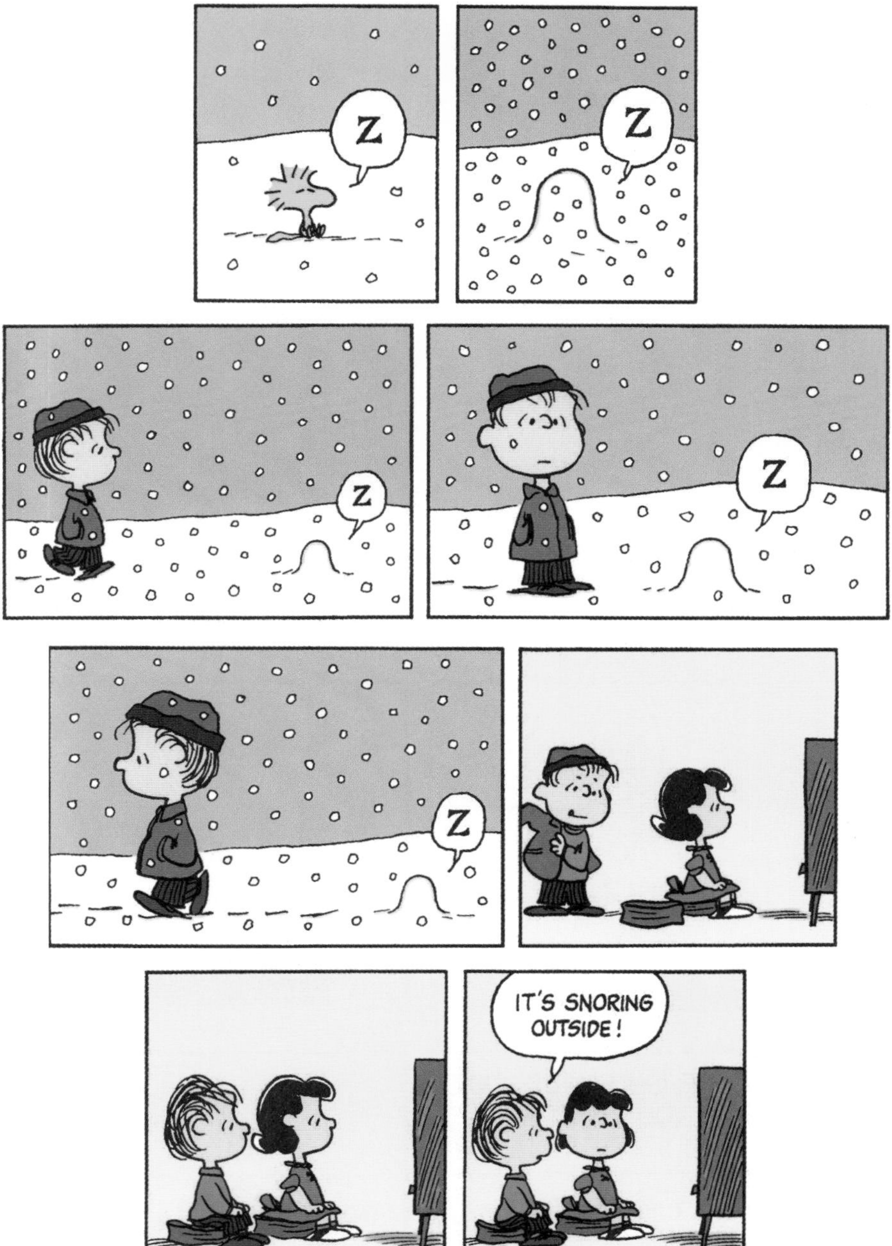
Z
Z
Z
Z
Z
IT'S SNORING OUTSIDE!
SCHULZ

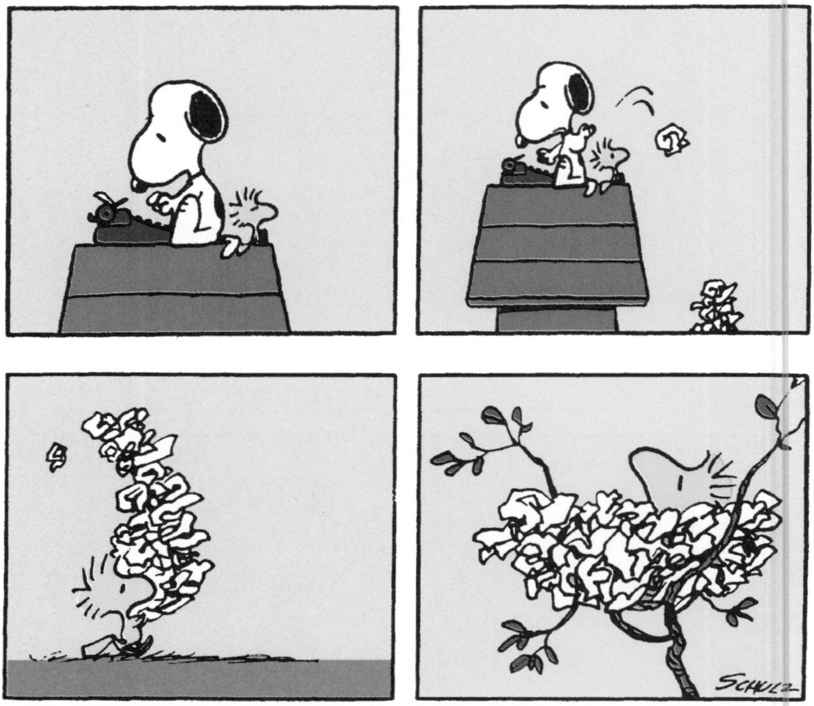

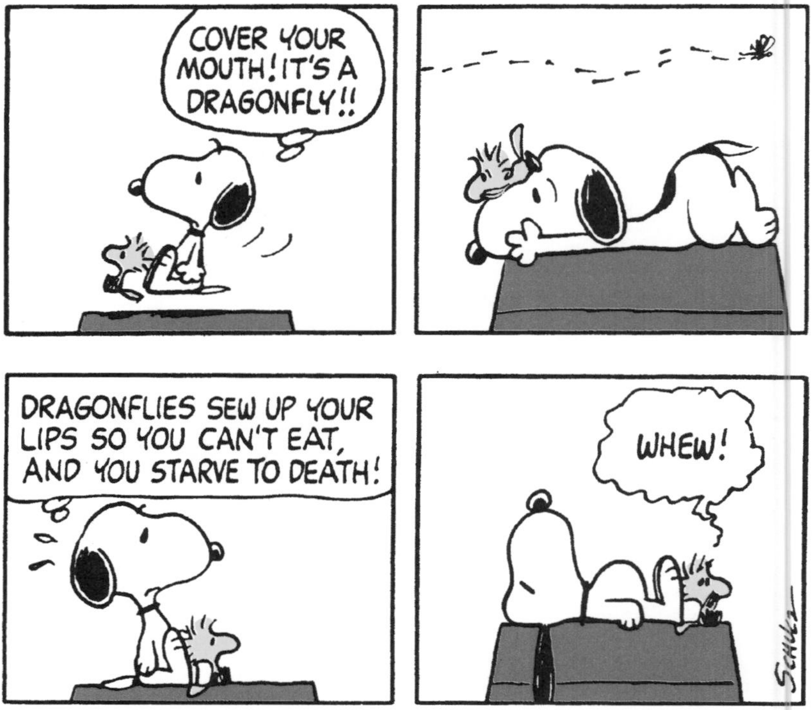

COVER YOUR MOUTH! IT'S A DRAGONFLY!!
DRAGONFLIES SEW UP YOUR LIPS SO YOU CAN'T EAT, AND YOU STARVE TO DEATH!
WHEW!

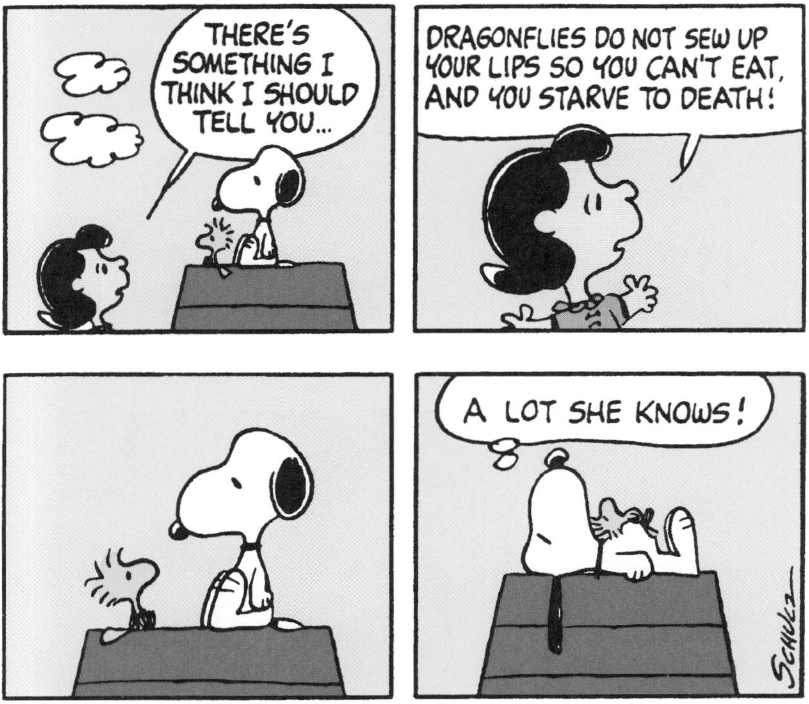
THERE'S SOMETHING I THINK I SHOULD TELL YOU...
DRAGONFLIES DO NOT SEW UP YOUR LIPS SO YOU CAN'T EAT, AND YOU STARVE TO DEATH!
A LOT SHE KNOWS!
SCHULZ

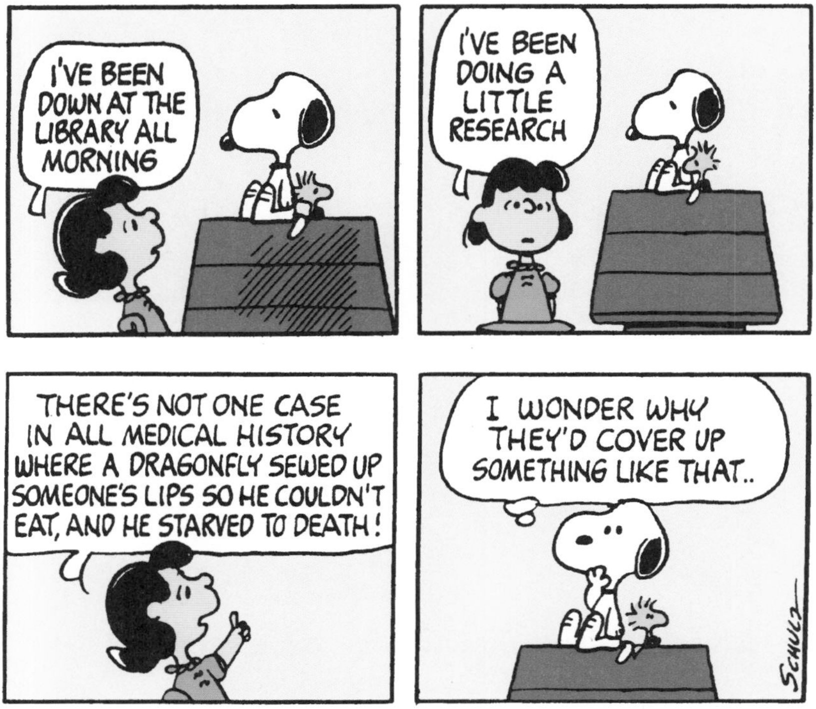
I'VE BEEN DOWN AT THE LIBRARY ALL MORNING
I'VE BEEN DOING A LITTLE RESEARCH
THERE'S NOT ONE CASE IN ALL MEDICAL HISTORY WHERE A DRAGONFLY SEWED UP SOMEONE'S LIPS SO HE COULDN'T EAT, AND HE STARVED TO DEATH!
I WONDER WHY THEY'D COVER UP SOMETHING LIKE THAT..
SCHULZ

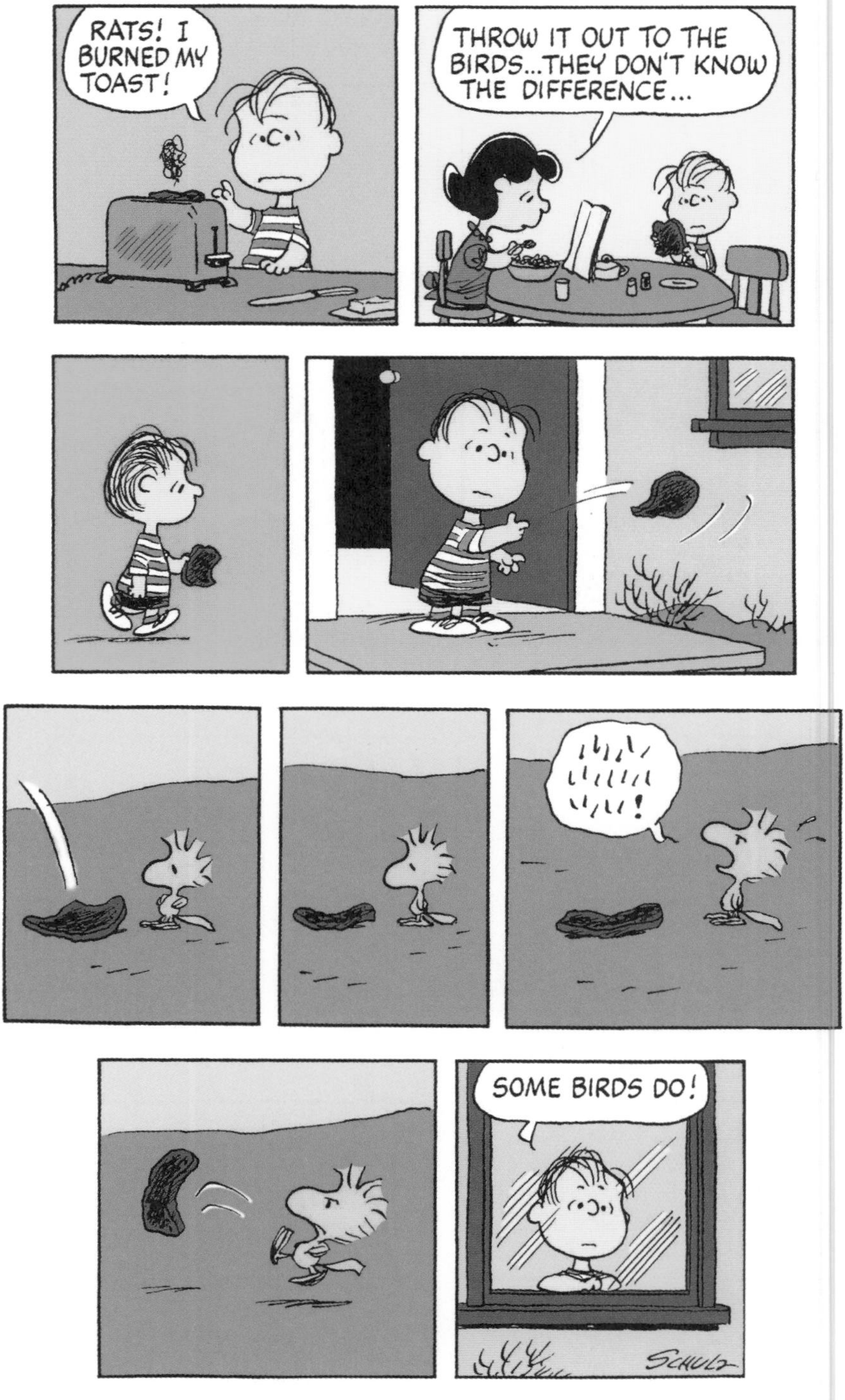
RATS! I BURNED MY TOAST!
THROW IT OUT TO THE BIRDS...THEY DON'T KNOW THE DIFFERENCE...
SOME BIRDS DO!
SCHULZ

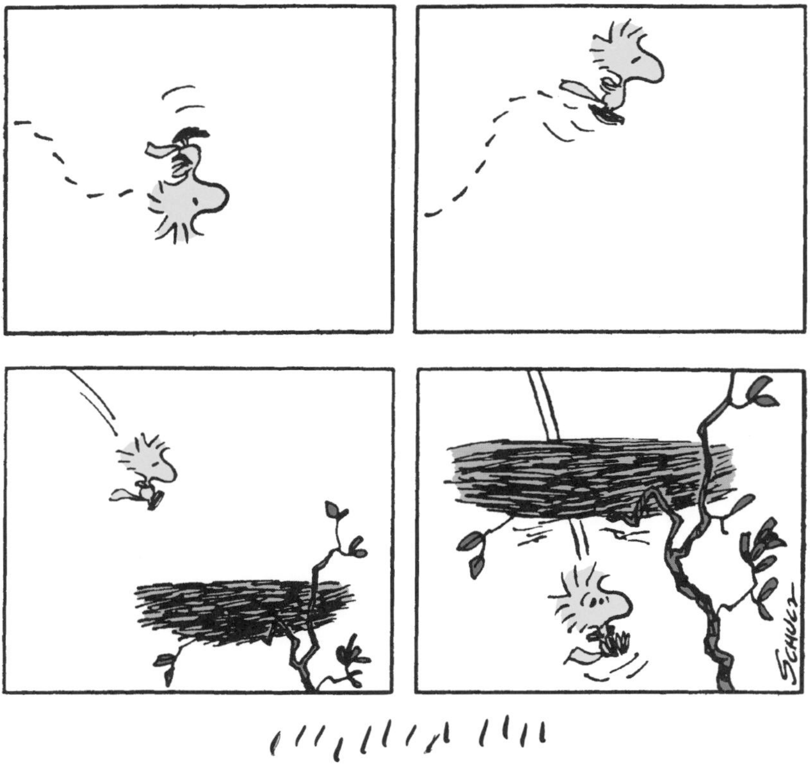

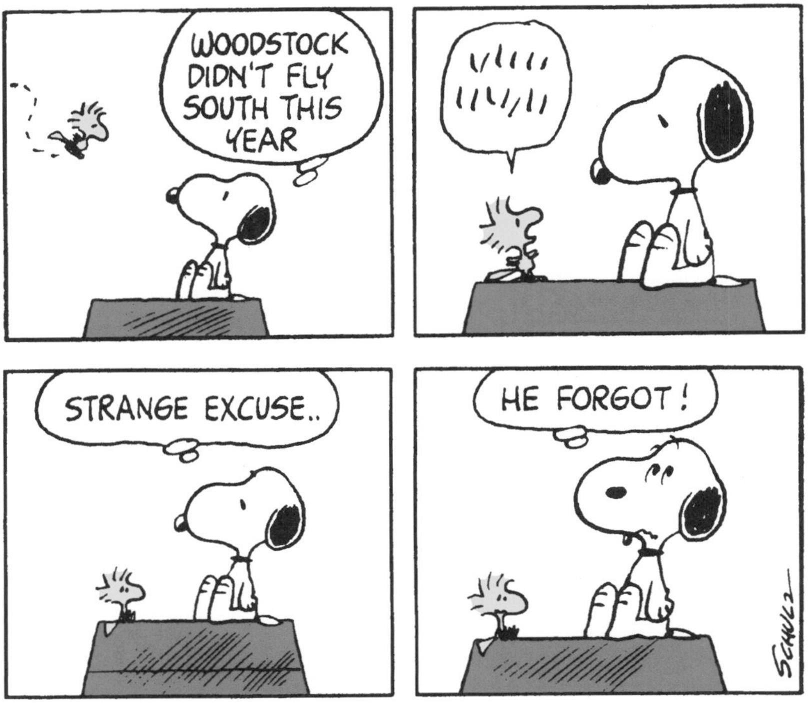
WOODSTOCK DIDN'T FLY SOUTH THIS YEAR
STRANGE EXCUSE..
HE FORGOT!
SCHULZ

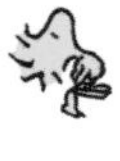

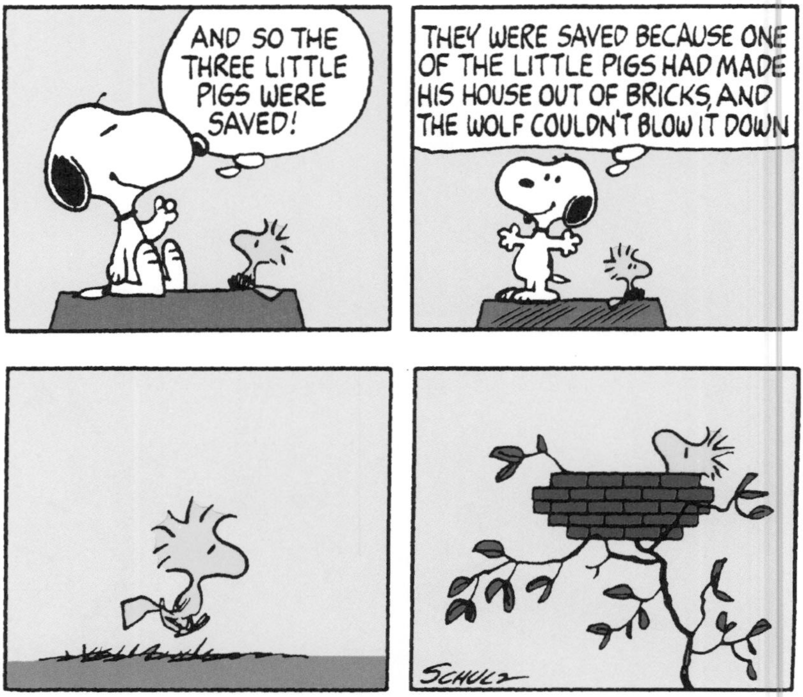
AND SO THE THREE LITTLE PIGS WERE SAVED!
THEY WERE SAVED BECAUSE ONE OF THE LITTLE PIGS HAD MADE HIS HOUSE OUT OF BRICKS, AND THE WOLF COULDN'T BLOW IT DOWN
SCHULZ

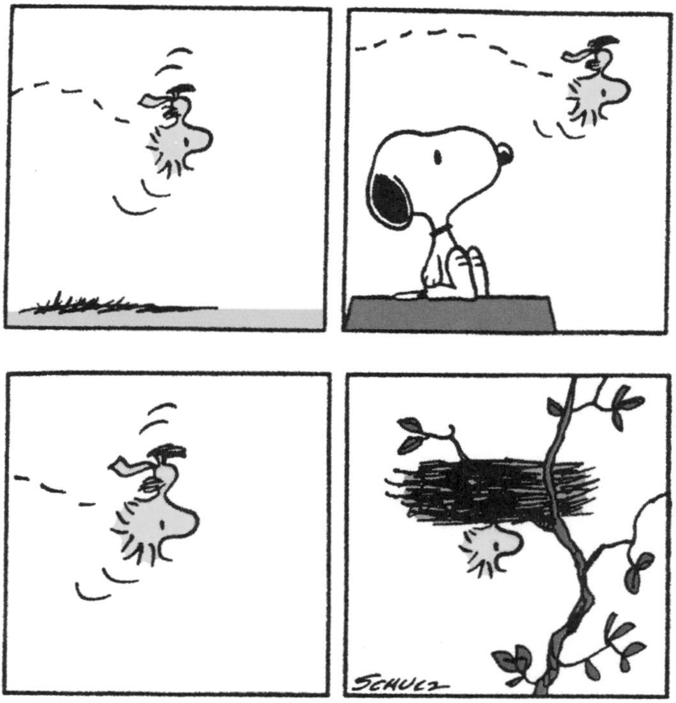
SCHULZ

SCHULZ

Z
SCHULZ

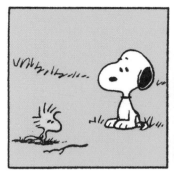

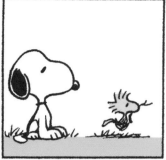

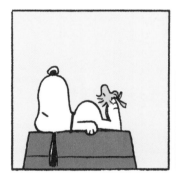

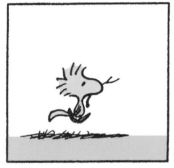

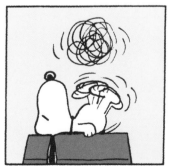

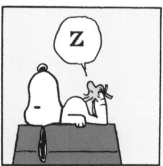

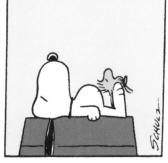

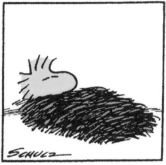

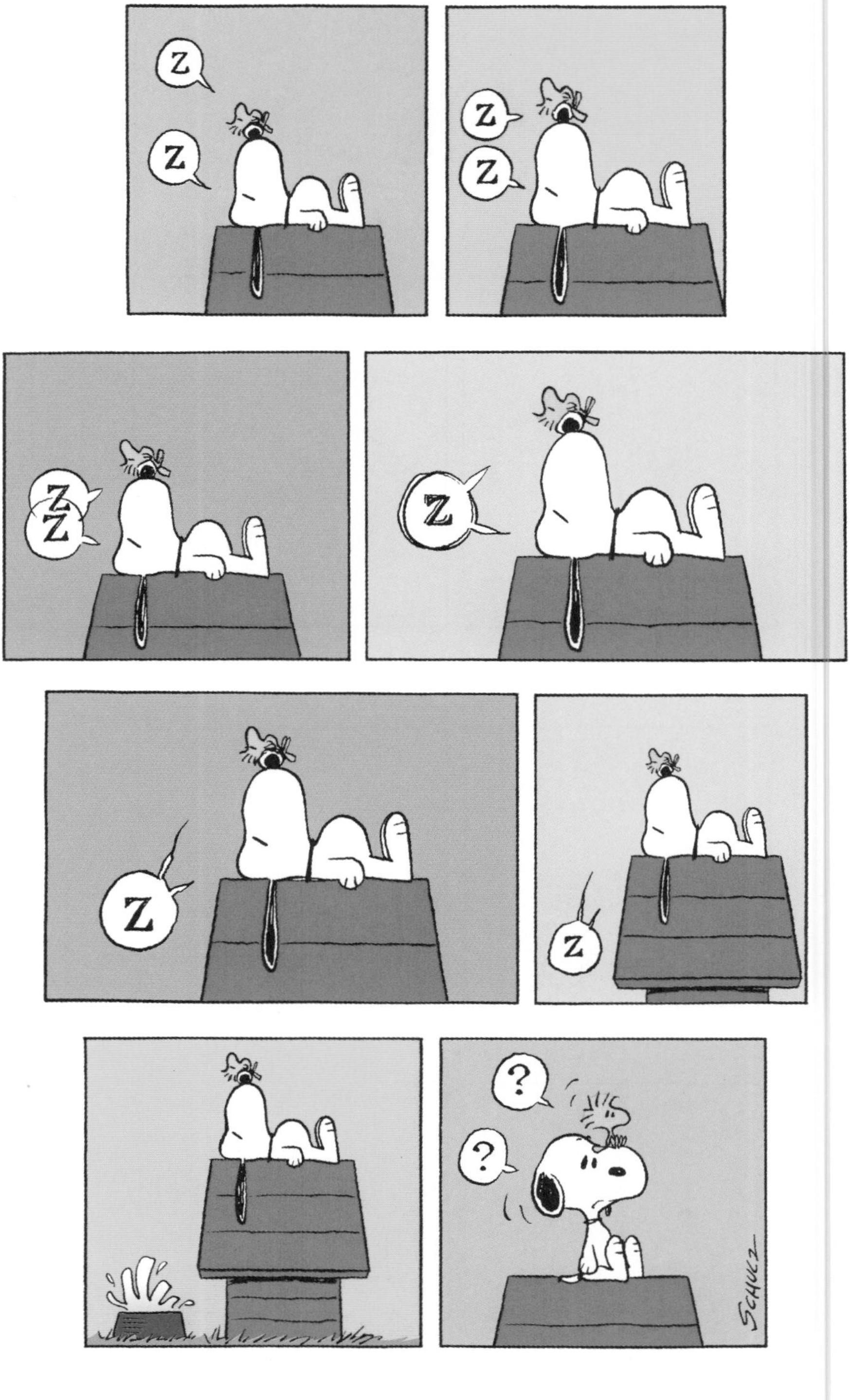
Z
Z
Z
Z
Z
Z
Z
Z
Z
Z
?
?
SCHULZ

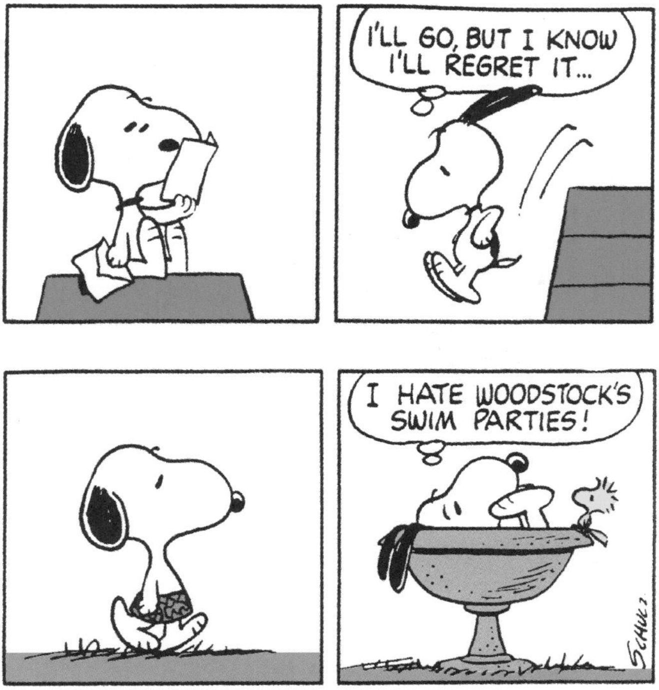
I'LL GO, BUT I KNOW I'LL REGRET IT...
I HATE WOODSTOCK'S SWIM PARTIES!
SCHULZ

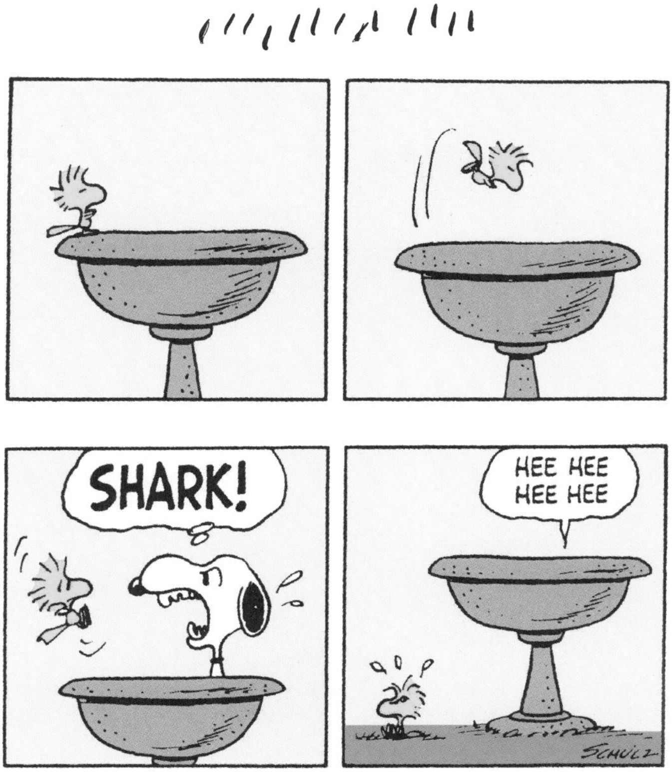
SHARK!
HEE HEE HEE HEE
SCHULZ

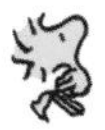

HEE HEE HEE HEE
WHY DO SOME PEOPLE THINK IT'S FUNNY TO TALK ABOUT WORMS WHILE YOU'RE TRYING TO EAT SPAGHETTI?
SCHULZ

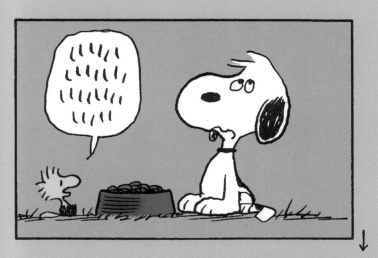

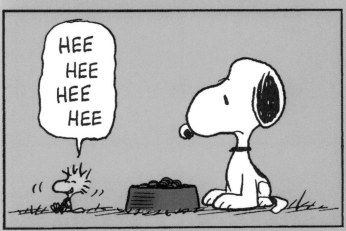

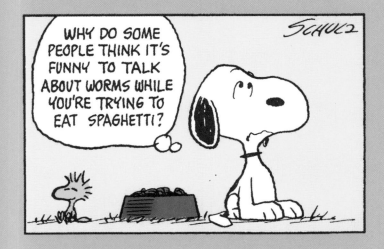

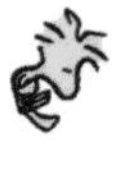

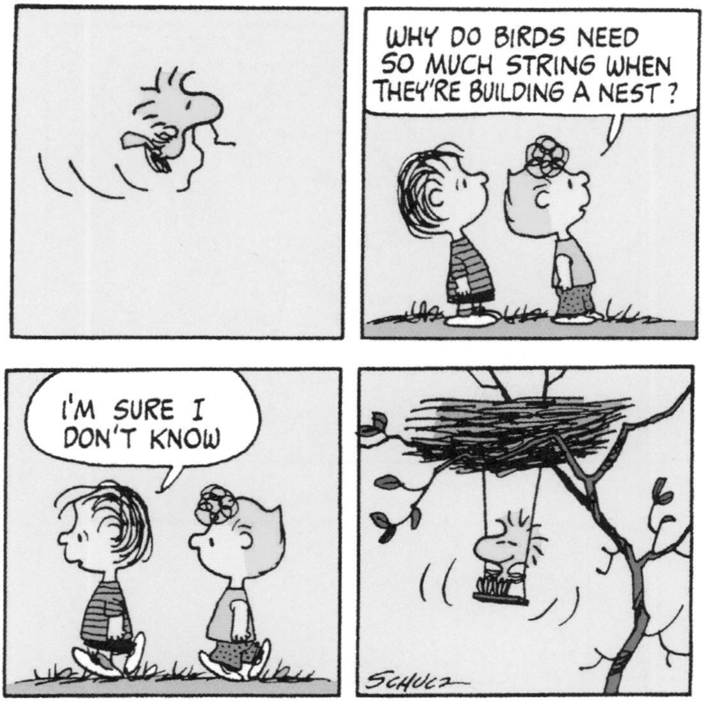
WHY DO BIRDS NEED SO MUCH STRING WHEN THEY'RE BUILDING A NEST?
I'M SURE I DON'T KNOW
SCHULZ

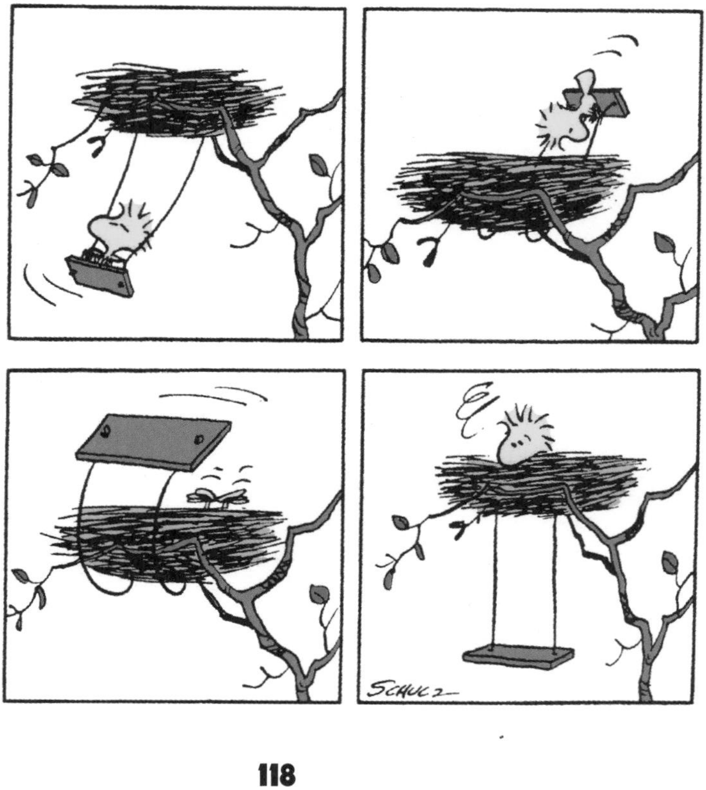
SCHULZ

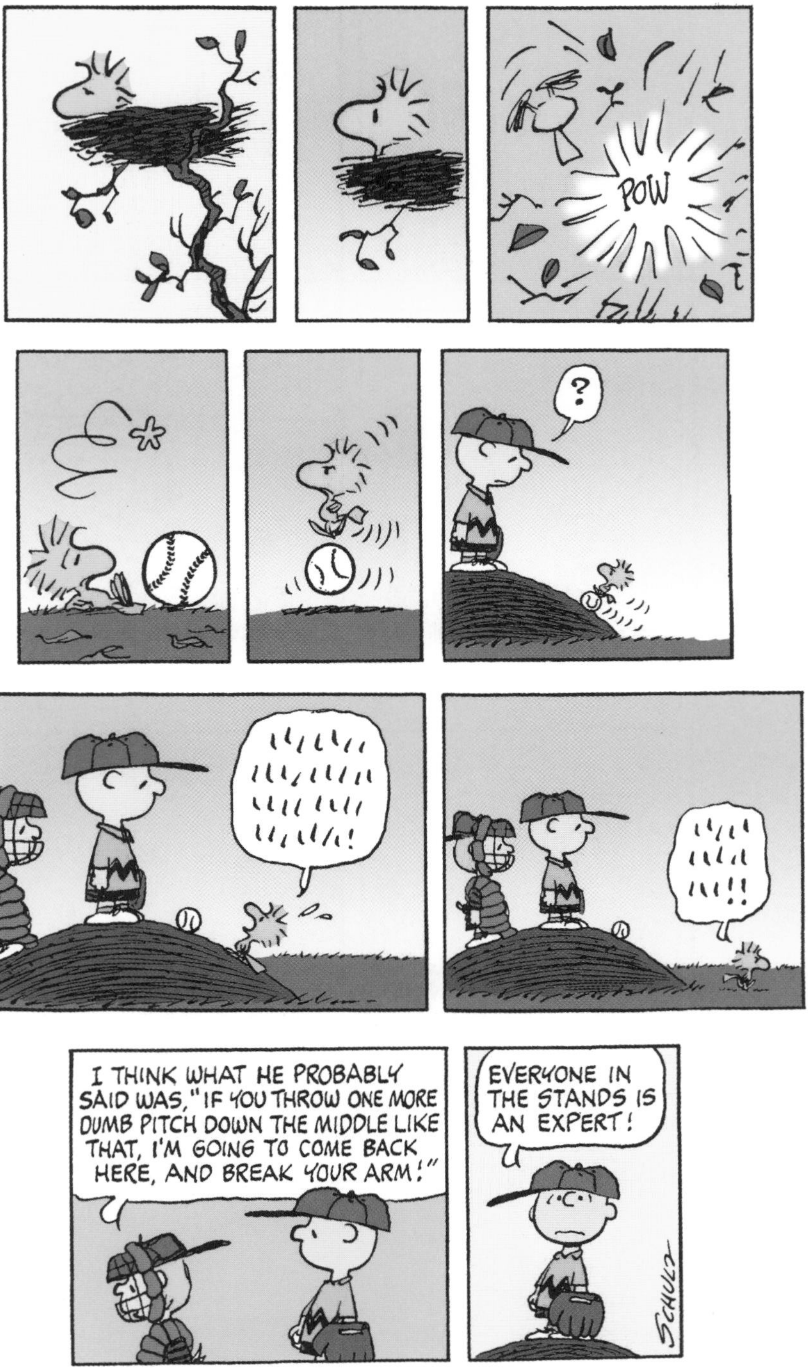
POW
?
I THINK WHAT HE PROBABLY SAID WAS, "IF YOU THROW ONE MORE DUMB PITCH DOWN THE MIDDLE LIKE THAT, I'M GOING TO COME BACK HERE, AND BREAK YOUR ARM!"
EVERYONE IN THE STANDS IS AN EXPERT!
SCHULZ

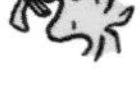

I FEEL SORRY FOR SOMEONE WHO HAS TO WIN AT EVERYTHING!

WEIRD!

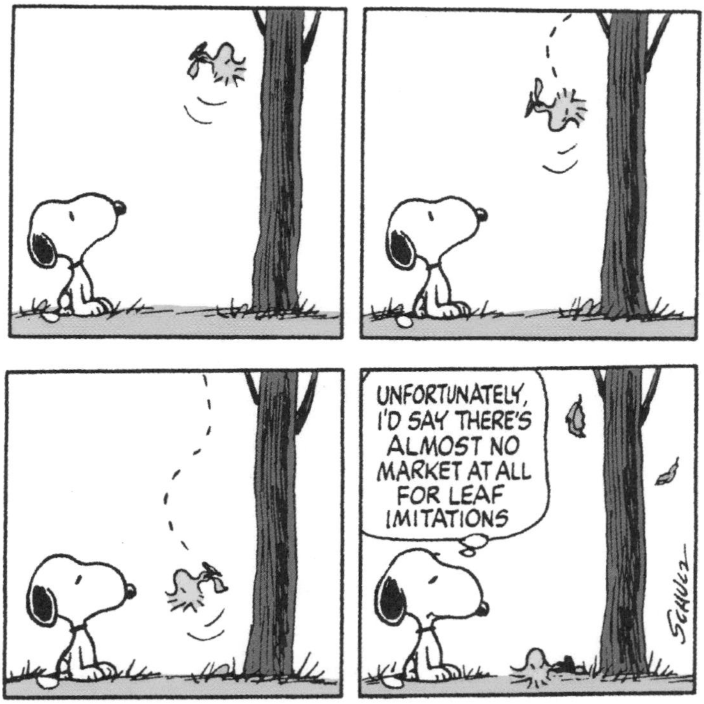
UNFORTUNATELY, I'D SAY THERE'S ALMOST NO MARKET AT ALL FOR LEAF IMITATIONS
SCHULZ

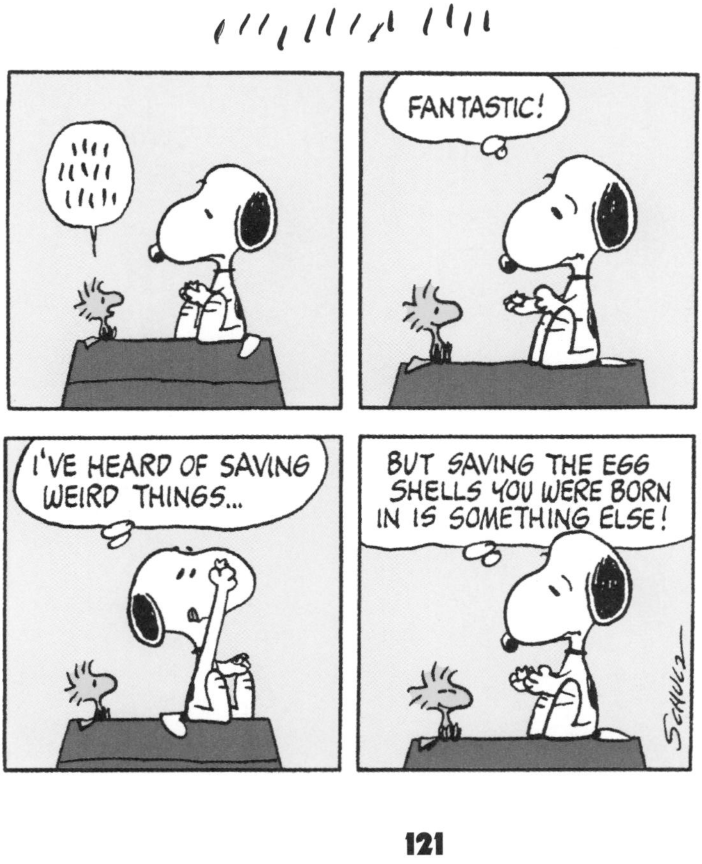
FANTASTIC!
I'VE HEARD OF SAVING WEIRD THINGS...
BUT SAVING THE EGG SHELLS YOU WERE BORN IN IS SOMETHING ELSE!
SCHULZ

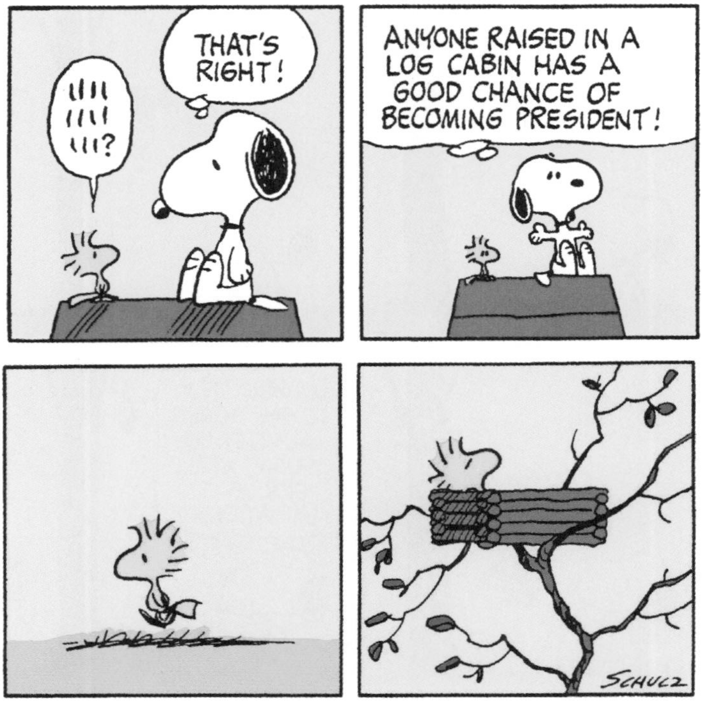
THAT'S RIGHT!
ANYONE RAISED IN A LOG CABIN HAS A GOOD CHANCE OF BECOMING PRESIDENT!
SCHULZ

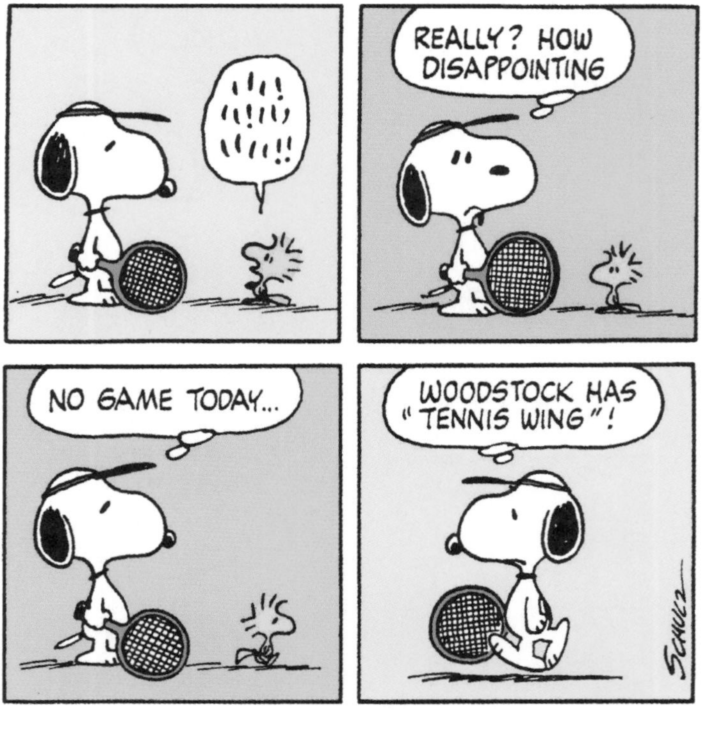
REALLY? HOW DISAPPOINTING
NO GAME TODAY...
WOODSTOCK HAS "TENNIS WING"!
SCHULZ

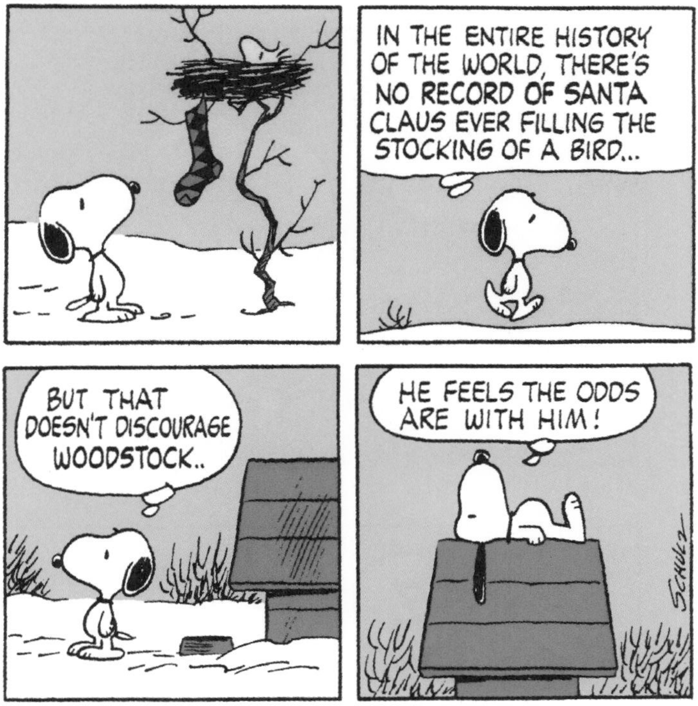
IN THE ENTIRE HISTORY OF THE WORLD, THERE'S NO RECORD OF SANTA CLAUS EVER FILLING THE STOCKING OF A BIRD...
BUT THAT DOESN'T DISCOURAGE WOODSTOCK..
HE FEELS THE ODDS ARE WITH HIM!
SCHULZ

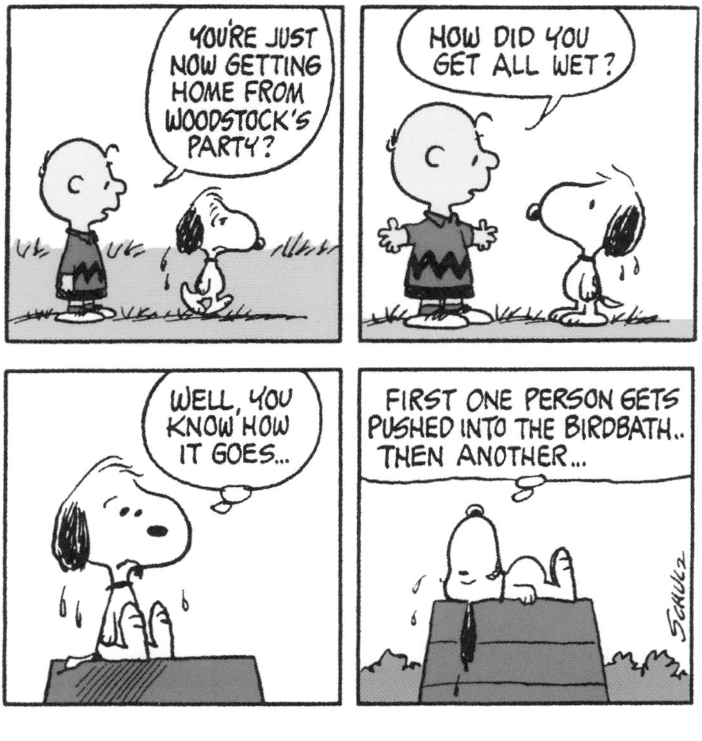
YOU'RE JUST NOW GETTING HOME FROM WOODSTOCK'S PARTY?
HOW DID YOU GET ALL WET?
WELL, YOU KNOW HOW IT GOES...
FIRST ONE PERSON GETS PUSHED INTO THE BIRDBATH.. THEN ANOTHER...
SCHULZ

YAWN
Z
Z
Z

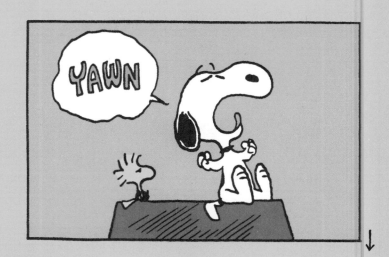

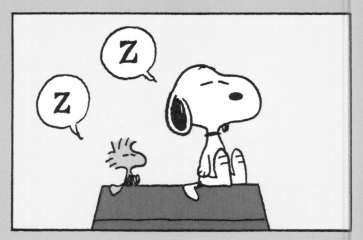

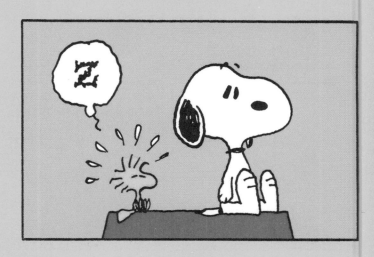

WOODSTOCK HAS SOME WEIRD DREAMS..

SCHULZ

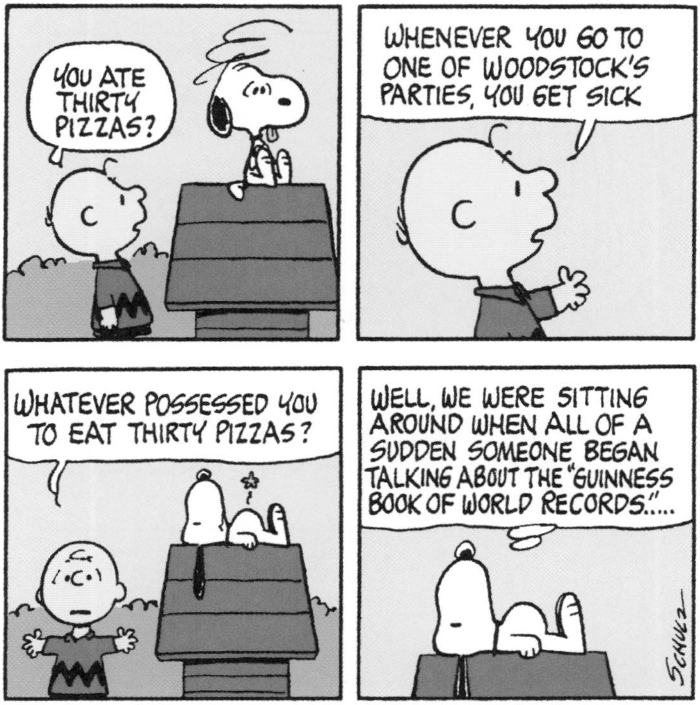
YOU ATE THIRTY PIZZAS?
WHENEVER YOU GO TO ONE OF WOODSTOCK'S PARTIES, YOU GET SICK
WHATEVER POSSESSED YOU TO EAT THIRTY PIZZAS?
WELL, WE WERE SITTING AROUND WHEN ALL OF A SUDDEN SOMEONE BEGAN TALKING ABOUT THE "GUINNESS BOOK OF WORLD RECORDS.".....
SCHULZ

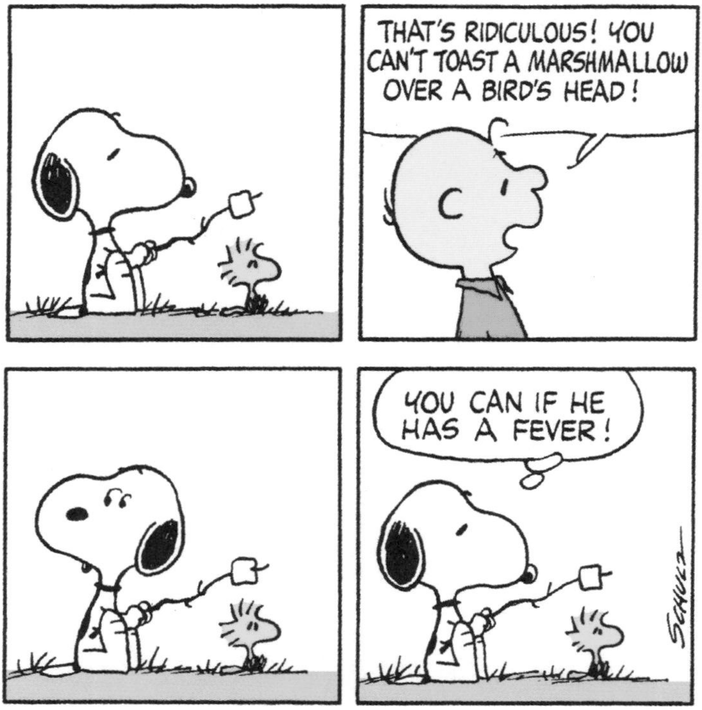
THAT'S RIDICULOUS! YOU CAN'T TOAST A MARSHMALLOW OVER A BIRD'S HEAD!
YOU CAN IF HE HAS A FEVER!
SCHULZ

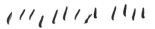

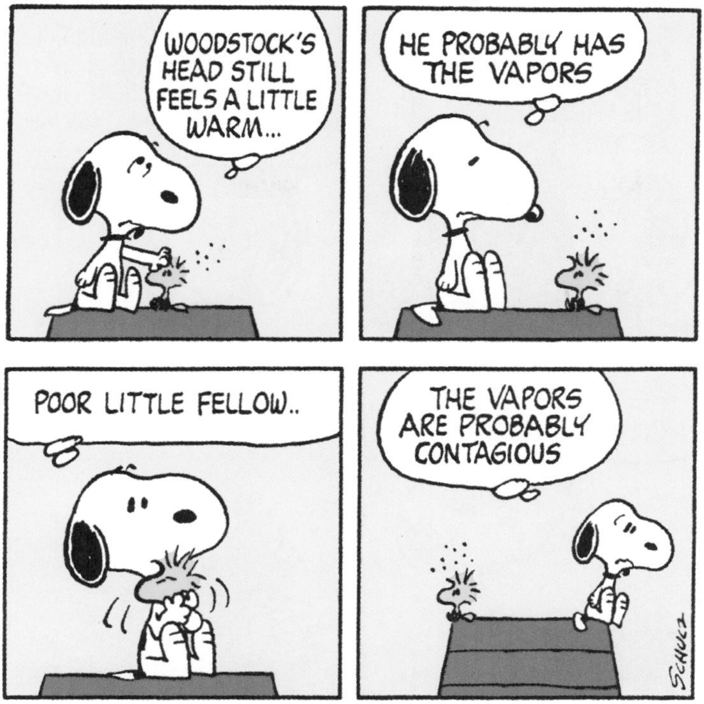
WOODSTOCK'S HEAD STILL FEELS A LITTLE WARM...
HE PROBABLY HAS THE VAPORS
POOR LITTLE FELLOW..
THE VAPORS ARE PROBABLY CONTAGIOUS
SCHULZ

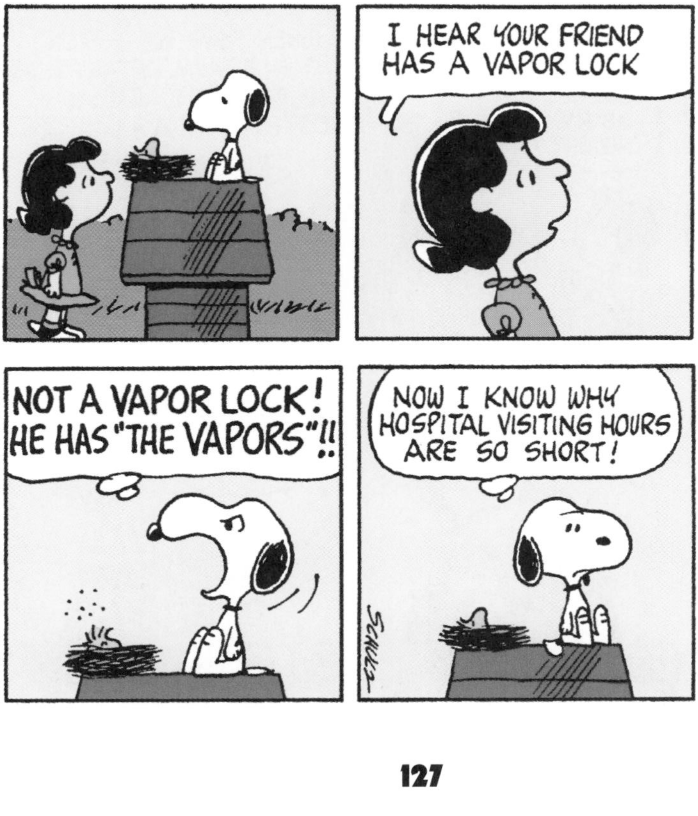
I HEAR YOUR FRIEND HAS A VAPOR LOCK
NOT A VAPOR LOCK! HE HAS "THE VAPORS"!!
NOW I KNOW WHY HOSPITAL VISITING HOURS ARE SO SHORT!
SCHULZ

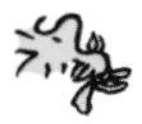

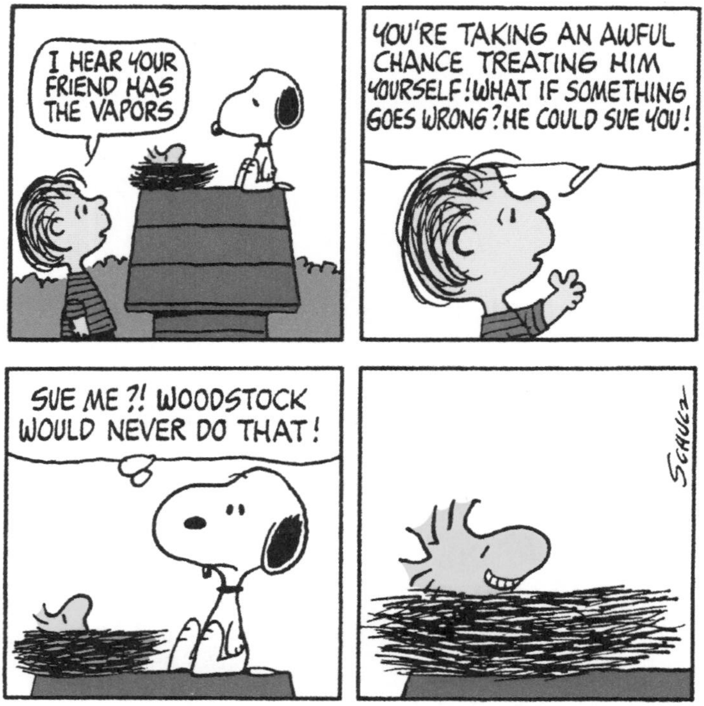
I HEAR YOUR FRIEND HAS THE VAPORS
YOU'RE TAKING AN AWFUL CHANCE TREATING HIM YOURSELF! WHAT IF SOMETHING GOES WRONG? HE COULD SUE YOU!
SUE ME ?! WOODSTOCK WOULD NEVER DO THAT!
SCHULZ

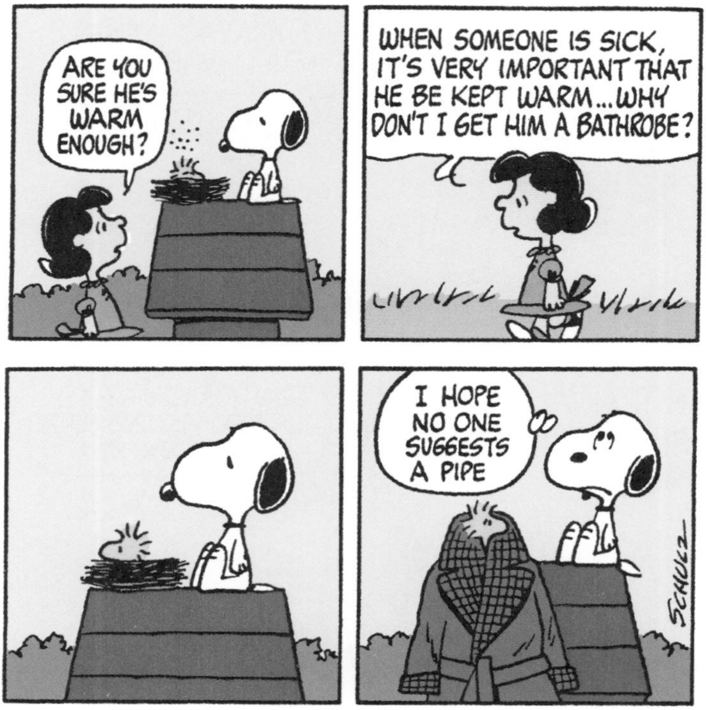
ARE YOU SURE HE'S WARM ENOUGH?
WHEN SOMEONE IS SICK, IT'S VERY IMPORTANT THAT HE BE KEPT WARM...WHY DON'T I GET HIM A BATHROBE?
I HOPE NO ONE SUGGESTS A PIPE
SCHULZ

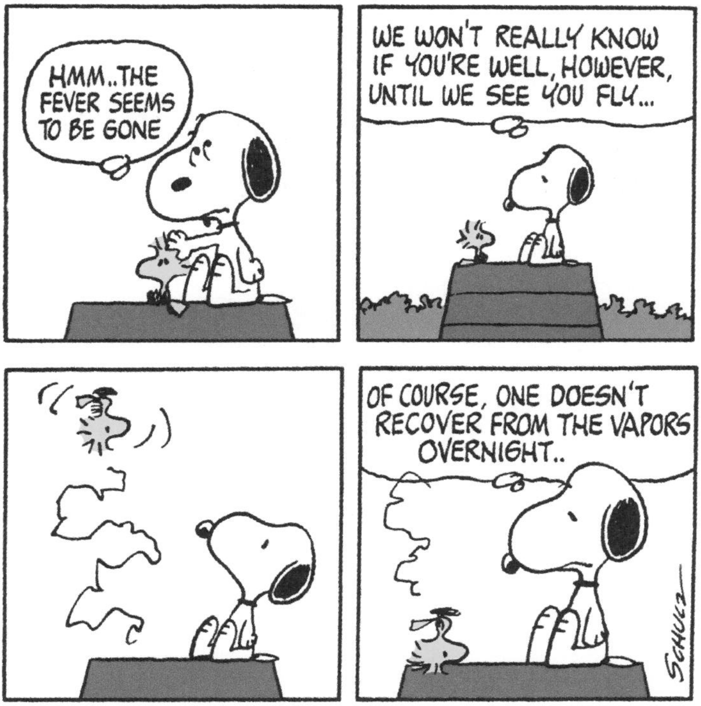
HMM..THE FEVER SEEMS TO BE GONE
WE WON'T REALLY KNOW IF YOU'RE WELL, HOWEVER, UNTIL WE SEE YOU FLY...
OF COURSE, ONE DOESN'T RECOVER FROM THE VAPORS OVERNIGHT..
SCHULZ

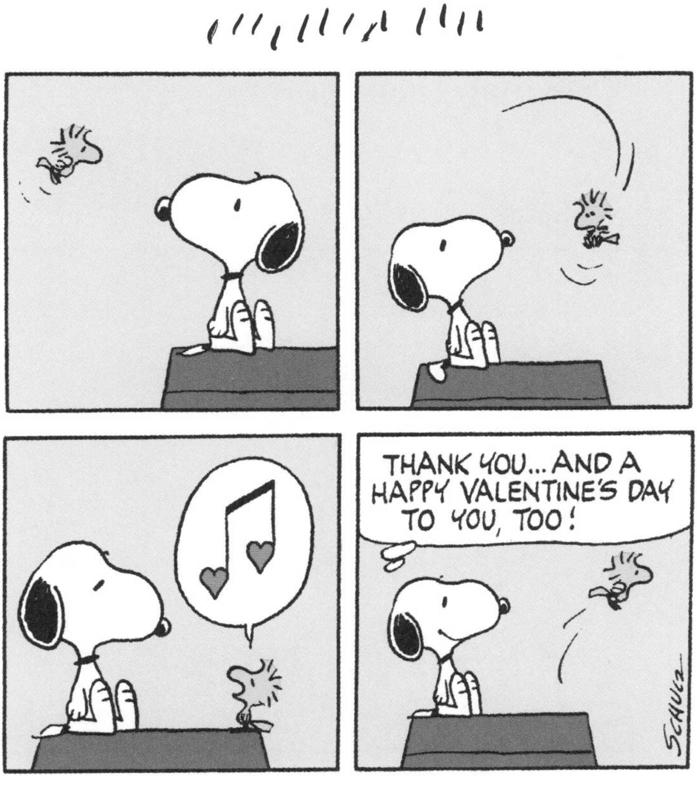
THANK YOU...AND A HAPPY VALENTINE'S DAY TO YOU, TOO!
SCHULZ

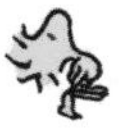

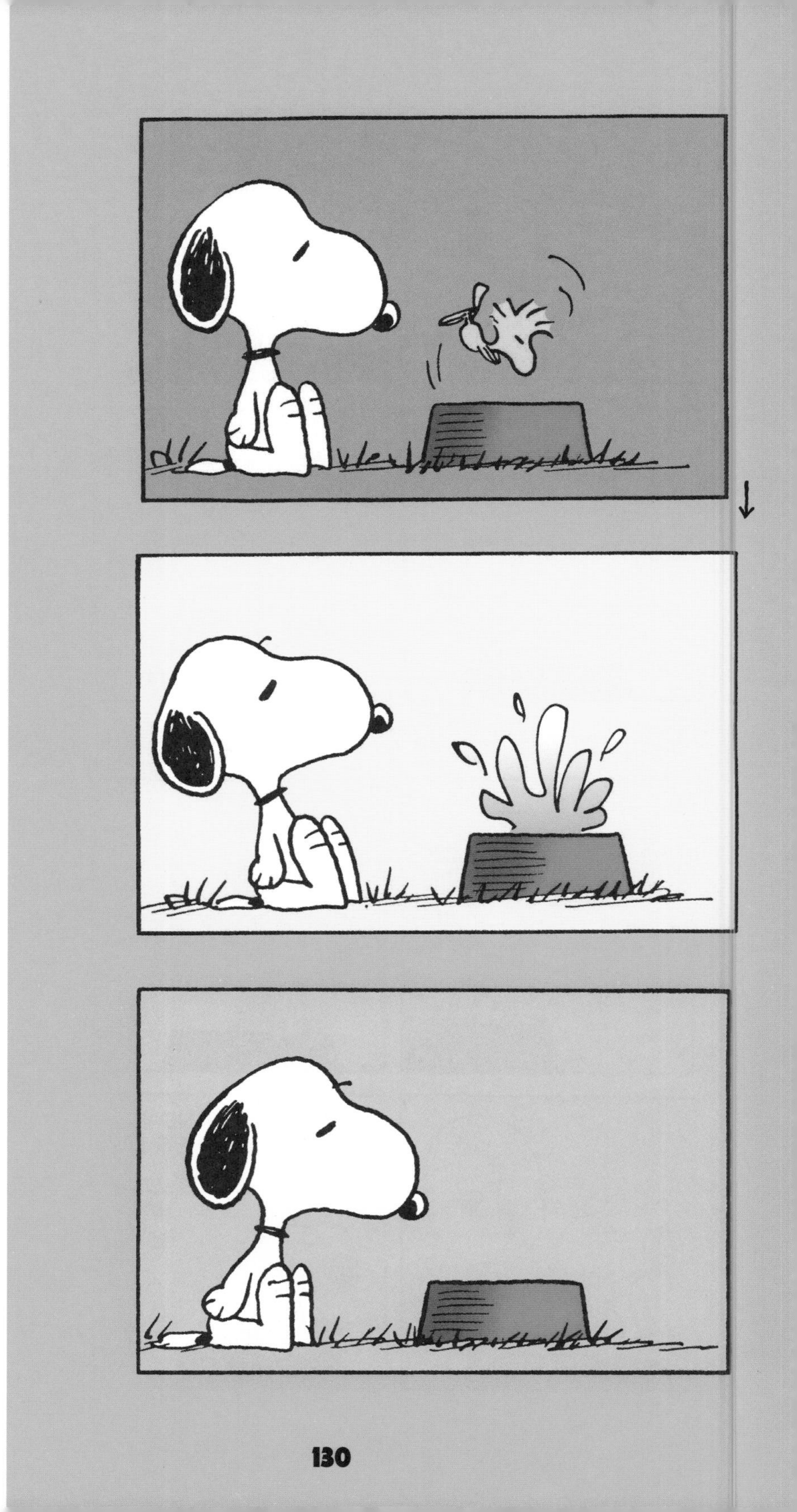

COFF KOFF
GASP
KOFF COFF
I KNEW HE COULDN'T DO TEN LAPS UNDER WATER!
SCHULZ

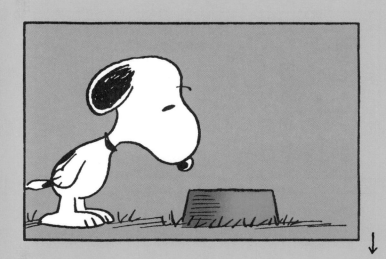

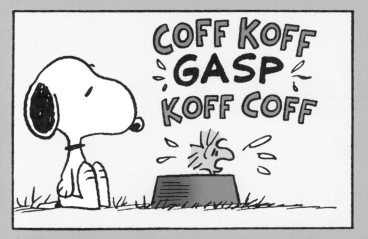

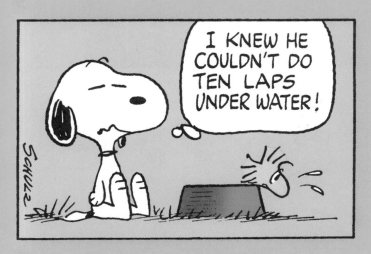

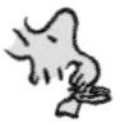

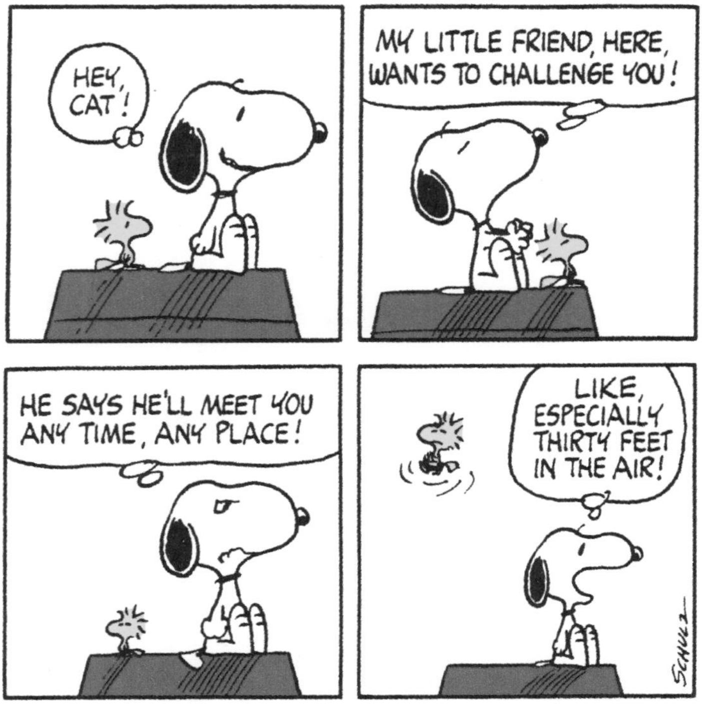
HEY, CAT!
MY LITTLE FRIEND, HERE, WANTS TO CHALLENGE YOU!
HE SAYS HE'LL MEET YOU ANY TIME, ANY PLACE!
LIKE, ESPECIALLY THIRTY FEET IN THE AIR!
SCHULZ

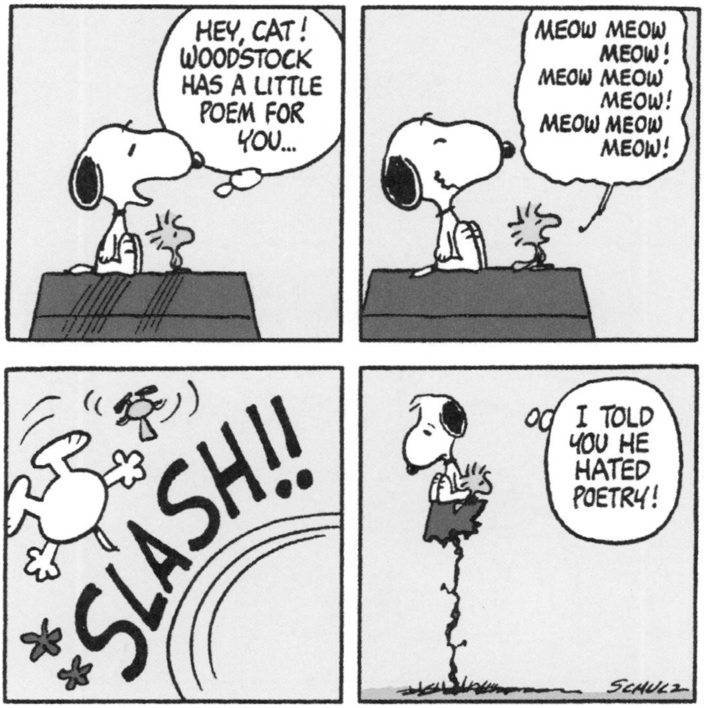
HEY, CAT! WOODSTOCK HAS A LITTLE POEM FOR YOU...
MEOW MEOW MEOW! MEOW MEOW MEOW! MEOW MEOW MEOW!
SLASH!!
I TOLD YOU HE HATED POETRY!
SCHULZ

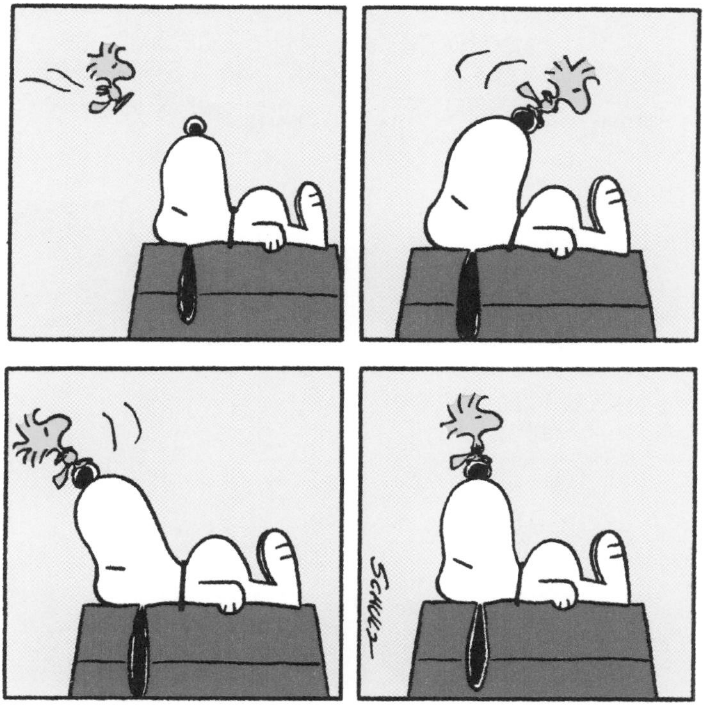

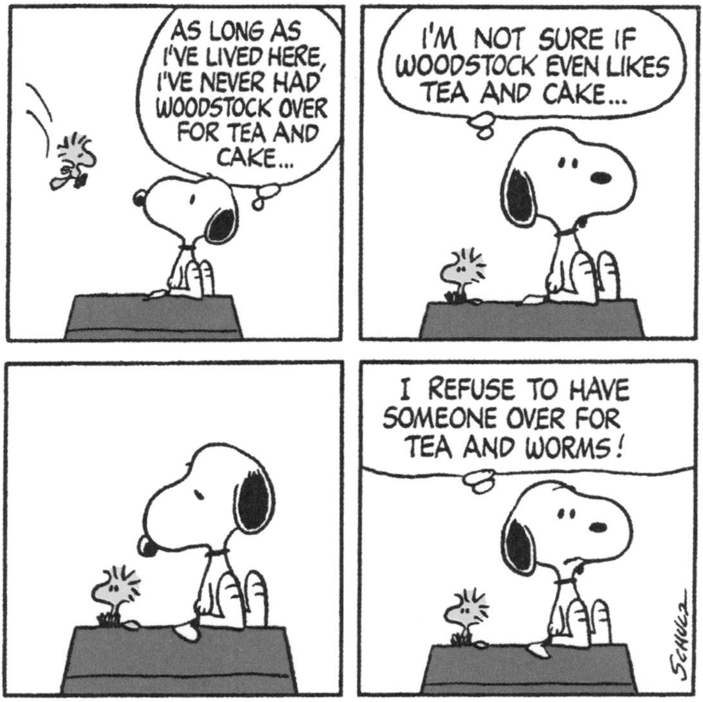
AS LONG AS I'VE LIVED HERE, I'VE NEVER HAD WOODSTOCK OVER FOR TEA AND CAKE...
I'M NOT SURE IF WOODSTOCK EVEN LIKES TEA AND CAKE...
I REFUSE TO HAVE SOMEONE OVER FOR TEA AND WORMS!

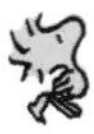

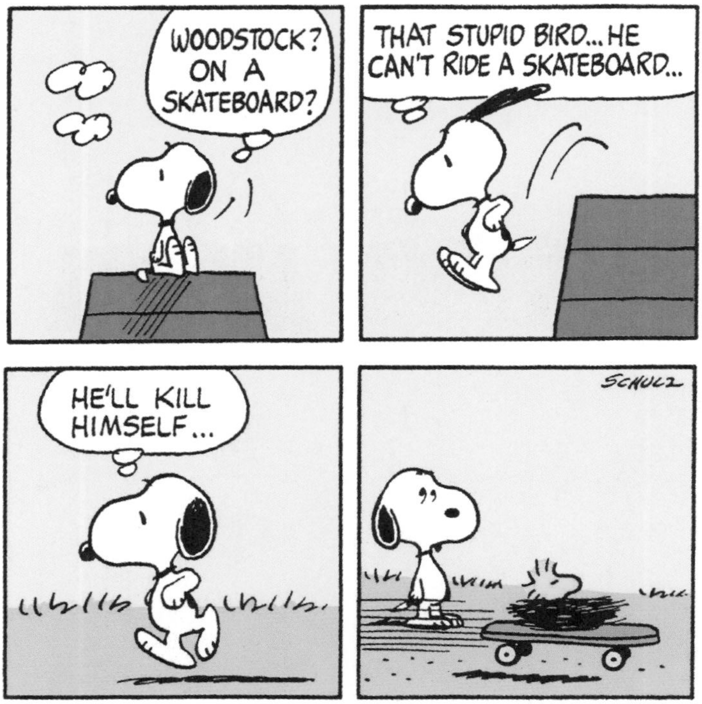
WOODSTOCK? ON A SKATEBOARD?
THAT STUPID BIRD... HE CAN'T RIDE A SKATEBOARD...
HE'LL KILL HIMSELF...
SCHULZ

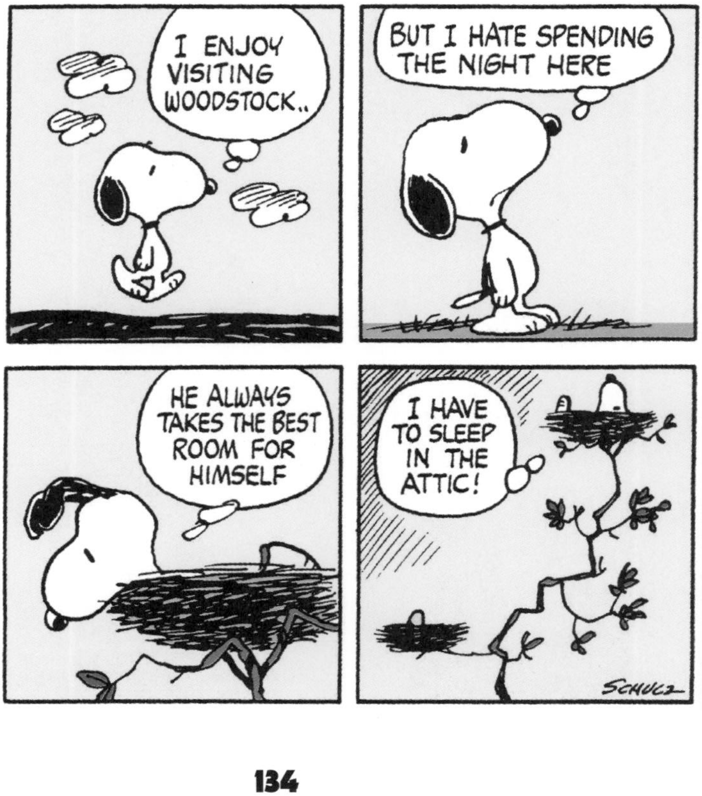
I ENJOY VISITING WOODSTOCK..
BUT I HATE SPENDING THE NIGHT HERE
HE ALWAYS TAKES THE BEST ROOM FOR HIMSELF
I HAVE TO SLEEP IN THE ATTIC!
SCHULZ

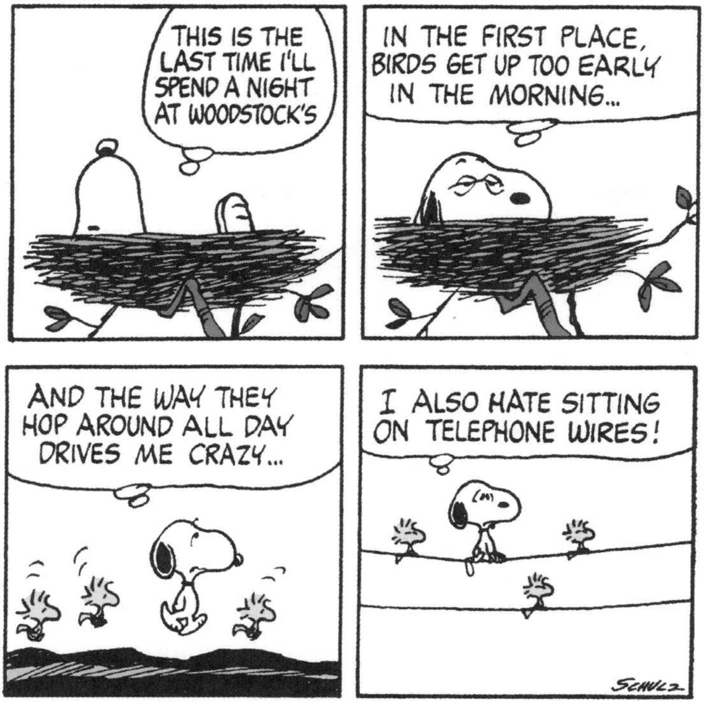
THIS IS THE LAST TIME I'LL SPEND A NIGHT AT WOODSTOCK'S
IN THE FIRST PLACE, BIRDS GET UP TOO EARLY IN THE MORNING...
AND THE WAY THEY HOP AROUND ALL DAY DRIVES ME CRAZY...
I ALSO HATE SITTING ON TELEPHONE WIRES!
SCHULZ

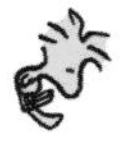

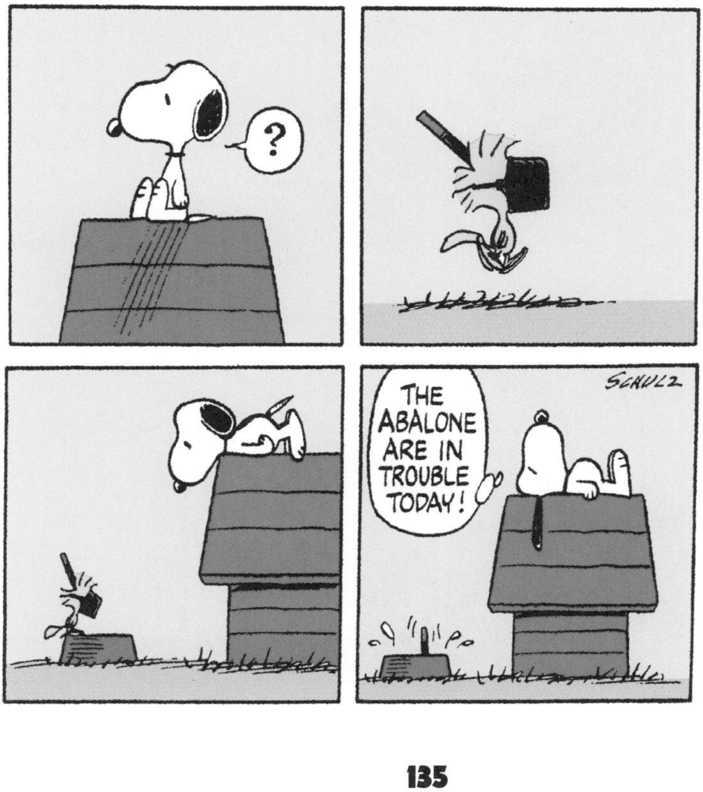
?
SCHULZ
THE ABALONE ARE IN TROUBLE TODAY!

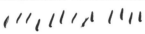

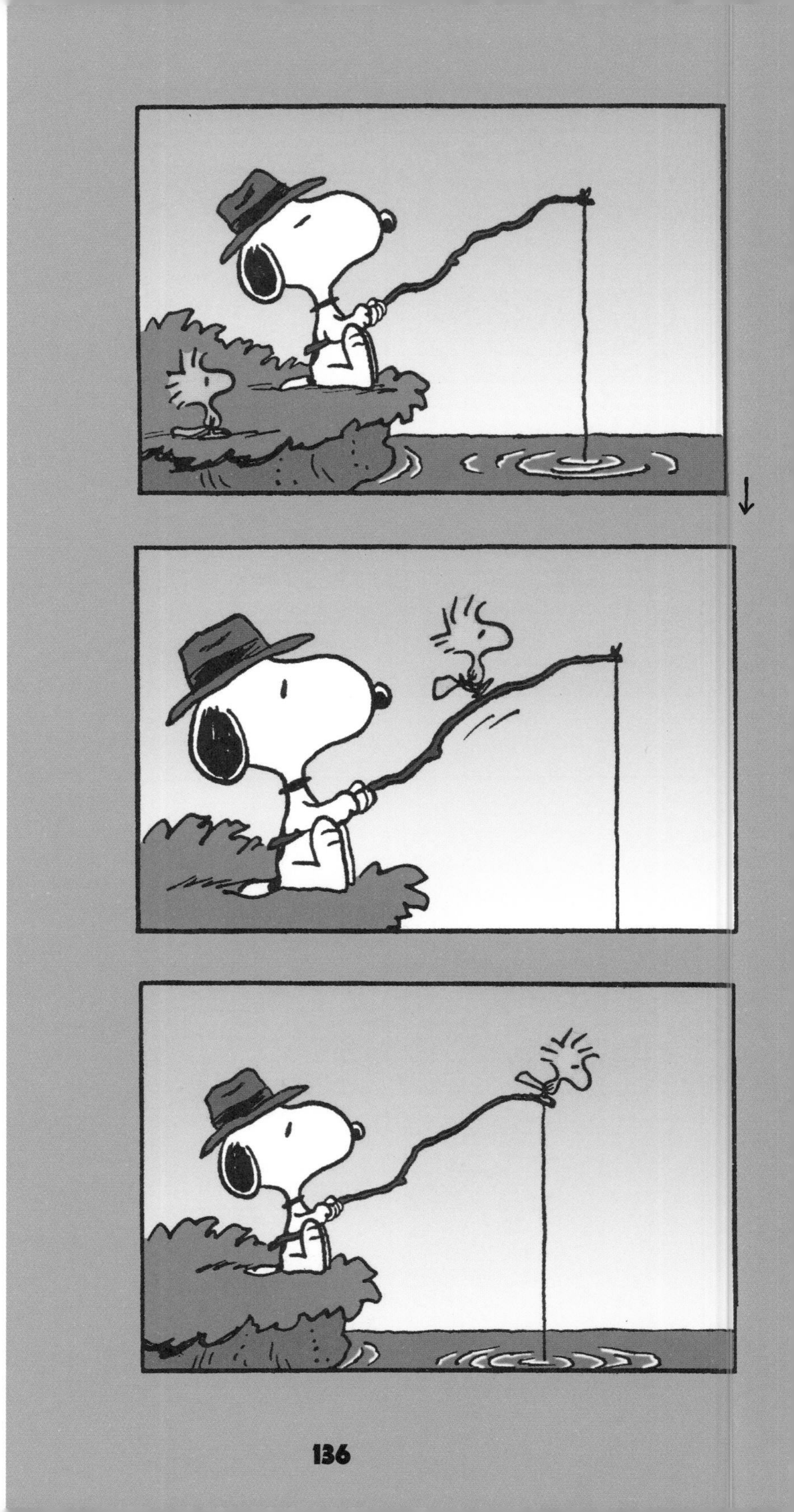

SCHULZ

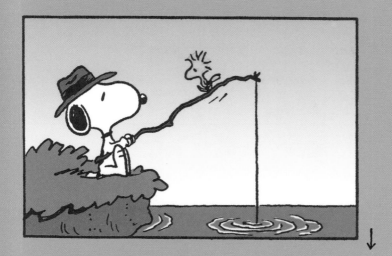

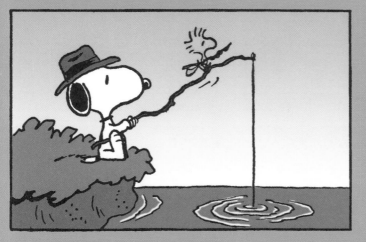

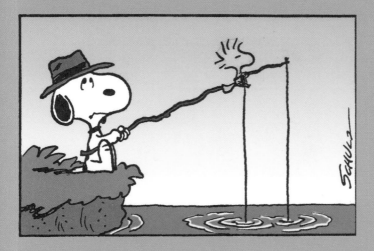

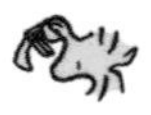

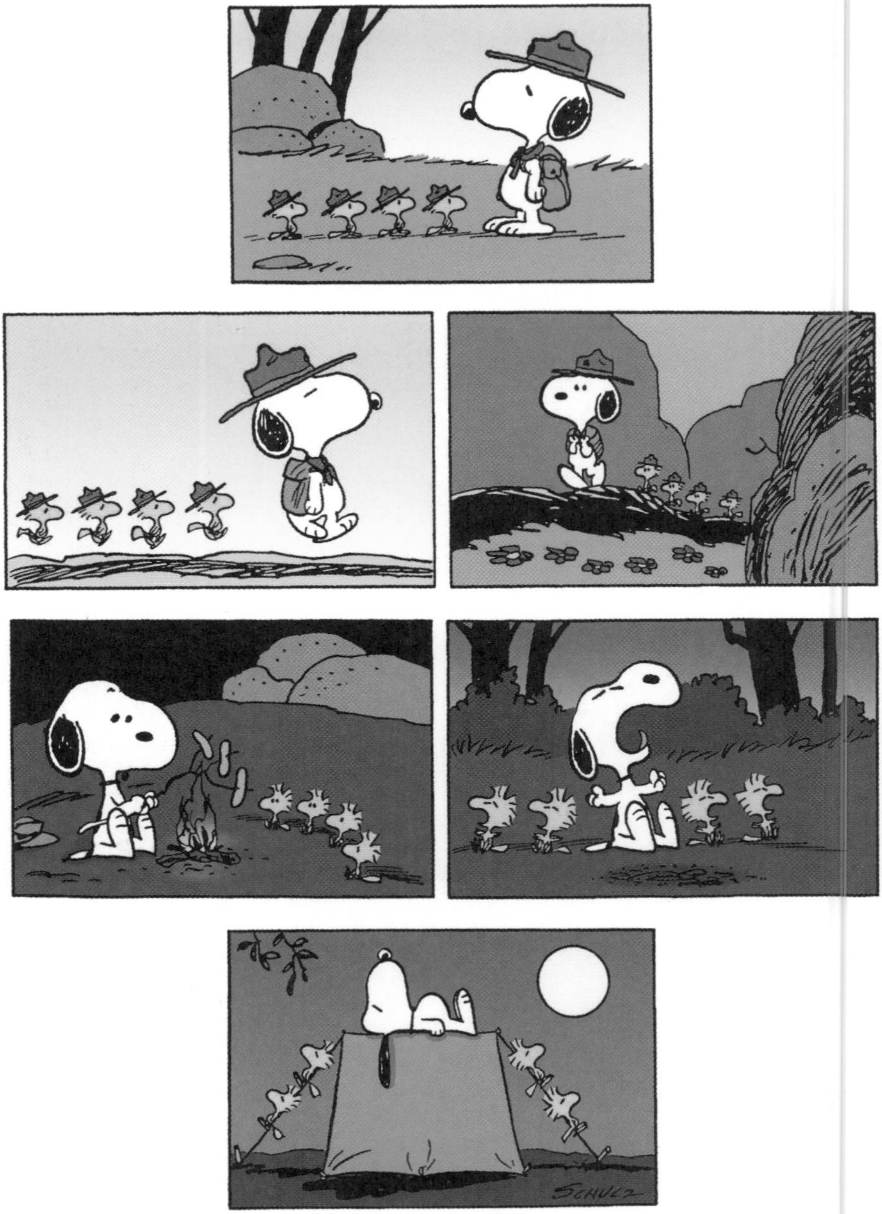

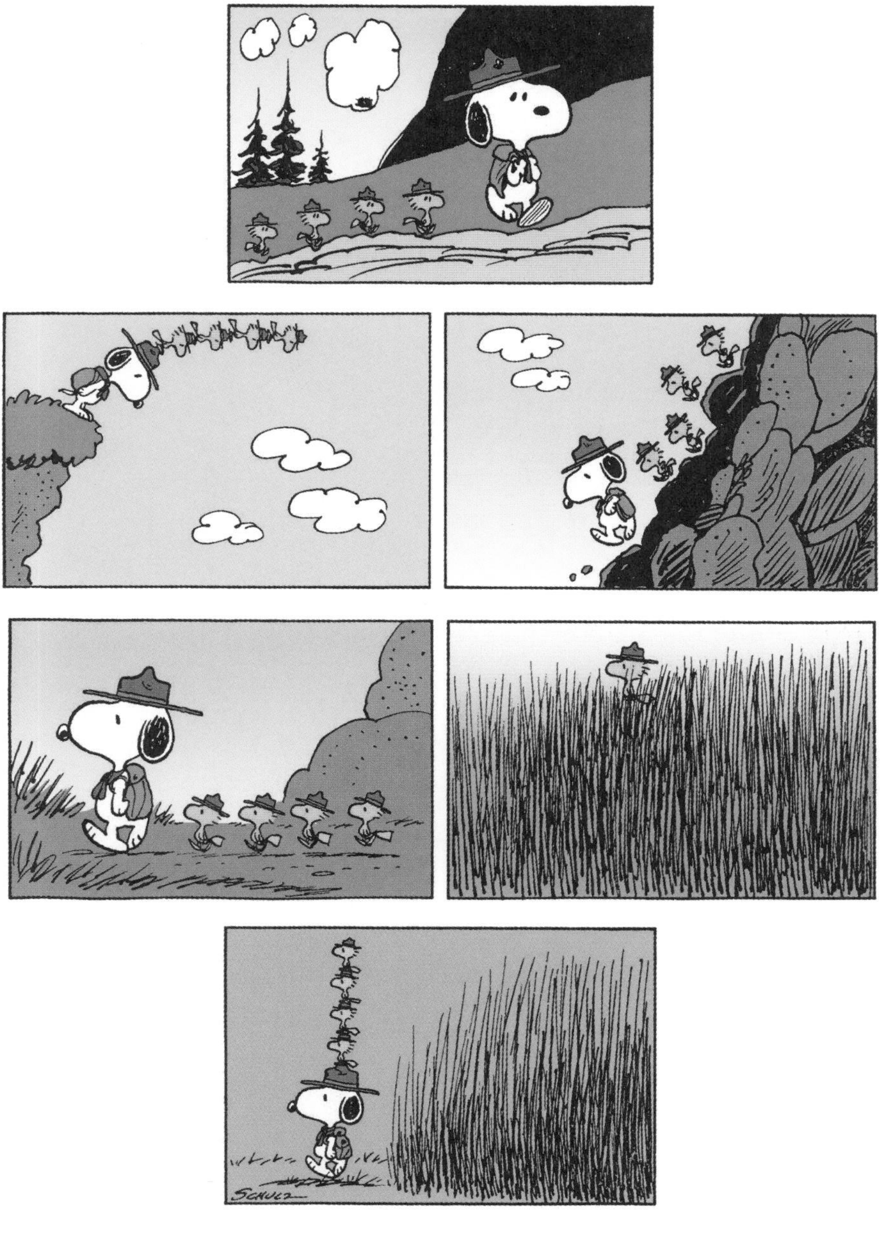
SCHULZ

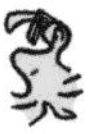

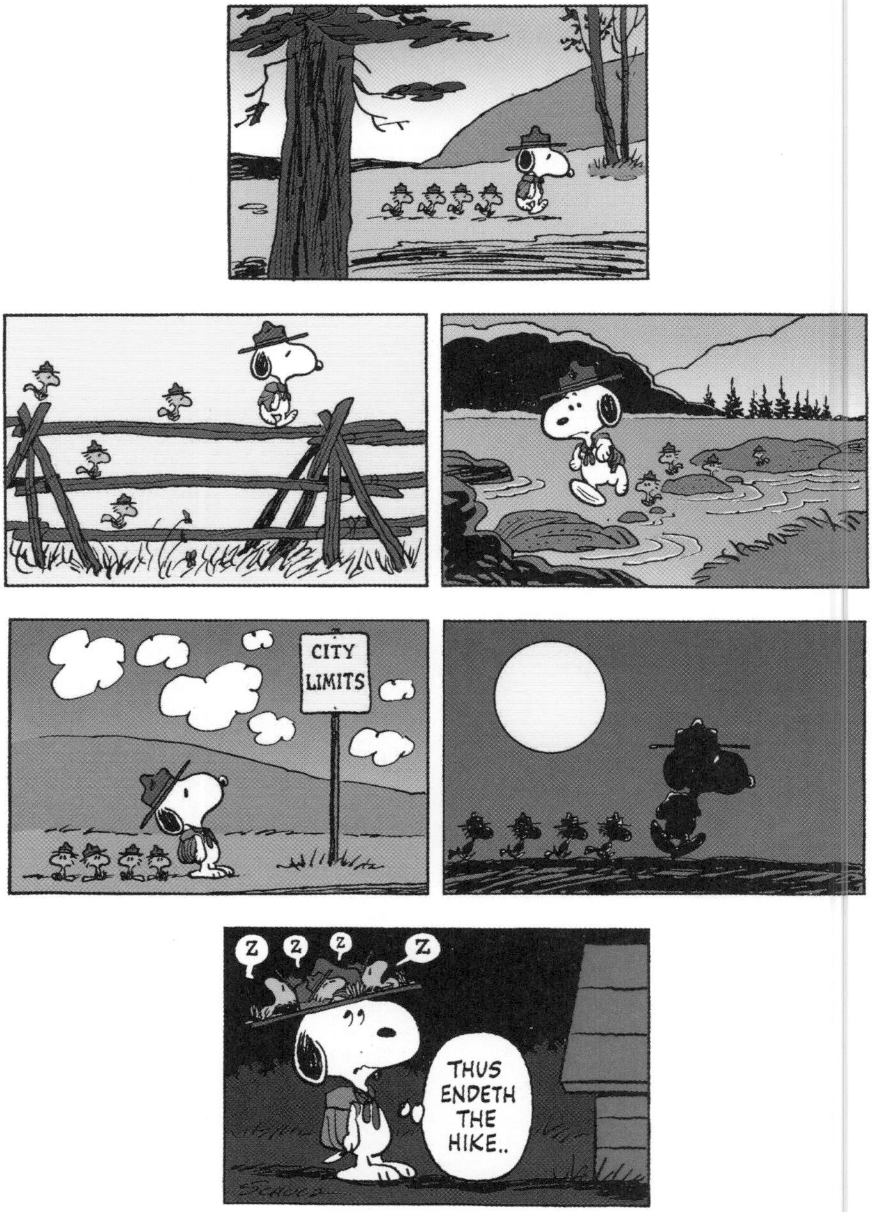
CITY
LIMITS
Z
Z
Z
Z
THUS
ENDETH
THE
HIKE..
SCHULZ

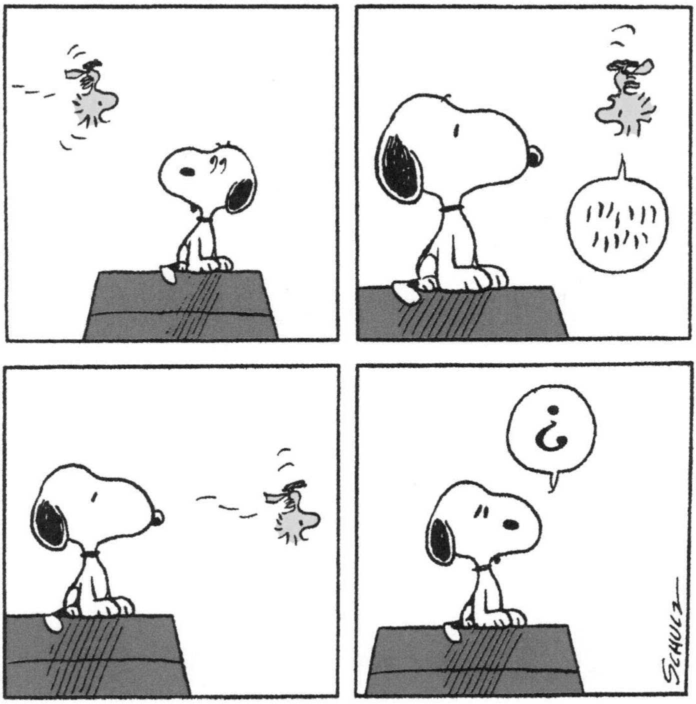
¿
SCHULZ

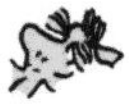

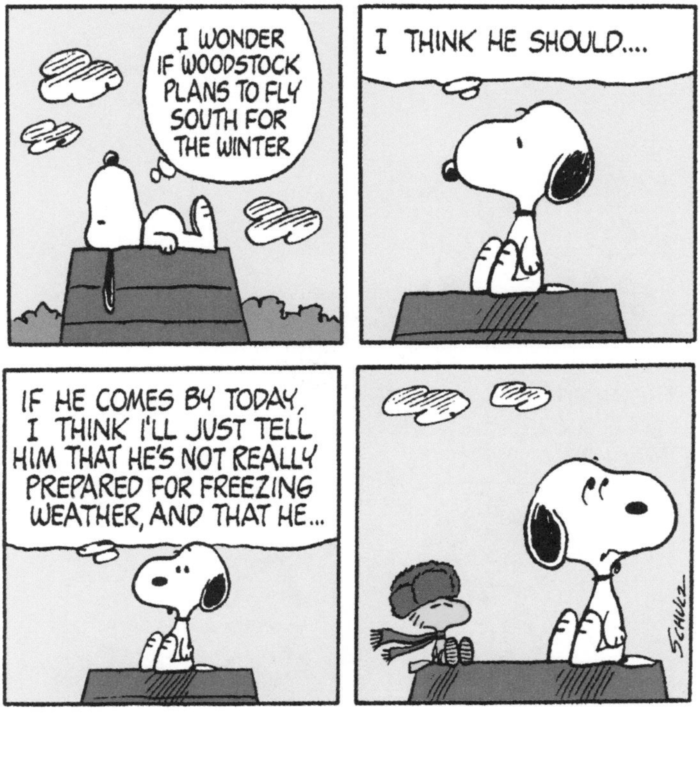
I WONDER IF WOODSTOCK PLANS TO FLY SOUTH FOR THE WINTER
I THINK HE SHOULD....
IF HE COMES BY TODAY, I THINK I'LL JUST TELL HIM THAT HE'S NOT REALLY PREPARED FOR FREEZING WEATHER, AND THAT HE...
SCHULZ

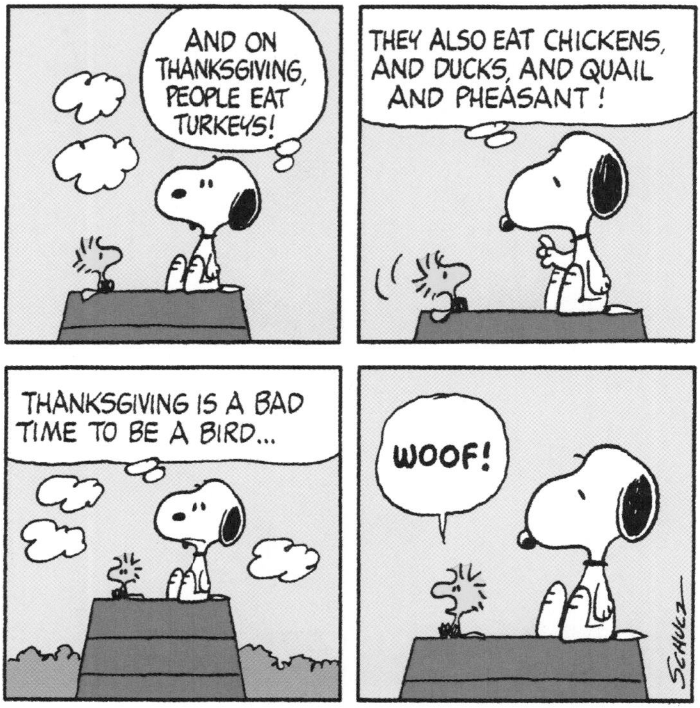
AND ON THANKSGIVING, PEOPLE EAT TURKEYS!
THEY ALSO EAT CHICKENS, AND DUCKS, AND QUAIL AND PHEASANT!
THANKSGIVING IS A BAD TIME TO BE A BIRD...
WOOF!
SCHULZ

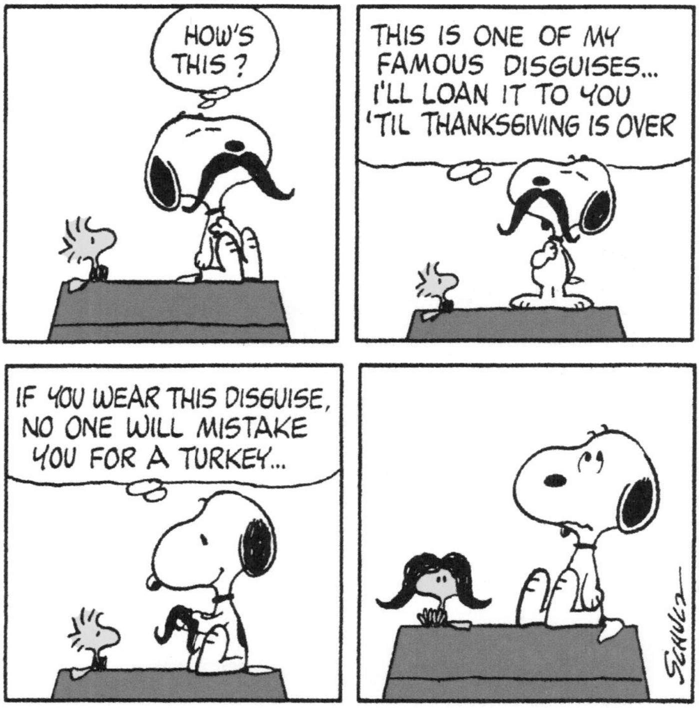
HOW'S THIS?
THIS IS ONE OF MY FAMOUS DISGUISES... I'LL LOAN IT TO YOU 'TIL THANKSGIVING IS OVER
IF YOU WEAR THIS DISGUISE, NO ONE WILL MISTAKE YOU FOR A TURKEY...
SCHULZ

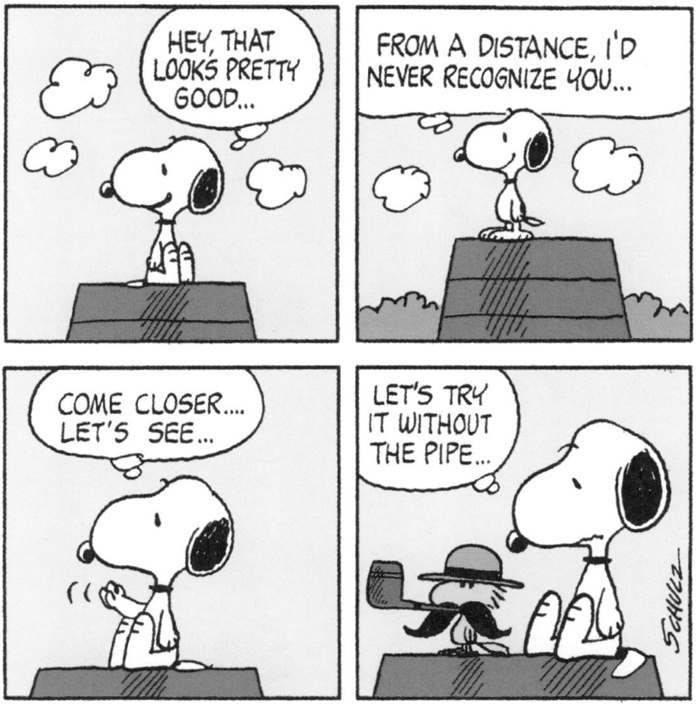
HEY, THAT LOOKS PRETTY GOOD...
FROM A DISTANCE, I'D NEVER RECOGNIZE YOU...
COME CLOSER.... LET'S SEE...
LET'S TRY IT WITHOUT THE PIPE...
SCHULZ

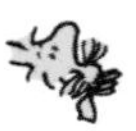

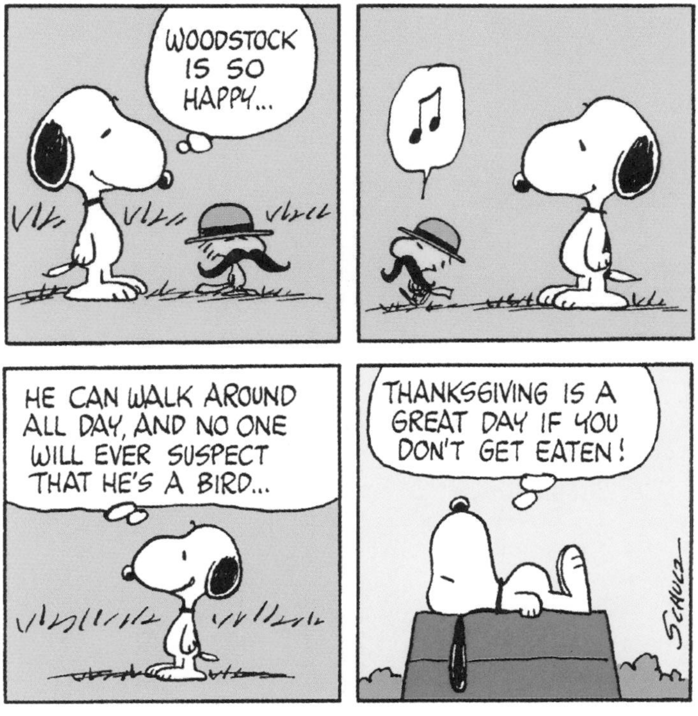
WOODSTOCK IS SO HAPPY...
HE CAN WALK AROUND ALL DAY, AND NO ONE WILL EVER SUSPECT THAT HE'S A BIRD...
THANKSGIVING IS A GREAT DAY IF YOU DON'T GET EATEN!
SCHULZ

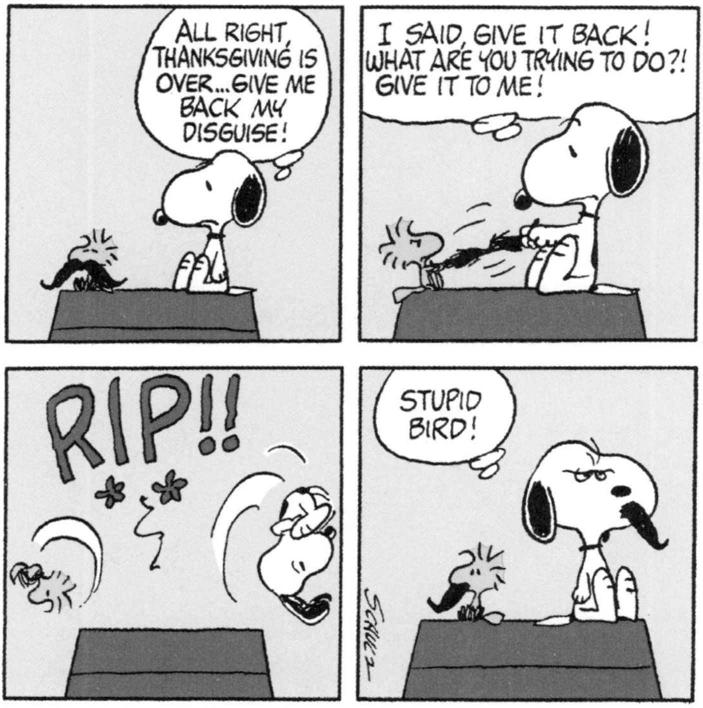
ALL RIGHT, THANKSGIVING IS OVER...GIVE ME BACK MY DISGUISE!
I SAID, GIVE IT BACK! WHAT ARE YOU TRYING TO DO?! GIVE IT TO ME!
RIP!!
STUPID BIRD!
SCHULZ

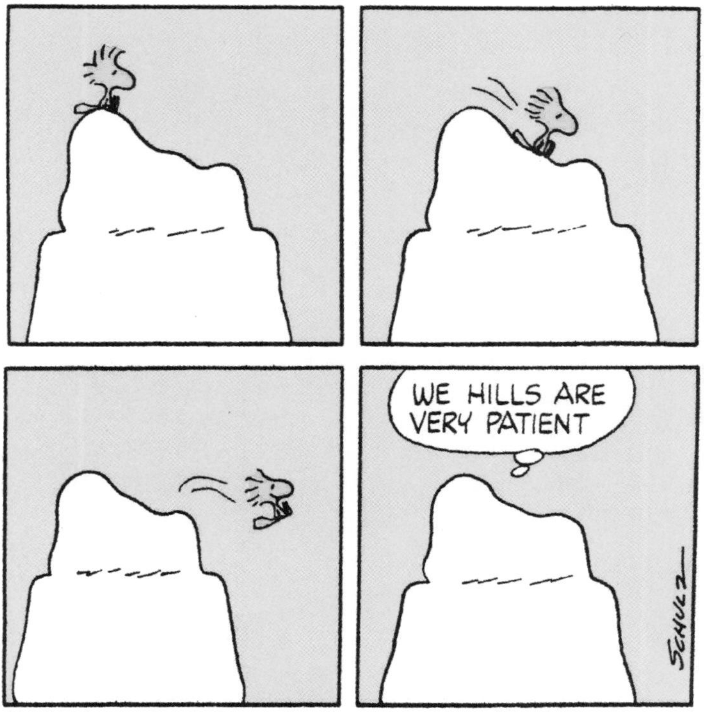
WE HILLS ARE VERY PATIENT
SCHULZ

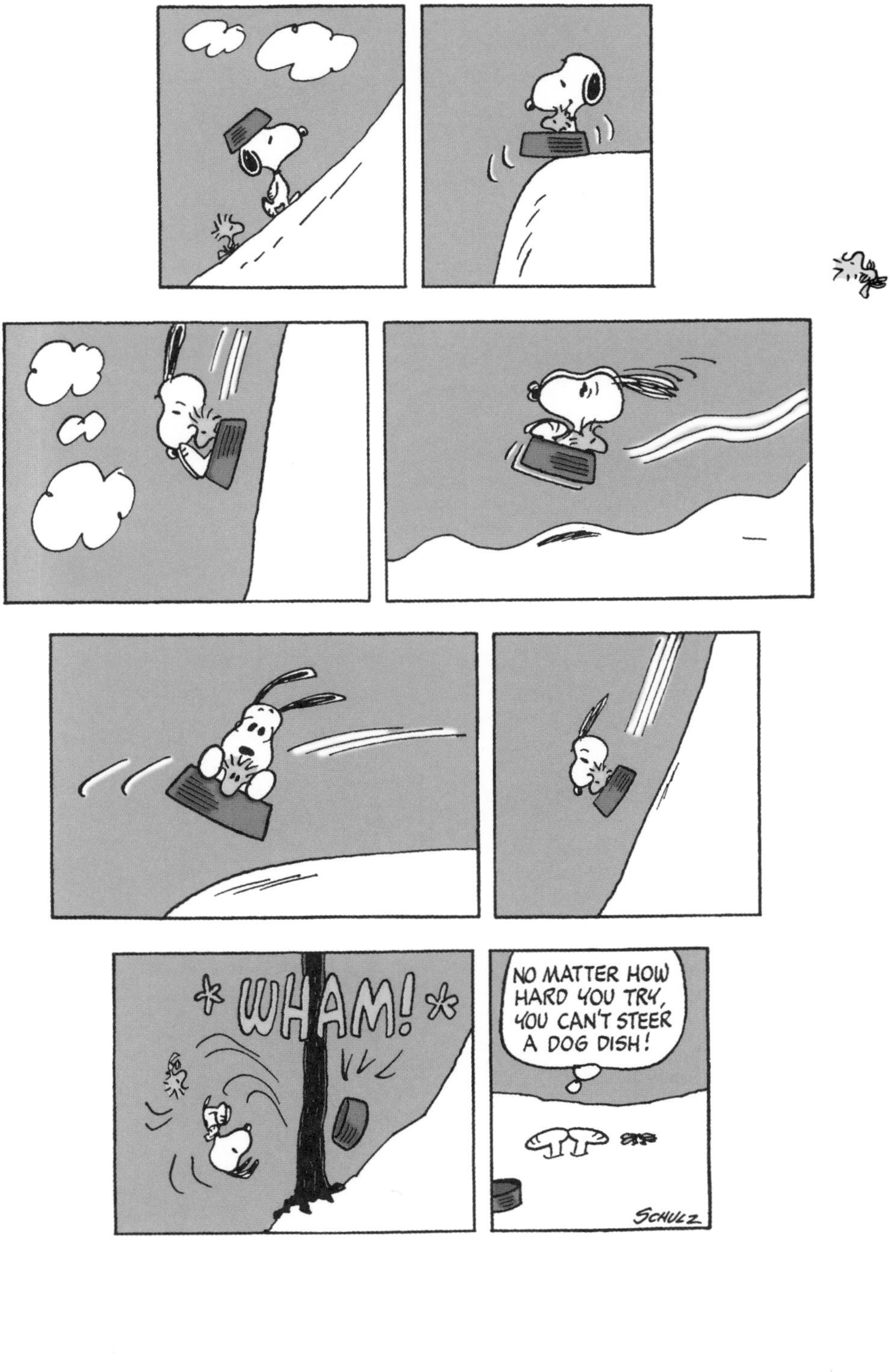
WHAM!
NO MATTER HOW HARD YOU TRY, YOU CAN'T STEER A DOG DISH!
SCHULZ

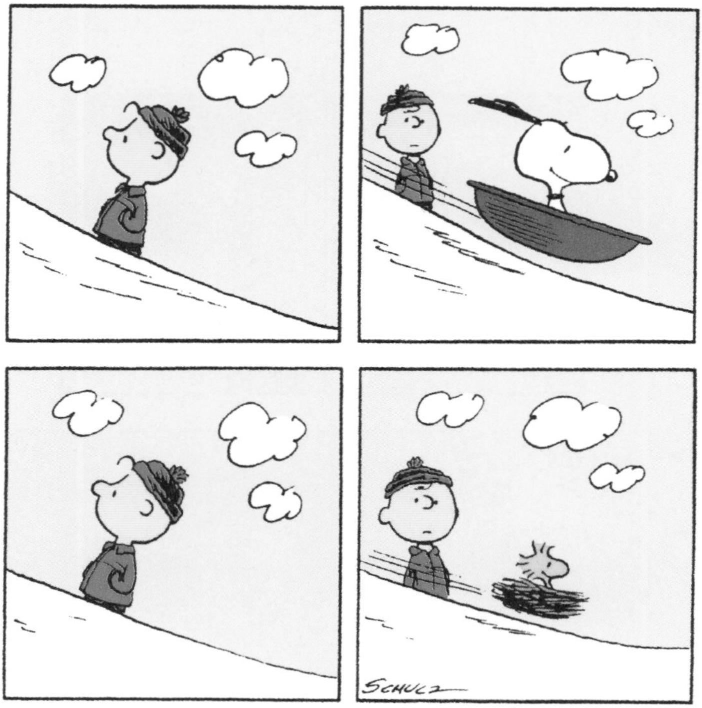

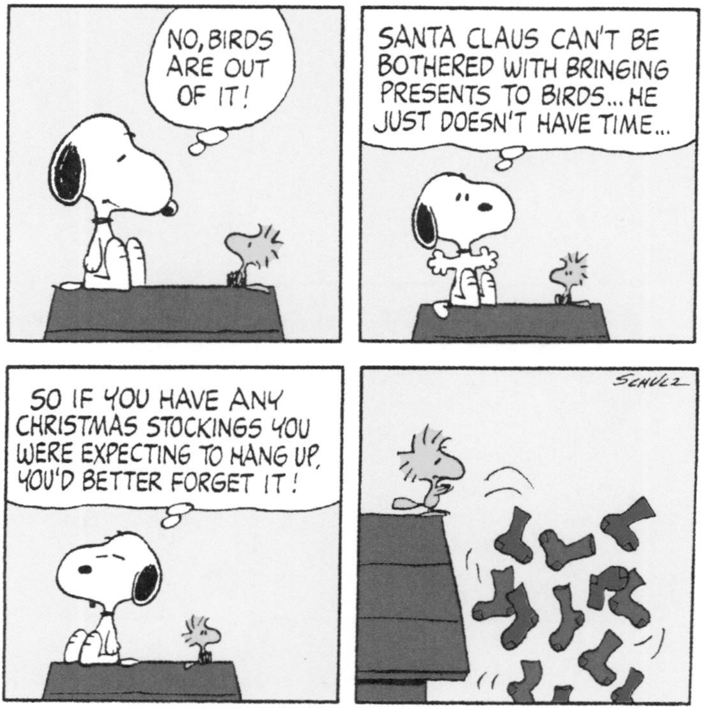
NO, BIRDS ARE OUT OF IT!
SANTA CLAUS CAN'T BE BOTHERED WITH BRINGING PRESENTS TO BIRDS... HE JUST DOESN'T HAVE TIME...
SO IF YOU HAVE ANY CHRISTMAS STOCKINGS YOU WERE EXPECTING TO HANG UP, YOU'D BETTER FORGET IT!
SCHULZ

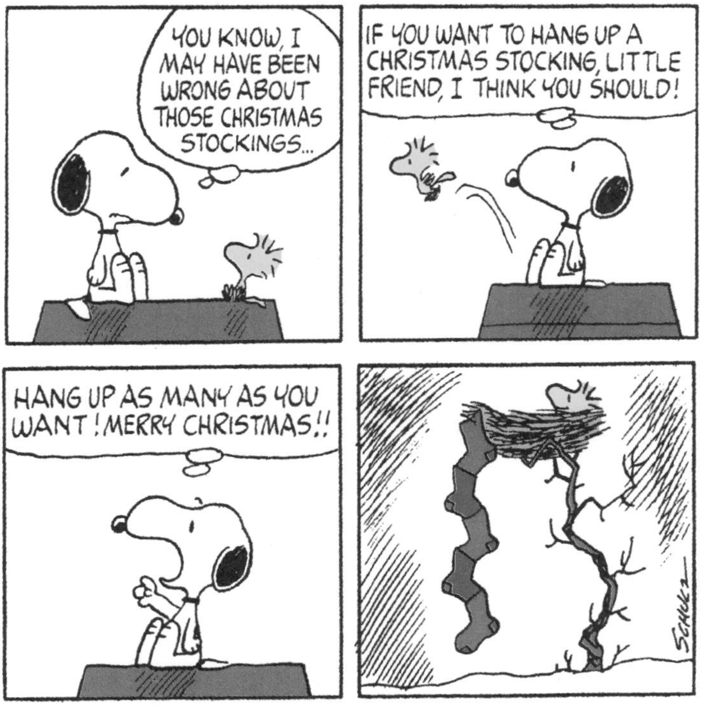
YOU KNOW, I MAY HAVE BEEN WRONG ABOUT THOSE CHRISTMAS STOCKINGS...
IF YOU WANT TO HANG UP A CHRISTMAS STOCKING, LITTLE FRIEND, I THINK YOU SHOULD!
HANG UP AS MANY AS YOU WANT! MERRY CHRISTMAS!!
SCHULZ

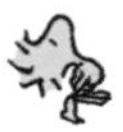

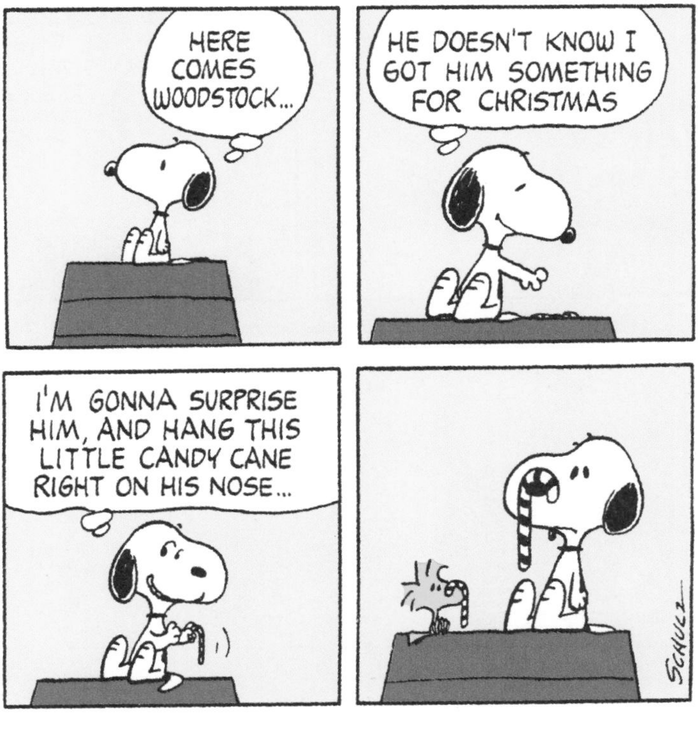
HERE COMES WOODSTOCK...
HE DOESN'T KNOW I GOT HIM SOMETHING FOR CHRISTMAS
I'M GONNA SURPRISE HIM, AND HANG THIS LITTLE CANDY CANE RIGHT ON HIS NOSE...
SCHULZ

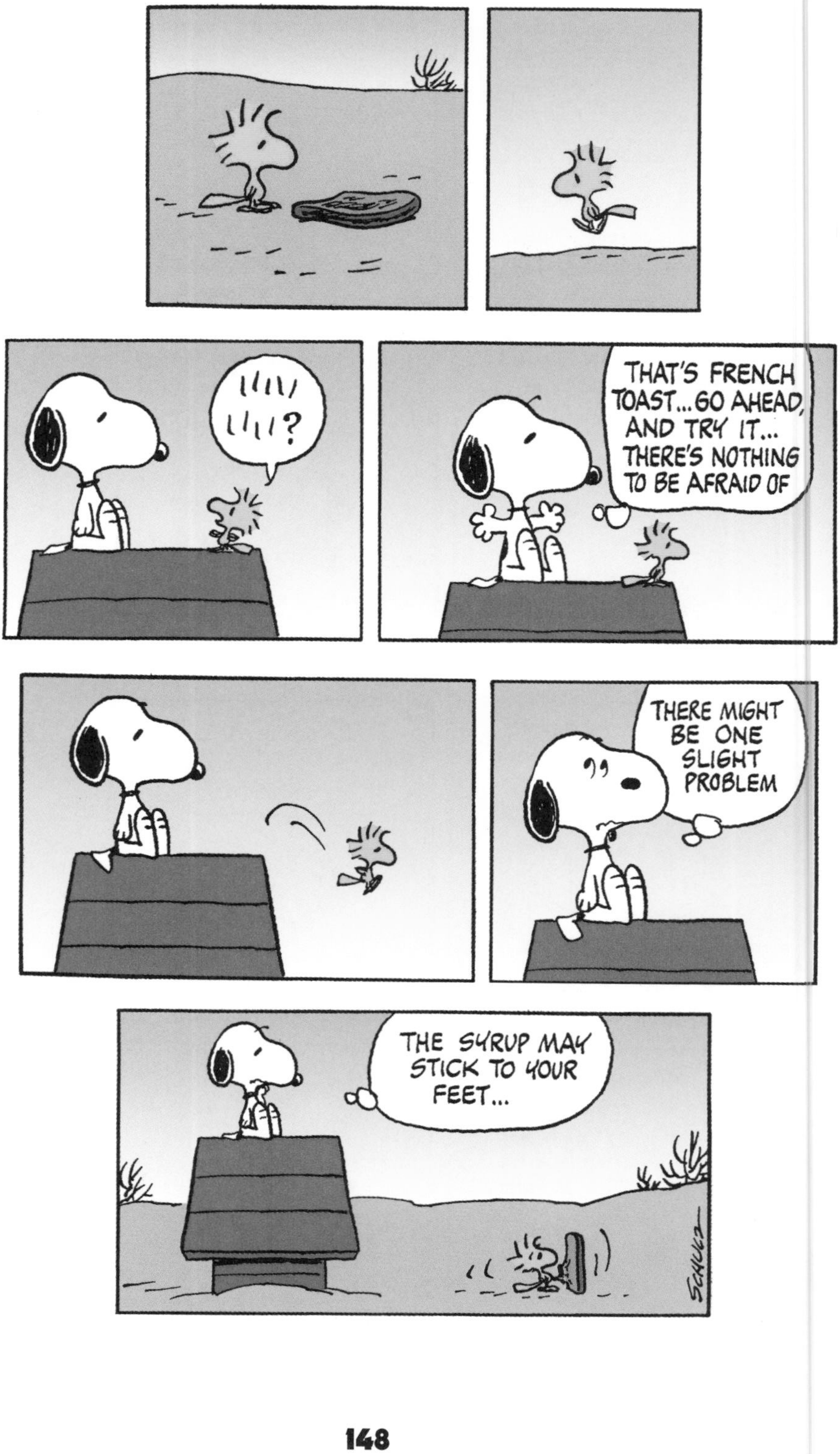
THAT'S FRENCH TOAST...GO AHEAD, AND TRY IT... THERE'S NOTHING TO BE AFRAID OF
THERE MIGHT BE ONE SLIGHT PROBLEM
THE SYRUP MAY STICK TO YOUR FEET...
SCHULZ

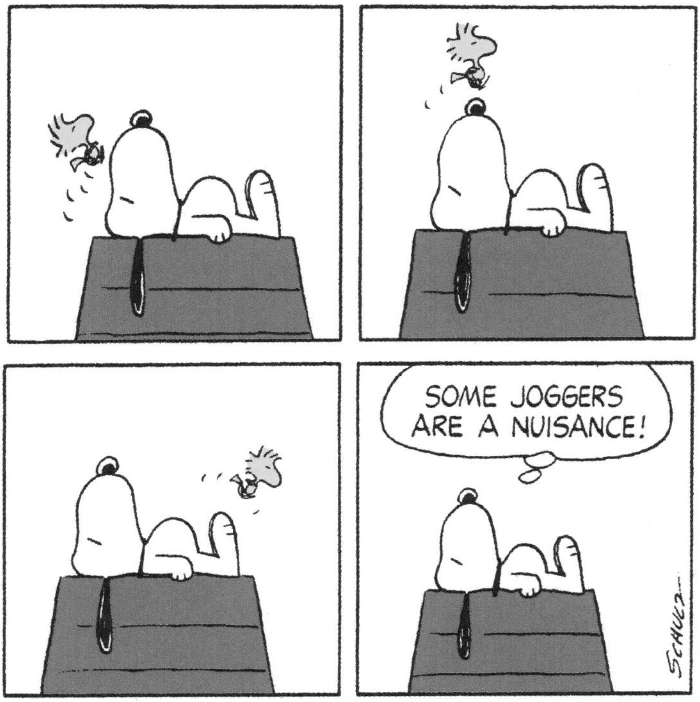
SOME JOGGERS ARE A NUISANCE!
SCHULZ

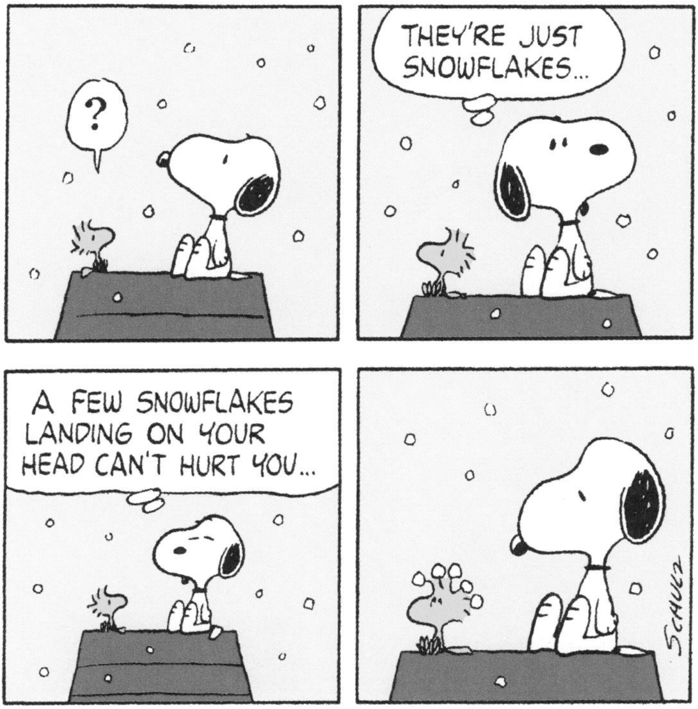
?
THEY'RE JUST SNOWFLAKES...
A FEW SNOWFLAKES LANDING ON YOUR HEAD CAN'T HURT YOU...
SCHULZ

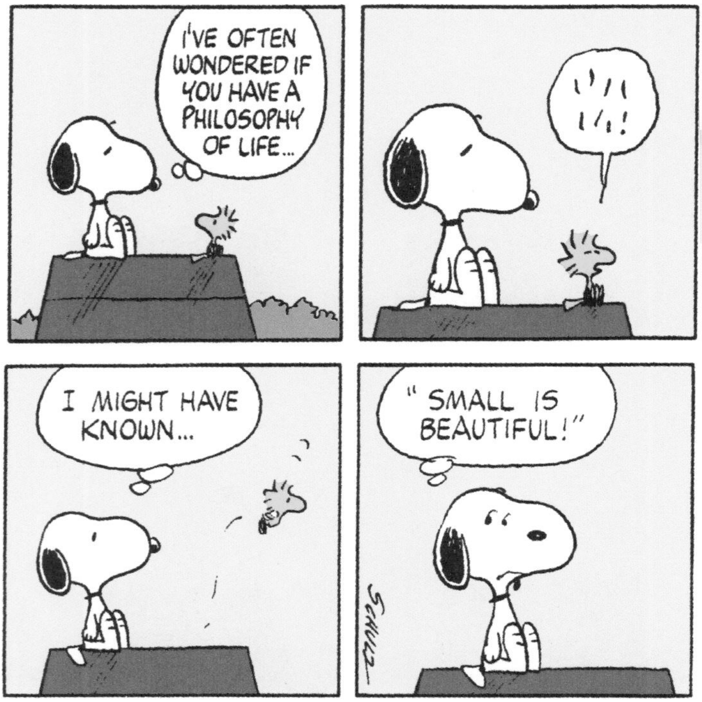
I'VE OFTEN WONDERED IF YOU HAVE A PHILOSOPHY OF LIFE...
I MIGHT HAVE KNOWN...
"SMALL IS BEAUTIFUL!"
SCHULZ

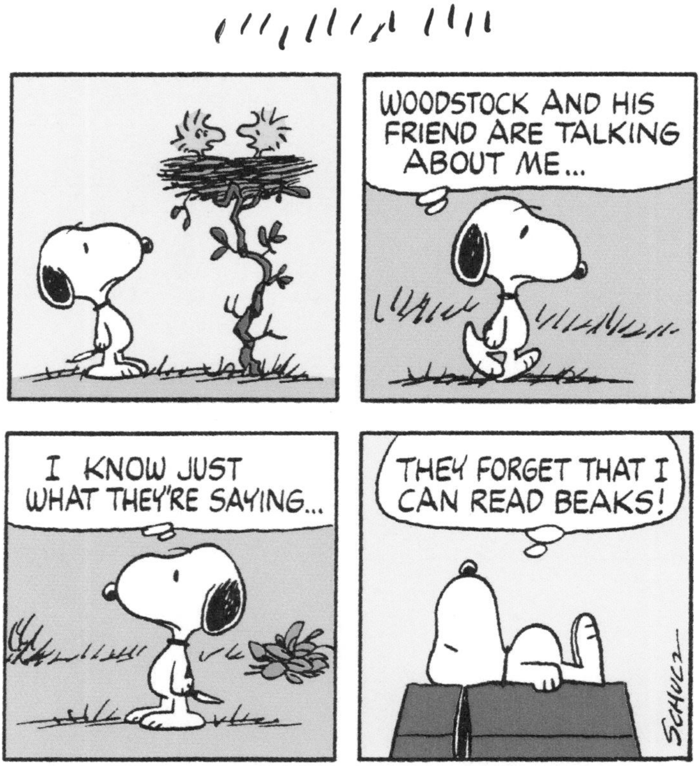
WOODSTOCK AND HIS FRIEND ARE TALKING ABOUT ME...
I KNOW JUST WHAT THEY'RE SAYING...
THEY FORGET THAT I CAN READ BEAKS!
SCHULZ

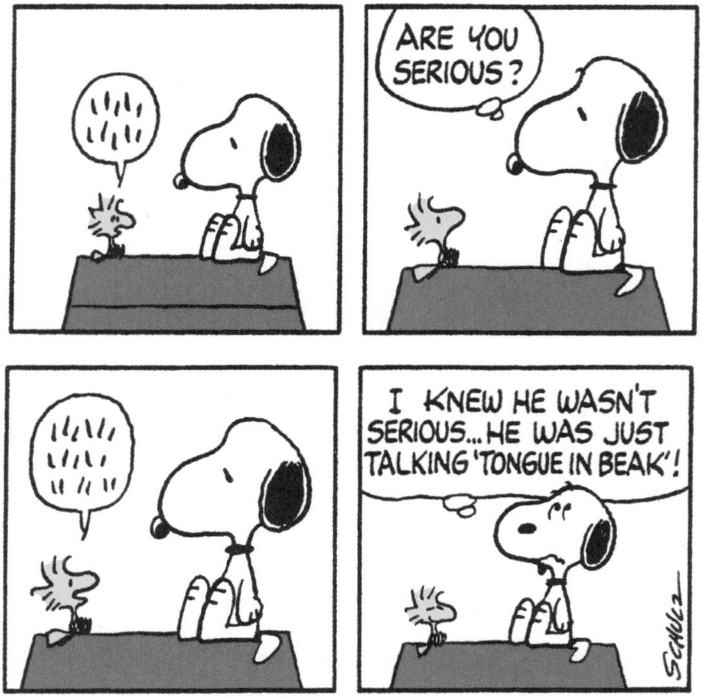
ARE YOU SERIOUS?
I KNEW HE WASN'T SERIOUS...HE WAS JUST TALKING 'TONGUE IN BEAK'!
SCHULZ

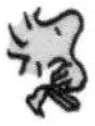

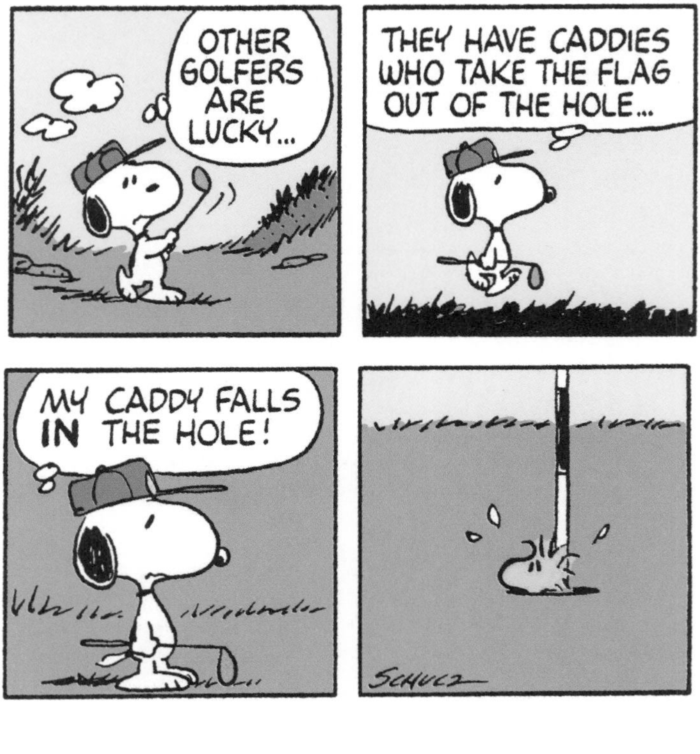
OTHER GOLFERS ARE LUCKY...
THEY HAVE CADDIES WHO TAKE THE FLAG OUT OF THE HOLE...
MY CADDY FALLS **IN** THE HOLE!
SCHULZ

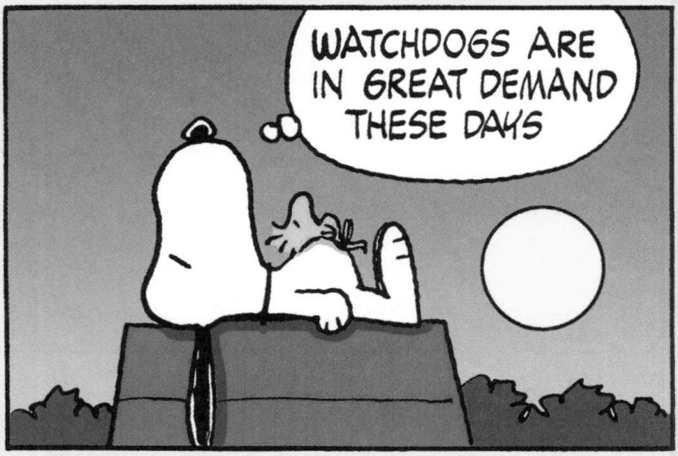
WATCHDOGS ARE IN GREAT DEMAND THESE DAYS

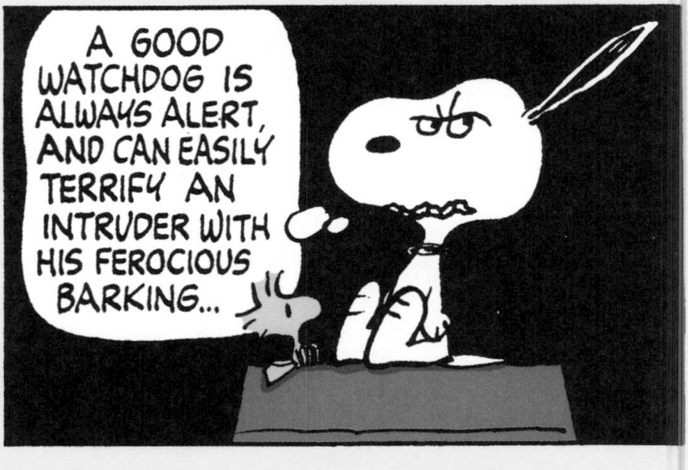
A GOOD WATCHDOG IS ALWAYS ALERT, AND CAN EASILY TERRIFY AN INTRUDER WITH HIS FEROCIOUS BARKING...

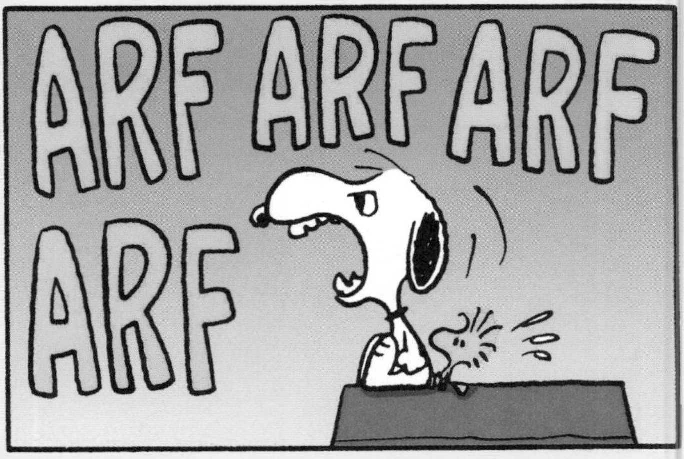
ARF ARF ARF ARF

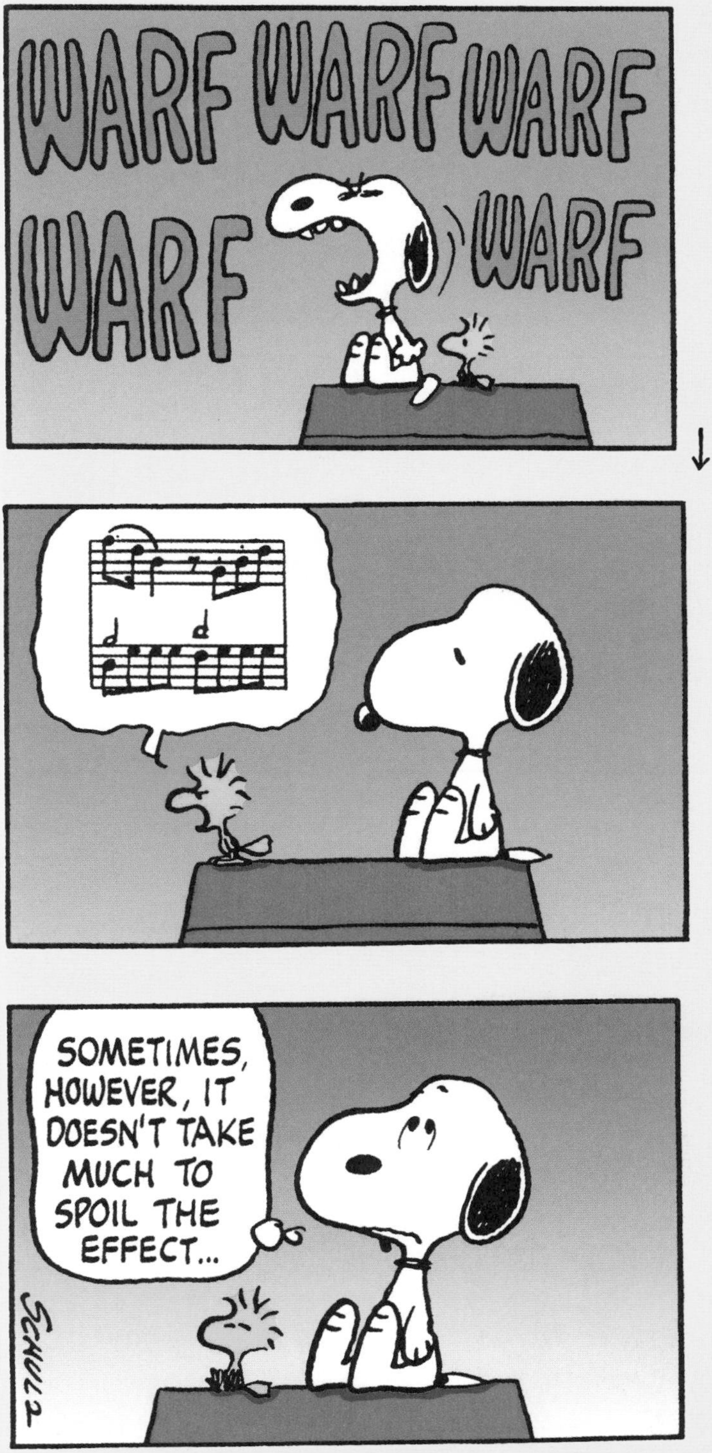
WARF WARF WARF
WARF
WARF
SOMETIMES, HOWEVER, IT DOESN'T TAKE MUCH TO SPOIL THE EFFECT...
SCHULZ

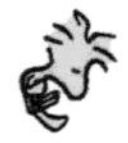

I WONDER HOW MANY YARDS IT IS TO THE GREEN...
TWO HUNDRED AND FIFTY-ONE YARDS!

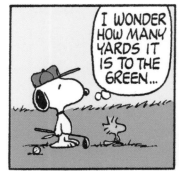

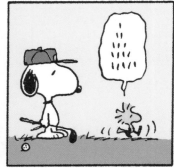

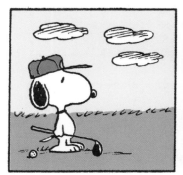

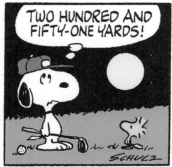

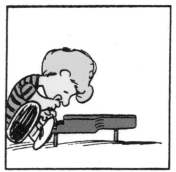

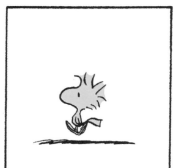

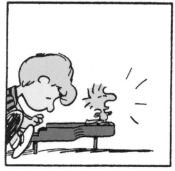

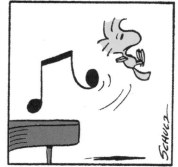

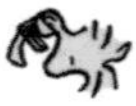

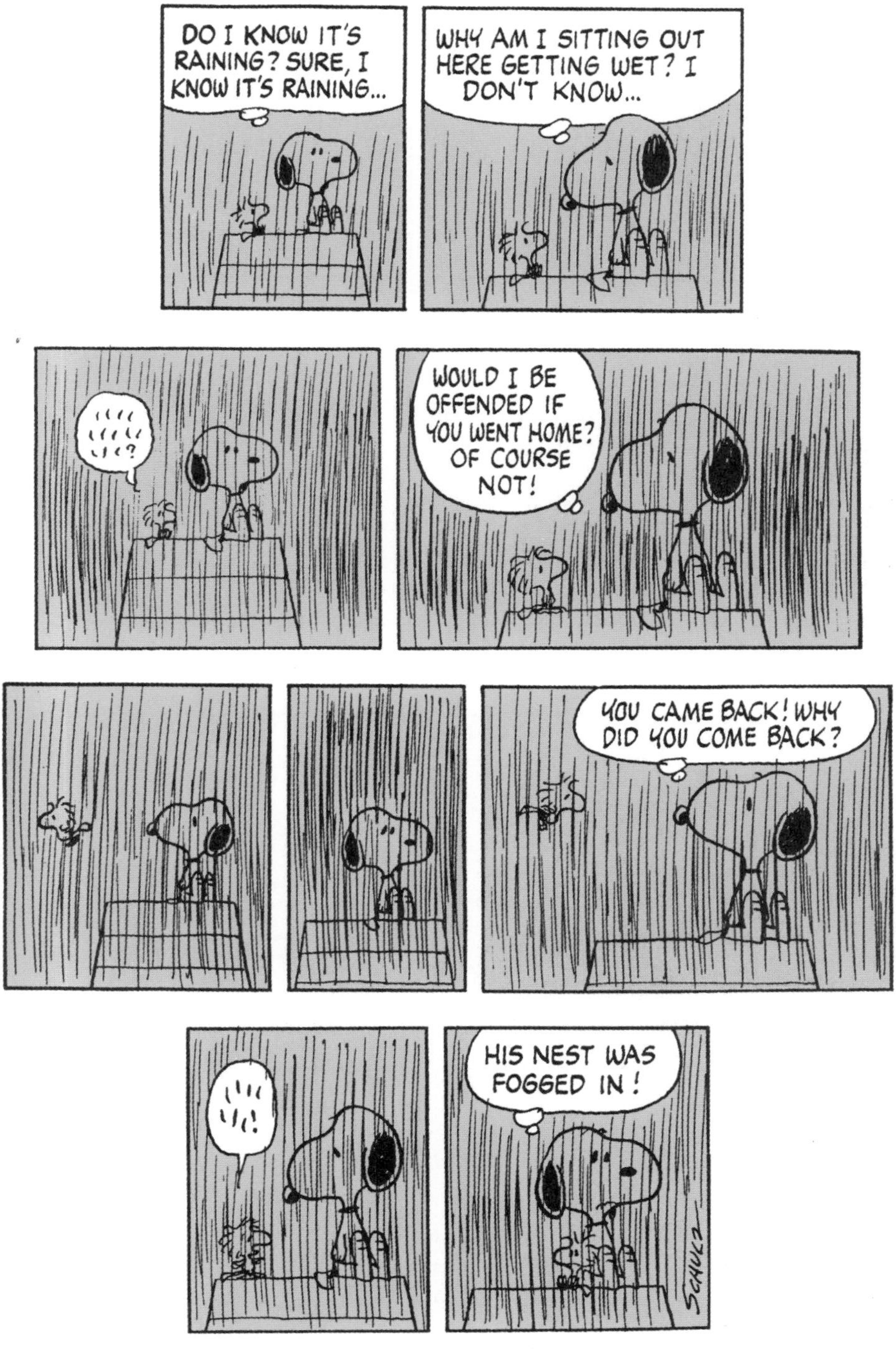
DO I KNOW IT'S RAINING? SURE, I KNOW IT'S RAINING...
WHY AM I SITTING OUT HERE GETTING WET? I DON'T KNOW...
WOULD I BE OFFENDED IF YOU WENT HOME? OF COURSE NOT!
YOU CAME BACK! WHY DID YOU COME BACK?
HIS NEST WAS FOGGED IN!
SCHULZ

SCHULZ

SCHULZ

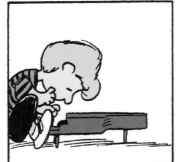

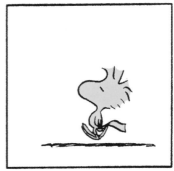

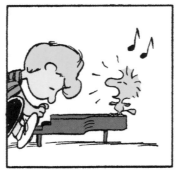

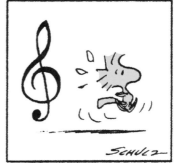

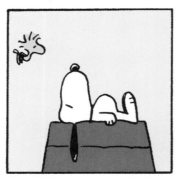

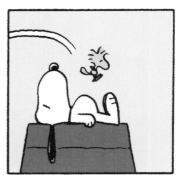

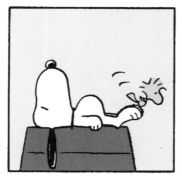

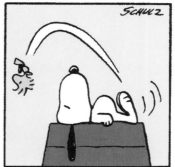

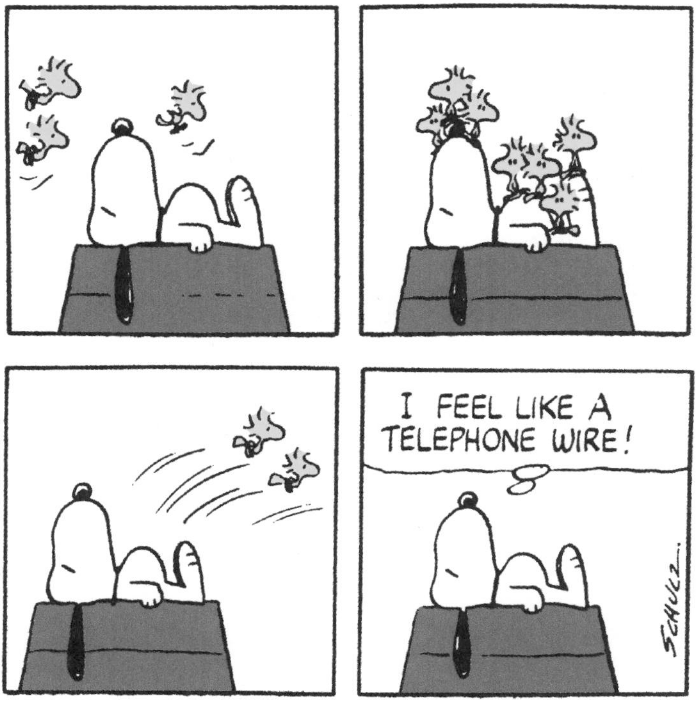
I FEEL LIKE A TELEPHONE WIRE!
SCHULZ

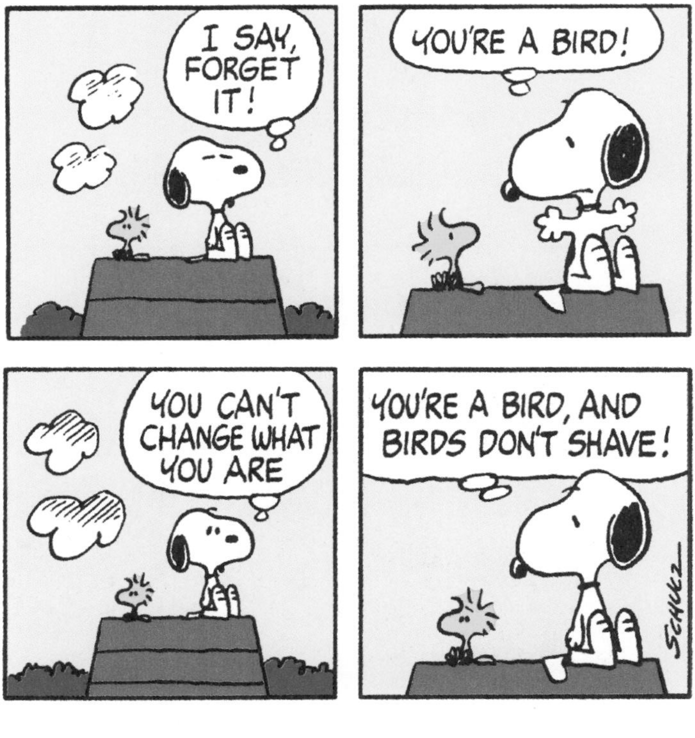
I SAY, FORGET IT!
YOU'RE A BIRD!
YOU CAN'T CHANGE WHAT YOU ARE
YOU'RE A BIRD, AND BIRDS DON'T SHAVE!
SCHULZ

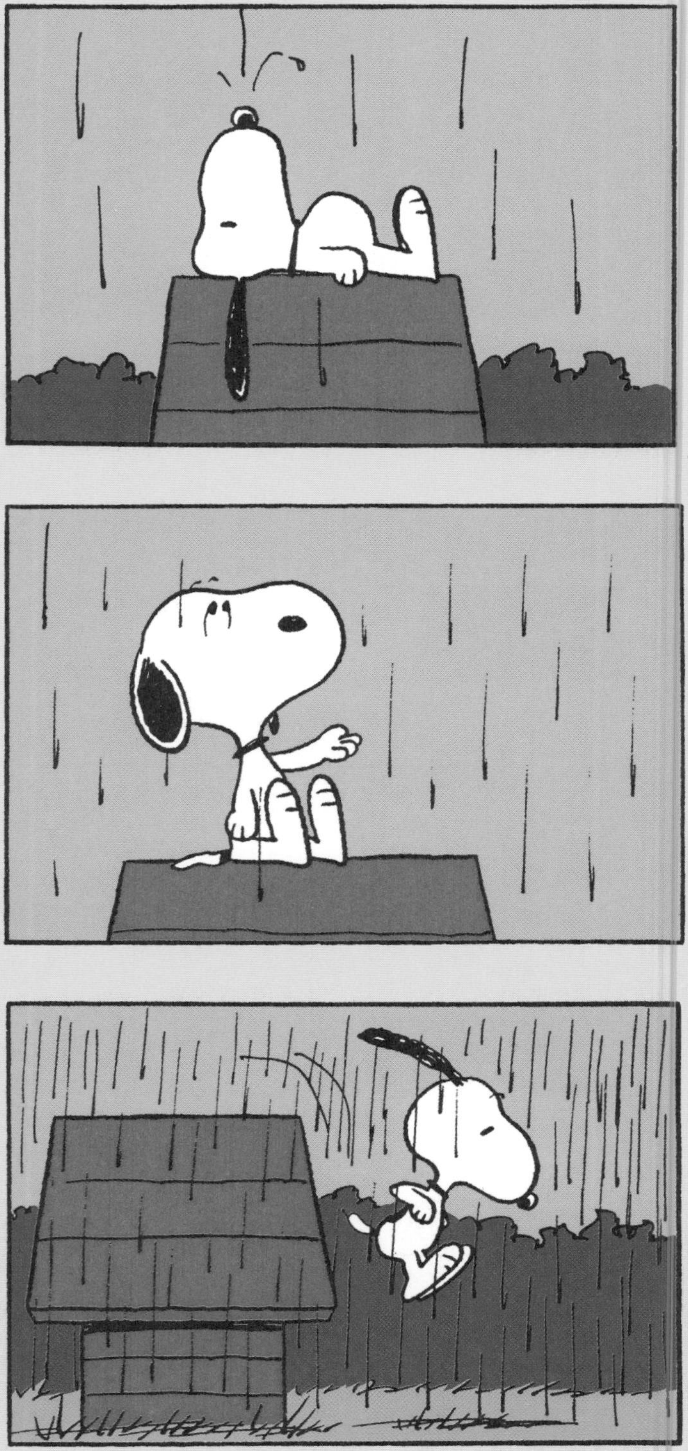

SCHULZ

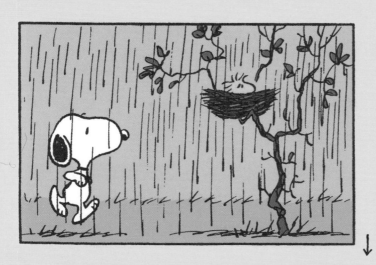

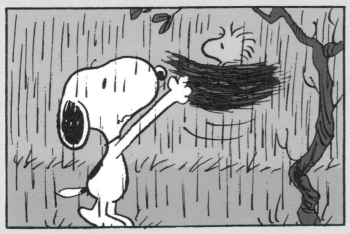

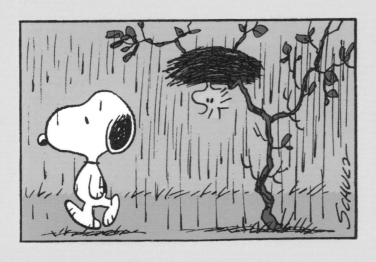

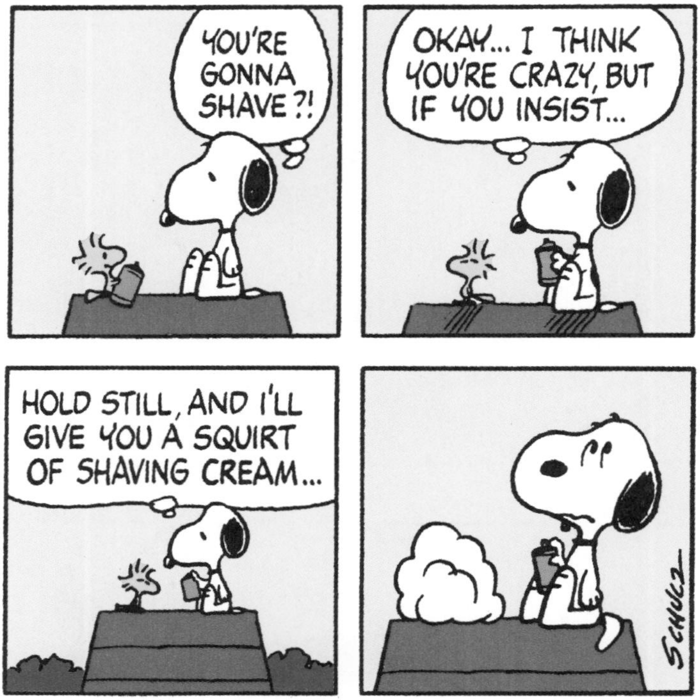
YOU'RE GONNA SHAVE ?!
OKAY... I THINK YOU'RE CRAZY, BUT IF YOU INSIST...
HOLD STILL, AND I'LL GIVE YOU A SQUIRT OF SHAVING CREAM...
SCHULZ

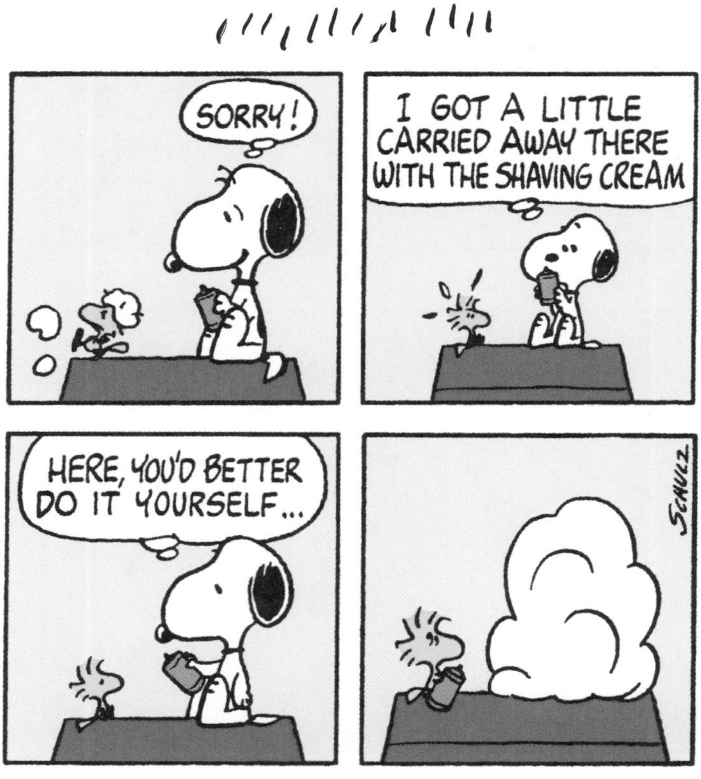
SORRY!
I GOT A LITTLE CARRIED AWAY THERE WITH THE SHAVING CREAM
HERE, YOU'D BETTER DO IT YOURSELF...
SCHULZ

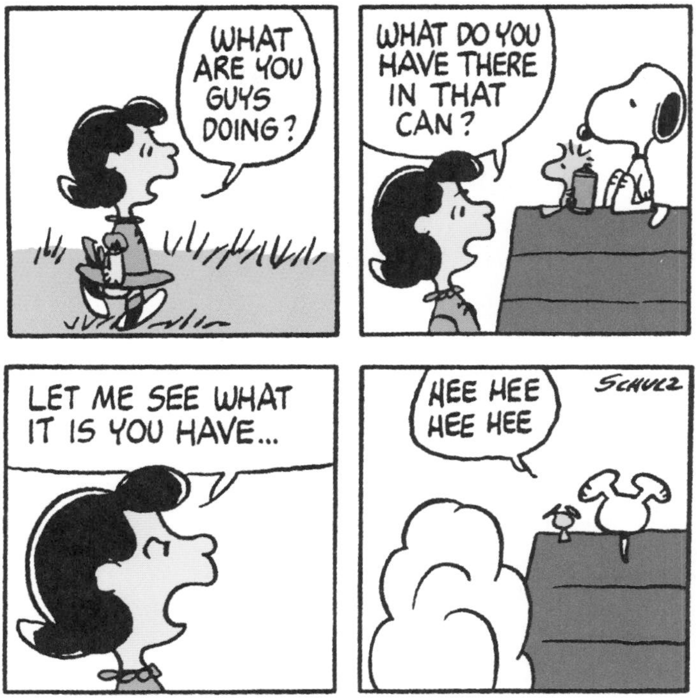
WHAT ARE YOU GUYS DOING?
WHAT DO YOU HAVE THERE IN THAT CAN?
LET ME SEE WHAT IT IS YOU HAVE...
SCHULZ
HEE HEE HEE HEE

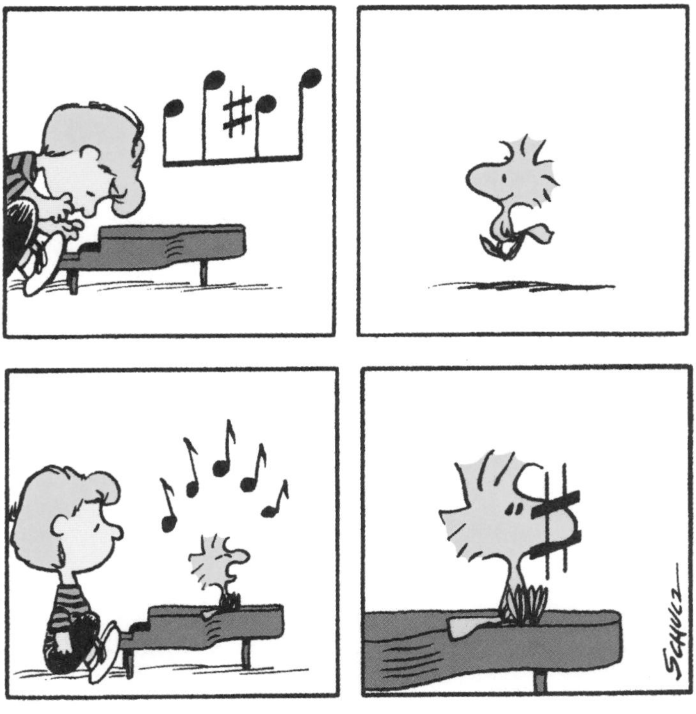
SCHULZ

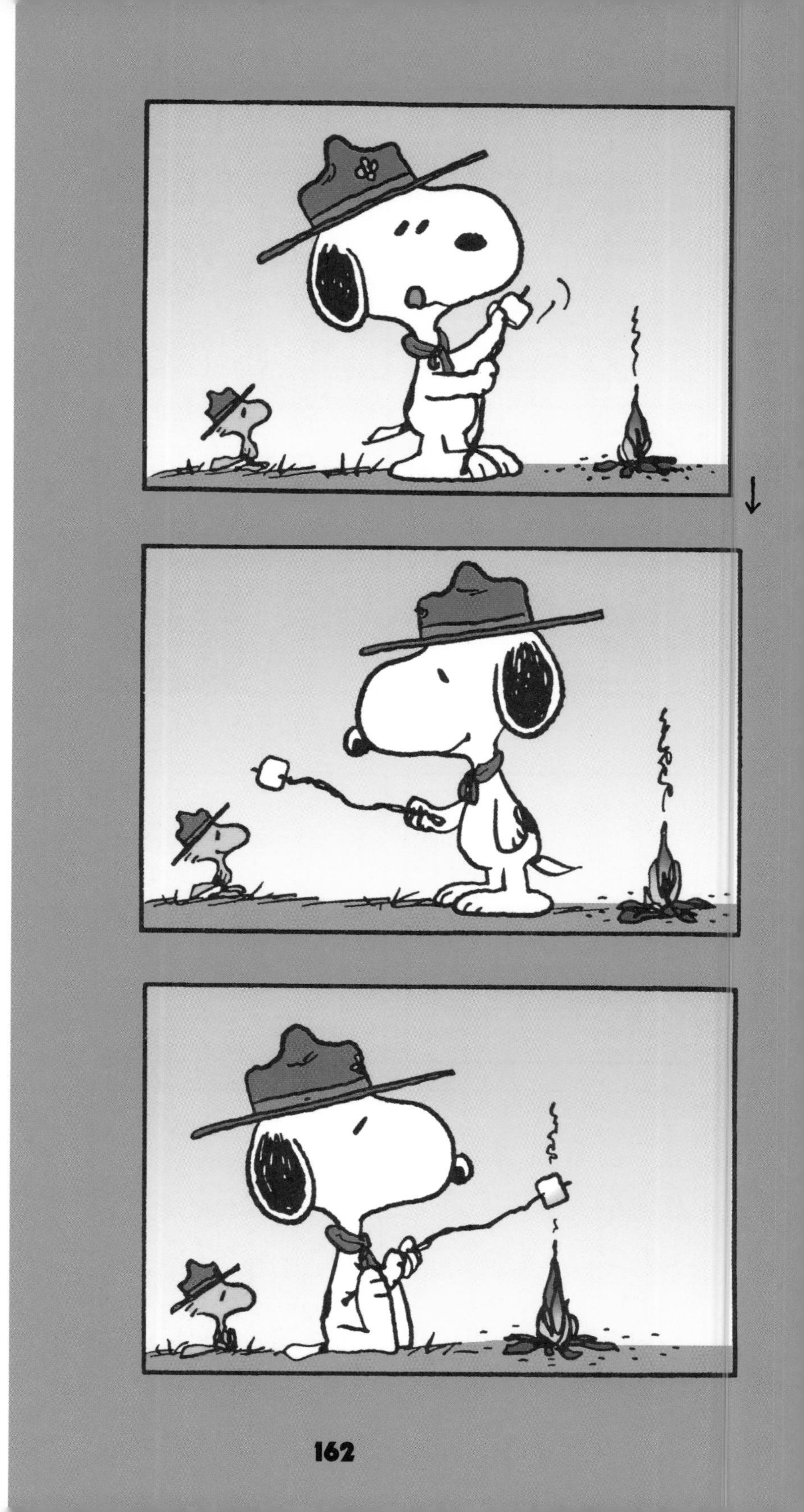

SCHULZ

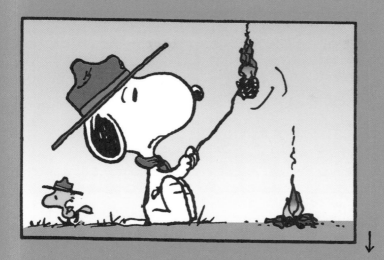

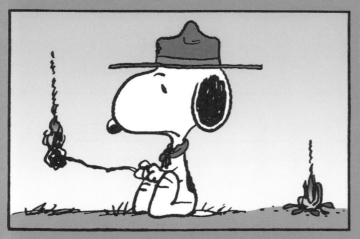

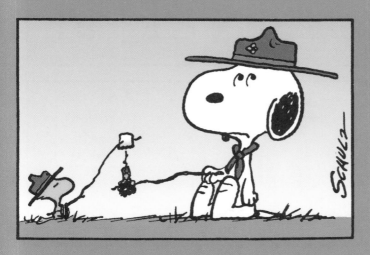

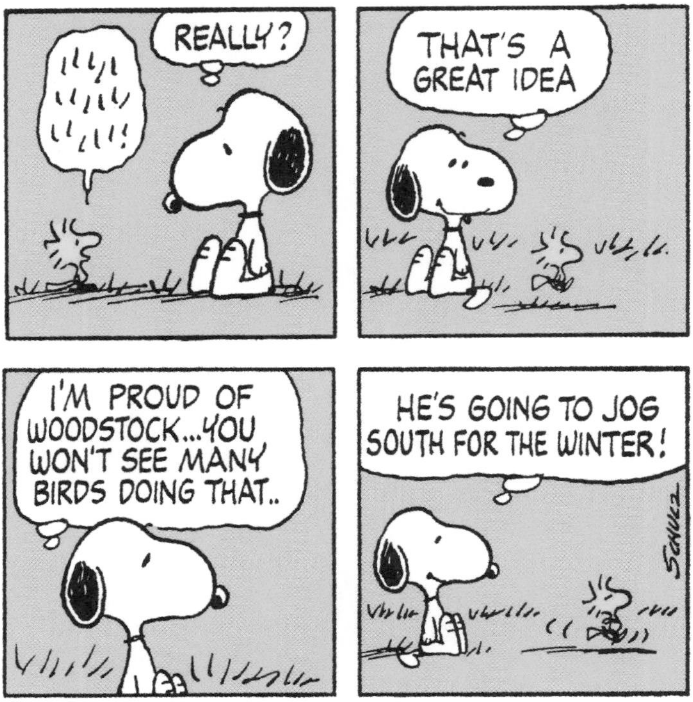
REALLY?
THAT'S A GREAT IDEA
I'M PROUD OF WOODSTOCK...YOU WON'T SEE MANY BIRDS DOING THAT..
HE'S GOING TO JOG SOUTH FOR THE WINTER!
SCHULZ

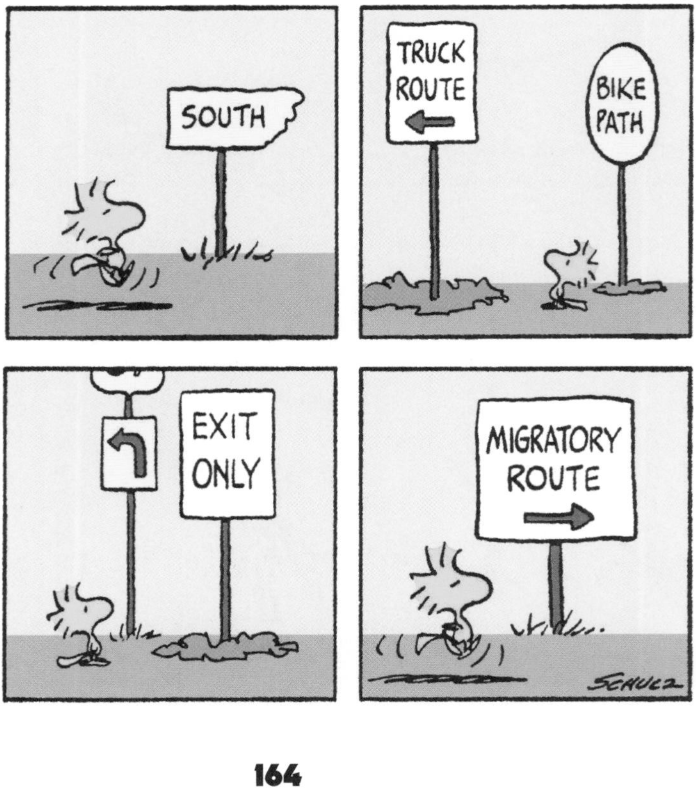
SOUTH
TRUCK ROUTE
BIKE PATH
EXIT ONLY
MIGRATORY ROUTE
SCHULZ

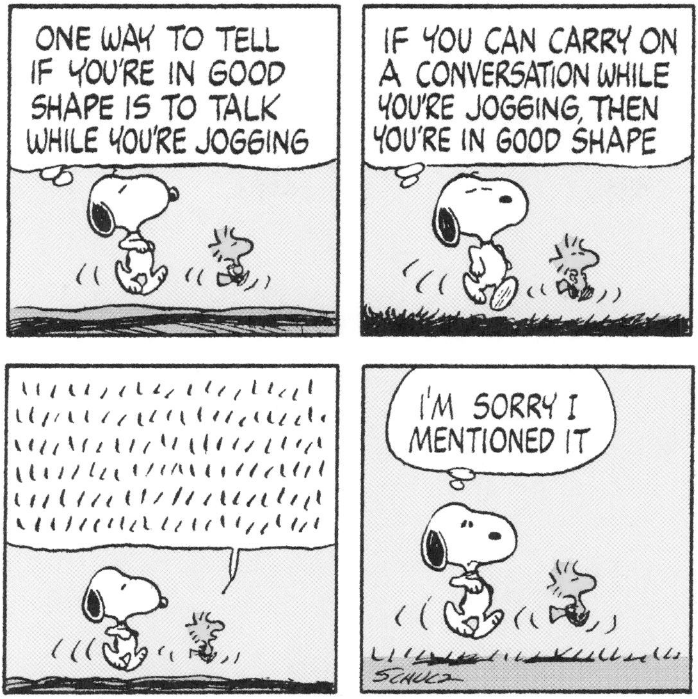
ONE WAY TO TELL IF YOU'RE IN GOOD SHAPE IS TO TALK WHILE YOU'RE JOGGING
IF YOU CAN CARRY ON A CONVERSATION WHILE YOU'RE JOGGING, THEN YOU'RE IN GOOD SHAPE
I'M SORRY I MENTIONED IT
SCHULZ

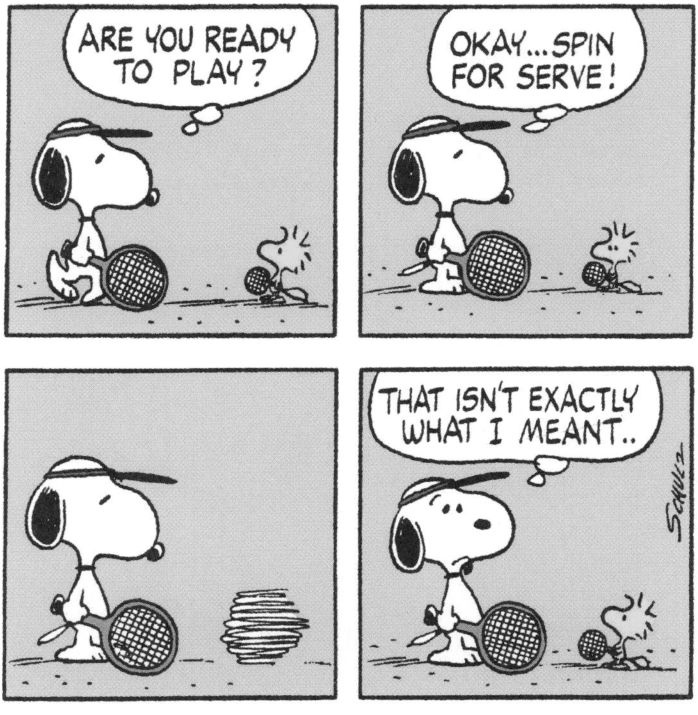
ARE YOU READY TO PLAY?
OKAY...SPIN FOR SERVE!
THAT ISN'T EXACTLY WHAT I MEANT..
SCHULZ

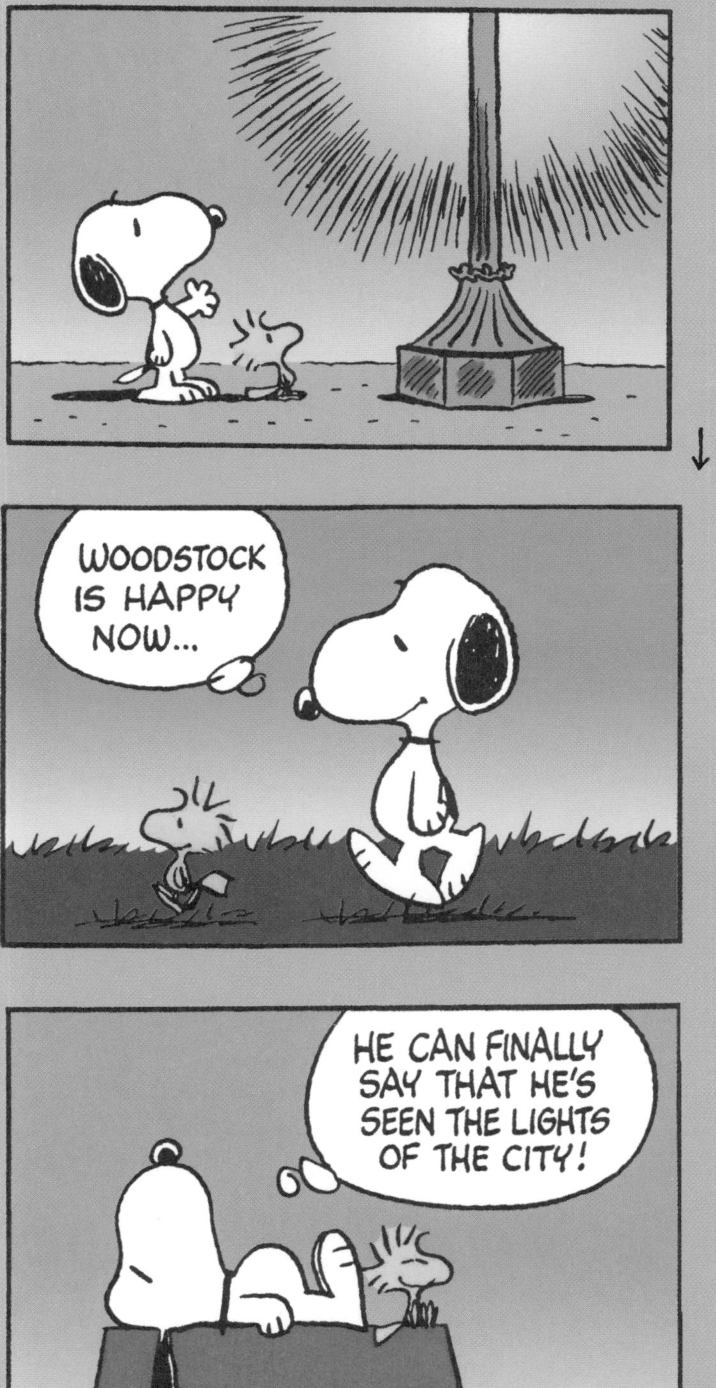
WOODSTOCK IS HAPPY NOW...
HE CAN FINALLY SAY THAT HE'S SEEN THE LIGHTS OF THE CITY!
SCHULZ

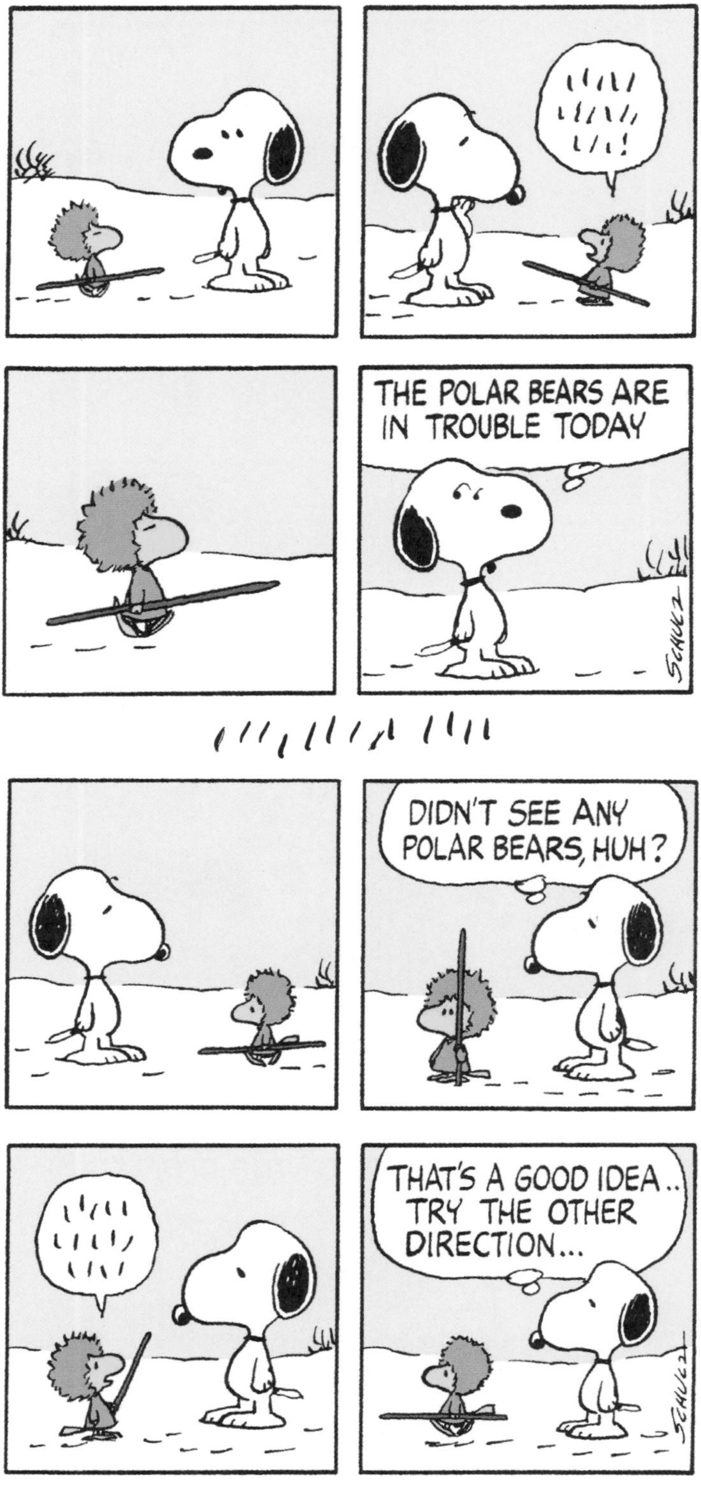
THE POLAR BEARS ARE IN TROUBLE TODAY
DIDN'T SEE ANY POLAR BEARS, HUH?
THAT'S A GOOD IDEA.. TRY THE OTHER DIRECTION...

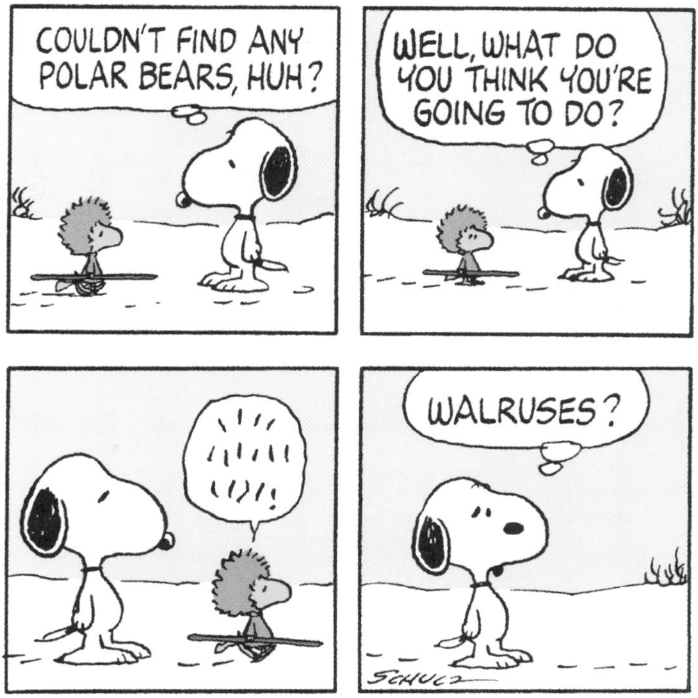
COULDN'T FIND ANY POLAR BEARS, HUH?
WELL, WHAT DO YOU THINK YOU'RE GOING TO DO?
WALRUSES?
SCHULZ

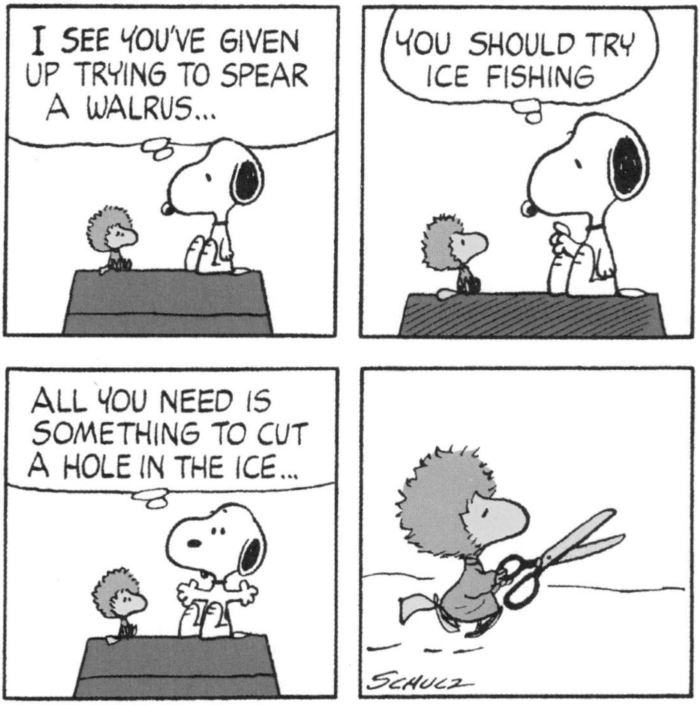
I SEE YOU'VE GIVEN UP TRYING TO SPEAR A WALRUS...
YOU SHOULD TRY ICE FISHING
ALL YOU NEED IS SOMETHING TO CUT A HOLE IN THE ICE...
SCHULZ

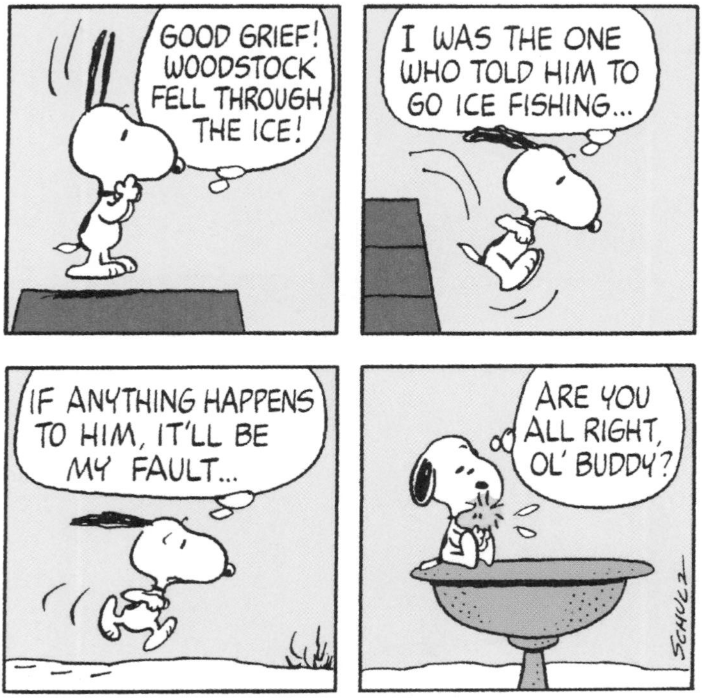
GOOD GRIEF! WOODSTOCK FELL THROUGH THE ICE!
I WAS THE ONE WHO TOLD HIM TO GO ICE FISHING...
IF ANYTHING HAPPENS TO HIM, IT'LL BE MY FAULT...
ARE YOU ALL RIGHT, OL' BUDDY?
SCHULZ

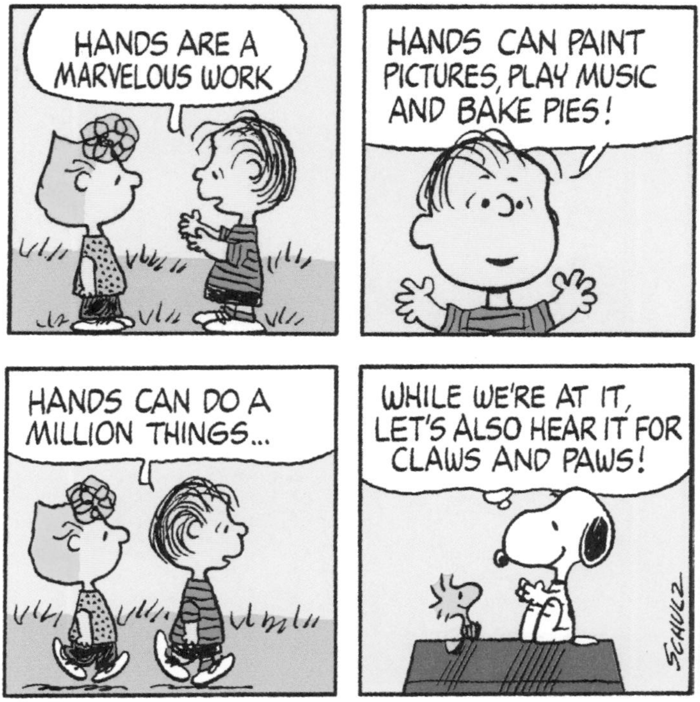
HANDS ARE A MARVELOUS WORK
HANDS CAN PAINT PICTURES, PLAY MUSIC AND BAKE PIES!
HANDS CAN DO A MILLION THINGS...
WHILE WE'RE AT IT, LET'S ALSO HEAR IT FOR CLAWS AND PAWS!
SCHULZ

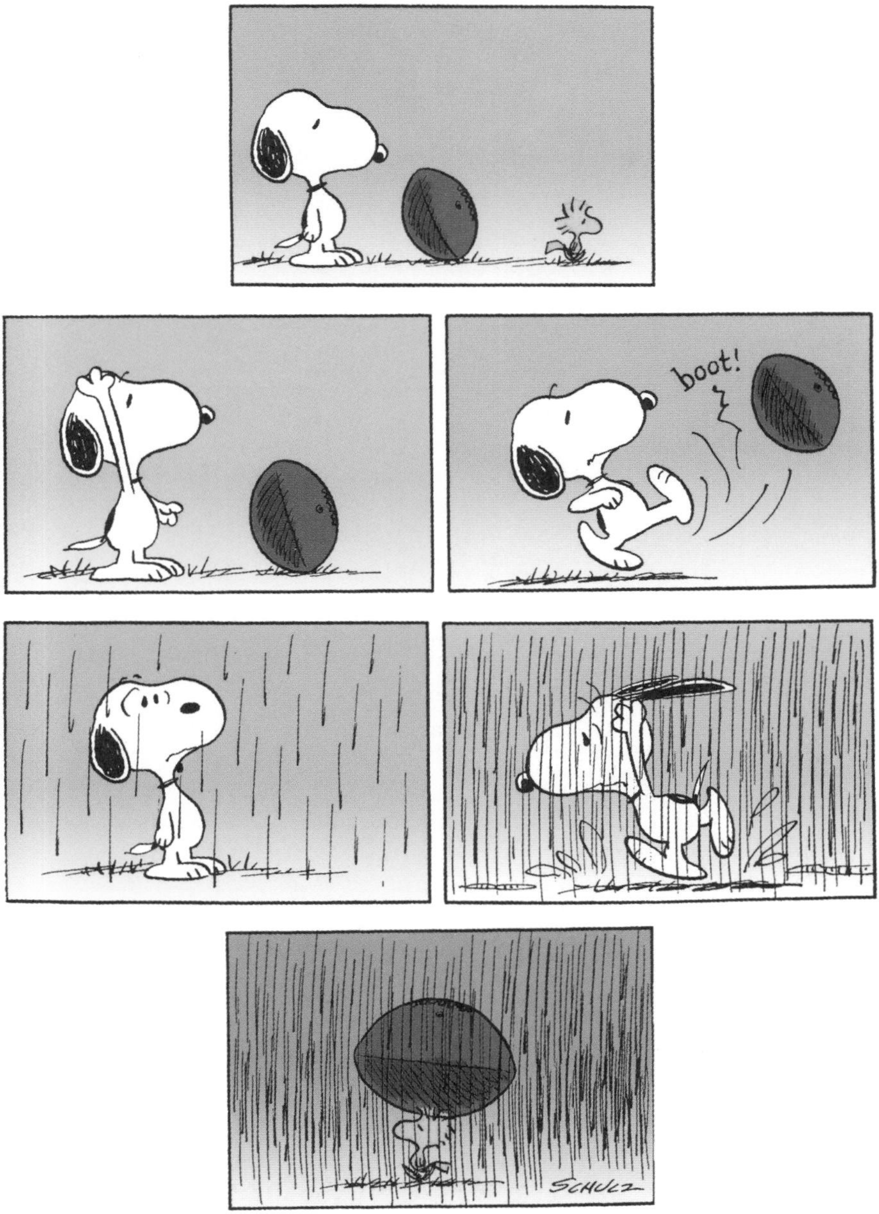
boot!
SCHULZ

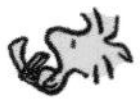

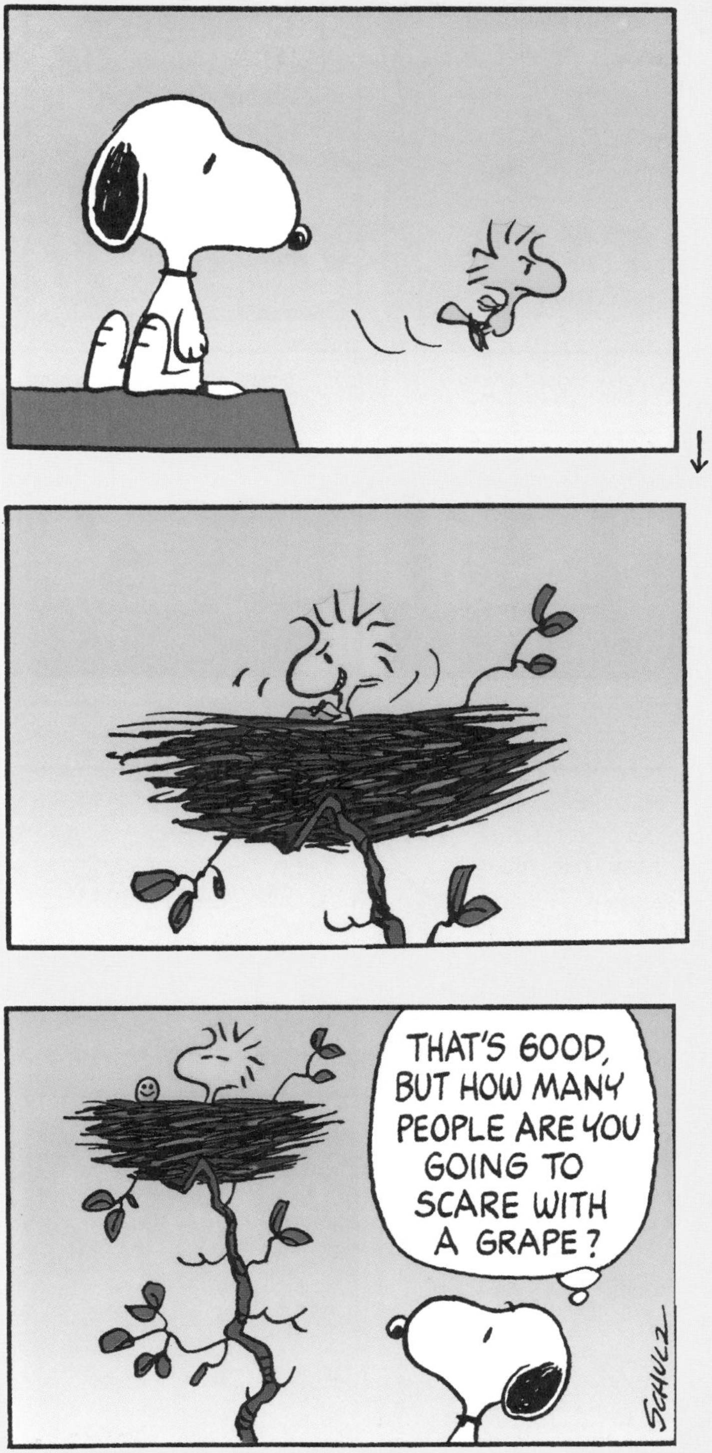
THAT'S GOOD, BUT HOW MANY PEOPLE ARE YOU GOING TO SCARE WITH A GRAPE?
SCHULZ

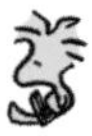

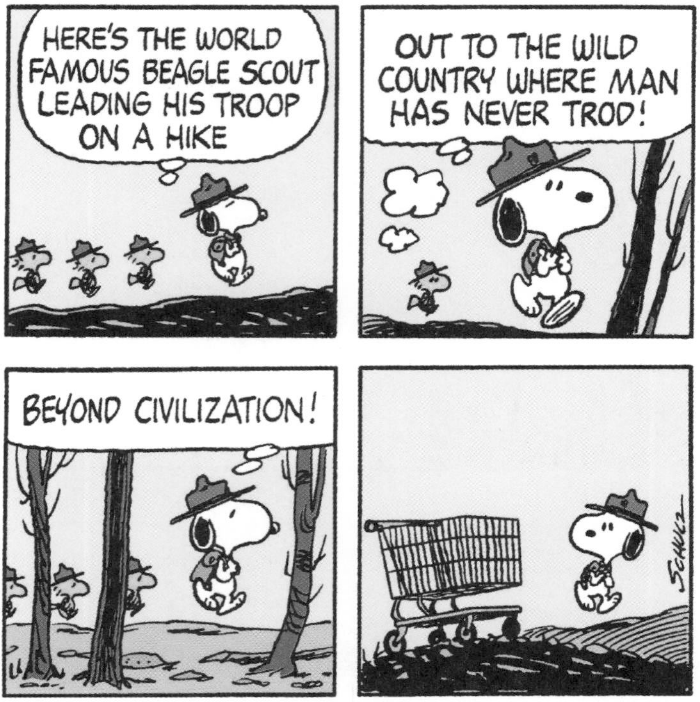
HERE'S THE WORLD FAMOUS BEAGLE SCOUT LEADING HIS TROOP ON A HIKE
OUT TO THE WILD COUNTRY WHERE MAN HAS NEVER TROD!
BEYOND CIVILIZATION!
SCHULZ

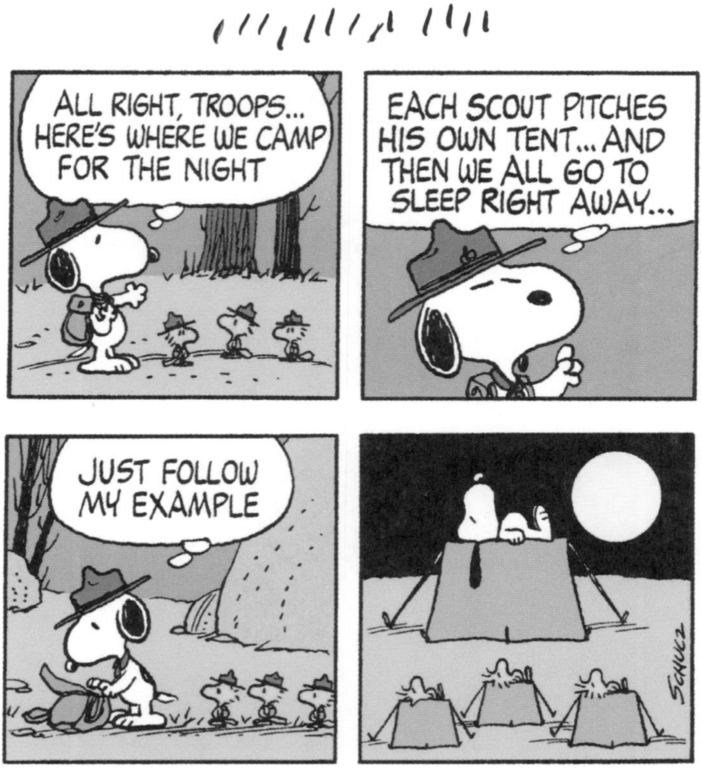
ALL RIGHT, TROOPS... HERE'S WHERE WE CAMP FOR THE NIGHT
EACH SCOUT PITCHES HIS OWN TENT... AND THEN WE ALL GO TO SLEEP RIGHT AWAY...
JUST FOLLOW MY EXAMPLE
SCHULZ

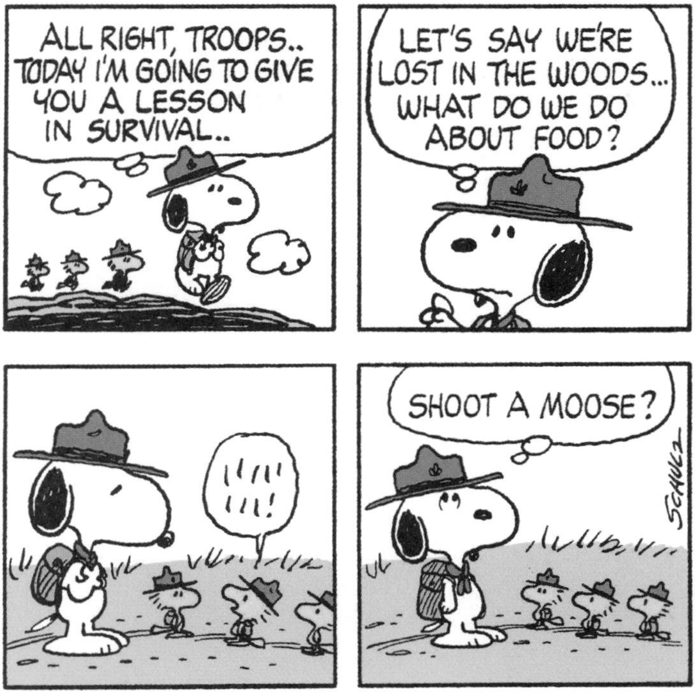
ALL RIGHT, TROOPS.. TODAY I'M GOING TO GIVE YOU A LESSON IN SURVIVAL..
LET'S SAY WE'RE LOST IN THE WOODS... WHAT DO WE DO ABOUT FOOD?
SHOOT A MOOSE?
SCHULZ

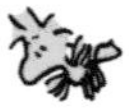

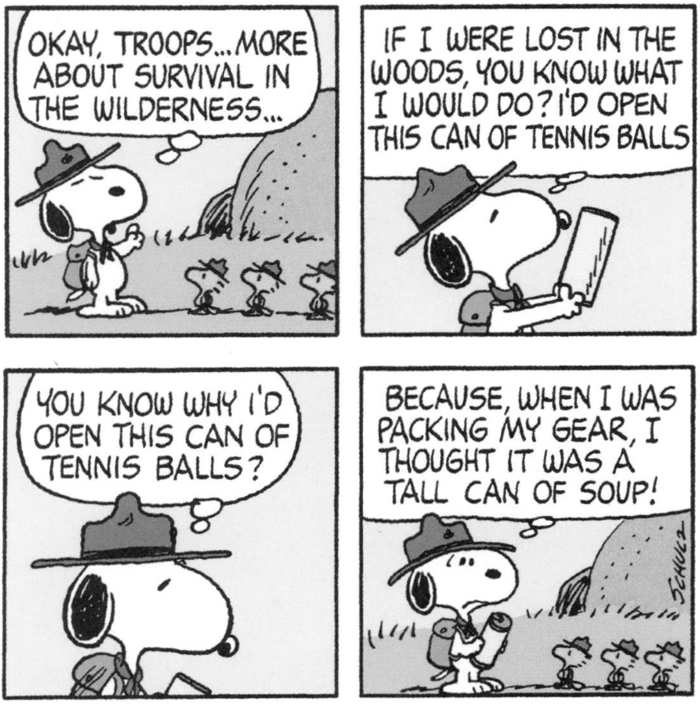
OKAY, TROOPS...MORE ABOUT SURVIVAL IN THE WILDERNESS...
IF I WERE LOST IN THE WOODS, YOU KNOW WHAT I WOULD DO? I'D OPEN THIS CAN OF TENNIS BALLS
YOU KNOW WHY I'D OPEN THIS CAN OF TENNIS BALLS?
BECAUSE, WHEN I WAS PACKING MY GEAR, I THOUGHT IT WAS A TALL CAN OF SOUP!
SCHULZ

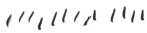

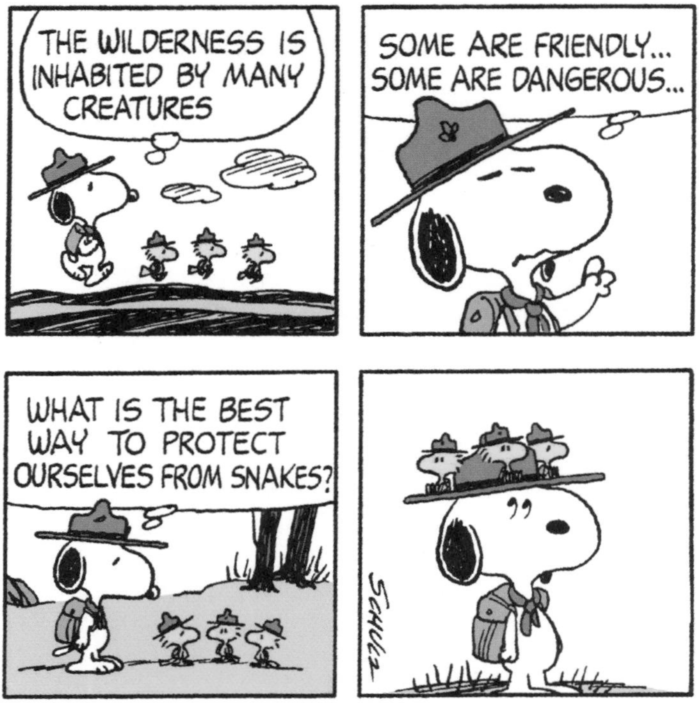
THE WILDERNESS IS INHABITED BY MANY CREATURES
SOME ARE FRIENDLY... SOME ARE DANGEROUS...
WHAT IS THE BEST WAY TO PROTECT OURSELVES FROM SNAKES?

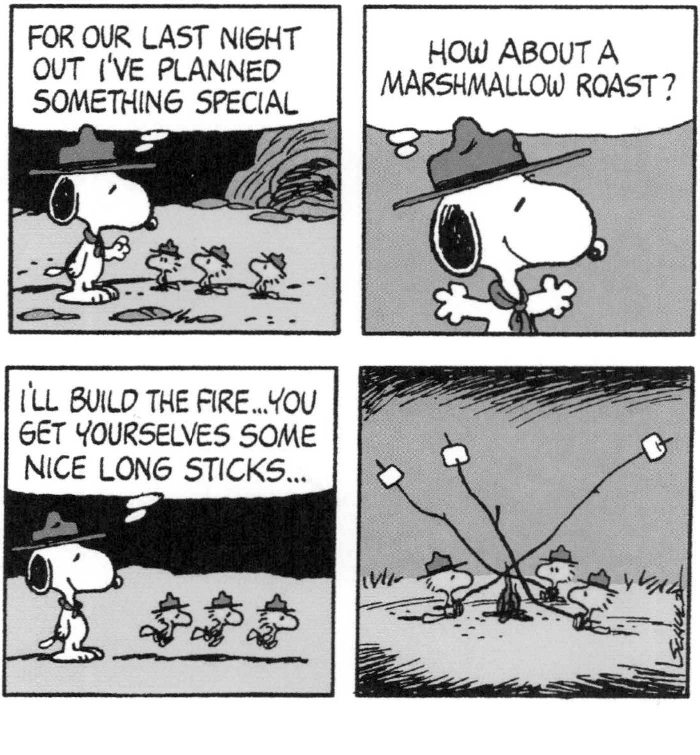
FOR OUR LAST NIGHT OUT I'VE PLANNED SOMETHING SPECIAL
HOW ABOUT A MARSHMALLOW ROAST?
I'LL BUILD THE FIRE...YOU GET YOURSELVES SOME NICE LONG STICKS...

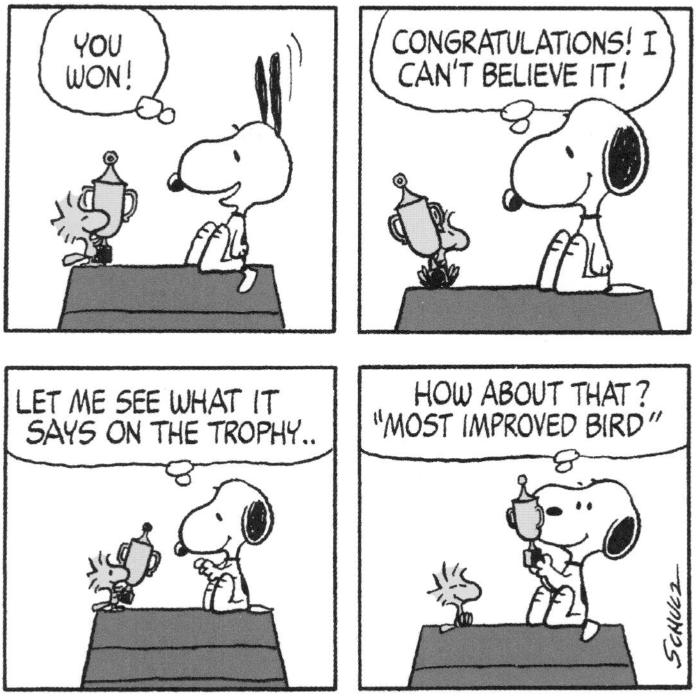
YOU WON!
CONGRATULATIONS! I CAN'T BELIEVE IT!
LET ME SEE WHAT IT SAYS ON THE TROPHY..
HOW ABOUT THAT? "MOST IMPROVED BIRD"
SCHULZ

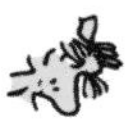

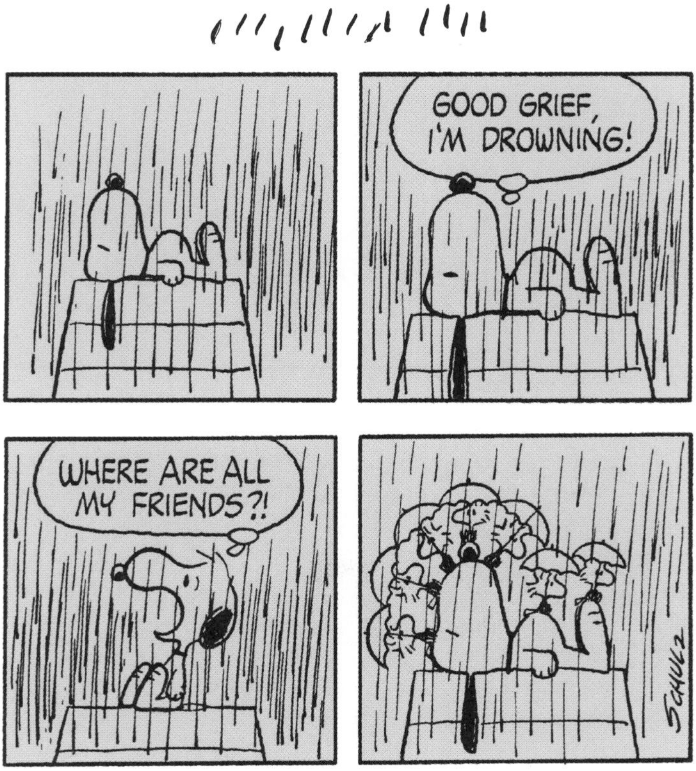
GOOD GRIEF, I'M DROWNING!
WHERE ARE ALL MY FRIENDS?!
SCHULZ

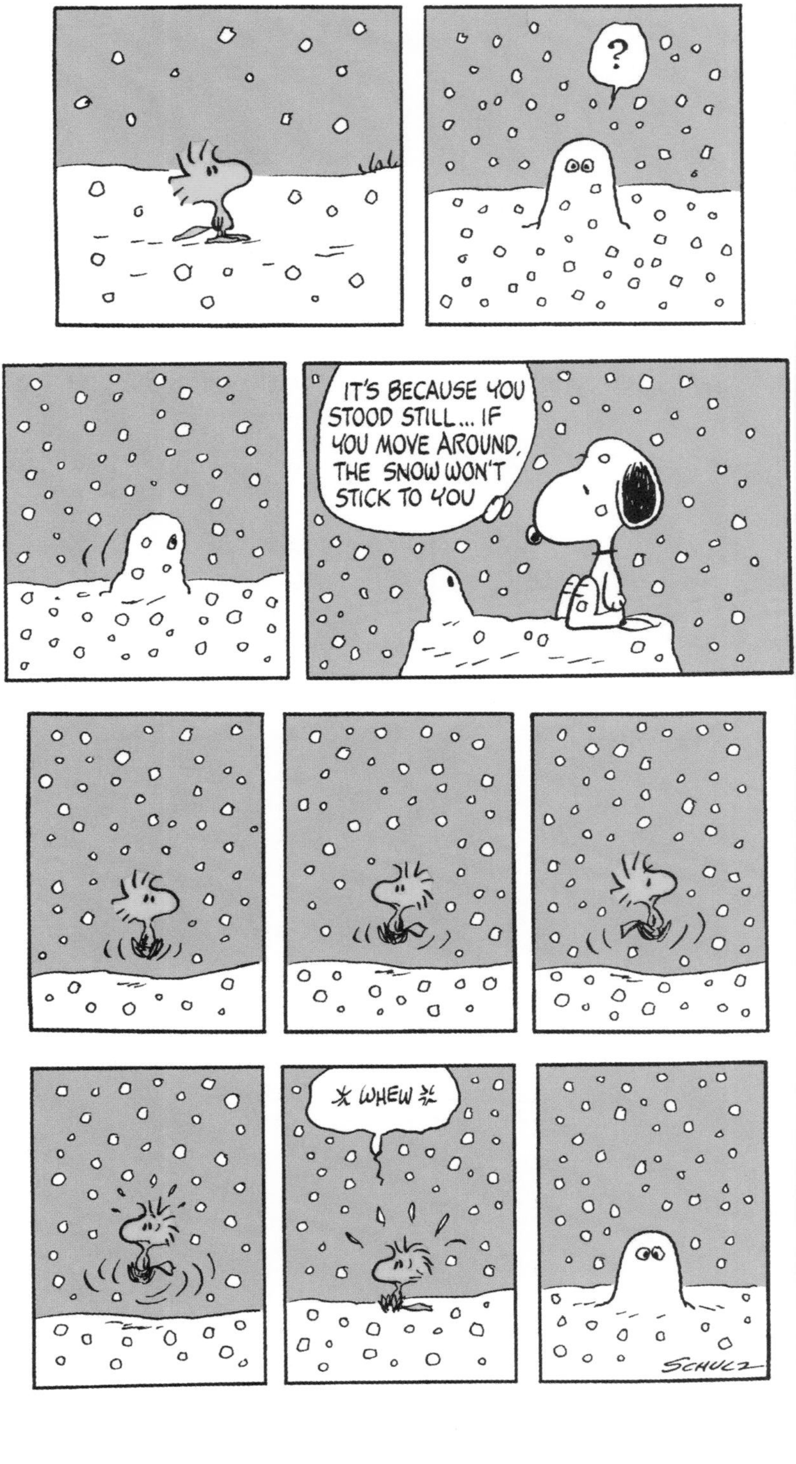
?
IT'S BECAUSE YOU STOOD STILL... IF YOU MOVE AROUND, THE SNOW WON'T STICK TO YOU
WHEW
SCHULZ

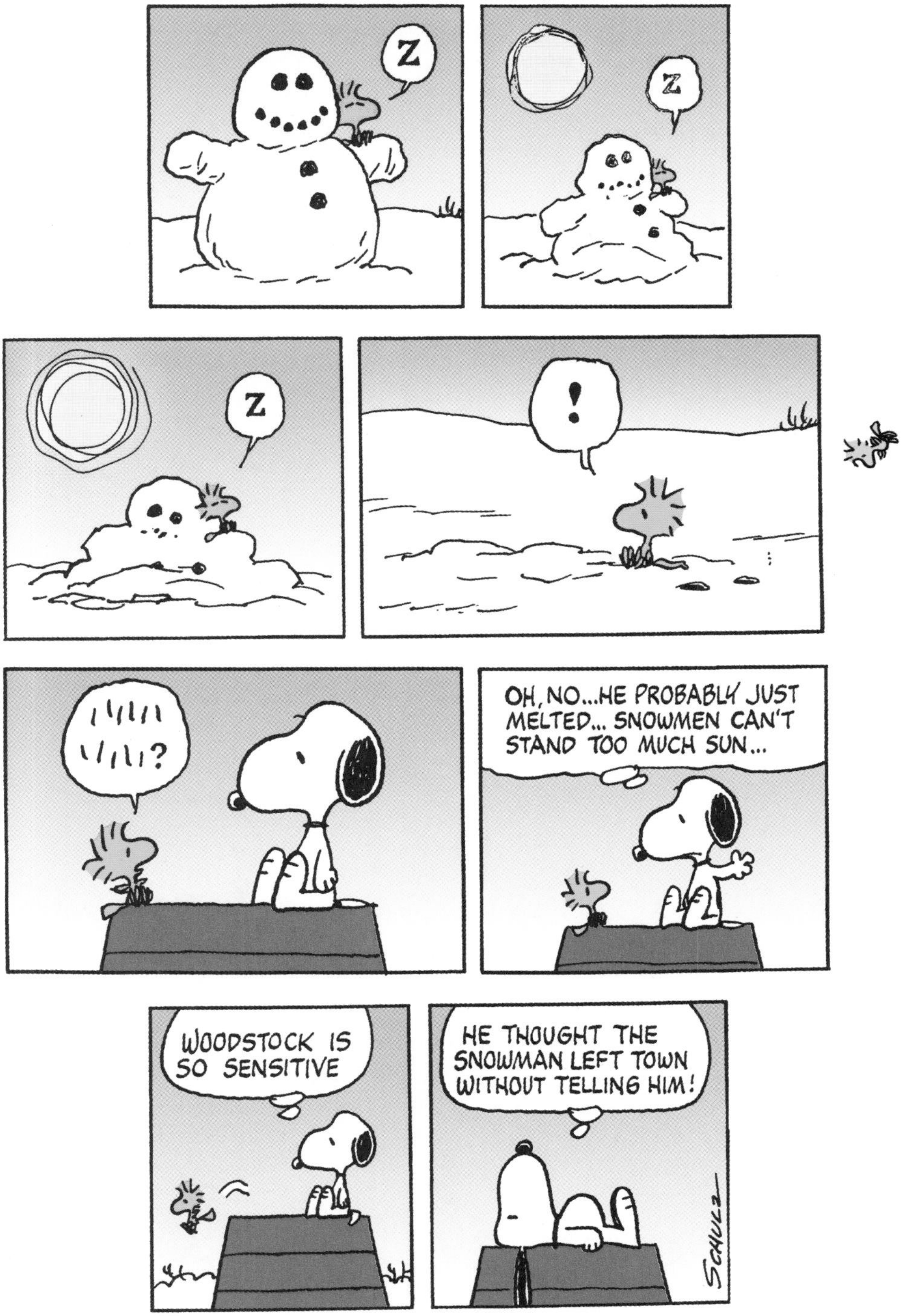
Z
Z
Z
!
OH, NO...HE PROBABLY JUST MELTED... SNOWMEN CAN'T STAND TOO MUCH SUN...
WOODSTOCK IS SO SENSITIVE
HE THOUGHT THE SNOWMAN LEFT TOWN WITHOUT TELLING HIM!
SCHULZ

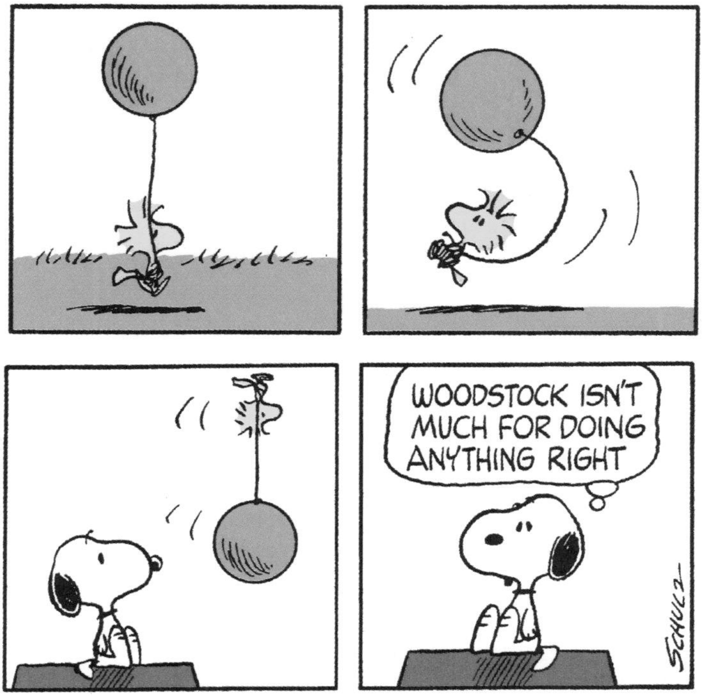
WOODSTOCK ISN'T MUCH FOR DOING ANYTHING RIGHT
SCHULZ

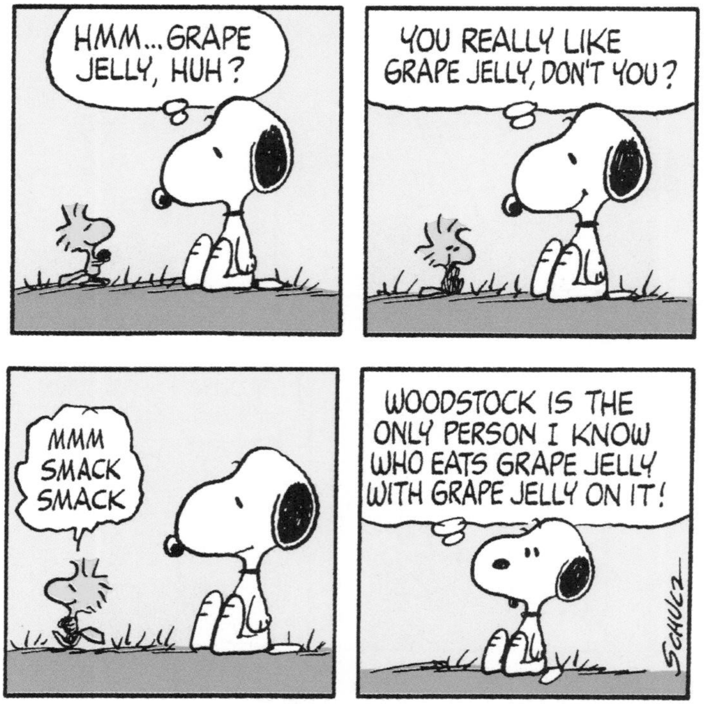
HMM...GRAPE JELLY, HUH?
YOU REALLY LIKE GRAPE JELLY, DON'T YOU?
MMM SMACK SMACK
WOODSTOCK IS THE ONLY PERSON I KNOW WHO EATS GRAPE JELLY WITH GRAPE JELLY ON IT!
SCHULZ

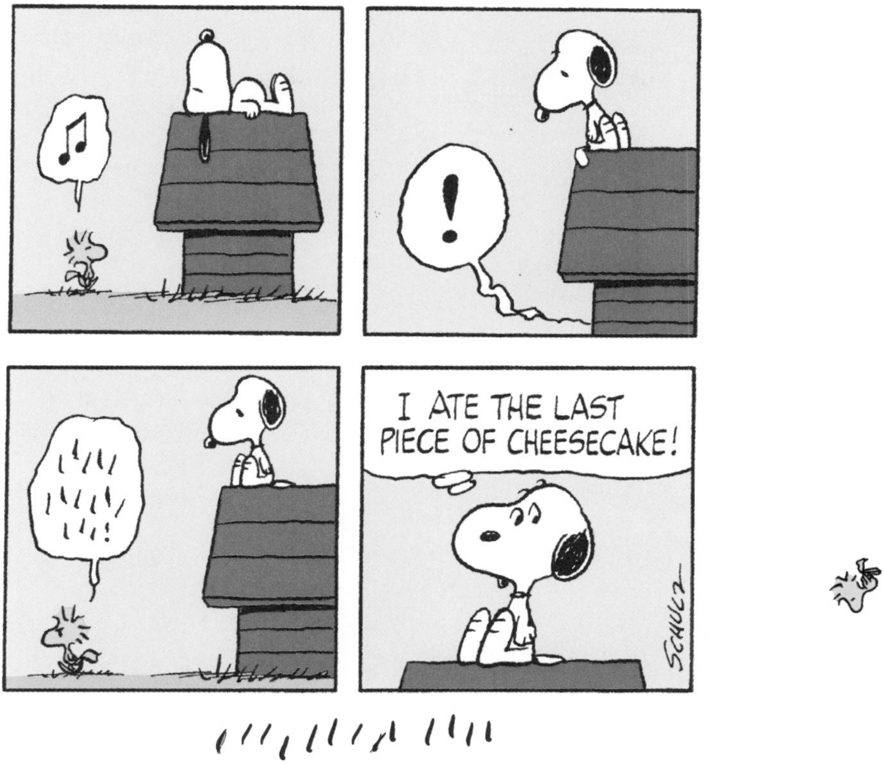
I ATE THE LAST PIECE OF CHEESECAKE!
SCHULZ

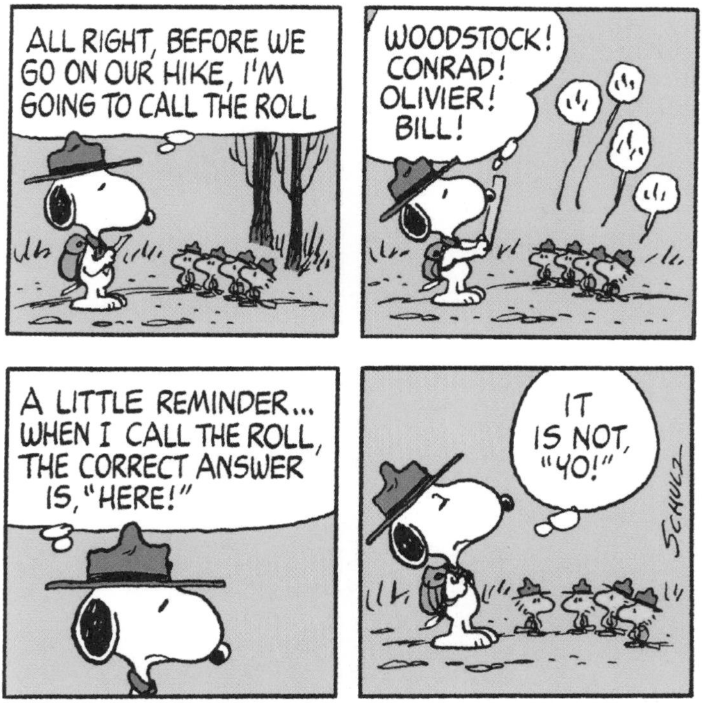
ALL RIGHT, BEFORE WE GO ON OUR HIKE, I'M GOING TO CALL THE ROLL
WOODSTOCK! CONRAD! OLIVIER! BILL!
A LITTLE REMINDER... WHEN I CALL THE ROLL, THE CORRECT ANSWER IS, "HERE!"
IT IS NOT, "YO!"
SCHULZ

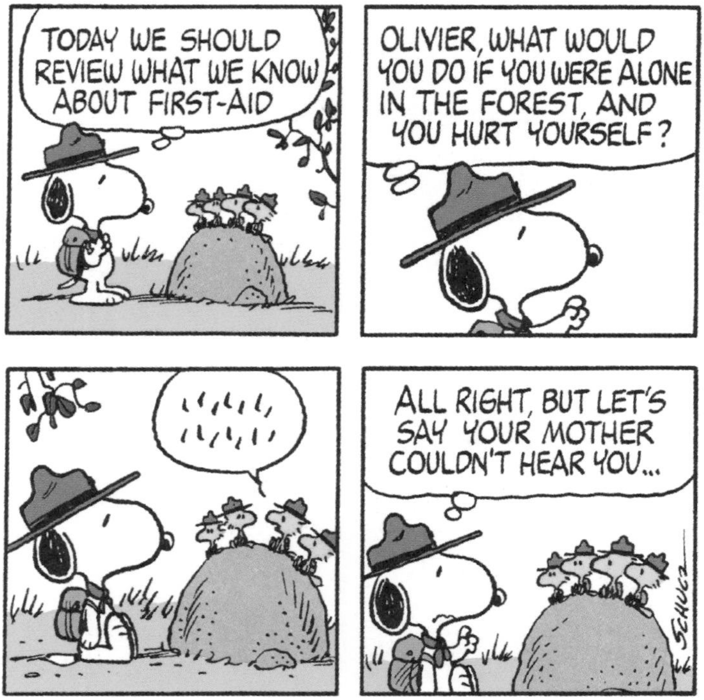
TODAY WE SHOULD REVIEW WHAT WE KNOW ABOUT FIRST-AID
OLIVIER, WHAT WOULD YOU DO IF YOU WERE ALONE IN THE FOREST, AND YOU HURT YOURSELF?
ALL RIGHT, BUT LET'S SAY YOUR MOTHER COULDN'T HEAR YOU...

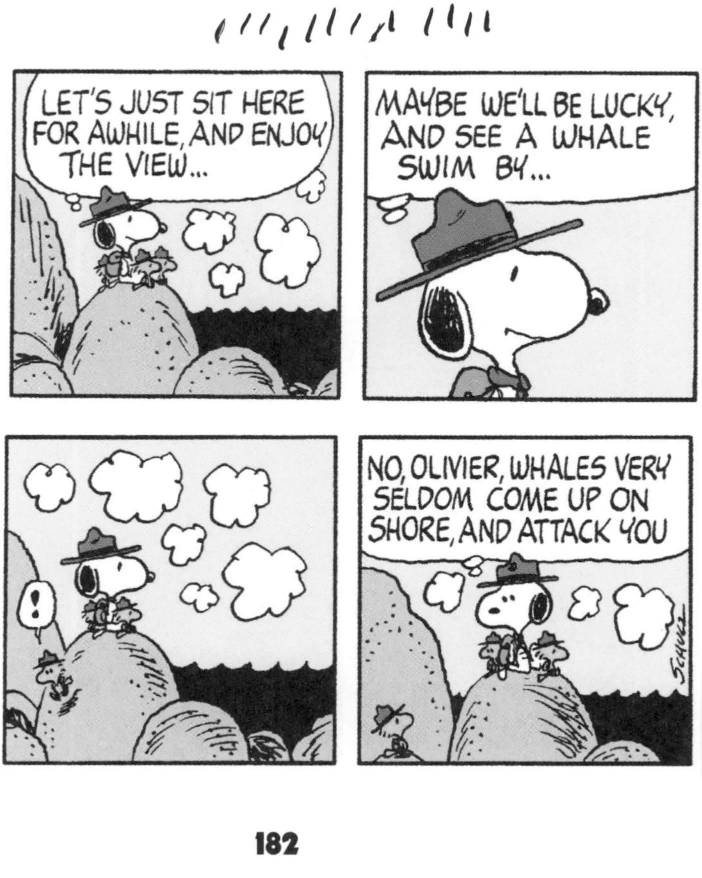
LET'S JUST SIT HERE FOR AWHILE, AND ENJOY THE VIEW...
MAYBE WE'LL BE LUCKY, AND SEE A WHALE SWIM BY...
!
NO, OLIVIER, WHALES VERY SELDOM COME UP ON SHORE, AND ATTACK YOU

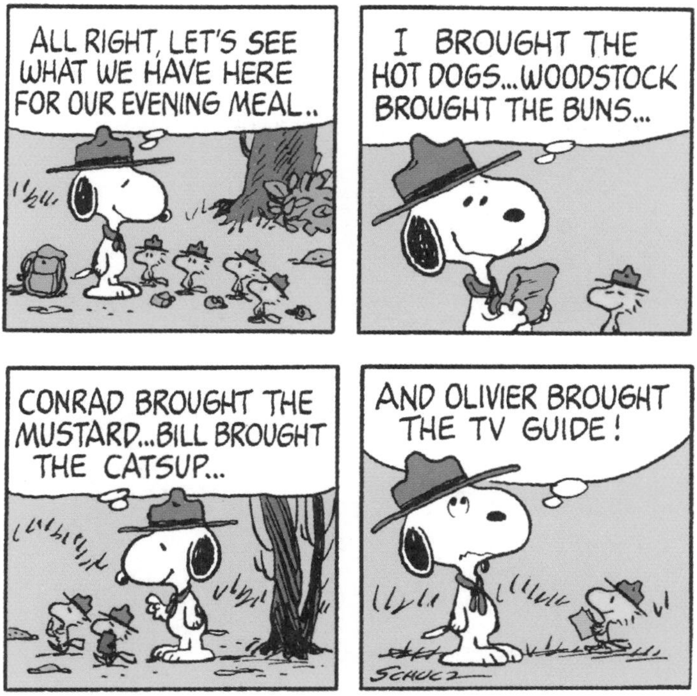
ALL RIGHT, LET'S SEE WHAT WE HAVE HERE FOR OUR EVENING MEAL..
I BROUGHT THE HOT DOGS...WOODSTOCK BROUGHT THE BUNS...
CONRAD BROUGHT THE MUSTARD...BILL BROUGHT THE CATSUP...
AND OLIVIER BROUGHT THE TV GUIDE!

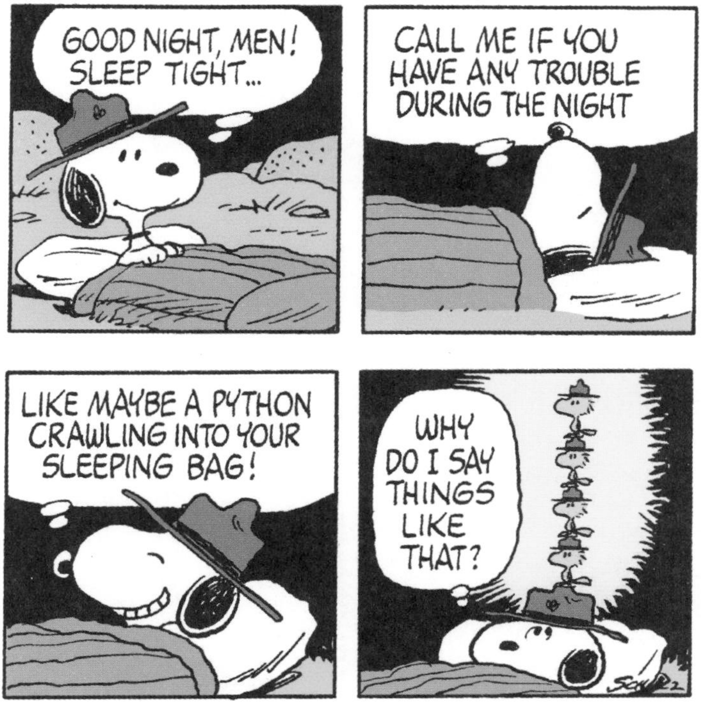
GOOD NIGHT, MEN! SLEEP TIGHT...
CALL ME IF YOU HAVE ANY TROUBLE DURING THE NIGHT
LIKE MAYBE A PYTHON CRAWLING INTO YOUR SLEEPING BAG!
WHY DO I SAY THINGS LIKE THAT?

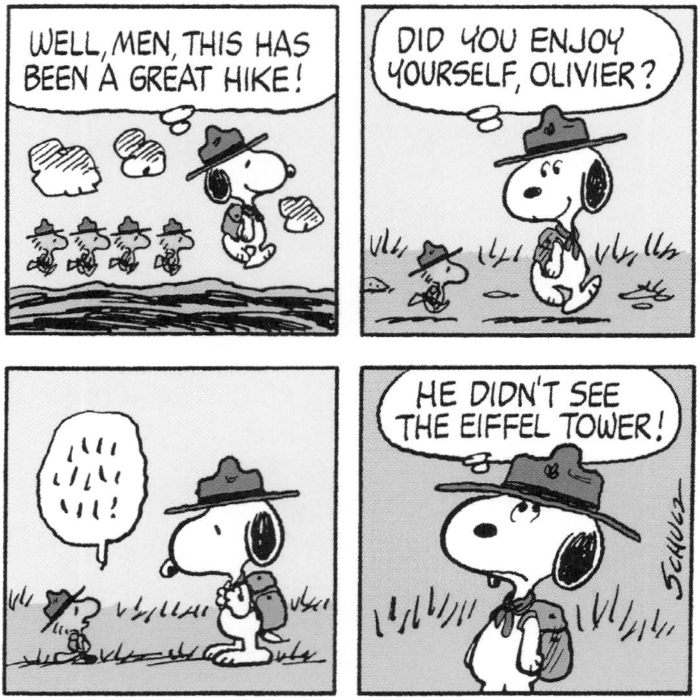
WELL, MEN, THIS HAS BEEN A GREAT HIKE!
DID YOU ENJOY YOURSELF, OLIVIER?
HE DIDN'T SEE THE EIFFEL TOWER!
SCHULZ

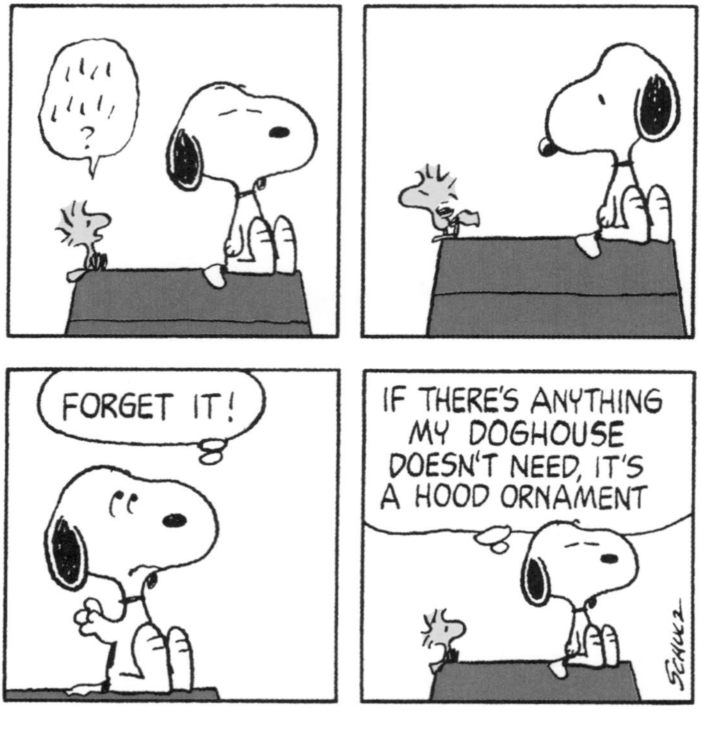
FORGET IT!
IF THERE'S ANYTHING MY DOGHOUSE DOESN'T NEED, IT'S A HOOD ORNAMENT
SCHULZ

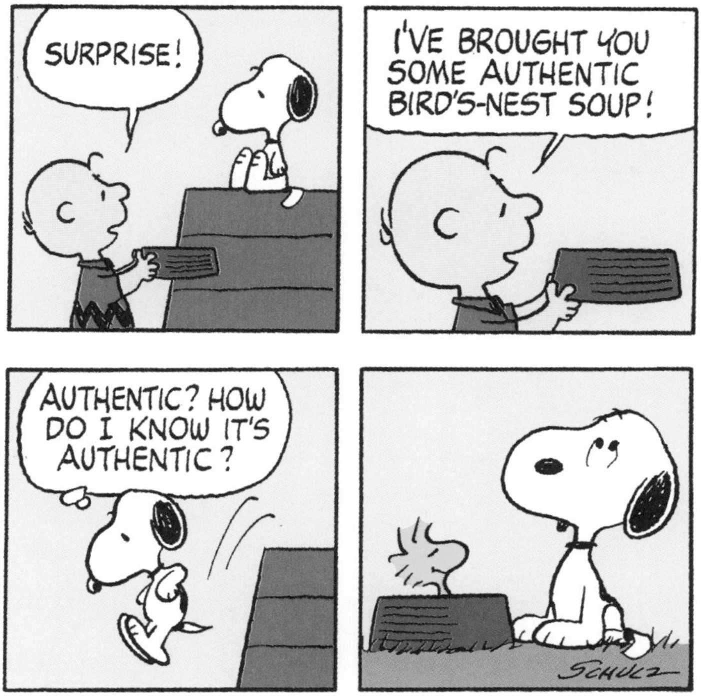
SURPRISE!
I'VE BROUGHT YOU SOME AUTHENTIC BIRD'S-NEST SOUP!
AUTHENTIC? HOW DO I KNOW IT'S AUTHENTIC?
SCHULZ

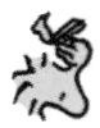

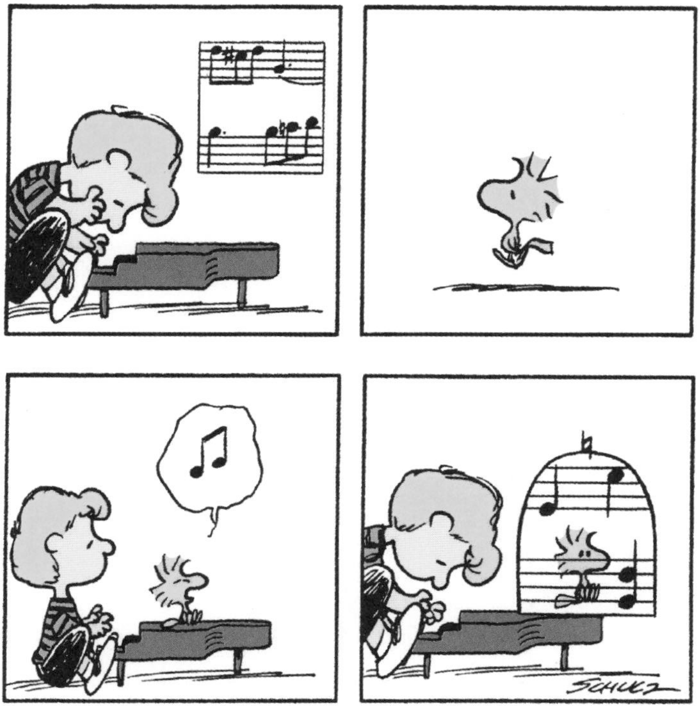
SCHULZ

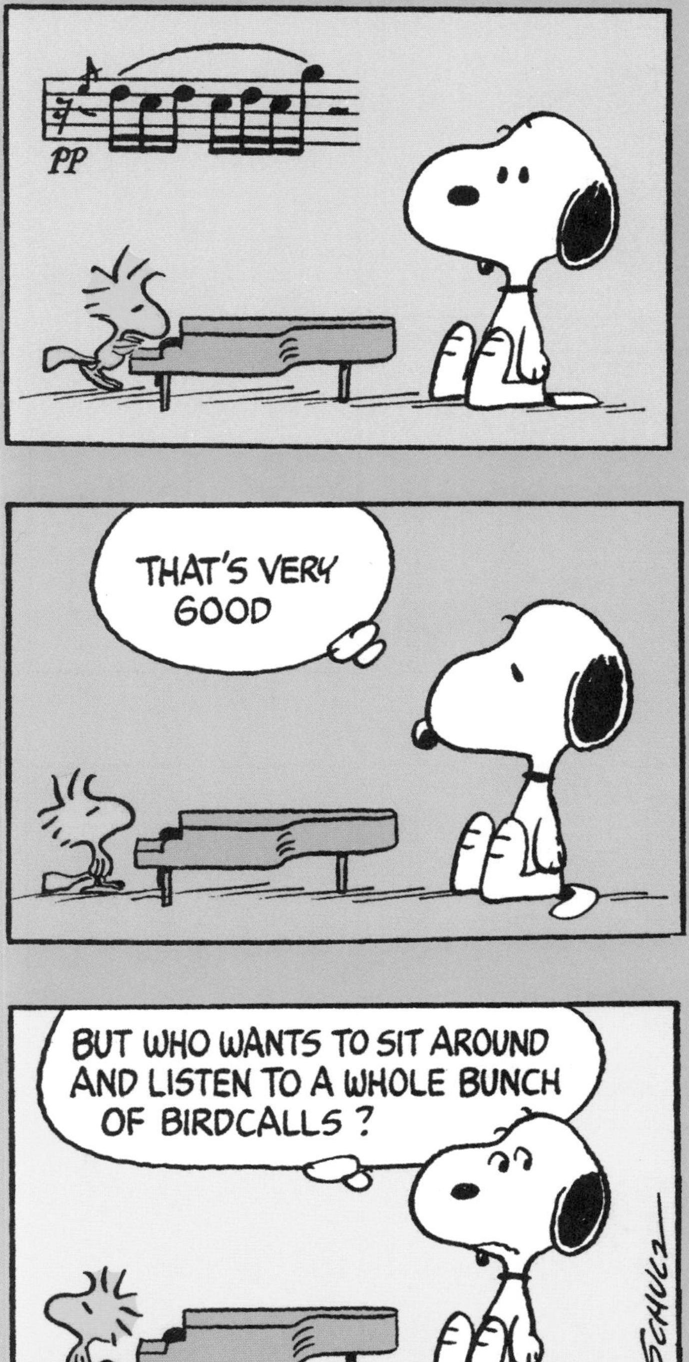
PP
THAT'S VERY GOOD
BUT WHO WANTS TO SIT AROUND AND LISTEN TO A WHOLE BUNCH OF BIRDCALLS ?
SCHULZ

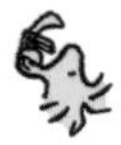

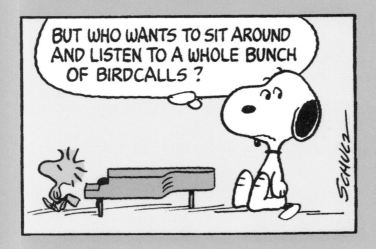

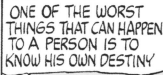

ONE OF THE WORST THINGS THAT CAN HAPPEN TO A PERSON IS TO KNOW HIS OWN DESTINY

ONE SHOULD NEVER TRY TO LOOK INTO THE FUTURE

I SAW YOU PEEK!

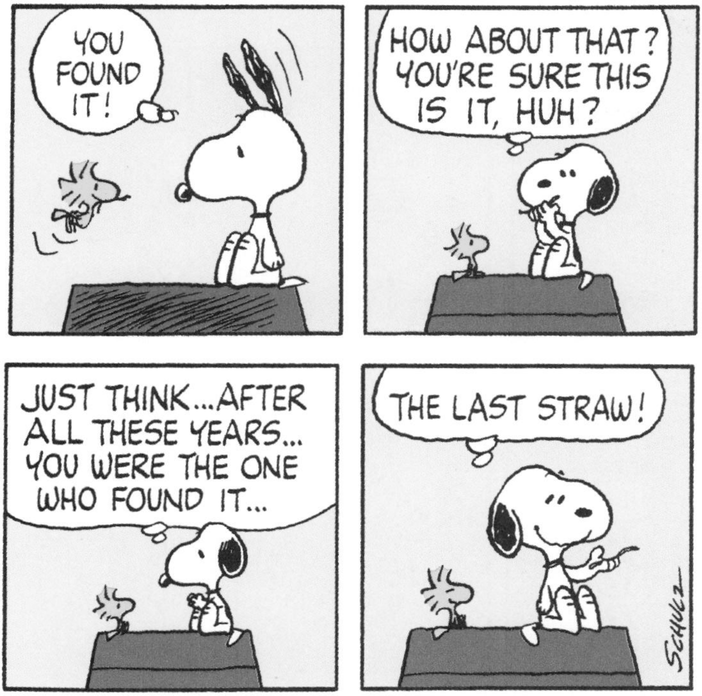
YOU FOUND IT!
HOW ABOUT THAT? YOU'RE SURE THIS IS IT, HUH?
JUST THINK...AFTER ALL THESE YEARS... YOU WERE THE ONE WHO FOUND IT...
THE LAST STRAW!
SCHULZ

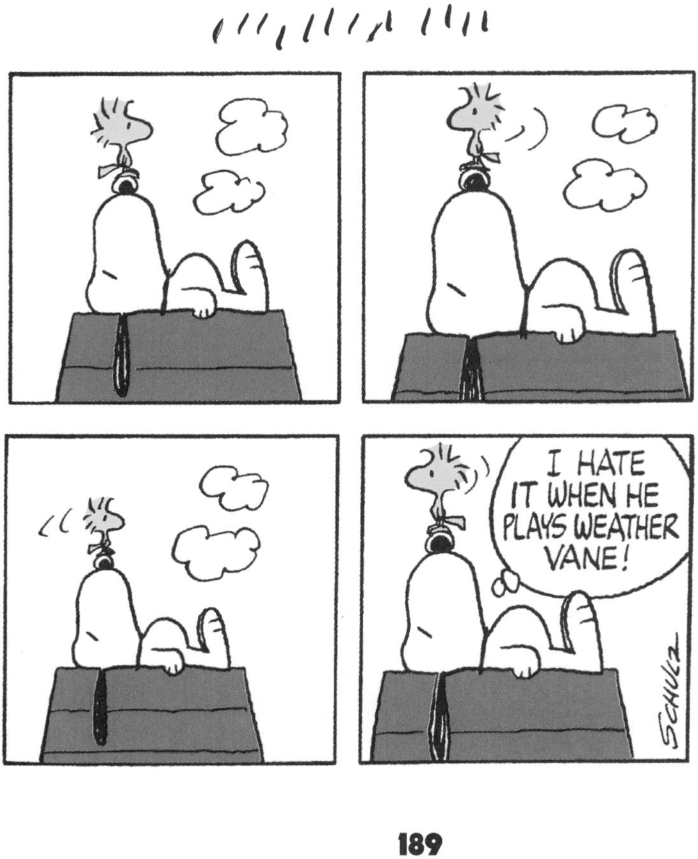
I HATE IT WHEN HE PLAYS WEATHER VANE!
SCHULZ

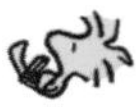

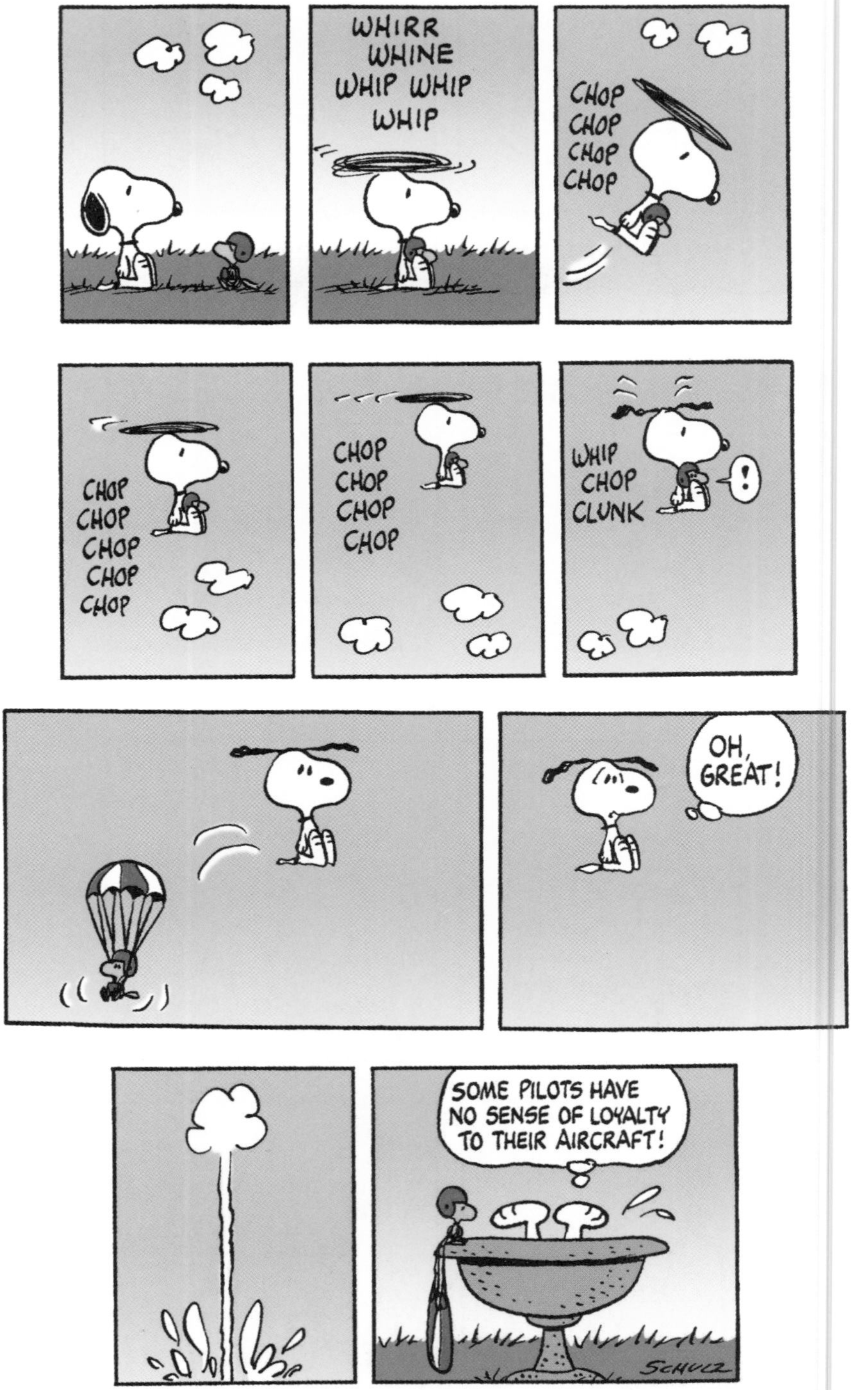
WHIRR
WHINE
WHIP WHIP
WHIP
CHOP
CHOP
CHOP
CHOP
CHOP
CHOP
CHOP
CHOP
CHOP
CHOP
CHOP
CHOP
CHOP
WHIP
CHOP
CLUNK
!
OH, GREAT!
SOME PILOTS HAVE NO SENSE OF LOYALTY TO THEIR AIRCRAFT!
SCHULZ

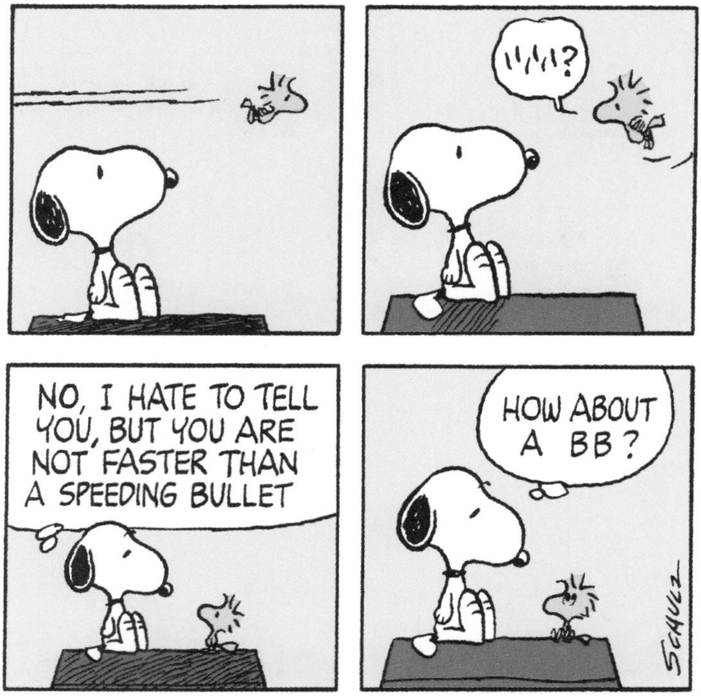
NO, I HATE TO TELL YOU, BUT YOU ARE NOT FASTER THAN A SPEEDING BULLET
HOW ABOUT A BB?
SCHULZ

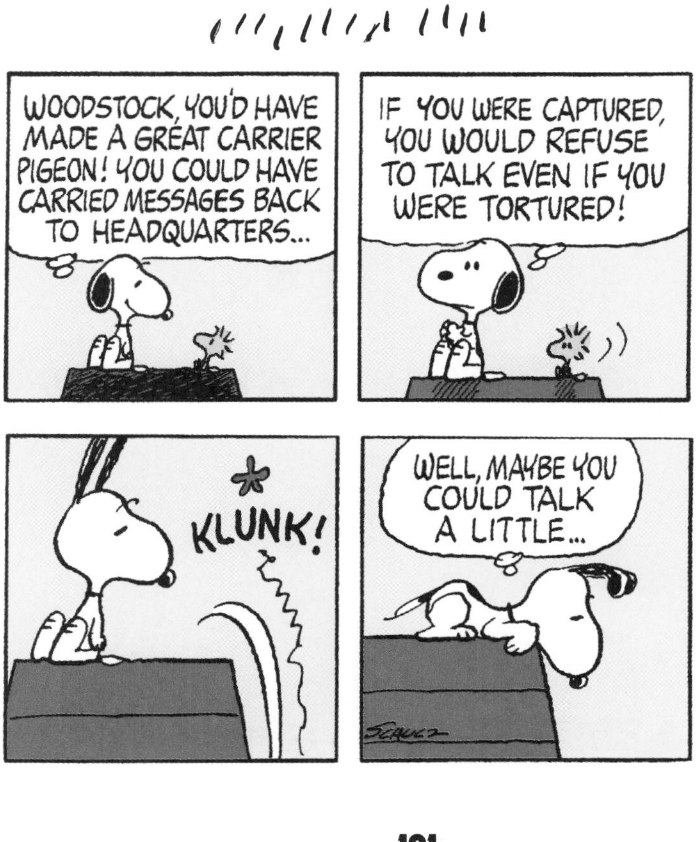
WOODSTOCK, YOU'D HAVE MADE A GREAT CARRIER PIGEON! YOU COULD HAVE CARRIED MESSAGES BACK TO HEADQUARTERS...
IF YOU WERE CAPTURED, YOU WOULD REFUSE TO TALK EVEN IF YOU WERE TORTURED!
KLUNK!
WELL, MAYBE YOU COULD TALK A LITTLE...

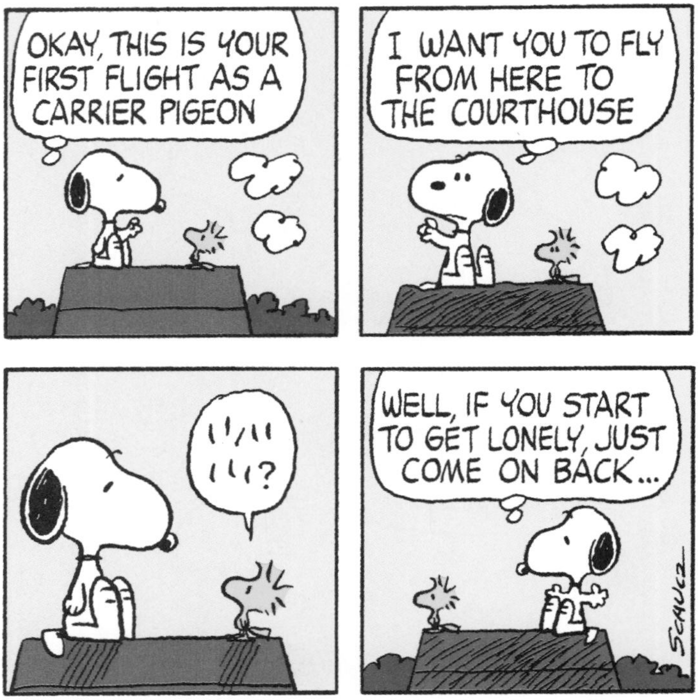
OKAY, THIS IS YOUR FIRST FLIGHT AS A CARRIER PIGEON
I WANT YOU TO FLY FROM HERE TO THE COURTHOUSE
WELL, IF YOU START TO GET LONELY, JUST COME ON BACK...

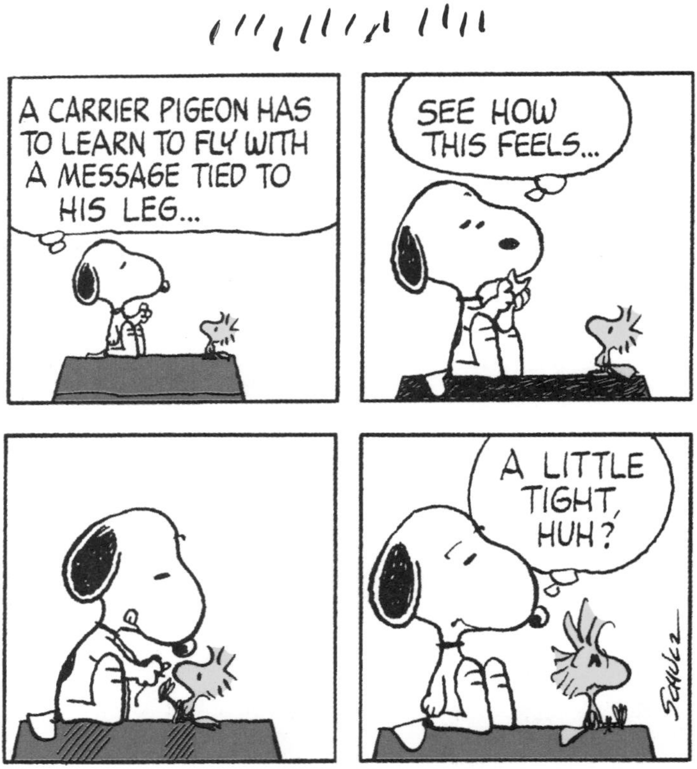
A CARRIER PIGEON HAS TO LEARN TO FLY WITH A MESSAGE TIED TO HIS LEG...
SEE HOW THIS FEELS...
A LITTLE TIGHT, HUH?

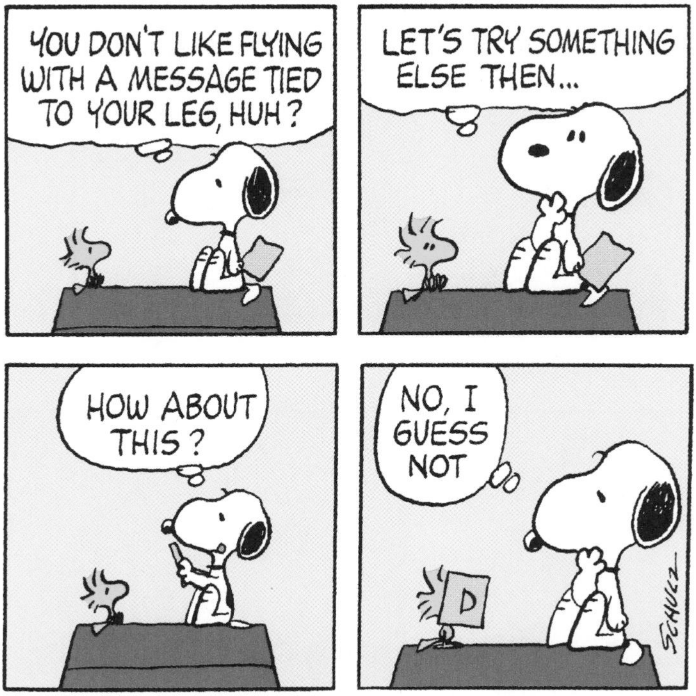
YOU DON'T LIKE FLYING WITH A MESSAGE TIED TO YOUR LEG, HUH ?
LET'S TRY SOMETHING ELSE THEN...
HOW ABOUT THIS ?
NO, I GUESS NOT
D
SCHULZ

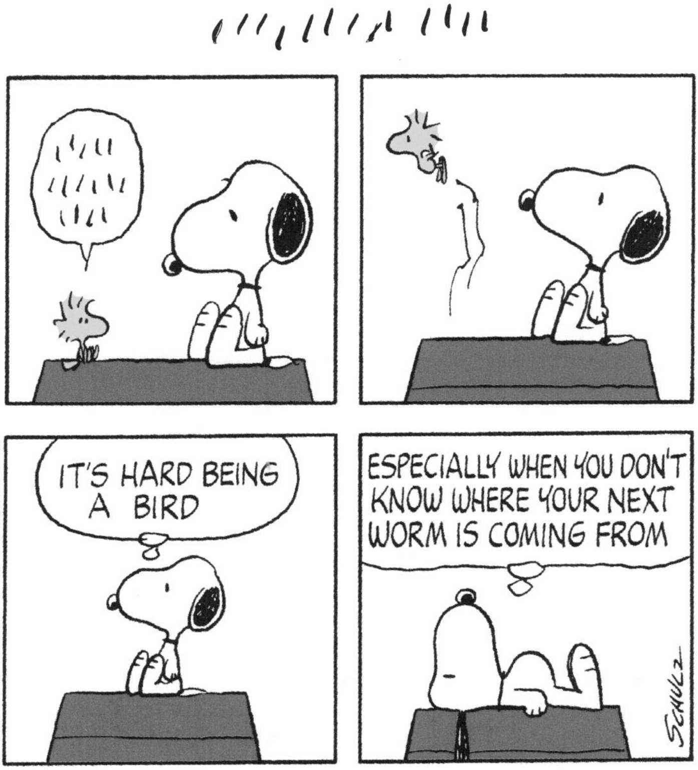
IT'S HARD BEING A BIRD
ESPECIALLY WHEN YOU DON'T KNOW WHERE YOUR NEXT WORM IS COMING FROM
SCHULZ

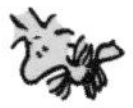

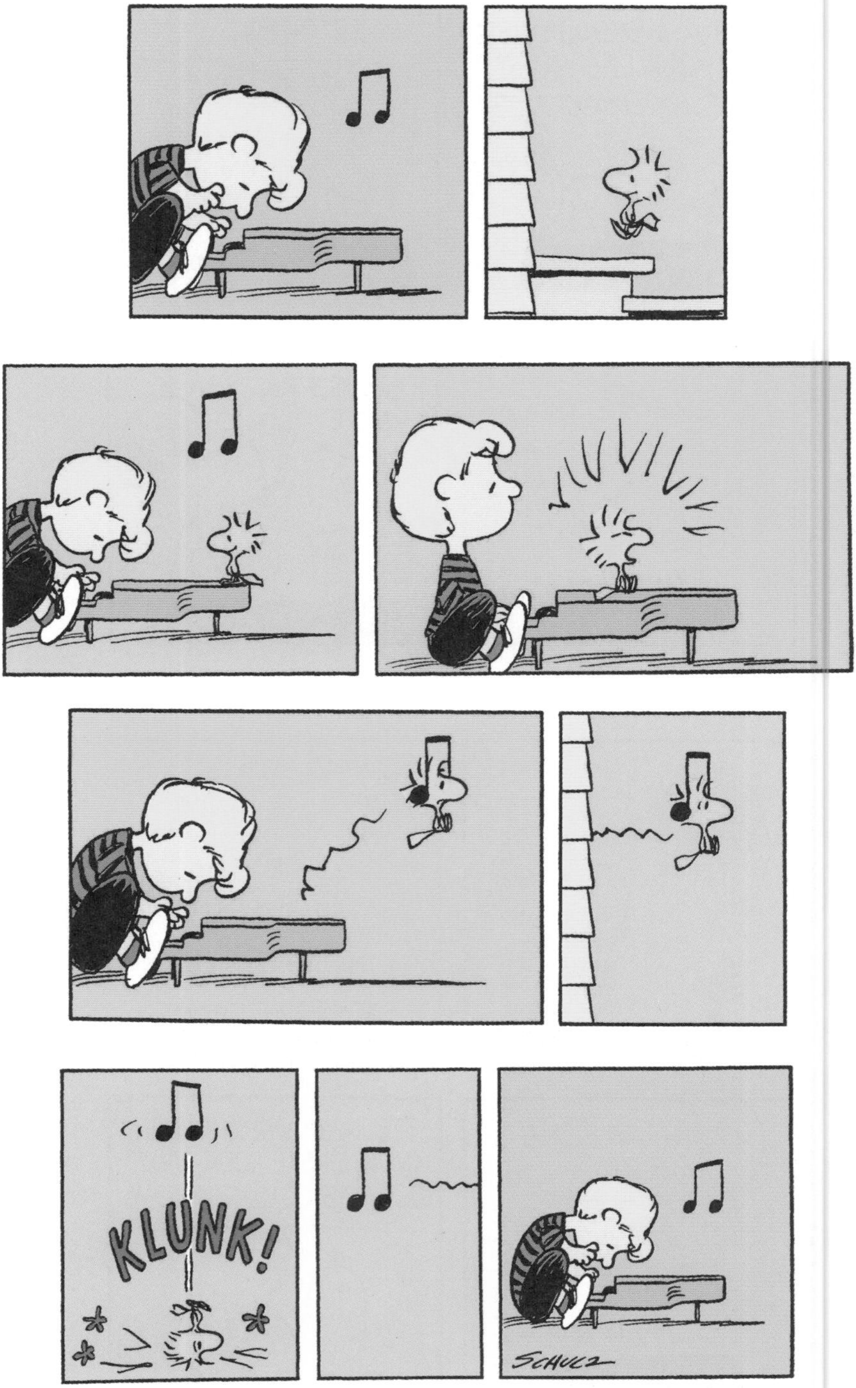
KLUNK!
SCHULZ

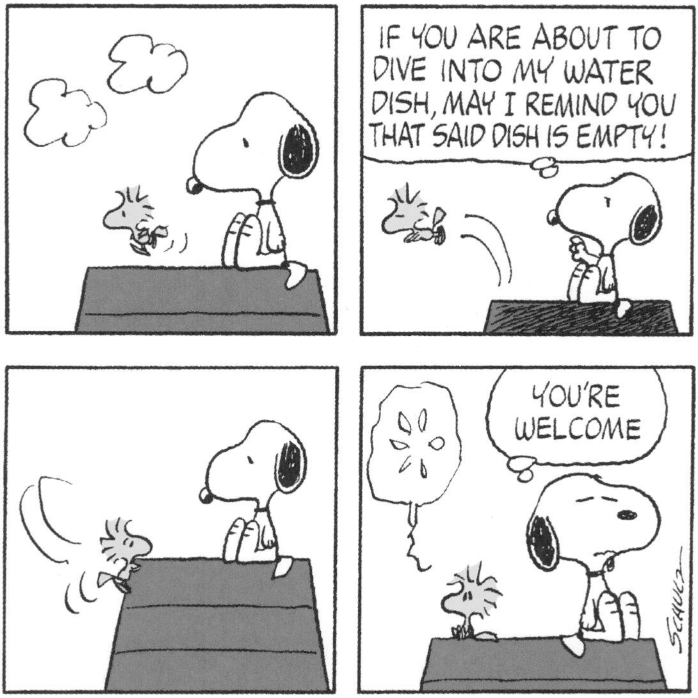
IF YOU ARE ABOUT TO DIVE INTO MY WATER DISH, MAY I REMIND YOU THAT SAID DISH IS EMPTY!
YOU'RE WELCOME

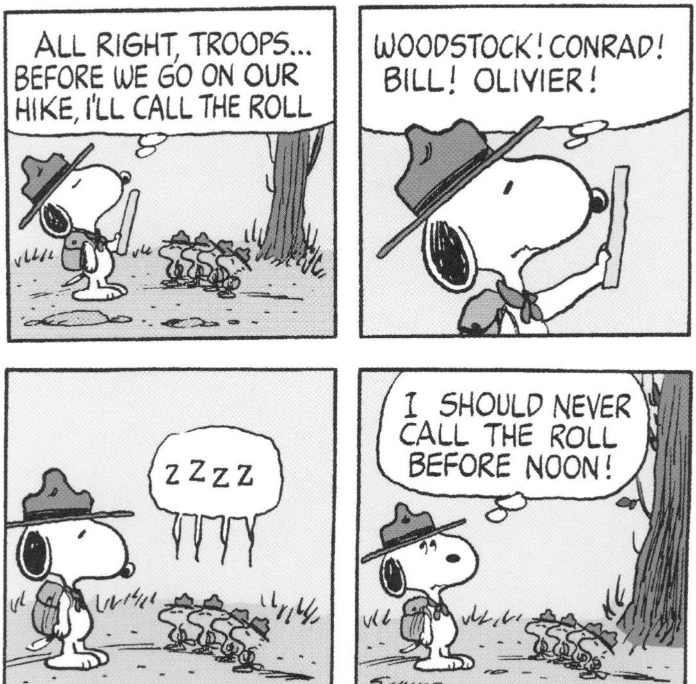
ALL RIGHT, TROOPS... BEFORE WE GO ON OUR HIKE, I'LL CALL THE ROLL
WOODSTOCK! CONRAD! BILL! OLIVIER!
Z Z Z Z
I SHOULD NEVER CALL THE ROLL BEFORE NOON!

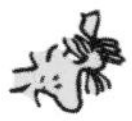

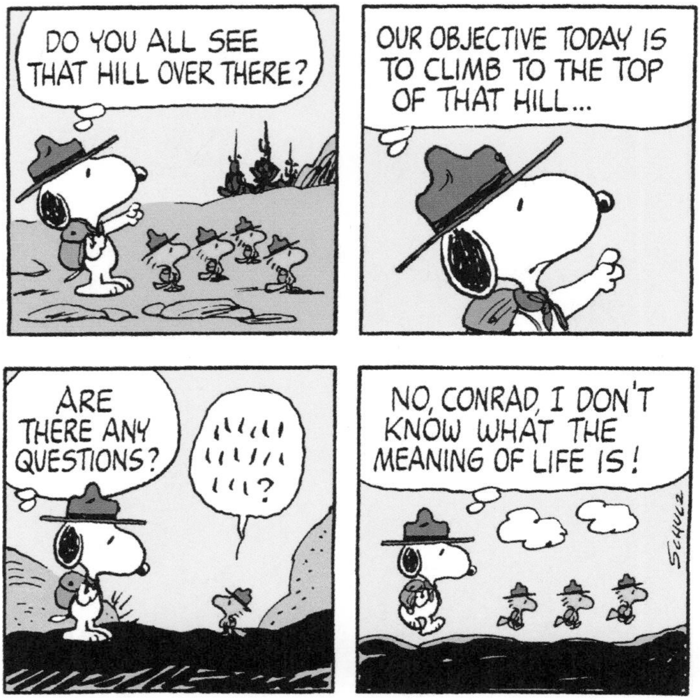
DO YOU ALL SEE THAT HILL OVER THERE?
OUR OBJECTIVE TODAY IS TO CLIMB TO THE TOP OF THAT HILL...
ARE THERE ANY QUESTIONS?
?
NO, CONRAD, I DON'T KNOW WHAT THE MEANING OF LIFE IS!
SCHULZ

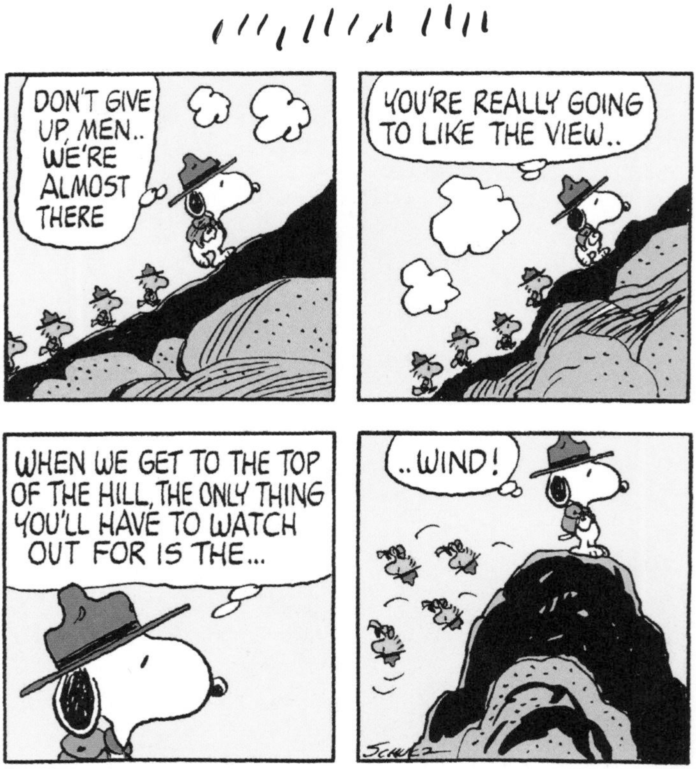
DON'T GIVE UP, MEN.. WE'RE ALMOST THERE
YOU'RE REALLY GOING TO LIKE THE VIEW..
WHEN WE GET TO THE TOP OF THE HILL, THE ONLY THING YOU'LL HAVE TO WATCH OUT FOR IS THE...
..WIND!
SCHULZ

WELL! DIDN'T I TELL YOU GUYS THERE'D BE A GREAT VIEW?
WE'RE ACTUALLY ABOVE THE CLOUDS...HAVE YOU NOTICED?
!!!! !!!!
SCHULZ

INCIDENTALLY, HOW DO YOU GUYS LIKE THE GRAPE JELLY I BROUGHT ALONG?
IT'S A NEW BRAND CALLED "SMIRK"
IF SOMEONE GETS JELLY ON HIS FACE, YOU CAN SAY TO HIM, "WIPE THAT 'SMIRK' OFF YOUR FACE!"
JUST A LITTLE JOKE THERE TO BOOST SAGGING MORALE
SCHULZ

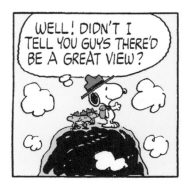

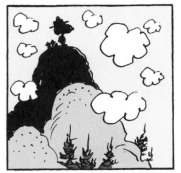

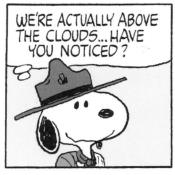

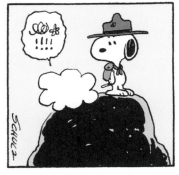

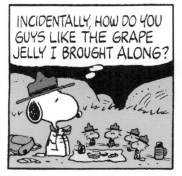

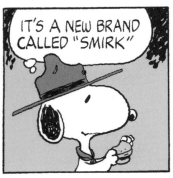

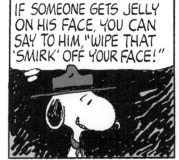

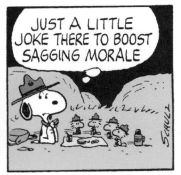

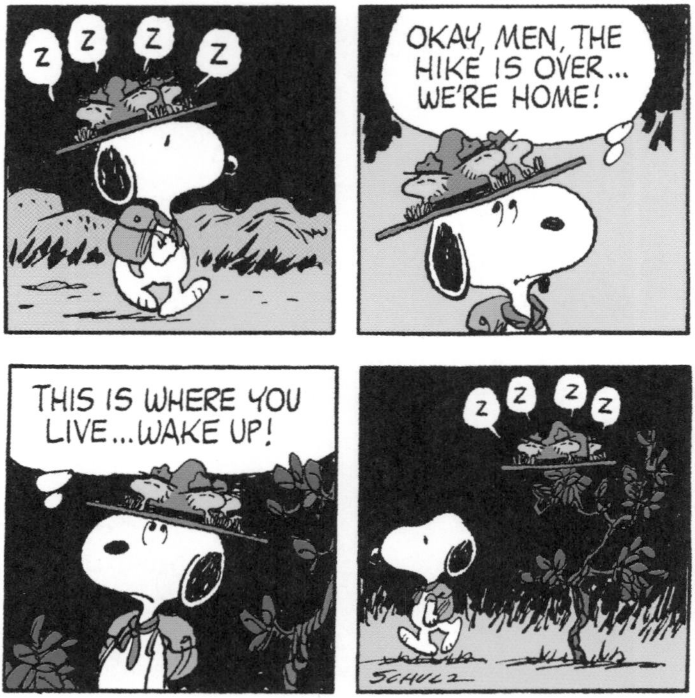
Z Z Z Z
OKAY, MEN, THE HIKE IS OVER... WE'RE HOME!
THIS IS WHERE YOU LIVE...WAKE UP!
Z Z Z Z
SCHULZ

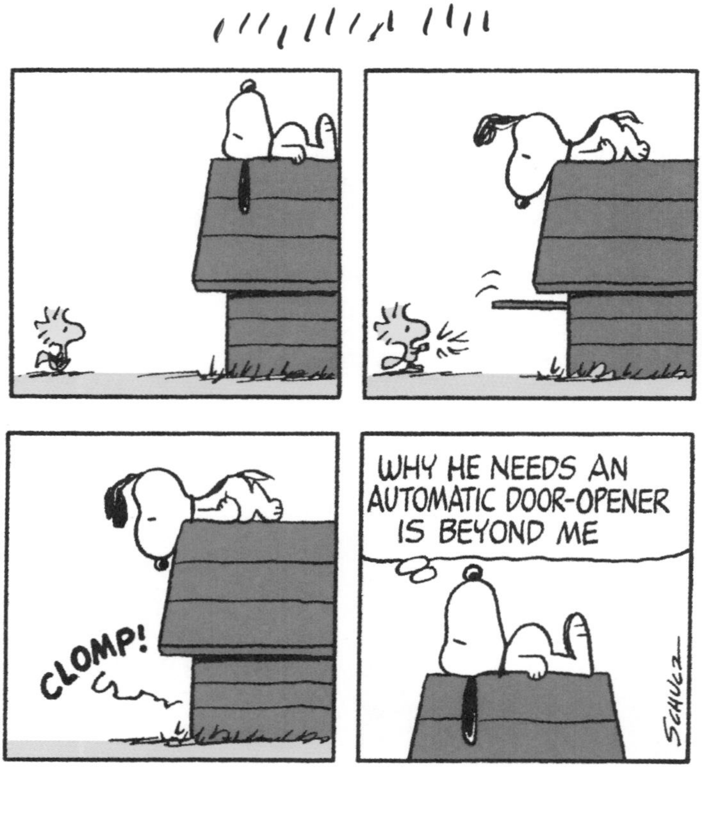
CLOMP!
WHY HE NEEDS AN AUTOMATIC DOOR-OPENER IS BEYOND ME
SCHULZ

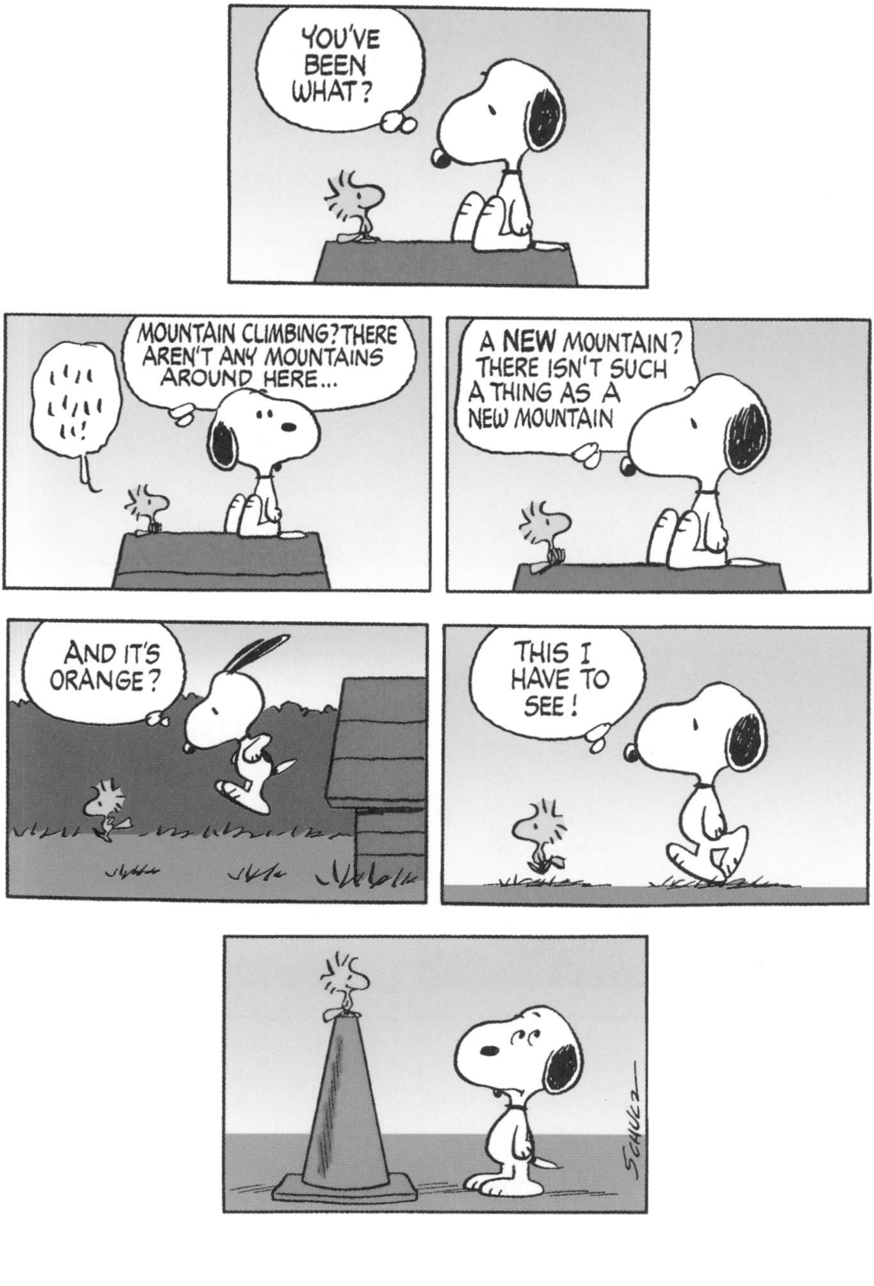
YOU'VE BEEN WHAT?
MOUNTAIN CLIMBING? THERE AREN'T ANY MOUNTAINS AROUND HERE...
A NEW MOUNTAIN? THERE ISN'T SUCH A THING AS A NEW MOUNTAIN
AND IT'S ORANGE?
THIS I HAVE TO SEE!
SCHULZ

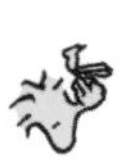

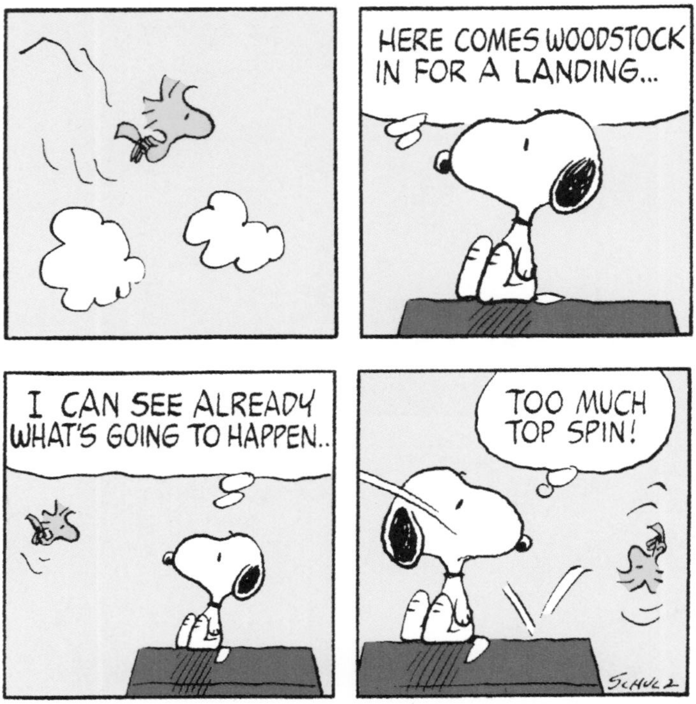
HERE COMES WOODSTOCK IN FOR A LANDING...
I CAN SEE ALREADY WHAT'S GOING TO HAPPEN..
TOO MUCH TOP SPIN!

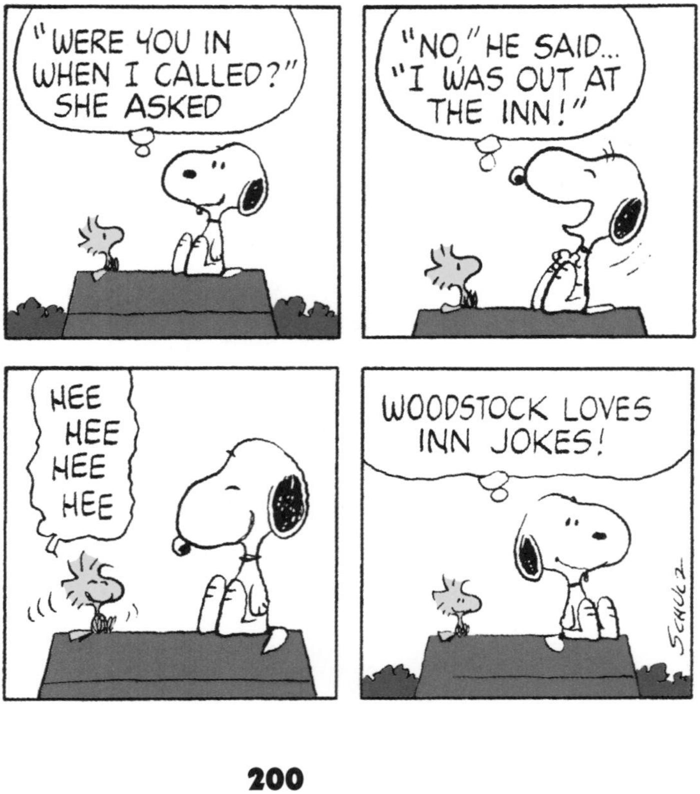
"WERE YOU IN WHEN I CALLED?" SHE ASKED
"NO," HE SAID... "I WAS OUT AT THE INN!"
HEE HEE HEE HEE
WOODSTOCK LOVES INN JOKES!

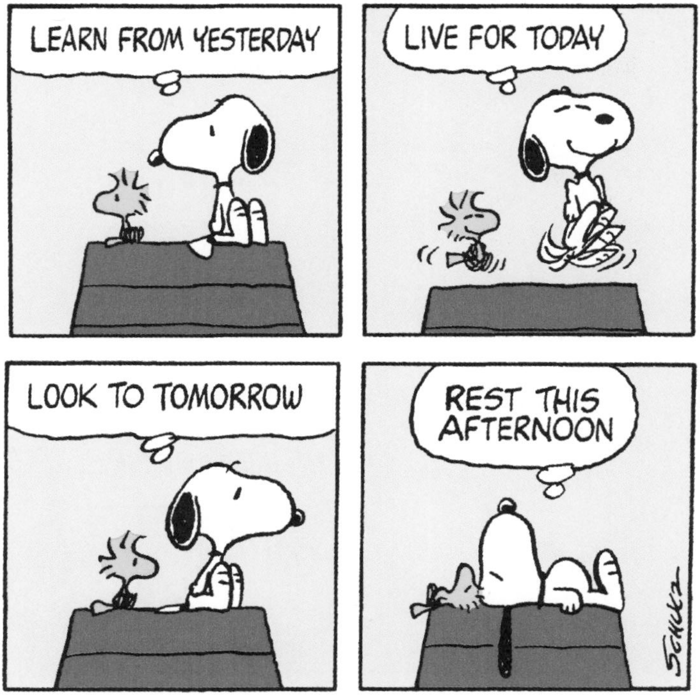
LEARN FROM YESTERDAY
LIVE FOR TODAY
LOOK TO TOMORROW
REST THIS AFTERNOON
SCHULZ

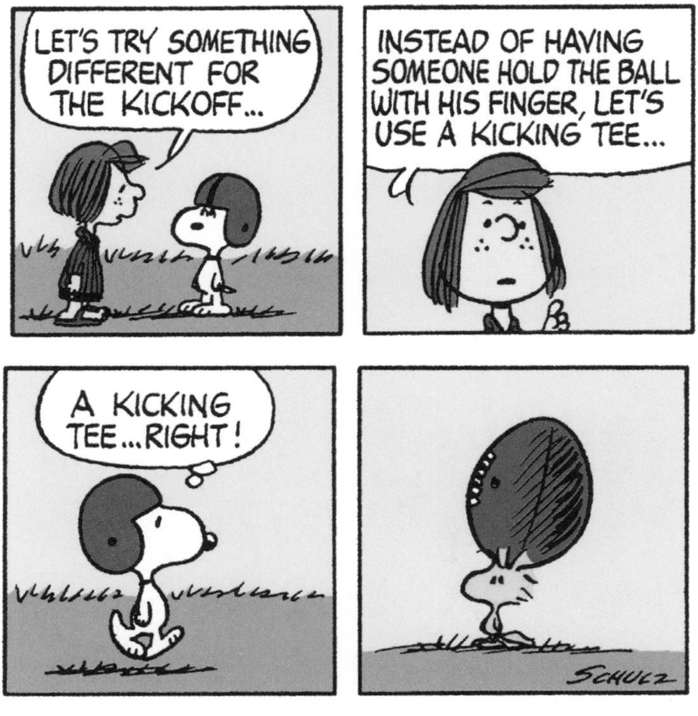
LET'S TRY SOMETHING DIFFERENT FOR THE KICKOFF...
INSTEAD OF HAVING SOMEONE HOLD THE BALL WITH HIS FINGER, LET'S USE A KICKING TEE...
A KICKING TEE...RIGHT!
SCHULZ

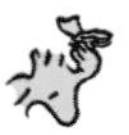

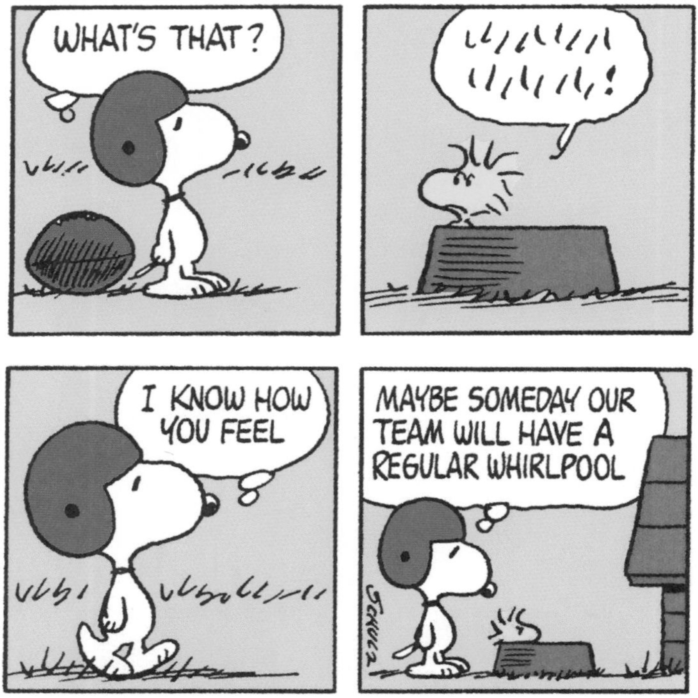
WHAT'S THAT?
I KNOW HOW YOU FEEL
MAYBE SOMEDAY OUR TEAM WILL HAVE A REGULAR WHIRLPOOL

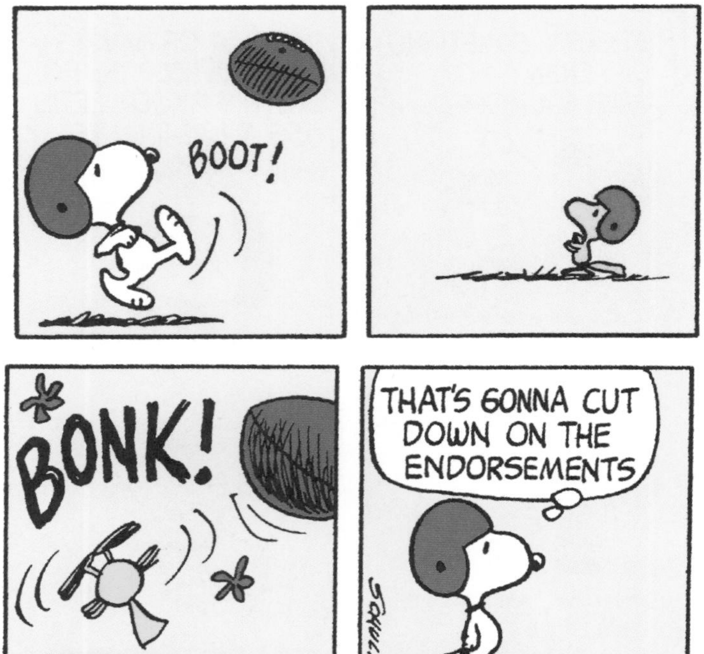
BOOT!
BONK!
THAT'S GONNA CUT DOWN ON THE ENDORSEMENTS

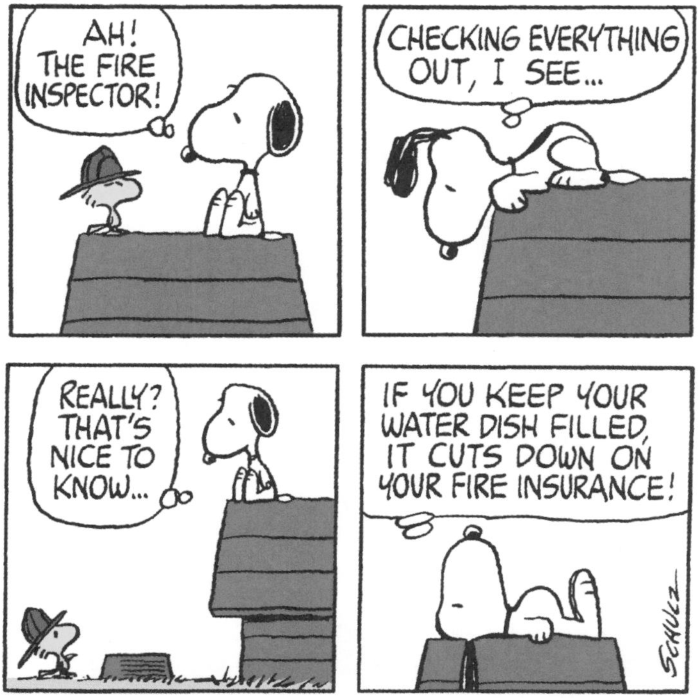
AH! THE FIRE INSPECTOR!
CHECKING EVERYTHING OUT, I SEE...
REALLY? THAT'S NICE TO KNOW...
IF YOU KEEP YOUR WATER DISH FILLED, IT CUTS DOWN ON YOUR FIRE INSURANCE!
SCHULZ

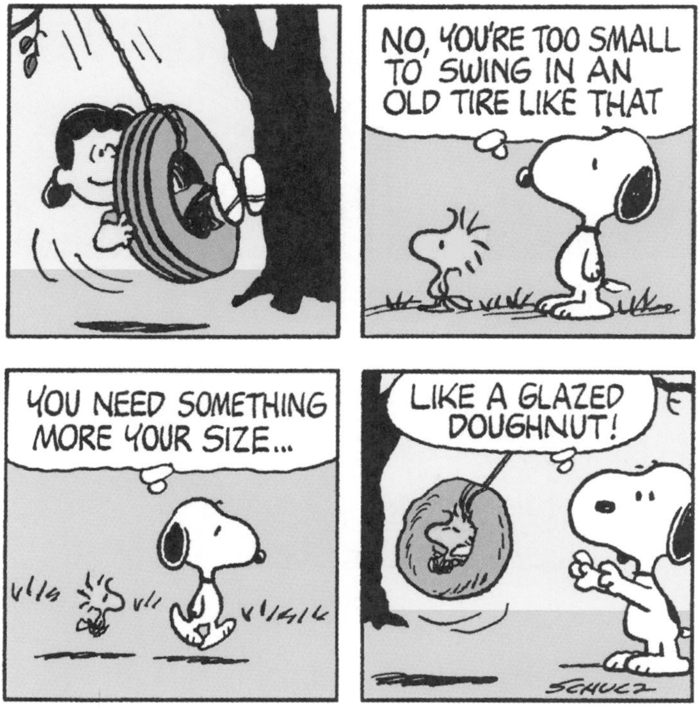
NO, YOU'RE TOO SMALL TO SWING IN AN OLD TIRE LIKE THAT
YOU NEED SOMETHING MORE YOUR SIZE...
LIKE A GLAZED DOUGHNUT!
SCHULZ

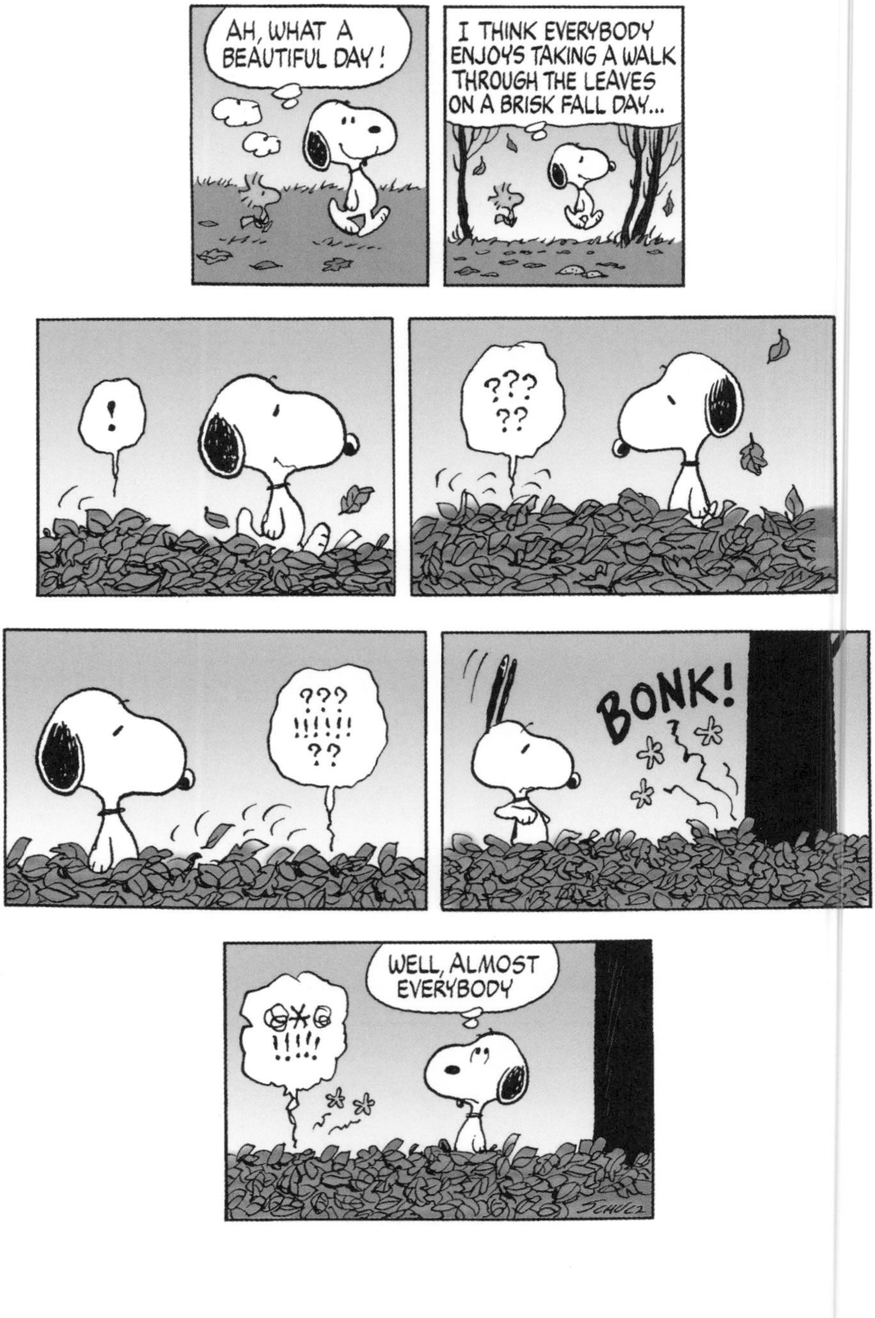
AH, WHAT A BEAUTIFUL DAY !
I THINK EVERYBODY ENJOYS TAKING A WALK THROUGH THE LEAVES ON A BRISK FALL DAY...
!
???
??
???
!!!!!!
??
BONK!
WELL, ALMOST EVERYBODY
!!!!!
SCHULZ

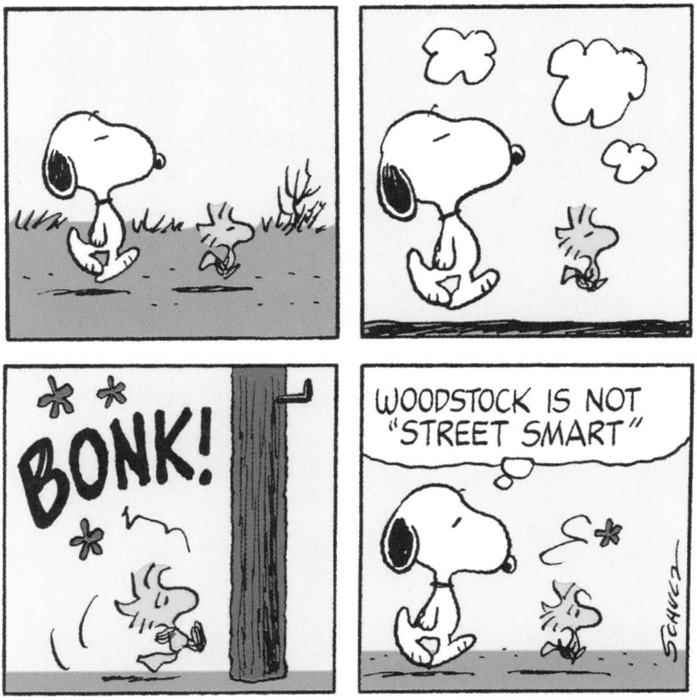
BONK!
WOODSTOCK IS NOT "STREET SMART"

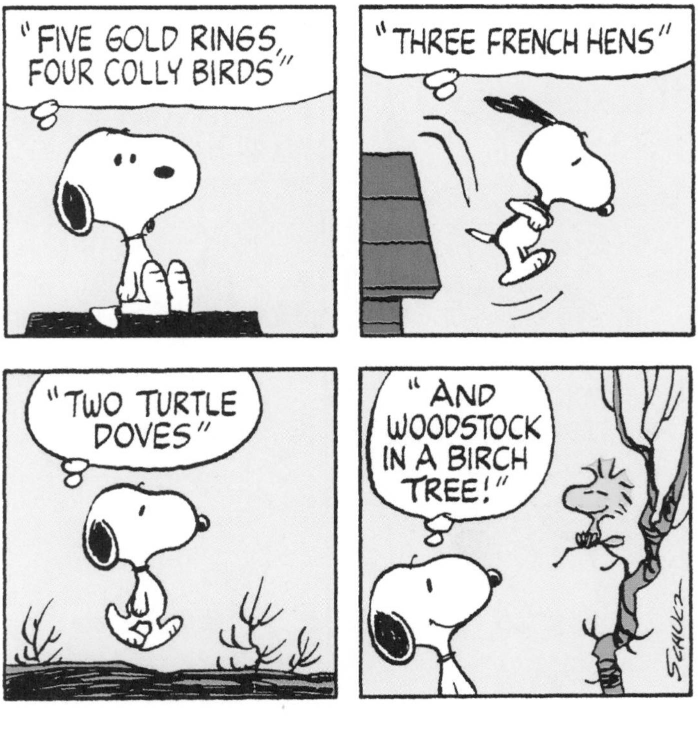
"FIVE GOLD RINGS, FOUR COLLY BIRDS"
"THREE FRENCH HENS"
"TWO TURTLE DOVES"
"AND WOODSTOCK IN A BIRCH TREE!"

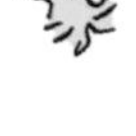

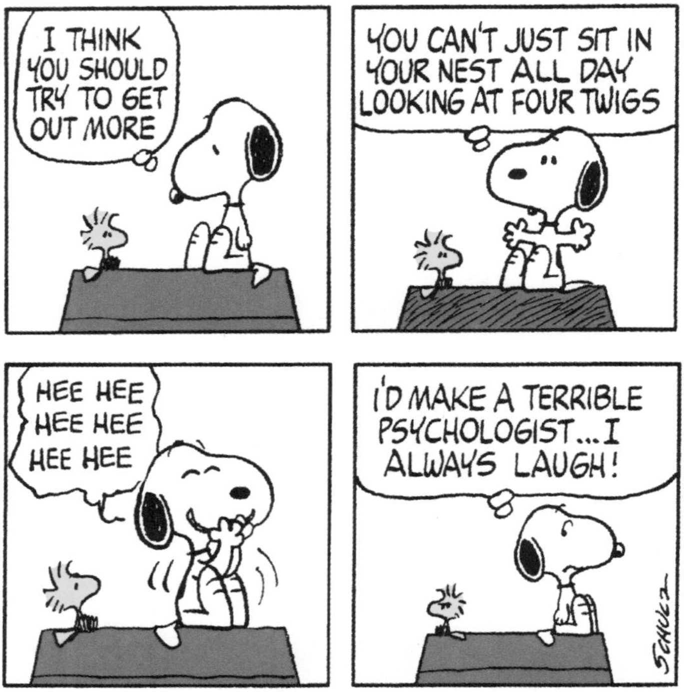
I THINK YOU SHOULD TRY TO GET OUT MORE
YOU CAN'T JUST SIT IN YOUR NEST ALL DAY LOOKING AT FOUR TWIGS
HEE HEE HEE HEE HEE HEE
I'D MAKE A TERRIBLE PSYCHOLOGIST... I ALWAYS LAUGH!
SCHULZ

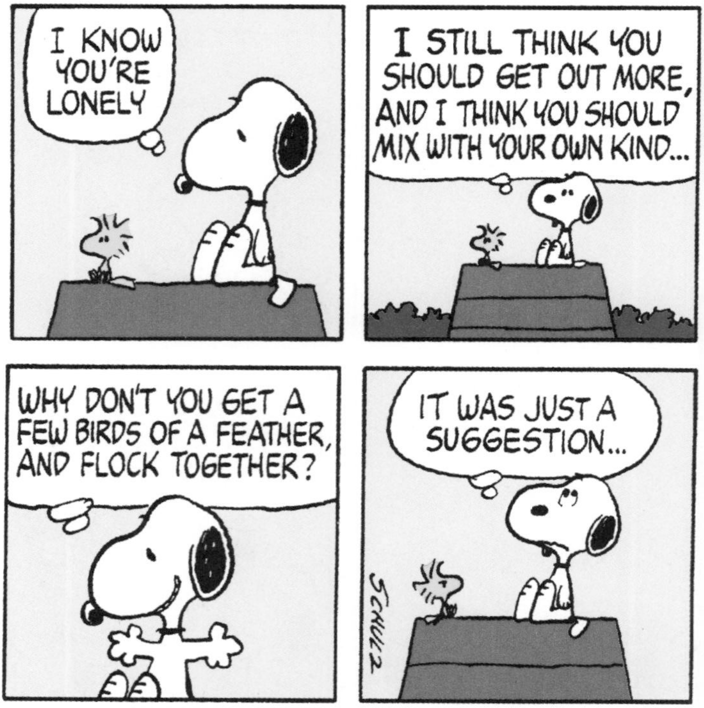
I KNOW YOU'RE LONELY
I STILL THINK YOU SHOULD GET OUT MORE, AND I THINK YOU SHOULD MIX WITH YOUR OWN KIND...
WHY DON'T YOU GET A FEW BIRDS OF A FEATHER, AND FLOCK TOGETHER?
IT WAS JUST A SUGGESTION...
SCHULZ

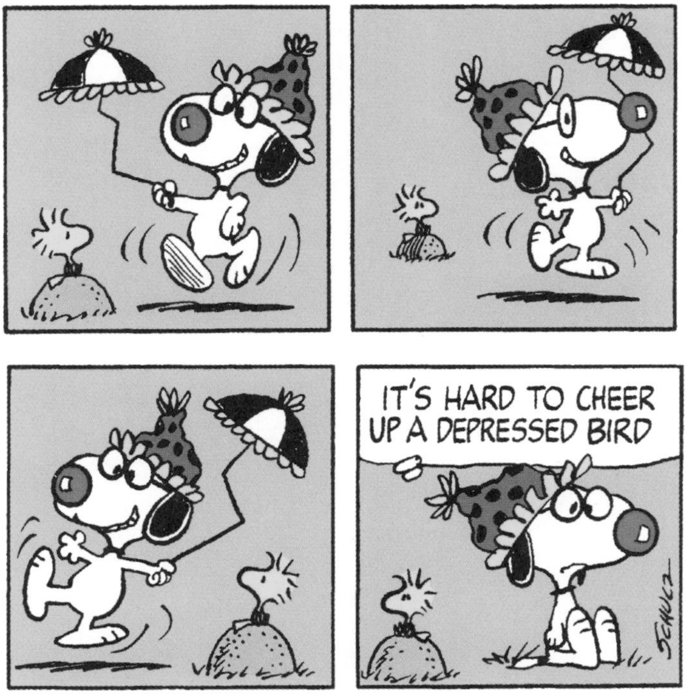

IT'S HARD TO CHEER UP A DEPRESSED BIRD

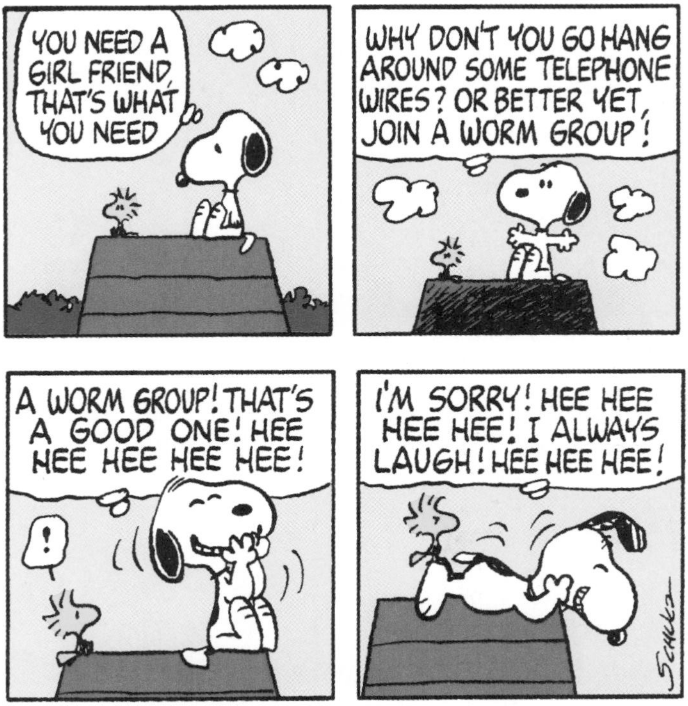

YOU NEED A GIRL FRIEND, THAT'S WHAT YOU NEED
WHY DON'T YOU GO HANG AROUND SOME TELEPHONE WIRES? OR BETTER YET, JOIN A WORM GROUP!
A WORM GROUP! THAT'S A GOOD ONE! HEE HEE HEE HEE HEE!
!
I'M SORRY! HEE HEE HEE HEE! I ALWAYS LAUGH! HEE HEE HEE!

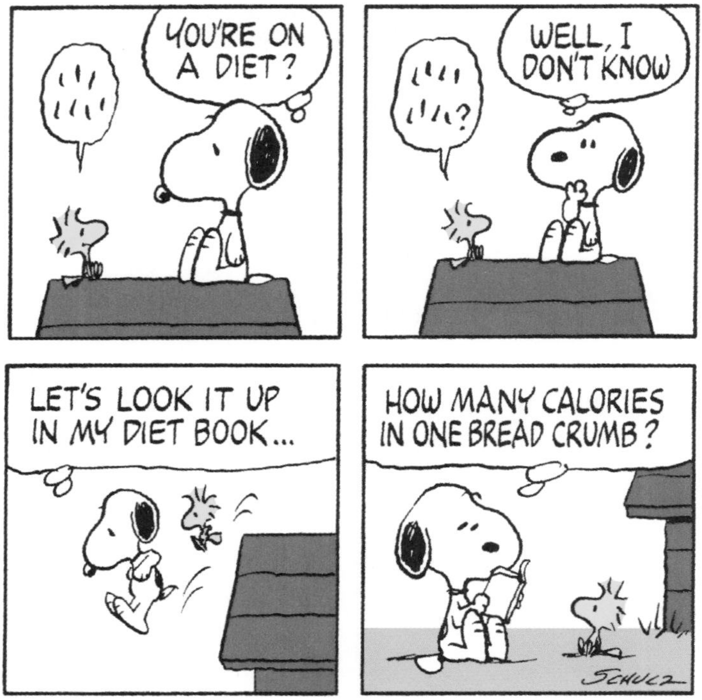
YOU'RE ON A DIET?
WELL, I DON'T KNOW
LET'S LOOK IT UP IN MY DIET BOOK...
HOW MANY CALORIES IN ONE BREAD CRUMB?
SCHULZ

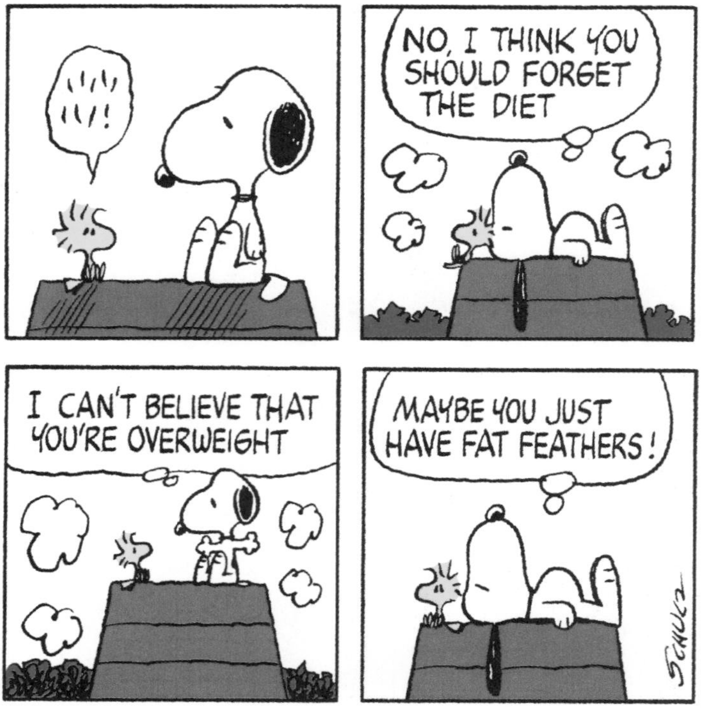
NO, I THINK YOU SHOULD FORGET THE DIET
I CAN'T BELIEVE THAT YOU'RE OVERWEIGHT
MAYBE YOU JUST HAVE FAT FEATHERS!
SCHULZ

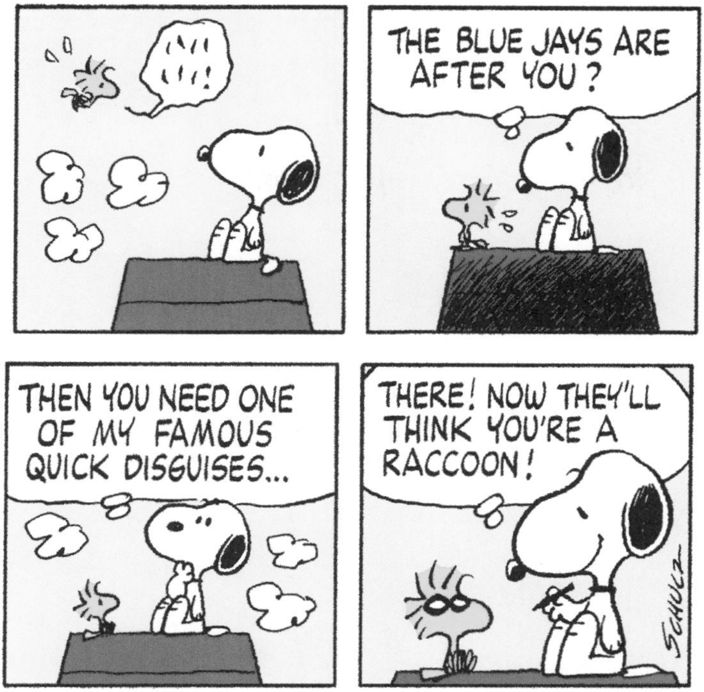
THE BLUE JAYS ARE AFTER YOU ?
THEN YOU NEED ONE OF MY FAMOUS QUICK DISGUISES...
THERE! NOW THEY'LL THINK YOU'RE A RACCOON!
SCHULZ

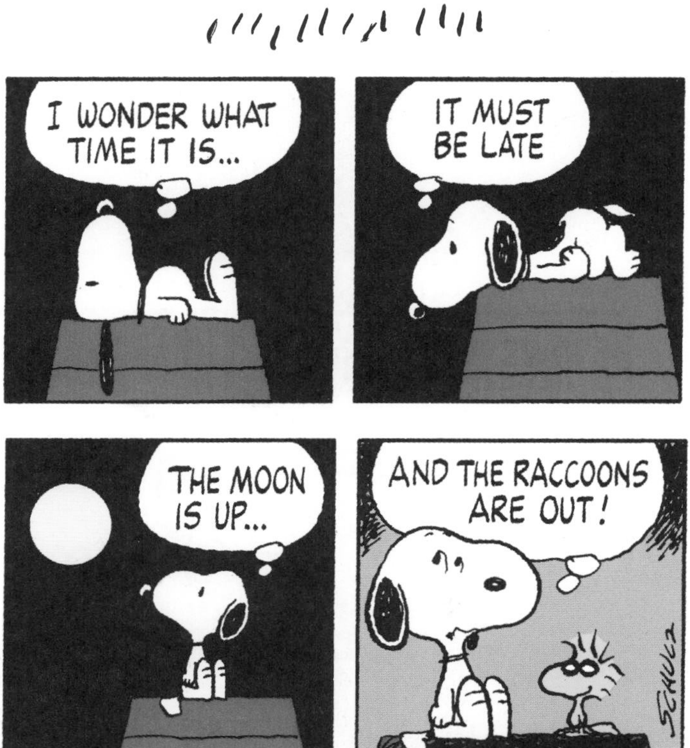
I WONDER WHAT TIME IT IS...
IT MUST BE LATE
THE MOON IS UP...
AND THE RACCOONS ARE OUT!
SCHULZ

YOU'VE BEEN ELECTED GRAND MASTER OF YOUR LODGE? HOW NICE!
IT'S A NEW ORGANIZATION? HOW INTERESTING
OVER TWO HUNDRED MEMBERS ALREADY? THAT'S GREAT! HOW OFTEN DO YOU MEET?

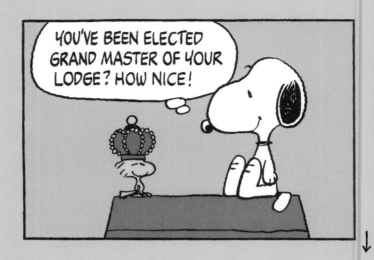

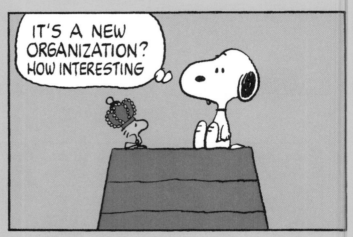

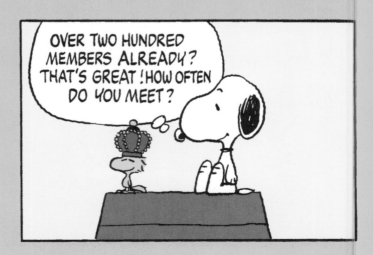

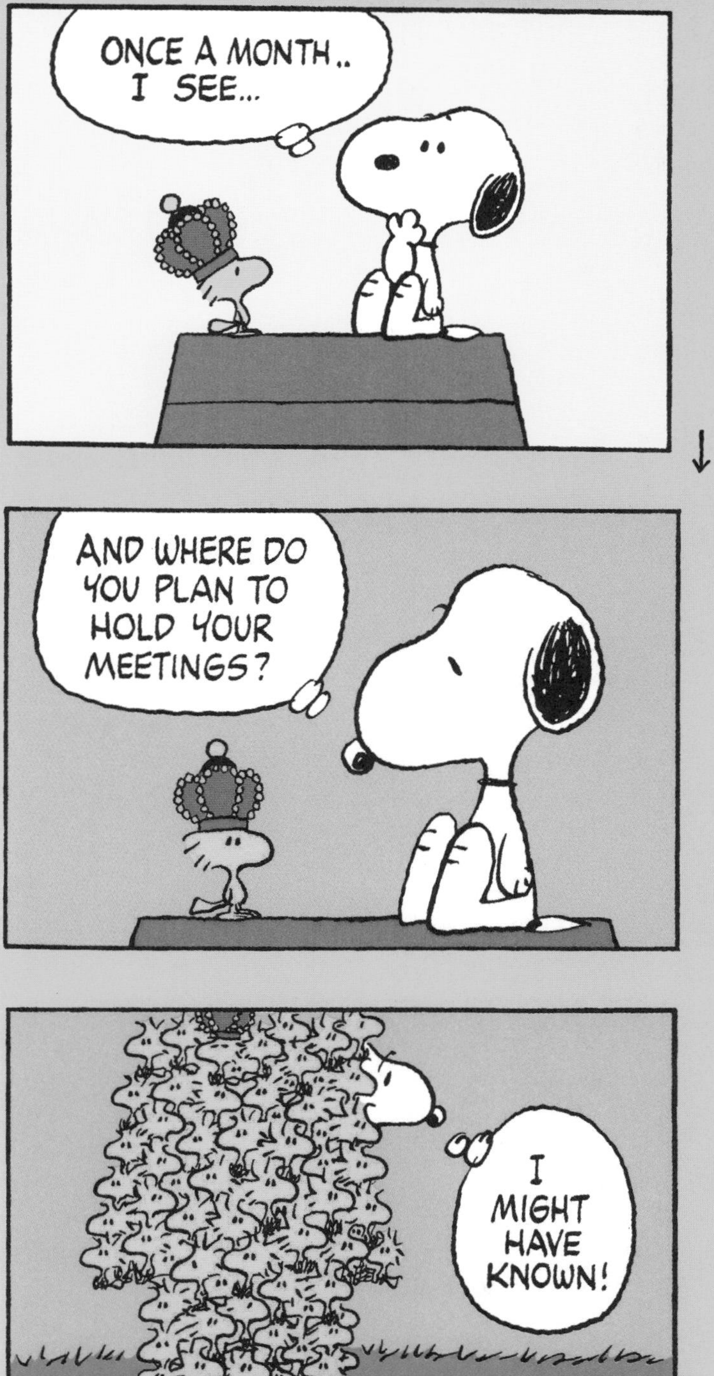
ONCE A MONTH..
I SEE...
AND WHERE DO YOU PLAN TO HOLD YOUR MEETINGS?
I MIGHT HAVE KNOWN!
SCHULZ

MORE TO EXPLORE!

In addition to all these great *Peanuts* cartoons, here are some cool activities and fun facts for you related to birds and comic strips. Thanks to our friends at the Charles M. Schulz Museum and Research Center in Santa Rosa, California, for letting us share these with you!

Make Your Own Bird Feeder from a Plastic Bottle

Woodstock and his feathered friends always appreciate it when people feed them. Here is an easy-to-make bird feeder from any size plastic bottle. (This is also a good way to recycle plastic bottles!)

MATERIALS: an empty plastic drink bottle with cap; two sticks about 10 inches long (or use two chopsticks); thumbtack; nail scissors; birdseed. OPTIONAL: acrylic paint, permanent markers, stickers

INSTRUCTIONS:

1. Wash the bottle and remove the label.

2. To make the perches, use a thumbtack to punch two holes opposite each other near the bottom of the bottle and cut small holes with scissors.

3. Insert a stick so that it goes through one hole and out the other side of the bottle. Repeat this to make the other perch go the other way across the bottle above the first perch.

4. Make the feeding holes. Use a thumbtack and scissors to make a small hole about one and a half inches above each perch, about one-third of an inch wide. The seeds will fall out if the holes are too big.

5. If you like, decorate the bottle with acrylic paint, permanent markers, and/or stickers.

6. Tie the string around the top of the bottle, below the cap.

7. Remove the cap and fill the feeder with birdseed. (A funnel will make this easier to do.)

8. Screw the cap back on and hang the feeder from a branch or a hook outside.

Make a Pinecone Bird Feeder

MATERIALS: one pinecone; peanut butter (or cashew or almond butter); plate; table knife; birdseed; string (about twenty inches).

INSTRUCTIONS:

1. Apply the peanut butter with the knife on the pinecone.
2. Pour a layer of birdseed on the plate.
3. Roll the pinecone on the birdseed firmly.
4. Tie the string to the top of the pinecone and hang outside.

Fun Bird Facts

- A group of larks is called an exaltation, a group of chickens is called a peep, a group of geese is called a gaggle, a group of ravens is called an unkindness, and a group of owls is called a parliament.
- There are approximately 10,000 species of birds in the world.
- Hummingbirds can fly backwards.
- Ostriches have the largest eyes of any land animal.
- The penguin is the only bird that can swim, but not fly. It's the only bird that can walk upright.

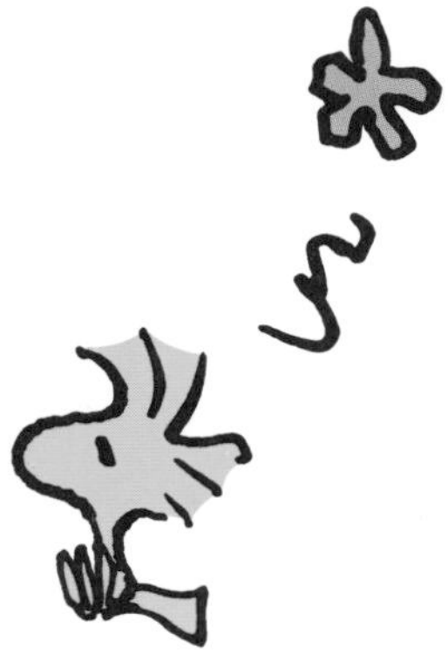

Make an Edible Woodstock's Nest

With an adult's help, make this sweet treat for you and your friends to enjoy.

INGREDIENTS: 1 5-oz. can of chow mein noodles; 1 12-oz. package of chocolate chips; 1 bag small jelly beans; peanut butter (or alternative cashew or almond butter); wax paper; paper plates. (Makes about 15 nests.)

INSTRUCTIONS:

1 Put a piece of wax paper on each plate.

2 Put chow mein noodles in a large bowl.

3 Melt chocolate chips in the microwave or over low heat on the stove.

4 Pour chocolate over noodles and mix.

5 Place a heaping tablespoonful of the mixture on the waxed paper on each plate. Have an adult test to see when it's cool enough to form the mixture into nests.

6 Stick the jelly beans down with peanut butter inside the nest.

Charles M. Schulz and *Peanuts* Fun Facts

- Charles Schulz drew 17,897 comic strips throughout his career.
- Schulz was first published in Ripley's newspaper feature *Believe It or Not* in 1937. He was fifteen years old and the drawing was of the family dog.
- From birth, comics played a large role in Schulz's life. At just two days old, an uncle nicknamed Schulz "Sparky" after the horse Spark Plug from the *Barney Google* comic strip. And that's what he was called for the rest of his life.
- In a bit of foreshadowing, Schulz's kindergarten teacher told him, "Someday, Charles, you're going to be an artist."
- Growing up, Schulz had a black-and-white dog that later became the inspiration for Snoopy—the same dog that Schulz drew for Ripley's *Believe It or Not*. The dog's name was Spike.

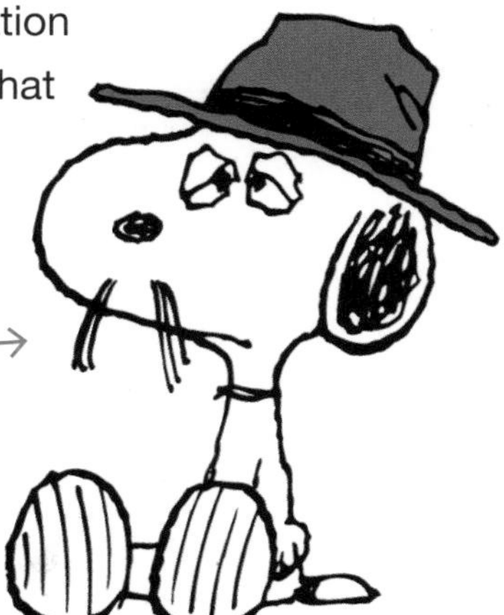

- Charles Schulz earned a star on the Hollywood Walk of Fame in 1996.

Learn How Woodstock Got His Name

"Woodstock was officially named on June 22, 1970. The little bird, who had been gaining prominence in the strip since 1967, was cleverly named Woodstock after the most famous rock festival of the 1960s. When asked why he had named the bird after the rock festival, Schulz pithily replied, 'Why not?'"

—from *Celebrating Peanuts: 60 Years*, Andrews McMeel Publishing, 2009.

PEANUTS
Tm. Reg. U. S. Pat. Off.—All rights reserved © 1970 by United Feature Syndicate, Inc.
I FINALLY FOUND OUT WHAT THAT STUPID BIRD'S NAME IS...
YOU'LL NEVER BELIEVE IT..
WOODSTOCK!
6-22
SCHULZ

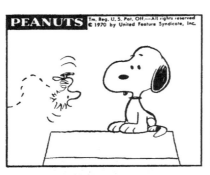

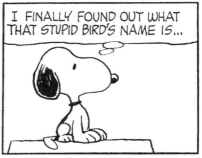

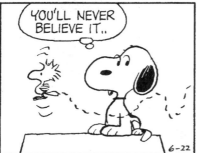

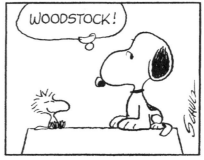

Learn How Comics Can Reflect Life

MATERIALS: blank piece of paper, pencil, markers or colored pencils

1. Make four blank cartoon panels, all the same size, on the piece of paper.
2. Look at the example below to see how Charles Schulz used his own life in his strips—even painful experiences like that of loss—and turned them into strips. Think of something that has happened to you at home or school that had a big impact on you.
3. Once you have decided on a story you want to tell, draw it in four panels. Remember, it should have a beginning, a middle, and an end.

An example from Schulz's life:

In 1966, a fire destroyed Schulz's Sebastopol studio. He translated his feelings into a strip about Snoopy's doghouse catching fire:

PEANUTS
SNIF?
I SMELL SMOKE!
SNIF SNIF
9-19
BAM! BAM!
BAM! BAM!
Tm. Reg. U. S. Pat. Off.—All rights reserved
©1966 by United Feature Syndicate, Inc.
WHAT IN THE WORLD.....
GOOD GRIEF!
MY BOOKS! MY RECORDS! MY POOL TABLE! MY VAN GOGH!
SOB!
SCHULZ

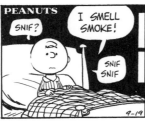

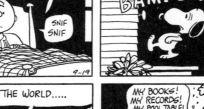

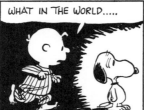

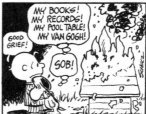

About the Charles M. Schulz Museum

The Schulz Museum and Research Center officially opened August 17, 2002, when a dream became a reality. For many years, thousands of admirers flocked to see Charles M. Schulz's original comic strips at exhibitions outside of Santa Rosa because his work didn't have a proper home. As the fiftieth anniversary of *Peanuts* drew closer, the idea that there ought to be a museum to hold all Schulz's precious work began to grow. Schulz didn't think of himself as a "museum piece" and was, therefore, understandably reluctant about accepting the idea. That left the "vision" work to local cartoon historian Mark Cohen, wife Jeannie Schulz, and longtime friend Edwin Anderson. Schulz's enthusiasm for the museum was kindled in 1997 after seeing the inspired and playful creations by artist and designer Yoshiteru Otani for the Snoopy Town shops in Japan. From that point plans for the museum moved steadily along. A board of directors was established, a mission statement adopted, and the architect and contractor were hired. The location of the museum is particularly fitting—sited across the street from Snoopy's Home Ice, the ice arena and coffee shop that Schulz built in 1969, and one block away from the studio where Schulz worked and created for thirty years. Since its opening in 2002, thousands of visitors from throughout the world have come to the museum to see the enduring work of Charles M. Schulz which will be enjoyed for generations to come.

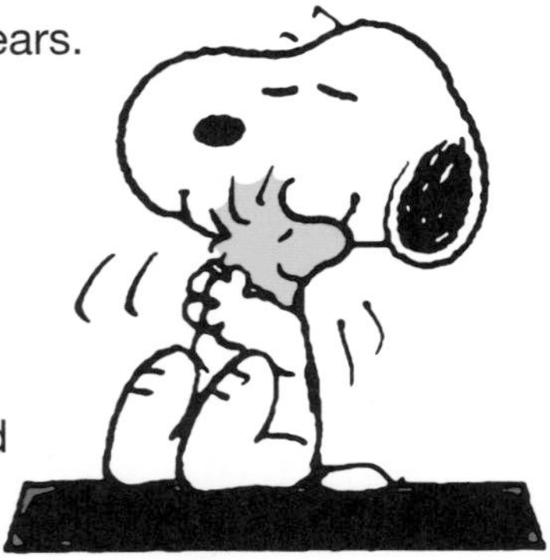

Even More to Explore!

These additional sources will be helpful if you wish to learn more about Charles Schulz, the Charles M. Schulz Museum and Research Center, *Peanuts*, or the art of cartooning.

WEBSITES:

www.schulzmuseum.org
- Official website of the Charles M. Schulz Museum and Research Center.

www.peanuts.com
- Thirty days' worth of *Peanuts* strips. Character profiles. Timeline about the strip. Character print-outs for coloring. Info on fellow cartoonists' tributes to Charles Schulz after he passed away.

www.fivecentsplease.com
- Recent news articles and press releases on Charles Schulz and *Peanuts*. Links to other *Peanuts*-themed websites. Info on *Peanuts* products.

www.toonopedia.com
- Info on *Peanuts* and many, many other comics—it's an "encyclopedia of 'toons."

www.gocomics.com
- Access to popular and lesser-known comic strips, as well as editorial cartoons.

www.reuben.org
- Official website of the National Cartoonists Society. Info on how to become a professional cartoonist. Info on awards given for cartooning.

www.kingfeatures.com and www.amuniversal.com
- Newspaper syndicate websites. Learn more about the distribution of comics to newspapers.

Andrews McMeel Publishing, LLC
an Andrews McMeel Universal company
1130 Walnut Street, Kansas City, Missouri 64106

www.andrewsmcmeel.com

www.peanuts.com

15 16 17 18 19 SDB 10 9 8 7 6 5 4 3 2 1

ISBN: 978-1-4494-5827-0

Library of Congress Control Number: 2014952151

Made by:
Shenzhen Donnelley Printing Company Ltd.
Address and location of manufacturer:
No. 47, Wuhe Nan Road, Bantian Ind. Zone,
Shenzhen China, 518129
1st Printing – 2/9/15

ATTENTION: SCHOOLS AND BUSINESSES
Andrews McMeel books are available at quantity discounts with bulk purchase for educational, business, or sales promotional use. For information, please e-mail the Andrews McMeel Publishing Special Sales Department:
specialsales@amuniversal.com.

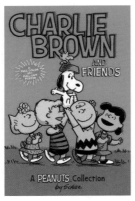

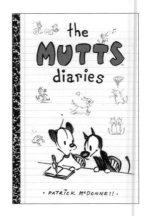

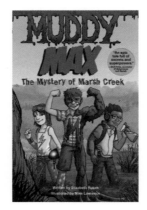